LOST IN WASTE

CATHERINE HAUSTEIN

CITY OWL
PRESS

LOST IN WASTE
Unstable States, Book Two

CITY OWL PRESS
www.cityowlpress.com

Cover Design by MiblArt. All stock photos licensed appropriately.

Edited by Christie Stratos

For information on subsidiary rights, please contact the publisher at info@cityowlpress.com.

Print Edition ISBN: 978-1-949090-66-6

Digital Edition ISBN: 978-1-949090-67-3

Printed in the United States of America

-- For those who've found love, and those still looking. It's out there, my friends.

PRAISE FOR CATHERINE HAUSTEIN

"Haustein creates her world with subtlety and intelligence which captures the imagination. Wonderfully entertaining, Mixed In delivers a powerful message with an admirable and honest grace. The reader can look forward to more tales from this author with anticipation. Well done!"
- InD'tale

"The author introduces an entertaining cast of characters, while warning us of what could be."
- Author Lee Joanne Collins

"Catrina bucks the typical trend you see of female scientists in pop culture. While she's a dedicated scientist, she refuses to let people see her as a one-dimensional nerd girl -- she also has aspirations for sex, romance, and having a family. This was a fantastic, sexy read, and the main character's struggles are very relatable for all women. Would definitely recommend!"
- Book Reviewer

"Hilarious, life-affirming, politically provocative . . . I loved seeing the world from the viewpoint of a chemist! A page-turner plot and clever writing."
- Cynthia Mahmood, Book Reviewer

"From romance to mystery to intrigue, Mixed In offers the reader a little bit of everything. Catrina and Ulysses's unlikely union sets the stage for all sorts of situations that occur throughout the book, keeping the reader interested from start to finish. Love how the author inserts tidbits of knowledge at the beginning of each

chapter! Love the dialogue throughout the book that builds the characters. Loved the book!"
- Ann V., Book Reviewer

"A unique love story that will suck you in, take you on a wild ride, and spit you back out on the other side with a smile."
- Karin A Van Wyk, Book Reviewer

CHAPTER ONE

I was high for a Midwesterner, six feet up on a poured concrete stage with fifteen feet of gold-and-green curtains behind me, held up by three giant concrete hands. Mom was in the mostly female crowd, standing in the town square among the Pesto women with their long ratty prairie skirts and the Cochton Enterprises employees in their polos and khakis. She mouthed, "Good luck, Cali."

Today's contest was a big one. I swear, the nation of Cochtonia had more competitions for its female citizens than an ear of corn has kernels, but we had to have some way to determine who was allowed to bear and birth a baby boy. After the great spill in Cochtonia thirty years ago, we still had more pigs than weeds. We still had more corn than our air had particulates. We even had insects, although it was an insecticide pipe that broke and shot its load into the Cedar River. Nine months later and beyond, people had baby girls now and then—I had been born three years after the incident—but a boy? Nope. Nobody had a male child without undergoing an expensive technique allowed for the best of female citizens, those awarded InVitro status.

A contest for InVitro status is why I stood six feet above the crowd on this cool spring day next to my boss in his supervisory role, and the Icon who had the fate of being my partner in this challenge. The Icon, Eve Whitehead, was low-level glitterati in the fledgling nation of Cochtonia. Her features were small and even. She might have been plain without makeup. She was muscular. I had to swallow my jealousy every time she moved her arms to fluff her perky mahogany bob or adjust the lacy beret she wore.

Eve was well known around Cochtonia. Her claim to fame was appearing in cautionary one-minute videos, where she disobeyed petty laws and did things like reading a paper book or planting a garden. For her crimes she was arrested by the Vice Patrol, the ubiquitous law enforcement group we citizens casually called Washers because they washed society of its human dirt. It was mandated that citizens log on to these videos each week. I'd already seen a lot of Eve. She was even better looking in person.

I worked as a chemist for Cochton Enterprises. Yet today I was with Eve on Team Beautiful and Damned. Looking at the downtown of the capital city of Cochtonville, with its red brick buildings and the gleaming Pavilion of Agriculture, bars, pawn shops, laundromats, and my mom's medic shop, I knew if we didn't win this contest, I'd be the damned. Living in Cochtonia and having a flunky lab job as I did was like living in a trench. InVitro status was the only way a female could dig her way out. I'd be Lady Van Winkle. I'd clear the family name, forever associated with lazy drunkenness. I'd have a genetically modified baby without the bother or expense of a husband who was certain to be older and on his second or third wife. Even better, it came with money and a chance at a house in a classy suburb. Mom could live with me in the luxury she deserved. *I* was going to be the best of citizens. Yes, I'd prove myself a success.

Carefully, I shrugged my supervisor's hand from my shoulder as he leaned into me and whispered, "Cali, forgive me if this becomes uncomfortable." My boss, once known as Richard Bux, had been a regular boss who wore polos and khakis. Last month he'd been promoted to the title of sir, and the new Sir Bux wore a uniform. He was more flighty than usual since he'd gotten his status as a member of the Order of the Pig, following which I'd been selected to participate in this competition. His shiny new Order of the Pig medal shook on his yellow sash across his new green suit. The pin was kind of like the British Order of the Garter star, but a hog instead of cross sat inside the gaudy burst of what I was sure was a thin layer of gold over plastic since we were resource poor. It was accompanied by three copper soybeans, one for each decade of devotion to Cochton Enterprises. According to his decorations, this man had served our nation well. Until recently, he'd been a father figure to me, more stable than my own father, and by that, I mean sober. But since he'd told me we were to be featured in the latest state-sponsored competition, he'd been weirdly touchy-feely and talked about how he cared for *me* rather than about my data. And he'd grown a scraggly goatee.

Previous contests were simple tasks such as a national anthem contest and bake-offs featuring cornmeal. The crowd was mildly interested in this event. Entertainment wasn't a thing in Cochtonia. We worked and were serious and consumed corn-based products. The people were mostly here for the food. In the sea of people, I caught Mom's furrowed brow as she stood next to the corn liquor stand set up by the Pestos at their all-corn food and beverage booth. She was there to watch my introduction but also to run interference in case my dad showed up and drank too much.

The Pestos, thus named because they were associated with pesticide application in Cochtonia (and sold a tasty corn-based sauce), were rural folk who came to town when there was a festival or announcement where they could sell their products in the town square—the only spot in the whole nation freely open to the public. Pesto women, their corn silk hair tied back in buns, were the only females in Cochtonia who seemed able to have children without any intervention these days, although all of their babies were girls. None of the kids were here, nor were their husbands, the pesticide appliers of the nation. The babies they blatantly nursed had bandanas wrapped across their eyes.

The Cochtonia manager, Norman Allen, a figurehead because

he was the last male conceived naturally, held up a microphone and spoke to all of us in his slow Iowa drawl. Cochtonia was once known as the state of Iowa and in the United States, but it had declared independence and broken away, and no one fought for our return. We were like a detaching skin tag. It first founded itself as a city-state called Cochtonville but expanded by foreclosing on farms, doing this quickly—before other countries could buy them, as was happening at the time—until it declared itself a new nation: Cochtonia.

A mosquito landed on Norm's head as he spoke. "We are having this competition because our nation isn't growing economically or population wise. We must work harder and smarter. Each team of two women will find a resource associated with their assigned project, along with a practical use for the site. I will now introduce the teams, although I'm sure you're all familiar with the Icons associated with each group." He slapped the mosquito.

As he introduced us, each team of two women stepped forward and greeted the audience.

"You all know Private Eye. She reminds you the Vice Patrol is always looking for criminal behavior. She and her science support will repurpose an abandoned library." A black-haired woman and someone who worked in the lab down the hall bowed to the crowd.

"The Icon known as Report 'Em Raw discourages unauthorized sexual conduct. She and her partner will find a use for an abandoned chicken farm." A thin-nosed woman and a blonde gave the crowd a thumbs-up.

"Icon Keep It Tidy and her colleague will find a way to use loose garbage and abandoned lots in our city. We know, although we highly applaud single use items, a creative use for them will encourage all to pick them up." Two women with neat buns and wrinkle-free rompers ran forward and did the splits as the crowd clapped.

"Our Beautiful and Damned Icon shows us the folly of disobeying Cochtonville's laws. She and her teammate will find a use for the WasteBin." I stepped forward and waved with a closed hand and forced smile as Eve did. My stomach was in knots. The WasteBin was a remote site filled with effluent from sewage lagoons. Everyone knew what was there—hog waste, garbage, and worthless rocky soil that couldn't grow corn. Getting there required a journey on rural roads. Some of them needed manual driving. Mom's face screwed up as if she was smelling it. We had the worst assignment of the bunch.

The manager took a dramatic pause before saying, "The prize will be InVitro status awarded in conjunction with the Corn Days Festival."

Upon hearing the words, the tangible consequence, I wanted to win as much as I wanted to breathe. Success was closer than it had ever been.

Eve grabbed me too tightly and cried, "I have always desired this. We can get our own men. Man rental is a perk of InVitro status!"

"Yuck," I said, looking at Sir Bux and Norm. "A perk I can do without."

"Silly, the rentals are probably robots. Where else would young men come from?"

Lady LouOtta Maliegene, a bobble-headed woman with InVitro status and a close-cut tailored dress, came from behind the curtains and took the microphone from the city manager. "Will all patriots join me in singing 'Bombs and Tassels'?" She'd won her status by writing this—the Cochtonia anthem. Her voice was bubbly, almost childish, as she nodded too much and flashed her huge teeth.

Norman Allen held up an image of a green square with yellow silhouettes of an ear of corn and a fat hog. This was our national flag. Immediately, as required, we all pressed our foreheads with our index fingers to show we were thinking of Cochtonia.

"Ohhh." LouOtta held the first note, a high C, to help the people of Cochtonia get started. This was the only song we were allowed to sing these days and we'd lost our sense of pitch. All joined in, finger to forehead. The smell of manure and insecticides drifted on a lazy breeze.

"Bombs and tassels, tassels and bombs,
Come father, come brothers,
Hear the sound.
As bombs and corn tassels burst around,
Defend our enterprise.
We will stand against enemies
And favor our friends
As we please.
We are the Cochtonians, right.
Defend. Defend and fight."

I was never sure who I was to fight nor had I ever seen a bomb or even a brother. Yet I sang because to not sing was to risk arrest.

We were dismissed to the backstage area. Sir Bux came up to us. "I'm giving you the best of resources for this competition. Cali, I've got permission to send you to the field with a UTI."

I clapped my hands together. "A Universal Testing Instrument? I've always wanted one of those!" A UTI was a handheld spectroscopic and chromatographic device. It detected a wide variety of atoms and molecules. Despite my shitty assignment, this gadget would give me an edge at figuring out what was in the sewage. From there, I'd find a use for it.

My mom rushed backstage and flew up to Sir Bux, giving him the stink eye.

"How can you send my daughter there? It's dangerous."

He opened and closed his mouth like a carp before blurting out, "Forgive me. The assignment was out of my hands. I care about Cali as much as you do."

A man in a white coat and white Stetson, a Vice Patrol agent, grabbed Sir Bux by his scraggly goatee. "You're sending my daughter to the WasteBin. If anything happens to her, you'll rot in prison."

My boss flailed his arms like a spotted cucumber beetle.

"Commissioner Whitehead, I can explain. It wasn't my choice. These orders came from the Cochtons."

"I, for one, am going to the WasteBin," I said. "I'm used to shit."

Eve linked arms with me. "I, too, wish to go. The WasteBin is my future."

"Medic? Is there a medic?" The city manager had the microphone and called from the front of the stage. "We have somebody down."

"It's just a Pesto," Lady LouOtta added. "No rush."

Mom backed away from my boss, and the Vice Patrol agent let go of his beard.

"I'm a medic. I'll handle it," Mom said. I followed her to the crowd, where a circle had formed around a Pesto woman collapsed on the grass next to a bawling blindfolded baby. Mom knelt beside her, took her pulse, and examined her eyes as the other Pesto women pressed close.

"She's damn weak," one said.

"I don't want her ugly baby," said another, holding her own colicky baby.

"She's a martyr," said a third.

Eve strode over. "The problem?" she said in a feminine voice.

"I suspect she fainted," Mom answered. "I need to get her to my clinic, XX Success, across the way."

Eve hoisted the limp woman to her shoulder as a Pesto woman shoved the fallen woman's baby into my arms.

"Let's go," said Eve.

The clinic bent around a corner on Maize Street. The building had once been a grocery store and had windows with six panes of glass, now covered with wooden blinds. Shelves packed with health and beauty products lined the walls. A bar sat adjacent to XX Success on one side, a laundromat on the other. Mom was a medic who treated minor injuries. She was an alternative to doctors for those who had few resources. Her patients rarely had the money to pay, but Mom made ends meet selling beauty products to the InVitros, who had money. She spent much of each day behind the counter with the glass display case that held wands filled with eyelash extenders and wrinkle smoothers and a Mercury purse—worth more than she made in a year.

"Thanks for your help. Put her here in the exam room." Mom indicated a screened-off area, not a room at all.

Eve and I waited on the other side of the wall. The baby bawled like a cat in heat.

"Don't be put off by the baby. We'll have nannies to help," Eve assured me. "It comes with InVitro status. Of course, you have to pay them, but not much, and we'll make publicity appearances for which we'll be paid."

The baby screamed so hard its bandana was wet from tears, and slobber flew from its tight lips.

"I'm not sure I like babies," I said, peeling the wet bandana from the baby's face.

We both gasped. The little girl had tiny eyes, the size of the quarter-inch gumballs in the machine by the door. I'd never seen such eyes before, but Mom had mentioned there'd been a rash of babies born with small eyes following the introduction of a new pesticide.

"It's true," Eve whispered. "The kids are mutated."

"Old man's a Duster. I'm late. Are you hip?" The Pesto had awakened and was talking in a harsh word salad. "The baby has pin eyes. She's up all night like a vampire bastard. She's not blind. The eyes are overly sensitive to light. I can't get a lick of sleep. I'm about to lose my mind."

"I'll take a look at her." Mom came from behind the screen. She grabbed a lollipop from the counter and unwrapped it. "Hold this in her mouth," she said, handing it to me. I did as instructed while she examined the baby's eyes with a penscope. She went back to talk to the woman.

"The reflection in her eyes is white instead of red. I could give you some drops to help her see without pain during the day. She might sleep at night after the treatment."

"Be cool, girl. *I'm* the sick one. I need a period restorer. Help me. I'm begging you as a martyr."

A Vice Patrol van pulled up in front of the store.

"It's Dad. Alright, I'm out of here," Eve said. "I'll see you tomorrow. Sorry to leave you with the baby." Her last sentence was insincere. She gave me a perfunctory hug as I clung to the baby, now nursing a lollipop.

As soon as Eve had gone, Mom called out. "Cali, lock the door. We're closed." She grabbed a device from her rack of gadgets before returning to the woman.

"A gun?" the woman said from behind the screen. "I thought I'd get a pill."

"I prefer physical methods to chemical ones. They're quicker and neater. Less painful. Faster too. Lean back and relax. It's just energy." A high-pitched pinging squealed out. The baby pinched her eyes together.

"You'll find relief in no time," Mom said.

The woman appeared from behind the screen, her blouse mussed, her hands on her belly. "I don't feel a thing."

Mom handed the woman a package of menstrual pads, Collection Pad brand. "That's the beauty of it."

"I got no money," said the woman. "I can't even pay for *this* with money." She pulled a ring off her hand and gave it to Mom. "It's cleared with the husband. He says if I have any more girls with tiny eyes he's gonna kill me."

"I'm not doing this for him. I'm working for you."

"Bitch, *I* wanted this. I can't go through having another tiny-eyed girl again. My own life is hard enough."

"I understand," said Mom.

"I knew I could trust you," the Pesto said.

Mom put the ring on the counter and pulled out another device from her rack of gadgets. She pointed a card-sized XRF gun at it, which pounded the ring with a stream of X-rays. Mom read the display. "It's copper," she told the woman. "I'll take it in trade.

Sometimes women come in and I have to break the news to them that their rings are mostly lead."

"I'm cool," the woman said.

"How about I treat the baby? Let's put some drops in her eyes while she least suspects it."

Mom opened a locked drawer and got out a massive book. Paper books—references included—were illegal. Officials needed to track everything we read, every page, every word for the good of Cochtonia. Books, all nonfiction, were online and updated frequently. Paper books were not only illegal, they were unreliable. Using a paper book meant one thing—Mom didn't want any trace left behind of these people getting a cure.

Mom put her finger on a page. "Yes."

"Is that a paper book? They're illegal," the woman said.

"No. It's an offline nonfiction reference," Mom replied. "I have to make the drug. It's nanoparticles. The opposite of making crystals."

"Spare the details, brainiac. I never went to school. Are you going to help her or not?"

"Yes. The waiting time on nanos is mercifully short." Mom hunched over the counter. She got out two jars and poured them together, then funneled them into a dropper bottle and shook it.

Mom pulled open one of the tiny eyes and added a dropperful of liquid. The baby startled awake and Mom put medicine in the other eye before the baby cried forcefully and filled her diaper.

"Damn, it made her poop," the Pesto said.

"I've got what it takes," Mom said with strained cheerfulness. "Let's change her before you leave."

The Pesto watched as Mom changed the baby and sprayed the dirty cloth diaper with ConTain, a scent remover we'd concocted together. The smell vanished. She put the diaper in a plastic bag and handed it and the blinking baby to the woman. Mom unlocked the door and ushered them out. On the sidewalk in front, a Vice Patrol in a long white coat and a Stetson decorated with pins of pigs and corn was getting an earful from a citizen of Cochtonville, a woman Mom's age. The Pesto went out to face them.

"What have you done?" the citizen said to her. "I know why you people come here."

"Got some eye drops for the brat and period pads for me. Is it any of your business?"

"Period pads. Officer. Take note." The woman snatched the Collection Pads from the plastic bag as the broad-shouldered Vice Patrol officer shifted her belt laden with devices uncomfortably.

"I won't take notes on such a delicate subject," she said.

The intruder pointed to Mom. "This woman is spreading regrets."

"Regrets I can deal with." The Vice Patrol agent took a No Regrets scanner from her belt. She passed it over the Pesto's cheek. A green light appeared.

"She's clean. No infections, not pregnant," the patrolman said, holding up the screen. "What kind of regrets are you talking about? What else does a woman have to regret? We've got plenty of deviants without you creating trouble with the savages." She grabbed the complainer by the neck and threw her to the cement. "You live in the greatest nation on earth. Act like it. Stop stirring up trouble."

"I have no regrets," said the Pesto as she and her baby swooshed past the fallen woman.

The woman, her chin bloody, called as she struggled to sit up, "You selfish Pest."

"Do *you* want this baby?" The Pesto turned and shoved the child at the woman, who shrank away at the sight of the tiny eyes. The baby smacked her lips diabolically as her mother held her out. "Take her and my husband and my life. Or shut the crap up, ya dig?"

"If you don't want your kids, keep your legs together."

"How about *you* dirty dance with my husband then? He's rough. Can you put your crotch where your mouth is?"

"This talk has to be illegal," the woman complained, wiping her chin.

"It is. Word Crime. I'm arresting both of you." The Washer pressed a gadget on her belt. A Washer van pulled up and Eve's dad got out. "What's happening here, Ursula?"

"Word Crime and being a nuisance, commissioner," said the Vice Patrol. She took the baby as Eve's dad escorted the swearing mother and the crying complainer to the van.

"What're you doing with the baby?" I asked in alarm.

"Don't bother about it. This kind of thing happens all the time," said Ursula. Eve's dad shut the door to the van.

"Get some rest," he said to me. "My daughter will win the contest and you're not dragging her down."

Mom and I walked to her old car, parked a ways from her shop.

"They resisted at first," Mom said as we swiped our sidewalk passes at the corner meter.

"The Pestos? Resisted what?"

"The takeover of their land by Cochton Enterprises. They slaughtered all of their animals. They poured ButtOut on their fields."

"The herbicide?" We crossed the street and spotted the car.

"Yes, but the scientists at Cochton Enterprises developed ButtOut resistant corn." We got in the car and closed the doors.

"I never learned this in school. I was told they were backward people who only partially appreciated the civilization we brought to them," I said.

"My dad told me. He was one of the scientists who worked on the resistant corn. He would've done anything for Cochton Enterprises. At the end of his life, he came to regret it. It's why I'm worried about your assignment. I don't trust Cochton Enterprises."

"Mom, I'll be fine. I'm twenty-five years old. If I'm going to be an InVitro, it may as well be now. I want to be a success. Don't you want to be a grandma?"

"I'm sure there's a catch. Be careful."

CHAPTER TWO

The moon rose full although it wasn't yet dark. My parents and I lived on a dead-end street next to a graveyard that was constantly sprayed for weeds. It was a miracle I didn't have tiny eyes. Even more of a miracle, or perhaps a horror, strange vines with sweet smelling flowers and popping seeds grew from the graveyard and into our back yard. Dad pulled them up and tossed them into his bonfires to keep them going, since wood was scarce in Cochtonville. They burned pungently and the smoke fanned my weird desire to run away from all of this.

A bird came and perched on Mom's lawn chair, right next to her ear. I brushed it away.

"Mom, even birds walk all over you. You didn't want to help that woman, did you?"

"Of course I did."

"It was illegal. It's not worth risking your business." Nervously I picked a stray graveyard flower. Its seeds popped into my hands. I picked another one.

"My business is helping women. Cali, you'll be off on your own and then what will I have? What am I even risking? If I get thrown into prison at least someone will take care of me."

"Until they execute you." I collected more seeds for no other reason than nervousness. I'd seen too many Vice Patrol and Pestos for one day. I absentmindedly put the seeds in my pocket and checked my phone. Sir Bux had sent instructions about tomorrow. *Be ready at eight. A driver will pick you up. Pack a small bag. Wear clothes for camping.*

A rabbit nibbled the grass beneath the lawn chair. Besides plants, animals came out of the graveyard. It had bushes and trees. I'd never dared go in there. In fact, I was afraid of shrubs because of what might be hiding in them. My dad, however, went through there to scavenge wood.

Dad, an old tomcat wearing a worn bathrobe and carrying a can of Coch Lite under one arm, came out of the soft glow of the door. He put the beer on the patio table, cinched his robe tightly, and stacked rotted wood in the firepit. The night was close and the air filled with carbon dioxide and heat, yet the whiskered man lit the fire, making the night hotter and closer as ants rushed from the burning log. He plopped in a chair beside Mom. Dad was an ancient man with a pronounced brow, a scraggly beard, and the genes to live practically forever, much to Mom's dismay. He was a person with few needs, a content man, happy to wear clothes decades old, and this gave him the aura of a scarecrow.

"Nice night," he said. "How was work?"

Mom tensed and the rabbit dashed off. "Work was brutal."

He replied with the aluminum two-snap of a beer can opening. "And the contest?"

"I'm being sent to the WasteBin." I was happier about this than I should have been. Leaving this dull life behind and having a challenge with a tangible prize had my blood whooshing through my head.

"Sounds like a load of crap." He took a swig.

"It for sure is. I have to find a resource to make the place special. I get a UTI."

"Have your mom take care of it before you go." Dad swigged his beer again. He could drink faster than irrigation drained an aquifer.

"It's a gadget, Dad. This is a great opportunity for me. The prize is InVitro status."

"You'd be set for life like I set up your mom." Dad had money from the sale of a family farm. The emphasis here was on *had*. He'd retired right after they married. We struggled now. Mom provided most of her services to the Pestos for nearly nothing.

"What are the odds of winning?" Dad asked.

"Twenty-five percent. Maybe a little less because the assignment stinks. I'm working with the best-looking Icon though."

"Her dad's a Washer," Mom added.

"Bum luck. Zip your mouth around her. She's not your friend. Keep it all business."

"Dad, she's not going to be friends with me even if I beg her. I haven't had a friend since the schools were closed."

"And Mom and I did a fine job of homeschooling you."

"Except all I learned about was science and not to trust anybody."

"The point is, zip it. The White Hand is always out looking for people like us with an eye on extermination."

"You're not making sense. Did you at least make dinner or did you spend all day imagining this junk?" Mom asked.

"I have to stay aware. And of course I made dinner." He went into the house.

"Mom, it's been thirty years. He's not going to change now."

"Like most women, I sacrifice. Like Aiyn Cochton. She died at her desk, you know. She died of overwork."

"The Cochtons give me the creeps. The only way I'm going to be like Aiyn Cochton is I'll never get married."

"It ruined my life. There are things people need to bring to a relationship: money, emotional support, physical support, care for the home—some combination of those things. When one person brings none of those things, there's no relationship."

"I have no interest in marriage, Mom."

Dad came from the house and onto the back deck with two

more beers under his arms, a pack of hot dogs, a stack of sliced cheese, and a bag of marshmallows. He teetered down the three stairs to the yard. He put the food on the patio table, then opened a beer and gave it to me.

"This is the life," he said. "Almost everything we need is here. We don't require a lot of fancy stuff. When the end goes down, we'll survive because we've done without." He shuffled into the yard and pulled up more plants and tossed them on the fire. They hissed as they burned.

He sat next to Mom. "Don't let this place get you down."

"There's an understatement—it's falling apart around me."

"I mean Cochtonville." He ripped open the hot dog wrapper with his teeth, stabbed a scrawny stick into the pack, and pulled out a hot dog on a stick.

"I know you women like to do things for yourself, so you can cook. Here Cali, one for you, too."

I put my hot dog into the fire and just left it there as it burned. I was metaphorically incinerating my life in this crazy city of Cochtonville in the nation of Cochtonia. People weren't even original when naming things here. I couldn't wait to leave. Of course, I'd have to return.

"What're you doing?" Dad asked as he unwrapped a slice of cheese.

"Dry ashing," I said, "is when you burn something until just the minerals are left. If you dissolve something in acid until just the minerals are left, it's called wet ashing. I learned it at work from my boss, Sir Bux, when he was sane."

"I'll be damned." Dad wrapped his toasted hotdog in the cheese and ate it in a couple of gulps.

Mom took the XRF, the device she'd used to determine the ring was copper, from her pocket. "Oh, damn. It's been such a long day I took this home by accident." She pointed it at Dad.

He held up his hands in fake alarm. "What is it?"

"A metal detector of sorts. I just gave you an X-ray. Your calcium level is mediocre."

"Mom," I said. "Is that healthy for Dad?"

"Put me in jail. What would it matter? My future's the same sameness."

Dad said, "Anybody want mustard?"

"You know what I want? I want one nice thing to look forward to. Something not a crappy house by a graveyard or a drunk for a husband or clients wanting what they don't need or needing what they shouldn't have to ask for in secret. I can see I'm not going to get it. Not one nice thing."

"Marshmallow anybody?" Dad said, ripping open the package.

Mom tossed her stick into the fire.

"Get me out of here. Anybody. Get me out of here." Mom paced the yard as Dad roasted a marshmallow. Mom walked to the house, irradiated the peeling paint, then examined the screen on her XRF.

"Damn, lead paint. I knew it. And I have been telling you for months to fix this board."

"It's just stained from the graveyard plants," he said.

"That's not tannins," Mom replied. "It's rotten."

"Always so negative. Can't you be content?"

The wobbly sound of a helicopter rumbled through the air above us as a glittery gold copter hovered into view. The Cochtons —Bert and Clarence, old men who liked to gaze on their domain from the air—were in the sky above.

"Hell no." Dad leapt up. "Not those freaking spies."

He ran to the deck and tripped up the first stair, and the second, and he tromped on the third. It broke in two and he tumbled onto the cement patio.

"I told you. This house is trying to kill us," said Mom. Dad lay there not moving.

"Dad, are you alright?" I cried.

"No. No, I'm not. My arm. Oh shit, it hurts like a butchered sow." He held it up. It was bent between the wrist and the elbow. "I think it's broken."

Mom scanned the bend with her device "There's a crack."

"What the hell?" Dad howled. "What's going on?"

"I've got to get you to the shop. I can set it with instructions from the manual."

"Cali, open another beer for me. It'll pass. Shit, the pain. Oh hell. No. I don't want to go into Cochtonville tonight with all the Washers. Fix it here."

"There are different kinds of splints. I need to look up the right one. I've got some pain meds, too. Cali, douse the fire and get in the car."

We drove through the streets of Cochtonville. Citizens were charged by the mile for the use of the roads, and of course, everywhere we went was tracked. On the surface, Cochtonville was any sleepy Midwestern berg. Above the houses, the sky still clung to powder blue. A Vice Patrol van silently followed us. They had a way of making you feel guilty even if you didn't do anything wrong. Ahead, the squarish Pavilion of Agriculture, the heart of the city proper, decorated with golden kernels of corn, loomed like a monster grain bin. Mom's shop was practically in its shadow. A few blocks up, a fire blazed on the sidewalk. The Washer van sped past us to investigate.

Mom parked behind her shop and we headed for the back. A Pesto crept from the alley doorway of the bar next door, which occasionally had male entertainment. This one was young with a smooth face as white and round as the moon. A tear-streaked girl with tiny eyes followed close behind in a pink bohemian blouse and a long brown skirt.

"Why were you closed?" the Pesto said. "It's Thursday night. Shops stay open Thursday night."

"We have an emergency," Mom said. "Please come back tomorrow."

"I need some help. I need help tonight. I'm late. I can't come tomorrow. I waited for an hour."

"Not now. I have an emergency. An emergency."

"You dumb old woman, I'm missing my rag."

"No," Mom said. "Not tonight."

The smell of the campfire smoke hung heavily in my hair.

"I'll help her, Mom," I said. I'd seen Mom give the period restore treatment earlier today. "Point and shoot."

"It's more complicated than it looks, Cali. You've got to focus on the right place to cause the disruption. Ma'am, we need to set my husband's arm first. Can you wait in the bar next door?"

"I'm not living like this another minute." The woman grabbed the girl by the sleeve and walked to the bar.

We rushed Dad into the shop and locked the door.

Mom put him in the chair behind the screen. "Alright, Cali, we're going to pull it into place. Hold it near the elbow and help me get traction. Pull in the direction of the bone."

Dad moaned.

"Stop reveling in your pain," Mom snapped. She pulled the crooked arm into place.

Dad roared. "This sucks!"

"Hush. Cali, read me the section about forearm splints."

"Splints are used to immobilize the injured area while allowing for swelling."

"Swelling!" Dad yelled.

"Just the instructions, please," Mom persisted.

"Once the fracture is in place, apply the loose gauze, followed by seven layers of padding."

"Where? Remind me of the position."

"The splint extends from the crease in the palm, across the palm and forearm, around the elbow to finger joints. Keep the wrist slightly extended."

Mom wrapped gauze from the middle of Dad's hand and across his elbow and to his palm.

"Wrap the arm for me with corn fluff."

I did as she told me.

"Bend your arm 90 degrees," she said to Dad.

She wrapped the bent elbow and Dad's upper arm with more gauze to hold it in the bent position.

"How about something for the pain?" I asked as Dad cried.

"Hell's bells. Anything."

` "Good idea." Mom went to her medicine cabinet and drew a syringe of medication. A woman outside screamed, "Fire!" Mom injected Dad with the sedative. A woman outside screamed, "Doctor!" As Dad relaxed in his chair, sirens cut the air. Someone called for a doctor again. A child cried out, "Maaaaamaaaa!"

"I'll see what the trouble is," Mom said. She stepped outside and I followed.

The air was thick with acrid smoke. The Pesto woman was crumpled on the sidewalk, her long skirt charred, the blouse ruffle burned, her hands and face red and weeping. The child stood sobbing. Hovering over them were two of the bartenders from the place next door, each in a tight dress, each holding a fire extinguisher, each talking to the commissioner, Eve's dad, with the Washer Ursula and another Washer, a plump guy named Barnabus.

"We're so sorry we sold her takeout booze," said the younger bartender, pulling the little girl close.

"She asked for extra bags. I should have known she'd incinerate them," said the older one.

Mom rushed to the burned woman. Her scalp was pink and blistered. Her clothes were singed and a burned plastic bag around her waist was melted onto her clothes. "What happened?"

The commissioner poked the burned woman with the toe of his pointed white boot. "She poured vodka on herself, wrapped her gut in plastic, and lit it. All her clothes went up. These people are nuts."

"Why would she do this? Everyone knows life is beautiful in Cochtonville," said the bartender, her red hair flopping across an eye.

"Third degree burns." Mom took off her sweater and covered the woman. "She needs an ambulance. Call somebody!" I'd never heard Mom or anyone command a Vice Patrol before. These guys had official carte blanche—total power with no repercussion. He could have shot Mom right there or done whatever he wanted to her. Dad, swaying in his flapping robe, his arm in a sling, gave a warning whistle. The patrolman raised his arm and pushed a button on his watch.

"As you wish. They're on their way. Ursula, the ATD #1." The assistant held up her All Things Device and the image of the Cochtonian flag with its corncob and fat hog on a green background burned our eyes. As required, we non-official citizens stood straight and pointed to our foreheads to indicate we were focused on Cochtonia. Mom rose slowly from her crouch next to the motionless Pesto and put her finger up too, if reluctantly.

"And ladies," the commissioner turned to the bartenders, "be honest. Do you see anything unusual?"

"What ya mean?" The red-haired bartender's fingernail dug into her forehead and she nervously pressed it. "A burned Pesto isn't every day. Maybe once a month."

"Use your brains," the Vice Patrol said harshly. "Cochtonia depends on your vigilance. Do you see anything else out of the ordinary?"

"Not out of the ordinary for me," the older bartender said slowly as she viewed Dad, standing and swaying, his robe flapping open. Not much was showing from my vantage point, a trace of navy boxer with a corn dog print.

"I don't normally see it on the streets," the younger one said.

"That's the spirit, Maven. Dame," he said, addressing Mom with a title a few pegs down from "Lady." "Dame Van Winkle, I'm sorry. Your husband isn't wearing pants beneath his bathrobe. He qualifies as a deviant."

"He does?" Mom said phlegmatically. "Scan him."

Barnabus ran No Regrets across Dad's bobbing forehead. Dad swatted the device weakly as it displayed a series of green lines.

"He's clean, but he's nearly naked. I suggest rehabilitation."

"Yes. Rehabilitation might work. Give it a try," Mom said, her eyes on the woman. The burned woman moaned weakly. Her daughter cried out, "Mommy! Mommy!" I reached for her.

"Don't touch her, girl," Ursula said to me.

"This woman needs fluids and pain medication. May I run

inside and get supplies?" Mom asked.

"Don't bother."

"May I get candy for the child?" I asked.

"Be quick."

I ran to the lollipop jar snatched one out, not sure it would be enough to comfort the child but helpless otherwise. I ran back to the gory scene. Dad yelled and flapped his arms helplessly as the commissioner hauled him to the Washer van.

"He didn't mean it," I cried. "He's forgetful. He forgot his pants. Mom, how could you?"

"Attention," Ursula said, and I put my finger to my forehead. The Pesto woman's skin was sloughing off. The commissioner closed the door to the Washer van. The Cochtonville streetlights blazed on—harsh white LEDs. The Pesto child cried out in pain and I cried, too.

"What's going to happen to him?"

"We'll rehabilitate him," said Ursula. "And meanwhile, your mom can live in peace." She patted Mom on the shoulder. "Should I change your profile to single?"

"No," said Mom. "Let me help this woman! I want to get her into my shop and give her an IV."

Ursula closed the flag app. With relief, we all lowered our arms. Mom fell beside the Pesto woman. "She's in critical condition. I can stabilize her but she'll need intensive care."

The child rushed to her mother. "Mom! Help my mom, you gawking jerks!"

Without the threat of the flag app, a crowd gathered—a few brightly dressed bar patrons and some Pestos. I handed the little girl the sucker. She put it in her mouth and tears ran down her tiny cheeks. I took her in my arms and stroked her tangled hair.

"Help is here," Ursula said as a green pickup truck pulled up.

Two attendants arrived and lifted the woman onto a stretcher and trudged over to the pickup. Her child followed, crying.

Mom said angrily, "That's no ambulance."

"I'm sorry. She's as good as dead," Ursula said, picking up the child and putting her in the bed of in the truck with her mother. "And the child is a liability of the state."

Two Pestos appeared from the darkness to confront the attendants. "You must give the body to us. She's sacrificed herself. We must let her rest in peace on our Cemetery of Martyrs," one said with a stony urgency.

Ursula touched the gun on her belt. "She's already loaded."

"Get her out," said Commissioner Whitehead. "It's cheaper to have them take her."

The attendants went into to the bed of the truck and returned with the woman on the stretcher. They tipped the stretcher and the woman plopped to the ground. The Pestos bent down, one taking her arms, another her legs, both facing the same direction. They stood together with the woman between them. She had to be dead by now. They walked across the street, stopping traffic.

"What about the girl?" I called. I appealed to the other Pestos hanging around watching the scene. "The child? Who'll take her?"

Another Pesto held out her arms and swept up the crying girl. "Exalt you, child. Your life is sanctified." The woman put the child in the truck and slammed the tailgate.

"Her society knows best." The commissioner saluted the truck and it pulled away from the curb.

The Pestos fell to their knees as the truck drove away.

"What's happening?" I cried.

"A Pesto child without a mother is released to the state," the commissioner said.

"Sucks to be her," Ursula said. She waved a gun at the crowd. "Enough out of you. Get to that filthy bar and stop gawking. And you," she pointed to the Pestos, "don't you have some land to till?"

The crowd cleared and the remaining Pestos left in single file, emotionless, their hands behind their heads with the middle fingers extended, blocking the honking traffic. I clutched my hands together, holding myself in loneliness and grief, hating myself for not running after the girl or my dad. I would, however, be running to a sewage lagoon, and the sooner the better.

CHAPTER THREE

When Mom shook me awake, it was still dark. Her pajamas were translucent, and her cheek had a pillow line.

"Someone's here for you."

"Already? Sir Bux said eight."

"She has identification." Mom looked brittle, like a cheap plastic doll left out in the sun. She needed to talk about last night, but there wasn't time.

I pulled on the green t-shirt and my pants from the night before. I'd fallen asleep right after I'd showered, and my hair puffed from my head like a dandelion. I brushed it as best I could and put the brush in my Perky Pig backpack—left over from grade school, back when we had schools—with a set of clean underwear, a white toothbrush and paste, sunglasses, binoculars, soap, and an extra menstrual pad should I be surprised or stuck in the field longer than I wanted to be. I hadn't time to add anything else.

I kissed Mom tentatively, not wanting to be emotional about this, and raced down the rickety front steps, hoping no one in the car would judge me or my house for our disrepair.

The pilot who stopped by my house in the company-owned self-driving rover was petite, pale in her reflectively white pants and shirt, as if she aspired to join the Vice Patrol. She introduced herself as Nell. She didn't look old enough to drive.

"Where's Sir Bux? He's not coming?" I said with suppressed relief.

She replied, "No. He's scared to go to the WasteBin and doesn't know how to use the UTI. I do, so I'm the driver and the teacher."

Eve, wearing her white beret and clothes matching mine but clean, sat calmly in the back seat and I scooted in with her. I was exhausted and hollow; all I had left was resolve to get this assignment started.

Thanks to sensor technology, Nell didn't have to drive for the first part of the trip. A microbiologist, she chatted about her work with microbial cures for leaf blight as the sun rose over Cochtonville's clean suburbs.

"Isn't the solution simply pesticides?" Eve asked.

"It could be, or we can create true antidotes, or even modified antagonists. That's what I'm working on," Nell replied. "Hey, aren't you the Beautiful and Damned?"

Eve blushed sweetly. "I am, but don't worry. This won't end in arrest."

"Your public will be disappointed if it doesn't," Nell said, renewing my fears of a disastrous end for our quest.

"I'm branching out. I'll be introducing Cochtonia to their newest opportunity instead of the newest threat," Eve said brightly. The car passed a massive gangly robotic row planter hogging the road.

"Ever been outside the city limits before?" Nell asked.

"No," Eve and I said, clutching each other as some sort of wide load sprayer driven by a hard-faced man came toward us on the other side of the road.

"We're headed into open roads. It's free to drive on country roads. No paywalls. Open your eyes," Nell informed us as we drove into farmland. "And hold your breath."

Agriculture made up the largest segment of Cochtonia, covering 8.7 million acres, about a fourth of what was once Iowa.

Farms lined the roads as the new corn popped up—each one a fountain of apple green promise. Shallow metal buildings appeared every ten or so miles and as we passed them, the air reeked of manure from the Confined Animal Feeding Operations holding hogs. Hogs, fed from our corn, were Cochtonia's main export. No other country wanted the pollution that came with cramming them together in buildings and holding their waste in ponds. The rest of the world regularly blamed Cochtonia for starting flu epidemics due to virus mixing between hogs and birds. Of course, the accusers bought our pork. When the ponds overflowed during heavy rains or broke due to construction flaws, or if they became full and needed a scheduled release, the sewage was channeled to the WasteBin. The WasteBin was the dump of Cochtonia and our destination.

At first the roads were straight. Farmhouses boasted new vinyl siding and the grain bins gleamed in the sunrise. The land was cut into well-organized cubes and we moved in one direction. Nell took the wheel, overriding the autopilot as the road's sensors dropped off and she veered around more farm equipment monopolizing the road. I studied the uniform beauty of the land, desolate and fertile, the sky ever stretching. Sameness, sameness. Corn, soybeans, corn, corn, corn. Sky, always sky above. Despite Nell's admonishment to open my eyes, I nodded off.

I woke with a start. My hand shot to my pocket. Those silly seeds were still there like lint. Nell took a sudden turn left and after a few miles, turned right, and right again and we swerved around a corner after. The road twisted and narrowed. The asphalt was as cracked as my driveway at home. The potholes had our heads bobbing. The houses were far between, and lead paint peeled from their boards baking in the sun. The transmission towers grew fewer. The grain bins were rusty. More cracks. More potholes. Fewer houses. No houses. No cracked asphalt. Only gravel. No towers. Only the fresh corn popping through the dirt. I allowed my head to bob and slump until again I fell into merciful sleep.

This time I woke with confusion. Nell slammed on the brakes and Eve grabbed my leg. We spun 360 degrees, the car fishtailing as gravel dust fell like the fallout. We'd come to a barbwire-topped polyethylene gate across the road. Nell held up a communication and identification device, and the gate opened. Coarse gravel hit the side of the car as we drove past towering foliage.

"These big plants—are they trees?" Eve asked.

"Sure are. Oaks," said Nell. "We've got these out here."

We drove over a creaky bridge spanning a tree-lined creek, rushing beneath us as we left the trees behind and entered a stretch of land bare of all vegetation with soil as rocky as the bottom of an aquarium.

"It looks like there's been a little too much ButtOut," I said, remembering the pesticide Mom had mentioned.

"No, fifty years ago it was an open pit coal mine," Nell explained. "The coal out here was wet and ashy and not valuable, so it closed down before Cochtonia was founded. The land was ruined and not worth reclaiming. That's why it's the WasteBin. Infertile land is useless."

"Until now," said Eve. "We'll find a use for it."

A mile or two of gravel later we came to an oblong building with a wide porch and a faded sign on the awning reading "Welcome Mart. All Needs Accommodated."

Nell pulled up in front, hers being the only car. A rusty bus sat in the side yard surrounded by thorny bushes with blood-red blobs hanging from them.

"Here we are," she said.

"We have to get out?" Eve snapped a photo through the car window. "It looks so run down. My dad always taught me no good comes from a ramshackle place."

"Looks okay to me." I opened the door and got out, happy to be more graveyard plant than a hothouse flower.

The Welcome Market had an empty cooler with the lid tossed open. The counters were mostly dusty with a stingy assortment of gum and bagged snacks.

"Nell," said the woman behind the counter. "I thought you'd never return. I'm at the end of my rope and my supplies here. Is it time?"

The woman's face was a mask of wrinkled skin. She was as slim as a straw and as white as a Vice Patrol uniform. I hadn't seen such an old-looking woman before. It was illegal to not get your face lifted in Cochtonville proper. Women went broke doing it. I couldn't decide if the creases were ugly or beautiful or if the saggy eyes were tired or wise. I tried not to stare.

"Not yet, My Lady," Nell said. "But surely the time will come."

"Nell," she said brightly, squinting at us. "Who have you got here?"

"A couple of fortune seekers sent by Cochton Enterprises. They're here searching for a resource to exploit."

Eve held out her hand, "I'm Eve, and this is Cali."

"What'll it be, gals?" said the woman, shaking Eve's hand. "It's been a while since I had people here who were up to any good."

"We've been assigned by Cochton Enterprises to study this place," I said.

"What do you want? What do you seek? What do you love?" The woman looked serious and paused, waiting for an answer.

"I love my freedom," Eve said, not missing a beat. "If we find something of value here, we'll win InVitro status."

"I'm sure that's good. Keep in mind there's always a catch in Cochtonia. And you?" She stared at me like a curious bird.

"I seek success," I said.

"You must be very young. As life progresses, you'll find more. More to love. For your sakes. Take it from someone who has lost half of everything."

"We were sent by Cochton Enterprises to look for resources," Eve repeated. "What can you tell us about this interesting place?"

"We've got feces, rocks, and non-perishables." She went to the shelf and tossed bags of corn nuts, two bottles of water, and some pork jerky into a plastic bag.

Eve pointed to a faded sign for Rainy Day Ale. "Do you have any of that? The sign says all needs accommodated."

"Ale is a want, not a need," the woman said. "But yes, I have well-aged Rainy Day Ale. The last beer truck came through ten years ago. This brand of beer was banned in Cochtonville for being subversive."

"I've heard. I want to try it."

"Don't keep it in the open. We get helicopters on occasion. Head to the shack at the top of the hill. It's nine hundred feet above sea level at best. Maybe you'll enjoy the view from there. I've come to appreciate it," the elder said. "We have a few residents. Don't let them scare you. They're harmless. They have a limited range." She handed me the sack of food while Eve hefted the six-pack of beer.

"As in shooting?" Eve asked.

"As in where they will travel."

"They're prisoners?" I said.

"We're all prisoners here although we've not committed crimes. Even the two of you in a way. Worst of luck to be sent here to look for anything of value, but I have hope for you. I'm sure your boss —it was a boss who sent you here wasn't it?—wants you to prove how much you want this. Bosses are like dog trainers, aren't they? Animals will do all sorts of things to help their masters. Cash only, by the way."

"Cash? Of course." Eve dug into her backpack while I took out the little cash I had in my pockets.

"Thanks. I owe you," I said to Eve when we got outside.

"When you want a ride back, you come here to telephone," Nell instructed us as she opened the hatch of the car.

"Here to telephone?" Eve said.

"The WasteBin is a dead zone in more ways than one," said Nell. "It's technologically dead, too. Once you go in farther, you can't be reached." She undid the three locks on a black box and carefully pulled out a belt and a holster. "I'll help you strap it on."

"Is this the UTI?"

"Sure is the Universal Testing Instrument." She buckled the belt around my waist. "Comfortable?"

"I'm made for this," I said.

"Now, draw the device from the holster. Keep your wrist straight. Get a sight on something you want to analyze. Then push the proper button. Select from molecular mass analyzer, atomic absorption, X-ray, infrared, ultraviolet-visible. You can sit on one wavelength or scan. They're all on the side."

"Let me record this," said Eve, getting out her pocket camera.

"Atomic," I said with conviction.

"Push the symbol on the side panel."

The panel had displays of a Bohr atom, a ball and stick molecule with a smiley face, a radiating bone for X-ray, a ruby blob for infrared, and a sun for ultraviolet-visible. I pushed the atom.

"Focus your beam on your target. Keep your wrist straight."

I held out the gadget. It was as heavy as a half-liter of ConTain scent remover but half the size. My arm wobbled. I was ham-handed.

Eve, camera recording, came near. "Use one hand to grip and your other hand to stabilize if you need to."

I pointed to the foundation of the building.

"Pull the trigger," Nell said cheerfully.

A rainbow of lines poured from the gadget, and with them I saw the light.

"Read the display on the side."

I eagerly read, "Calcium, silicon, oxygen."

"It's old cement," said Eve. "My eye is telling me."

"Yes, concrete. May you find more interesting samples than concrete," Nell said.

"The important thing is I did it."

"You've got the gist of it. Dial, aim, shoot, read. It'll store your data and send it wirelessly to your computer back at work. Be sure to use a backup drive at the end of each day. It can be glitchy."

"This is the gadget of my dreams. It's going to change my life." I put it in the holster. "What should I analyze next?" My head swirled with the thought I would be selecting what to study on my own.

Nell said, "It's in your hands. May you find what you are looking for here. I have a couple more devices for you both. These are not heavy. Turn off the camera and save your juice. Here you go. No Regrets 2.0." She gave Eve a pink plastic wristband.

"No Regrets? My dad has one of those, but it's silver, bigger, and not wearable. But what good will this do me out here in the WasteBin? Am I likely to run across some deviants?"

"Probably not. This new device will suppress your menstrual cycle." She handed me one. "You, too. No need to be uncomfortable out here. One last thing, vaccines."

"Vaccines?"

"You can't walk around here near hog slop without a series of vaccinations to keep you from catching E. coli and a whole host of nasty stuff."

She took a cooler from the car and handed us a series of sugar cubes. We ate one for each vaccination and chased them with a dose of liquid to ward off poison ivy.

"Anything else you need from me?" she asked.

"Where do we start looking?" I said. "There isn't signage here."

She gestured to her left as the wind ruffled her fine hair. "Do as My Lady says. Climb the hill and use the shack as a base. Look around. You'll find something." Nell sounded confident as if she knew this place. "Be creative. You wouldn't have been chosen if Cochtonia didn't want something from you they thought you could deliver. Friends, it's been a pleasure. Enjoy the ways of the wild."

"I have one more question. You work for Sir Bux?" I said.

"I do. In microbiology."

"Does he ever..."

"Yes. He does. Appreciate your time here. Away from him." She picked up her pack, jumped in the car, and left us in a cloud of particulate matter. It was hot, and the heat and dust strangled us.

"How do we call her when we need to go back?" Eve said. "What's the number?"

"I don't know. We can't let superfluous details stop us. We have to show we want it," I said, trying not to let the black hole in my stomach take over my head. What *were* we to do? We had to accomplish something and get ourselves home again. What *was* out there?

We walked. Eve carried the sack of snacks in one arm and swung the six-pack with the other. I scanned the sky for the helicopter the woman had mentioned. Skies were clear. This wasn't even flyover country. The rocks crunched beneath our feet as the sun beat on our heads.

"This assignment will be a piece of cake. Let's climb to the top of the hill and look around. We can have a few beers and let the creative juices flow," she said.

Our feet dug into the limestone, and rocks tumbled down the hill as we walked to the shack. Eve moved steadily without breaking a sweat. She chatted as I stuck with heavy breathing and short answers. No matter how much I panted and sweated, my heart rose with the freedom of walking without having to stop and enter a credit card each block as we did in Cochtonville, where even sidewalks had tolls.

"What a lonely existence that woman must have out here," Eve said. "I don't know if it's a privilege to get old or a sentence."

"Peaceful here."

"Maybe she's being punished. Only people with something to hide deal in cash. Which is why we must succeed. We need independent money to keep ourselves up and secure our freedom. Have you ever looked through the List of Husbands?"

"No!"

"My dad showed it to me for motivation. Page after page of dull old men with hairy nostrils. If I had a kid with one of them, I'd toss it in the dumpster."

"Lazy men."

"Not my dad. He's an alpha male and bossier than Sir Bux. I don't need a man like him or a lazy one. I want to be on my own, doing things on my terms, at least for now."

Halfway up I sat in the dust to rest. Eve sat beside me.

"I'm drenched," I said. No matter how hot and uncomfortable, despite my heart laboring under the stress and humidity, I clung to my determination and to the raw emptiness here as the wind's fingers played with my hair. Between this earth and sky were few complications and every opportunity.

"Try this a sec," Eve said, removing her beret and putting it on my head. It provided immediate shade; a waterfall of cool washed over me.

"Wow," I said in awe.

"It's HotNot, like the Vice Patrol wears. It's illegal for average citizens, but my dad had my mom shorten his coat and she saved the extra fabric."

"It's amazing."

"We can share it and everything we have."

"How about jerky? I haven't eaten today."

"Me neither."

We sat in the dirt together, gnawing the dried meat.

I laughed at the crudeness of it all. "We're eating like animals."

"The ways of the wild," Eve said, ripping off a blob of jerky with her teeth. Before long, we'd eaten all five ounces.

CHAPTER FOUR

A weathered wooden building with a cracked picture window overlooked a sewage lagoon, dark water in an abandoned mine pit from the days when coal was king. This was an overflow pit, the largest holding pit in Cochtonia, and it doubled as a municipal waste disposal site. Piles of broken couches, ripped stuffed animals, analog clocks, and wet cardboard surrounded the pit. Plastic bags blew in the wind.

"This is one ugly sight. A lake of pig shit and garbage," Eve said with a tone of casual disappointment. "And an architecturally unappealing shack. This place smells worse than the portable toilets at the Harvest Festival. How can I make this into a destination?"

A flick of my hand brought the UTI to life. "Hydrogen sulfide, ammonia, carbon dioxide, and methane," I read. "Not the freshest air."

I pushed open the door to the shack. Inside were two wooden chairs.

Eve put the sack and beer on the floor. "I don't see any beds."

"We'll sleep on the floor. We've got to want this. Let's explore outside and return to the shack if we become faint. I'll set the UTI to alarm us if it detects high levels of those gases when we go out."

"What's this dirty thing?" Eve said, looking at the stone fireplace with a dusty braided rug in front of it.

"A fireplace. You burn wood in it. Wood is dead trees. There are logs and smaller branches called kindling. My dad does it. Or did. My mom had him hauled away for being useless." Not anxious to talk about my parents, I opened my pack and took out binoculars. I looped the strap around my wrist. "Let's look for resources and opportunities."

We pulled the chairs outside the shack and sat with a view of the pit. The water below was brown with a stiff foamy crust like meringue. In addition to garbage, it was surrounded by rocks, and in the distance, a patch of trees stuck out like coarse hair. A small cabin sat at the edge of the green. The sky was a strip of blue, peacefully beckoning. I relaxed into this place. It was eerily serene and energizing. To live and die in Cochtonville, never escaping the city limits, always under the watchful eye, would be a tragedy.

"This is freedom," I said, dizzy with the excitement of possibility, or maybe the hydrogen sulfide.

"Not yet," Eve replied. "Being left out in the open like discarded porch furniture is hardly liberating."

"Being away from Sir Bux and Cochtonville is freedom enough for me. We can do this. I feel it. Success is all around us. The water is a resource. It can be used as fertilizer," I said. "Let's check what's floating there." I unclipped the UTI. I pushed a ruby-sheened button and pointed the device at the water, pulled the trigger, then read the screen on the barrel. "Lipids. Fat. Not what I expected." I pushed the mass/charge ratio button, adjusted the range to everyday inorganics and blipped it again. "Fats with a layer of ammonium nitrate. How strange. One might expect ammonium nitrate from the manure, but who would imagine such fats to be in water?"

"What kind of shit hole is this?"

"I'm trying to find out. Let's see how thick it is and what's beneath it. We could create a nutrient profile. People could put it on their lawns if they wanted a slick fertilizer."

"We have to do something about that stench. Neutralize it or something."

"I can ask my mom. She makes a scent container."

"We need to come up with a way to make this a destination. There aren't any destinations in Cochtonia beyond events like the Harvest Festival, Corn Days, Cochton Enterprise's New Year's Eve party, and Cochtonville Days."

"What's going on with the cabin? Do more people live out here?"

Three geese flew over, honking asthmatically.

Eve said, "Maybe it's a hunting cabin and this could be a hunting range. Shoot your goose and we will cook it to order. We can develop the shack into a restaurant. Your goose is cooked—to perfection."

A goose landed on the lagoon, cracking the frothy surface of the water. The bird honked in alarm and fell over with a brown and white wing jutting up.

"Or maybe not," I said.

"Tragic. This could be a resort for people who hate birds."

The gas detector alarmed.

"The bird cracked the crust and released the gases," I cried as a rotten egg smell burned my nose.

We stumbled into the shack. Eve bent over, holding her stomach. "Why would people come here? I'd say we should go home, but I don't want a husband."

"We can't give up so soon." I held up the binoculars and looked out the window. "The crust has healed itself already. We can go back out."

I wondered if I'd been mentally affected by the gas release. Figures darted between two piles of garbage. My dad had told me tales of abominable snowmen who lurked in the desolation of the Himalayas. Why wouldn't there be such creatures here in this abominable place? "We're not alone. Things are out there on the other side of the pond, upright things on two legs."

"Somebody else is beating us to the punch! Damn it. No."

The binoculars shook in my hands. Two stocky men, shirtless, walked down on the gravelly slope to the water's edge. They wore tiny shorts and hiking boots. They had visible muscles and flat abs. One was a redhead with a shock of tangled hair; the taller one had dark curls cascading down his neck. The men stood in the sun, gawking at the bags of trash strewn about.

"You-you have *got* to s-see this." I handed Eve the binoculars.

"What am I looking at?"

"Next to the water line."

"It's—it's men. Non-dad men," she gasped.

"Who are they?" I said. "Are these the residents?"

"I hope so. Those are men, and boy are they. The residents are men!" She gripped the binoculars and watched the men.

"They look kind of stupid. I mean, they are staring at bags of garbage," I said.

"I'm not in it for conversation. Viva the country! I'm going to get one," said Eve, words tripping from her mouth. "I hope he can't talk. The men in Cochtonville have way too much advice. Oh, those butts of theirs. Help me, those guys have muscles. They're tossing bags into the pit."

"Each toss, a crack in the crust. We need to stay inside until they're done." I was frightened by my own excitement at the testosterone-infused arms and legs of the men. It had been so easy to be a child, growing up and saying I wanted to be an InVitro and work for Cochton Enterprises. Suddenly, I had doubts, piled onto the doubts of yesterday.

"Where will we hide them?" Eve scrutinized the shack.

"Hide them?" I said, puzzled by her scheming. "You sincerely mean to kidnap them?"

"Entice them. I'm sure they'd rather be here than next to a mine pit filled with manure, don't you think? It's my patriotic duty to import these men-type creatures."

"What will we do when we have them?"

"We kiss them, you fool. Do you think they are savages we can tame? Let's name them Fred and Barney. Are you with me?"

"I guess. I mean, I'd like to meet them if they are kind."

"We'll lure them over. We've got to get them to cross the manure pond."

"My turn for the binoculars," I said as a large-wheeled garbage truck rumbled to the side of the manure pit and dumped a load of bulging plastic trash bags and a couple of dead hogs. The men tossed them one by one into the pit, moving away carefully after each toss. Eve snapped a few photos. Although the distance was great, her phone was equipped. She studied the photos. "These for sure are two good-looking males."

"Why are they here? This is the most inefficient way to get rid of trash," I said. "Machines would work much faster."

The pair stopped when they came to a ripped white bag. I watched them discuss what to do with it. They opened it. A body was inside dressed in brown and pink like the kid I'd seen the day before—the girl whose mother committed suicide. The redhead picked her up while the sexier one ripped open another plastic bag and fished out an empty laundry detergent bottle. Again, the men discussed. They left in the direction of the trees, with the girl in their arms.

"Are they taking people away?" asked Eve.

"Yes. A girl."

"Is she alive?"

"I think so."

"Should we tell anybody about this?"

"There's no one to tell. It was a Pesto. No one is going to care."

"I might not care either," Eve said. "They cause a lot of trouble."

It grew dark and having nowhere to go, we spent the night in the shack. I'd never been away from home overnight before. Cochtonia was a small country surrounded by a wall to keep people in—or out depending on who you asked. To lay there with another person, a person who could be a friend who might be on my side, was more delightful than I could imagine.

"Do you work alone?" I asked Eve.

"I'm part of a team," she replied.

"Do you see them? Work with them? Hang out with them?"

"Not really. We work through messages."

I wasn't sure I should disclose my thoughts. "Can you see what's happening? Sir Bux is isolating us."

Eve considered my theory for a moment. "You're right. He intends to break us down and make us dependent on him. My dad does it to my mom. He says if she gets out and works it will hurt his pride. Well, Sir Bux made a mistake, didn't he? We've got each other." She fluffed the pillows. "These are softer than I'm used to."

I tested them with the UTI. "No corn fiber at all. Cotton and of all things, goose down."

"We'll have to make do. I hope I can sleep. These are not slick at all."

We settled on the rug, so close our bodies touched. Eve was warm and smelled like a wild animal might. Even though raccoons scratched on the window, we slept.

Early the next morning, Eve sat in a lawn chair and took photos of the manure morass. I walked restlessly around the shack and toward the pit as I haphazardly tested the composition of anything I could get in the sight of the UTI.

"Limestone, limestone, limestone. We need a sustainable resource and something Cochtonia cares about. Limestone is so yesterday," I said in disappointment.

"It could be a prison. This place loves prisons."

"Of course. It's the only thing to do with a dump like this." I held up the binoculars and watched the farther shore with anxiety.

Again, my hands shook. The men were back, once again in their short shorts and now in muscle shirts. What was written on the shirts? I focused the binoculars. Cochtonville Market. They were poking through the pile of garbage bags, taking out a book and throwing a broken chair in the pit.

"Their clothes are made from plastic bags," I said as the rotten egg smell drifted on the wind.

"Interesting. If they were prisoners of the state they'd wear uniforms. What are they doing?" asked Eve.

"Throwing trash in the manure pit same as yesterday. They open the bags, poke through the contents, then pitch them. I'll never complain about my job again."

"We've got to get them to look our way. Life can get better for all of us." She lifted her t-shirt.

"What are you doing?"

"Sending a clear signal."

"Hold on."

"They're looking, aren't they?"

Eve put down her camera and held up an ale and a bag of corn nuts. The men squinted across the water and then tensed. Yes, they had seen the temptations. They exchanged words. Eve stretched. The men were fixed upon her. I studied their expressions through the binoculars. I wasn't good at reading people and had limited experience with men. Were they mad? Curious? Their faces were rigid masks, their skin slightly pinker than yesterday. They spoke to each other, then stood. They knitted their brows and strained their necks for a view. One picked up a rock and threw it to the other, who caught it with a dive. He held it up, then stood straight and threw it as hard as he could to the other who made a show of catching it as he fell dramatically to the dirt.

"They for sure see us," I reported. "They're showing off."

Eve rearranged the snacks, putting them more prominently in front of the chair. "My turn for the view." She held out her hand. I gave her the binoculars and helped myself to corn nuts.

"What the heck?"

"Are they tossing a rock?" I asked.

"No. They are holding up a stack of paper and cardboard and waving it our way. Are they shipping something?" she said. "No. They're showing us trash! I think they're insulting us." I didn't want to tell her it sounded like a paper book since they were illegal. Mixed feelings tumbled all over me. Men with books? Yes, I was intrigued. This curiosity wasn't going anywhere safe.

Eve narrated enthusiastically. "The primitive men are opening the cardboard. It might be a paper book. It has words on it. Plato's Republic? What kind of direction is that?" Eve put down the binoculars. "Maybe it's a destination where we're to meet them. Is it a bar or something?" Eve held up her beer and motioned for them to come over, which appeared impossible given the vast manure pit between us.

I took the binoculars from her lap and focused on the men. Yes, it was a print book with pages that had words on them. "It could be some kind of directory," I said. "Like a contacts list. A census of a territory."

"Written on paper? How could it be useful? There's no search function."

"In any case, it might not be trash. They could be trying to impress us." The men stuck out their chests. They gestured to the cabin by the trees.

"It's their house over there."

They pointed at the sky. Dark clouds rolled in from the west. I handed Eve the binoculars and reached for my communication device to check the radar. It was without service.

The wind came up with a rumble of thunder like water through old pipes.

"Do you think it's going to get bad?" I asked Eve. It was a superfluous comment. The sky opened up and pelted us with hail.

CHAPTER FIVE

The cabin window rattled as rainfall sounded like bacon sizzling and spattering.

"The hail has stopped," said Eve, as she looked out the window overlooking the lagoon.

"Let's put out bottles to catch the rain. We drank all the water."

"Okay. We can't live on beer alone." Eve took off her shoes, her shorts, her green t-shirt, and finally, her lacey undergarments. "I don't want damp clothes," she explained. She scampered outside, an empty beer bottle in hand. I stripped and joined her.

The pounding rain flipped our nipples to high beams and washed us free of the dirt of this place. We put the empty beer bottles on a rock to catch the rain water. Fresh water wasn't something to take for granted out here.

"Is this freedom?" I asked as rain poured over my body. "If so, it's cold."

"It's a form of freedom. Is it success?"

"No. I'll know success when I see it. It won't be chilly."

Back inside, charmed by our resourcefulness, thrilled with my nakedness, I braided my limp hair and tied it with a strip of plastic from a corn nuts bag before getting dressed.

The afternoon grew colder. Eve stood in front of the fireplace fluffing her short bob.

"Where do we find wood at a time like this? This place is a wasteland. The nearest trees are miles away. We should have gotten wood yesterday. The men were showing us the distant trees and their kindling, warning us to get some," I said.

"Their savage nature has them in touch with the earth and sky. Cali, they are so young! My mom says there's nothing better than a young man in your bed. They can make you moan like you're gonna die."

"Sounds painful," I lied. One of us had to keep rational or we'd never get our project done. "Plus, we don't have beds here."

"And love—it's like having rabies. You go mad with desire. You crave them and fear them at the same time."

"No thanks."

There was a knock at the door, and we jumped out of our mostly clean skins.

"Hellooooo." Two male voices in harmony!

"It's them," Eve said breathlessly. "It's them. They're here. Quick. How do I look? Brush your teeth."

I opened my pack and hurriedly scrubbed the bits of corn nuts from my teeth with my dry toothbrush while Eve did the same.

"We are at your command," came a deep voice. Someone peeked in the picture window. I screamed in surprise and he ducked away. Eve opened the door. Yes, they were men. However, their duds were just as they looked from a distance: made of old plastic bags wrapped around their bodies into makeshift clothes. Both their shorts and their sleeveless shirts shouted the stores from which the plastic bags had blown after they were used just once, if that: Cochtonville Market and Solomon's Hardware.

For having her fantasy realized, Eve was abrupt.

"What do you want?" she said. "And who are you?"

"We're called Layal and Remmer. We note you are new here and offer you the gift of warmth," said the sexy one with the curly hair. He shoved the other one playfully. "Tell them."

The tangle-haired redhead, was obviously shyer. He looked at the ground, or maybe at our legs as he spoke. "You signaled a willingness to mate with us when you showed yourselves. But if you aren't ready, we can wait. We aren't beasts. We are men, although we are lonely and live like beasts."

Eve put a hand on her hip. "Feeling good and wanting to attract you doesn't mean we want to mate. It's a leap of logic."

"Logic appeals to us. We'll take note," said the bold one.

"Tell us who you are."

The great-looking one spoke up. "I am Layal. Have you been told your name should be Truth? For truth is beauty."

"Yes, many times, but not so directly." Eve was attractive but the flagrant flattery was off-putting.

"Beauty is a true mark of quality. You show good breeding," he replied.

"On the contrary," said the shy one. "Beauty is cultural, and culture is local truth, not universal. Beauty can't be truth." He looked to me for approval. I smiled uneasily. Layal had already gotten under my skin. This other one, Remmer or perhaps I could call him Rem, was more open-minded. Still, I was disappointed by their introductory remarks. Perhaps they lived as beasts, but they were as full of judgment as any civilized male. I was anxious to get them on their way once they left their gift.

"The truth is, we could say the night is beautiful, but it's cold and smelly. Are we going to stand with the door open forever and let the hydrogen sulfide pour in?" I said.

"You're right," said Eve. "We're being rude. Please do come in and put your wood wherever it goes."

"Do you want the logs in the fireplace?" Remmer asked me.

"Yes, please."

He unwrapped the wood, a mixture of small logs and kindling, and stacked it in the fireplace. He took the other bag from Layal, opened it, and arranged this log and kindling to the side of the hearth.

"Would you like the bags?" he asked. "Or will you be leaving the area soon?"

"We're not here for long," I said.

With flourish, Layal took an ancient lighter, reading Iowa State Fair, from the front of his pants and lit the fire.

"We bring the fire," he said.

Eve held out her hands, seeking the warmth of the flames. "How can we thank you? Besides mating." Her eyelids fluttered so fast I nearly sensed convection.

"You had appealing food and drink," Remmer said.

"You saw it?" Eve sounded proud of her scheme.

"Yes, we see well. Our eyes feasted on the view. We didn't want to come until we had something of value to offer." Layal tossed his curls and waved his hand at the fire. "Do you like it?"

Eve looked him up and down. "Yes."

"We came because of your signaling, but we are forbidden to breed without permission," Remmer added.

"Isn't everyone?" Eve said with a smile.

Layal, standing behind Eve, said, "I hope to defy orders someday."

"I'm with you. Freedom is my goal," said Eve, turning to face him. "We don't have much of it where we come from. Do you like beer? There are four left."

"I relish anything that comes from your lips." Layal brushed her mouth with his finger, making me glad about the various vaccinations we'd received. Eve relaxed, as if she'd reached her melting point. Her eyes on Layal, she floated to the bag of supplies on the floor and grabbed two bottles. She unsnapped the bottle caps. "We only have two chairs."

"We will be your chairs, my Truth." Layal sprawled in a chair and patted his lap. Eve scooted aboard, plastic crinkling, as she and Layal giggled together as if they hadn't met a few moments ago. Unsure what to do, I studied the floorboards pretending I knew something about wood. Remmer did the same.

"Hey," said Layal. "Does somebody bite? Pull up a chair. Both of you."

"Come on, Cali, it's not every day we see men," Eve said. I was curious, with my stomach in knots at the sight of these guys. However I was hugely humiliated by the lack of enthusiasm I was receiving compared to Eve. It wasn't as if this would mean a half acre of mud once I was an InVitro. I wasn't going to beg a man wearing plastic bags, who may have hauled off a little girl for criminal purposes, to let me sit on his lap, no matter how curious I was, no matter how much I longed to throw caution to the worn wood floor and stomp on it. I had to stay rational.

Layal said, "Remmer, you are being impolite. Remember your manners."

"I'm at your service," he said to me.

This was worse than nothing. Now I had to give him an order or something.

"Have a seat," I said stupidly. "Enjoy your beer."

He sat stiffly, his hands on his knobby knees, fear in his eyes. Fortunately, a log fell from the fire and saved me from having to decide if I would sit on his lap. I ran to the fireplace and pushed the hot log in with an unburned one.

Remmer ran after me. "Do you need any assistance?"

"No, I can handle fires. My dad makes them all the time."

"You have a dad?" He blinked rapidly as if he was going to cry.

"He's out there somewhere." I didn't want to go into detail.

We sat on the rug in front of the fire and sipped our beer. Remmer made a face. "Fermented. This is an old drink. You must come drink from our cistern. It captures the freshly fallen rain."

"I'd like that," I said. I was half crazed with thirst. We'd finished our bottles, the other ones were still outside catching rain water, and I had no desire to drink from the WasteBin no matter how many vaccines I'd received.

Not to be outdone, Layal said, "As I will drink from your well, dear Truth. Drink to me only with your lips and of this beer I'll need no sips." The two leaned together and partook of each other's lips, lapping whatever chemicals the other held with their mouths.

Remmer and I shared a bag of corn nuts, watching this unfold. The sad thing was, I could imagine this type of interaction taking place between my parents, with my dad gushing about the beer and my mom's lips. Even worse, I was bubbling with toxic jealousy —my friend was being lured away from me as I sat un-kissed.

"These are tasty. I don't get a lot of salt," Remmer said.

"Do you have enough to eat out here?"

"Yes, what we can gather. Are these from the store?"

"Yes. Do you go there? It's not far."

"It's out of our territory."

We sat munching for a minute, the fire dancing and snapping before us, this man eating the corn nuts one by one, his muscles bulging, his musky scent tempting me to say something.

"Remmer, is it?"

"Yes, although you may call me anything, for Remmer is not my true name. I don't remember my true name. We were renamed with palindromes when we were taken from our parents. What's yours?"

"Cali. Cali Van Winkle." I was sure he hadn't been around enough to know "Van Winkle" was synonymous with a lazy drunk.

"I like your name." He had a large goofy smile. For someone who wore plastic bags and worked with garbage, he was happier than I expected. I appreciated his mellow voice and big eyes— without much eyelash.

"What's in a name?" I said. "It's just a placeholder." The firelight flickered across his face. I might as well have been walking on the moon, I was so high being this close to a young man. "It's a shadow of reality," I added. "A name can't contain an individual."

Rem held up his hand and the shadow fell on the wall. "What if you couldn't turn around and see the fire, all you saw was the shadow? How much would you know about me?"

"I'd know you had a fine profile." It was true. He had a strong chin.

"Could you touch me? Could you really know me?"

"Yes, I could touch you. My shadow and yours could *merge*," I said, the last word sounding embarrassingly like a whispered moan.

He either didn't notice or ignored my slip to spare us embarrassment. "If you were in a box and could only look forward, what would you know? Would you know about the world or would you know only shadows?"

I was wet beneath my arms and elsewhere. This fire and this guy were an uncomfortable mix. I had to say something. His crazy talk was something a person with little science background would come up with.

"I would know your image." Slightly emboldened by his inaction, I reached out my arm and my shadow fell across his to emphasize previous my point. "I would know as much as you know of me. Would it be fair if one knew more than the other? It wouldn't be equitable."

"We could turn around together. We would see the truth."

"No. We would see a fire." These strange thoughts were unsettling me. Why would a guy who lived by a manure lagoon be so ponderous? "Do you have all day to sit and contemplate?" I asked.

"Yes. We've been waiting for a more complicated assignment since we were exiled here a few years ago. This existence is intolerable. It's not what we were bred for."

"You were bred?"

"We're Crispers. We've got some traits inserted by Cochtonville's unique process."

"You're modified?"

Layal surfaced from his latest kiss to join in the conversation. "We have it tattooed on our behinds. May I show you?" Without waiting for an answer, he stood, pulled down the butt of his plastic bag shorts and wagged his rear.

"Oh, stop wiggling it so I can read," Eve said, holding out her hand to touch his flank, her voice as delighted as a child's. "Clustered regularly interspaced short palindromic erotic repeats.

Erotic. That's a new wrinkle on the Crispr process. Do you know what that means?"

He fell to his knees in front of her. "It means I am at your service in every way. I drink from your lips. I worship the temple of your body." He ran his hands across her legs. "Let us share the movement of our souls."

She pulled away from his touch. "Not so fast. I had a little editing myself. I was an experiment, too. It's why my name is a palindrome."

"No," I said with surprise. "I thought due to the shortage of males, there are only male modifieds as of now and those are mostly babies."

"I'm not a Crisper, with an e. I was slightly modified for promotional purposes. Tell me more about the *erotic* modification. There are more men like you?" she said eagerly, tilting her head and gazing at Layal.

"Better than us, we were told when we were banished."

Remmer said, "Our parents were paid volunteers—my dad was a scientist working for Cochton Enterprises. By golly, he's darn disappointed I was created to be erotic, but he's loyal to the company and Mom's just happy I turned out healthy—as far as I can remember them."

"My father, I have been told, is a well-respected scientist and employee. We recall little about our parents. We were sent away for training as children," Layal said.

Remmer added, "Crisper modification has been going on for a while, but it was kept under wraps while the process was perfected. In addition to our looks, we were bred for our stamina and discernment—robots aren't good at that yet. As you know there were spills in the past. The consequences included few males being born and those born unable to breed without assistance. You would think we'd be more elevated in society. No. We're commodities, or if you prefer, luxury goods." My heart swelled for this poor man, handsome, strong, and a product or perhaps a service. I moved my hand to my chest to quiet the beating.

"We are cheaper than robots, warmer than robots, more flexible than robots, but things went wrong."

"Wrong?" I asked, venturing a sympathetic hand on his thigh. My heart leapt at the intimate contact.

Remmer didn't move toward me, nor did he move away. "*We* went wrong. Yes, we question. We philosophize. We think too much."

"It's not your only problem," Layal added before diving in to Eve's face once more.

"Layal in particular *talks* too much. It was a mistake. A side effect. The people who created us wanted to remove the genes that cause people to wonder about the meaning of life. It was a failure. We've doubted our purpose in life."

"The next generation doesn't question," Layal said. "And they are taciturn. Women prefer them. They're for select women. You aren't select? I find that unbelievable."

"We're working toward it. It's why we are here," Eve said, her eyes gleaming.

"We're rejected. Now we're disposing of the trash of Cochtonia. We can't leave. We barely scratch out a living." Layal marked this remark with a pitiful sob.

"There's nothing better for you to do? You look perfectly healthy," I said, meaning "sexy."

"We're healthy but isolated. We live in an abandoned miner's cabin. We're lonely," said Remmer. His directness made my heart skip a beat.

Layal cried, "You are our air, our lifeline to the world. Oh, dear Truth. You are my angel."

At his excessive dramatics, Eve jumped from his lap. "However, the rain has stopped. We've learned enough for tonight. Will you be returning for a visit?"

"Returning? You mean we are leaving?" Rem moved away from me, as if he had caused this curve.

"They have to go?" I said. To cover my disappointment, I added, "Of course, they must. We have an assignment after all." To snap myself out of it, I imagined splashing my face with cold WasteBin effluent. It wasn't as if we needed these men for anything.

"I'm not ready for this smash," Eve said, talking casually now that she was out of Cochtonville's spotlight. "We don't know you well enough."

"Let's remedy the situation. How about we have you for dinner?" said Layal.

"A dinner we prepare for you," added Rem.

"I'd love it," I said, my stomach already rumbling.

Eve held up her hand. "I don't think I can eat. It smells like the manure out there."

"It smells," I said, wiping imaginary WasteBin water from my face as I gave her support.

Layal leapt up and took her hand. "Where we live has no smell and no flies. It's a two-mile walk. We'll be by tomorrow to escort you. And I will be only half alive until I drink from those wells that are your lips, dear Truth."

"I too, will be dead until tomorrow," she said with a swoosh of eyelash. "Go, so I may long for you."

After they had left, Eve stretched out on the rug in front of the fire. "Men. Can you believe it? We didn't even have to pay for them."

I attempted to regain my equilibrium. "Fascinating, but we wasted time. You didn't take one video and I had nothing at all to test. This is a setback."

"I wonder what they're going to serve tomorrow. How do wild people eat?"

"Was kicking them out your way of flirting?"

"Of course. My mom told me about playing hard to get."

"We don't know them and we're in a new place. We're as vulnerable as eggs on a sidewalk." The thought of eggs had my mouth watering.

"Eggs on a sidewalk. How would that even happen? Chickens are in confinement operations. Everyone knows that. You aren't making a bit of sense. Oh, Layal is such a doll. Never have I been talked to so intellectually. My mind is free to have new ideas."

"It's the beer, don't you think?"

"It's the man! Such words! And you know what he told me? If we don't have purpose, we can allow nature to take its course. I shall be without purpose from this day forward."

"Like the woman at the Welcome Mart," I said. "She's what happens to you when you don't have a plan."

"I know. He's trying to get me to mate with him. It's silly and yet," she stretched on the rug, taking up most of it. "It could be my only chance to experience love. If it goes wrong, my dad can save me."

I was ragingly jealous. She'd kissed a man for most of the night, he was trying to get in her pants, and she had the luxury of yes or no along with a rescue in her pocket.

"We're letting them lure us astray from our goals." I grabbed her camera. "I'm going to record you acting stupid."

She snatched it back and tossed her head playfully. She had no sense of my frustration. I wasn't beautiful. To hell if I was going to be damned. I needed this venture to produce something.

"Maybe we should ask the eight ball." She opened an app on her phone. "Eight the great, should we capture a mate?"

An eight ball floated onto her screen. It asked, "Mate? As in someone on a boat?"

"Of course not. A mate as in a man to love."

She tapped the ball, then looked at the floating cube in the transparent virtual window as it spun and then floated up.

"Does Cochtonville have corn?" it said.

She cheered. "A yes!"

"One sample is never enough," I said.

"One is enough if the answer is what you want."

"No, that's bias. Tap it again."

` "As sure as summer has crop dusters."

"Three times."

"You can count on it."

She hugged me with firm assurance. "Cali, we have time for fun. It's our chance to be free to love. We can take what Cochtonia denies us—the power to be female."

We cuddled together on the rug. She was burning hot, or maybe it was the flickering fire. I was lonely and it made no sense. I wasn't alone, yet I was isolated, alone in the most intimate way. No one talked about mates in Cochtonia. Eve had a point. Something was taken from us in Cochtonia. The chance to love had been stolen.

The fire rushed up the chimney, taking my sanity with it. There was writing in the haze. *I will experience love if it's the only thing I do.* I blinked. My imagination was playing tricks on me. I was already halfway there, half mad. Evidence: I'd forgotten to ask about the girl.

CHAPTER SIX

For breakfast, we sat on the rug and shared the fifty grams of corn nuts, two hundred calories at best, and the sixty milliliters of water we'd collected in the ale bottles. It might have been better not to eat; my stomach hurt like it was consuming itself.

The picture window was dotted with flies. They congregated on the cracked glass, as if trying to force their filth inside. The WasteBin stretched out before us, barren, smelly, and so far, chemically uninteresting. Any plan to use this faced an obvious barrier: getting power and plumbing out here would be expensive and Cochtonia wasn't known for providing public services. To have a winning proposal, we'd either have to prove public good or private profit or at best, both. This all hinged on a resource to make exploiting the place worth something, but who needed limestone when there was plastic?

"I'll walk to the Welcome Mart," I said, "if we've got any cash."

"You can't go. The men are coming. Oh, I can't remember when I've had such immediate needs." Eve touched her cracked lips. "Food, drink, sex...there's no room for creative thought. All I can imagine doing with this place is flushing it."

"We're better than this." I grabbed my UTI and holster from the floor and strapped them on. "There's something out there. I can feel it. I'm going to try multiple hierarchical sampling." I opened the door and a buzz of flies flew in. Eve screamed and took off her sneaker to swat them. I slammed the door behind me and marched steadily toward the pit, taking a measurement every ten steps. My goal was to make a chemical grid of the entire area. If there was anything of worth here, I'd find it.

The place was crushingly silent. No voices, no birds, no announcements from the Vice Patrol, only a random buzz in my ear from a curious fly. I walked in this manner until I was dizzy from the stench, hunger, and thirst. When I considered jumping into the pit for a swim, I knew I had to turn back before I gave in to temptation. What was I thinking? I couldn't even swim. I marked the spot with a rock, went ten paces to my left, measured, and started toward the shack again. Ten steps. Measure. Ten steps, measure. This was time consuming. I'd be better off looking for a needle in a haystack—I could draw it out with a magnet or centrifuge. What was I searching for? Unless I found a mother lode of plastic, Cochtonia wasn't going to care about the resource.

With every ten paces my motivation grew. I was flipping angry about this assignment when other teams had been sent to an old library or to pick up trash. I was going to shove this in Sir Bux's face somehow, and I would for sure fall in love along the way. I wasn't going to let Remmer's reticence put me off. I'd take full advantage of this shitty locale. My feet crunched on the rocks. Each step grew distractingly louder.

"Seven, eight, nine, ten." I pushed each button on the UTI, unleashing a barrage of energy onto the dull dirt as the gadget collected data on its composition. While at a standstill, the sound of footsteps continued. My scalp crawled. I discreetly switched the UTI to X-ray. Whatever it was following me, I'd give it a burn it wouldn't forget—or I'd run like hell. I wasn't sure which yet. Up on the hill, Eve hurried toward me from the shack. Something tapped me on the shoulder. Frightened, I whirled around, my gadget in hand.

"Made ya look!" Layal's sly, thin smile made me wish I'd beamed him.

"I could have X-rayed you!" I put the UTI in the holster. "Don't mess around. You could get hurt."

"Hear that, Remmer? She's the hurting kind. Think twice, my compadre. Ah, here comes my baby."

He held out his arms and Eve rushed into them. They spun together, enjoying the momentum of her forceful embrace.

"Hello," I said to Remmer, doing my best to sound confident. "I was gathering data." I didn't feel at all cute. My braid was crooked and my clothes were dusty. I looked like I wasn't even trying. To make things worse, he'd combed out his hair. He *was* trying. I would have to overcompensate.

Layal spoke over the brief silence. "Your pitiful shack baking in the sun is uncivilized. We're here to show you how to live out here in the wild. Come, let's feast together and celebrate our acquaintance."

"We're ready," said Eve, taking his hand. We proceeded with only the clothes on our backs and the UTI.

The walk was two miles or so across rocks interspersed with scruffy bushes, taking less than an hour by my estimation. My thirst gave me a dull headache and a muddled intellect. Layal pointed out the log cabin as we walked to it.

"We were banished from Cochtonville and relocated to this area," Layal explained. "We took residence in a home that was a domicile for miners before the coal ran out. We repaired it and cleaned it."

"There's no need for coal with Cochtonia biofuels," Eve said. "This area is remote. It's been abandoned. I take it you are the only people here."

This comment brought my mind around to the girl. I was sure I'd seen them take her. Would she be waiting for us?

"There are others," Layal said. "They are not worth meeting. They offend the sensibilities."

By the time we got to the log cabin, my thirst was acute. The men were smart enough to understand our needs and quickly dipped orange polyethylene glasses—the type children might drink from—into water from a plastic garbage can and gave it to us. The water was light and clear with a faint plastic aftertaste. My headache dissipated quickly. We'd only been in the wild for a day, thankfully. Finding a resource and application wasn't going to happen quickly. We needed these guys to show us the ways of the wild.

The cabin was constructed from notched logs filled with cement and was as square and sturdy as a Cochtonia hog. It had windows on each side, a narrow wood door, and a chimney in the rear.

Inside, it was one large room covered with a rug made from braided plastic bags and included a table with mismatched legs, set with red, yellow, blue, and purple plates. Two plastic chairs, and a park bench with a slat missing were pulled up to the table. Two lounge chairs sat by the fireplace. A steep wooden staircase led to a loft with two piles of blankets, a stack of books between them.

"You have paper?" I asked, afraid to utter the word "books."

"We dispose of contraband in the manure lagoon. At times we found paper with thoughts, bound up with two covers, which makes them pleasant to hold. I can't say I understand all I read. There is context though," Layal said. "And they make a good room divider."

"It's so cozy and spartan and a bit wicked," Eve said, squeezing Layal's arm, ignoring the books as she gazed into his eyes.

He said, "Our life is easier than it may appear. It takes just half a day to collect our food. On occasion, we trade goods for meat. We have much time to ponder. Too much time perhaps. We know what we are missing."

"This has been my goal, to relocate to a wild area and live in peace," I said. This had never been my goal, but I wasn't lying—a sudden peace had revealed itself here, away from it all. My words were more of a wish than a lie, a grasp at a credulous fantasy that I might both fall in love and have a future besides Cochtonville, where people ended their own lives rather than succumb to the harshness of the days.

Remmer, who had been standing with his arms dangling, perked up. "Yet we haven't the experiences with the vast stream of humanity to settle on any conclusions about life's meaning. We are what we do, and I do nothing. Nearly nothing."

"That's not enough?" I asked.

"Of course not. I need to be my own purpose."

Layal was uncomfortable with the silence following our exchange. "Shall we eat, Truth and Cali Van Winkle?"

It was a lusher meal than I'd expected—dandelion greens with walnuts and oil drizzled over, and meat they identified as squirrel. Layal and Eve sat close to each other as we ate with our fingers and licked them afterward. At this point, I could have eaten cardboard. The squirrel was tough but deliciously sweet, the greens fresher than anything I'd had at home, and the walnuts so bursting with flavor and oil—I thought I might cry.

"I rarely eat anything green," Eve said. "Where did you get all this?"

"We live in a unique habitat that's ours for the grazing," Layal said.

"The life you have is one I seek. Quiet. Simple. I envy you," Eve said.

"You're welcome to stay with us. See if our ways suit you. There's no rule against bringing people from the outside in. We can't leave or I would follow you anywhere." Plates finished, the two melted together in an embrace.

"Here they go again," I said to Rem. I allowed myself to study him, to meet his tawny eyes, hoping he'd follow the lead and embrace me.

He scratched his neck. "Golly, those two want to be alone. You and I could..."

I leaned toward him eagerly.

"We could pick raspberries. I know a patch of a unique and hardy species."

"What are raspberries?" I said, disappointed.

"They are delicious, that's what they are. Let's go. I'll teach you about raspberries."

"The two of us?"

"Go on," Layal said. "He doesn't bite."

I followed Rem to the backyard. A pile of discarded plastic containers and bags sat near a fire pit. He selected an old gallon ice cream bucket and grabbed a plastic bag blowing past his foot. He lined the bucket with the bag and again, we walked, toward the patch of trees untouched by the mining long ago.

Trees weren't popular in Cochtonville. "Nothing good happens in the shade," we were taught to say, and it was true, they were foreboding. This area's neglect had spared them. Once in their onerous canopy, I'd need to put my trust in this man I'd met yesterday. Brashly, more dogged to get away from the raptures of the Beautiful and Damned than concerned for my own safety, I walked on, one hand on my belt and the other in my pocket where the rough seeds of the cemetery plants rubbed my skin through the thin fabric of my pants. Irritated, I tossed a pinch onto the ground and then another as we marched along until at last, I couldn't feel any. My fingers held onto their jasmine scent, and tossing those seeds released a keen euphoria. Everything became interesting and fresh. I trusted Rem as he skipped along—a wild man in polyester. The sun was on our backs. I was so free.

Another plastic bag blew past us.

"Grab it," he said, and he ran after the bag. I joined him, our shadows dancing and crossing each other's, intimately merging. The bag spent time playing with us as we tried to make trash into treasure. Finally, he stepped on it and held it up in triumph. "A gift from nature. We use these when we go trading."

"Trading? What's this barter?"

"We meet traders at a rock and exchange goods. They are better hunters. Layal and I gather because we are better at it than the traders. They don't do as well with their hands as we do nor do they have the attention spans. Gathering takes a few hours as you will see, while hunting requires short bursts of speed. We weren't made for speed. I suppose you could say we hunters and gatherers depend on each other without living together."

"Why don't you just live together?"

"You'd have to meet them to understand."

My heart pounded as I beheld his amber eyes, so much clearer and brighter than any man's I'd seen before. The combination of these with his red hair made him an exotic creature. His youth and freshness had me simmering with want. Of course, with the gene insertion technology I could choose whatever combination I desired for my future son if I reached InVitro status. It would be this, these eyes, that tousled hair, if I ever made it home to seek my status and success.

We came to the patch of trees and their shadows. He stepped into the woods and I followed. Here, hidden by the awning of oaks, a patch of wild canes twisted together and burst with ruby caps the size of golf balls made from droplets of glistening gel.

"Careful, the canes scratch," Rem said, plucking a berry and handing it to me. "Eat it."

"Are they safe?"

"Of course. They were developed by My Lady."

"My Lady? The woman at the Welcome Mart? I saw this same plant there growing near an old bus."

"Yes, she was a scientist once, banished here, as we were, with her raspberries. We're forbidden to see her, although she watches us from the shack on the hill."

"She's suspicious. I wonder what she did wrong."

"Who knows? We met her when we came here. The authorities who transported us were standoffish to her. She bragged about her colossal raspberries and urged us to partake as we were taken away to be released. They emphasized we were to keep our distance. She overtly preferred Layal. Doesn't everybody?"

"Not me."

"You are too kind." He picked a raspberry and bit into it, juice running across his fingers and down his dimpled chin like thin blood.

I put mine to my lips. The scent was subtler than food in Cochtonville, which had added synthetic aromas. I nibbled it. The sweet, tangy burst wasn't as powerful or tantalizing as a candy and the aftertaste was understated and light.

"It's fructose," I said. "Less concentrated than I'm accustomed to."

"Of course. It's fruit. You can linger over it. You can spend an hour nibbling and not get a bellyache."

"I'm used to immediate satisfaction."

"You've got plenty of time out here. When you pick raspberries, there's little else you crave. You focus on them. They are a currency here, and you can spend all you want on yourself, but they don't last long. We'll need to set some aside to trade for food that sticks with us like a friend."

"I don't get it."

"Meat. We trade some of these for meat when we are called."

We picked for an hour or more. Time fell away and shadows began to darken as we ate nearly as much as what went into our bucket with the plastic bag inside. The berries may have been less sweet than candy, but they had a mixture of subtle flavors. At last I succumbed to my curiosity, dialed the mass to charge ratio on my UTI, and hit them with some laser ablation. My hair fell around my face as I read the data. *Ethyl formate and p-Hydroxybenzyl acetone.*

"Are these things even healthy?"

"Of course. What do you eat in your city?"

"Pork, beef, chicken, corn, soybeans, and anything made from them." I kept reading. "Anthocyanins, sophorosides, glucoside, glucorutinoside, and rutinoside. Do we need any phytochemicals that can't be found in corn and soybeans?"

"Don't know. They're luscious though."

He picked a berry and lifted it to my mouth, his fingers lingering over my lips so carefully, it was as if he was going to precisely deliver an aliquot of delightful.Rainbows poured from his eyes. Until this week, I couldn't remember anyone other than my parents giving me anything at all except work to do. Out here in the wild, Eve had bought supplies to share and now this man was handing me fruit, his skin brushing mine. I took the berry without hesitation.

"They must be healthy," I said.

"All natural. Barely touched by humanity." *Like him.*

"My turn," I said. I reached into the tangle of canes and plucked the fattest berry I saw. "Open up." He did as I commanded. I positioned the berry in his mouth and stretched up to consume the other half. My No Regrets 2.0 flashed a green smiley face as he closed his lips and closed his eyes.

His eyes popped open and he jumped back, fruit falling from his mouth. "What is that thing?"

"A device from my company."

"They require you to carry much."

"It's all good. It tells me things. It says you're safe." We leaned together. My heart was beating like a piston pump. Sweat poured down my back. A farm bell rang in the distance. I hadn't heard a real farm bell before—only the broadcast version before the Cochtonville Farm Report. I knew they'd been used decades ago on family farms, but there were no family farms anymore—everything belonged to Cochton Enterprises. It called out as a ghost from an eerie past none of us had ever lived. Remmer straightened.

"Hear that? It's the traders. Good news," he said. "We'll have meat tonight. You're staying, aren't you? We'll feast."

"I'm staying, but where is the bell coming from? It's kind of spooky."

"Oh, if you only knew. Quick, more berries." He grabbed his bag and plucked as much as he could. I worked beside him, each knobby berry a little brain between my fingers, until each plastic bag was full.

"Follow me. And don't let them put you off." He led me through a patch of woods and to a little river about eighteen feet wide, strangled with sediment and crossed by a path of stepping stones. "Climb on my back and keep dry," he said.

He bent down and I mounted him, my mind racing to places it had never been as my legs tangled around him and my arms reached around his neck. My bag of berries dangled across his chest as I pushed my breasts into his body in an effort to stay on. Oh, who was I kidding, I did it for the sensation. He was slick in his plastic suit, and with each step I feared I'd slip as he walked steadily across the knee-high lazy river. Closer I pressed. Harder I pressed. The water beneath my dangling feet, his hands clasped under my rump while his bag of berries dangled off his elbow. We reached the bank and his hands slacked. I slid gently behind him onto the rough sand.

"Thank you for the piggyback."

"Humans are cooperative breeders and human females appreciate help and cooperation. I learned that in a discarded anthropology text."

His technical talk about human breeding had me intrigued. I understood Mom. She'd followed her instincts to dump an uncooperative mate. This was a little too personal. I changed the subject.

"Thanks for the lift. I enjoyed the ride."

"Me, too. It's the closest I've been to a flesh-and-blood woman since I lost my mom," he said, blinking rapidly. "Come on. Not much farther. Through these woods."

The trees hovered over with their leaves hanging at me. I hadn't seen so many in one place before, and although it made for cooler air, it was sinister.

"It's getting dark."

"Not much moonlight among the trees," he said. "Those we are meeting, however, prefer the dark."

CHAPTER SEVEN

"Here's where we wait." Remmer and I sat on a flat rock the size of a telecom box next to the trees.

Two girls and a dun-colored dog pushed their way through the trees and stood before us. They resembled the Pesto girl with button noses and eyes the size of dimes, but they were older and all the worse for it. Their loose dresses were woven strands of plastic bags. Their hair was matted and they smoothed it with dusty hands. The shorter one with frizzy blonde curls—so thin and tangled they looked like smoke—carried a limp turkey by the legs. The dog, the size of a lab, hung next to the taller girl, who stroked its head.

"Hey, you red-headed stepchild, we need a trade," the short one said. "Your berries for this turkey. Ya dig?"

"Hey, NezLeigh. How fresh is the turkey?" Remmer asked, walking forward, the moonlight highlighting his tight shorts with the green Cochtonville Market logo across his butt. "It's not flapping."

"Strangled tonight. Still warm. Nice evening for a roast. Not a cloud anywhere. We were planning to eat it ourselves, but we want to show you mercy. We need fruit. We're scurvy and turd-plugged and have another mouth to feed, as you know. We're here to deal, but this turkey is worth more than those bloody bags of berries, ya dig?"

"Let's see you pluck it," he said. "Pluck it to show it's fresh."

"Damn, we told you it was warm. Don't you believe it?" NezLeigh threw the turkey on the ground and stepped on the neck with her bare feet. The taller girl, with darker scraggly hair, pulled the legs until the head popped off and lay raw and red in the dirt. The dog leapt forward and crunched it between its jaws.

"Good work, Kola," NezLeigh said to the tall girl with broad shoulders and gangly arms.

Blood dripped from the neck as Kola held up the turkey. NezLeigh tugged out the wing and tail feathers as the smell of raw meat mingled with the blood. She tossed her fistful of feathers on the ground. "You standing there like you're a boss? We're not gonna do it all. Get your limp hands over here."

Remmer handed me the bags of raspberries. "Keep this tight. They steal."

He tugged on the feathers as a musty smell rose from the bird. Feathers stuck to his hands, sweaty from gripping the plastic sack. Within three minutes, the stark skin of the turkey shimmered pink like a new baby. Remmer took one sack of berries from me and held them out to Kola, who snatched them away.

"Who's the worthless chick?" Kola said, flipping her tangled hair with her dusty hand.

"Bring her again and we'll toss you over that rock and strangle you, you son of a bitch. You got it?" said NezLeigh.

"I'm here to trade in goods, not personal advice." Remmer's voice broke. "And, by golly, you never knew my mother."

"This trade's not done. These berries are smashed, Crybaby."

"Don't talk to him like that. The berries are fine," I said, surprised by my rescuing instincts. It was because I hated these little jerks, not because of him, right?

"Only weaklings cry about losing our mamas. Give us your other bag while he mops his eyes."

I knew what these Pestos did—got services first and paid later.

Sometimes their rings were copper, but other times they were lead. I gave her the bag of berries, determined to step in if she stole everything.

"Hand over the turkey," I said. My hand went to my gadget belt. I didn't have a weapon, but I had a visible spectrometer and could pop 450 nanometers into those sensitive eyes of hers if she failed to deliver or came after me.

NezLeigh hid the bird behind her back. "We're not done with him yet and you're not his next of kin. Catching a turkey takes skill. You gotta call." She let lose a squawk. "You gotta kill. It's more dangerous work than picking berries. We could have gotten a wing in the eye. Give us each a kiss, bawler, and we'll call it even."

"Bawler the baller," Kola added.

Remmer slapped a mosquito. "Golly, you girls are too young to have such thoughts."

"Fine excuse. We're too ugly to get you to take off those tiny shorts. That's what you're saying. Pucker up or we'll rip them off you, panty-waist."

Remmer put a hand to his mouth. "Where'd you get your ideas? I picked the berries fair and square. Got a nasty cut. Your hands would be skinless if you did it. Be sweet and give me the bird before it gets too dark and we get bit up."

"Bummer, Crybaby. You want us to hurry so you can get some nookie."

That was enough. I drew my UTI from my belt and grabbed her hair in case she tried to run off without finishing the barter.

"Let go you fucking sweat hog." She slapped me with the raw turkey, its soft flesh pounding me. It hurt like being run into by a drunk, which I'd experienced. It wasn't brutal but it dented my pride and spattered me with blood. I held my UTI and struggled to get a good angle. Her plastic bag dress was slippery as slime and hissed as it rustled, like gas from a leaky valve. She was a wiry, wily thing and whatever age she was, I was sure she was small for it. She bit my arm. I yelled in surprise as she broke my grip. Her face filled with fury. She pulled a sharpened popsicle stick from her hair and lunged at me. In this dirty place, cuts *could* be as dangerous as a wing in the eye. I'd thought this through, my attack. I aimed. I pushed the button. The UTI poured forth blue light, right in her tiny eye. It was enough to stop her without doing permanent damage. She dropped back, wailing and holding her eye as the turkey plopped to the dust.

"Who's the crybaby now?" I said, making a show of putting the gadget in the holster.

NezLeigh held her injured eye. "I'll get you, bitch, and that thing you shot me with."

Remmer snatched the turkey from the lunge of the slobbering dog and slung the carcass over his shoulder. He grabbed my hand and we turned our backs on them, walking quickly.

"Hey, girl, life is shorter than his stupid pants. Get it while you can," Kola yelled to me as we left. "Don't make any ugly babies."

"They are just kind of mean," Remmer said as we walked away.

Yeah because the only power a woman has in society is her attractiveness. These girls are forging a new path. They can't trade on their looks, so they are getting what they can, and damn it, I admire that as much as I hate how they treat Remmer. "They aren't going to get anywhere being mean," I said, not wishing to wallow in my sympathy for them.

"You okay?"

"I'm worried about bruises. I don't imagine you have ice here." I wasn't so much concerned as I was seeking praise for my bold action. Someone had to put NezLeigh in her place.

"Only in the winter. What about the bite?"

"It didn't break the skin and I've had about every vaccination there is. It surprised me though. She's vicious. How did you meet those little jerks?"

"The girls? We have orders to look in the trash for salvageables. We found the girls in a pile of garbage. We are supposed to throw all biomass in the pit. We let them go free instead, and for a while they hung around catching mice and bats. We got some meat on our bones and they liked our berries. They can't see well enough to pick for themselves, and they can't just take their time because berry seasons are short. Even though we gathered nuts and dandelions for them, they decided they were better than we were and ran off to form their own camp, coming to barter when they needed it."

At last, my worries gushed out. "Do you find kids in the trash often?"

"Not much, but when we do, we give them to her. NezLeigh has her own gang hidden somewhere in the woods. The girls prefer to stick together."

"Did you find a child the other day?"

"Yeah, a little one. She was weary, weepy, and starving. We fed her, gave her water, and did our best not to frighten her. She went to NezLeigh when we got the squirrels."

"I saw her hauled away back in Cochtonville. I did nothing because I was afraid. Thanks for saving her."

"Everyone out here has been hauled away, except you and Eve. And I'm often afraid. This is a frightening place." He put his arm around me and we walked to the camp.

The sky was in its final throes of green-gray light. The berry stains on my hands looked like blood, and Remmer smelled like rust and meat. We got to camp and Rem used a cottage cheese container to dip water from the garbage pail-turned-cistern and leaned across the coals to pour it into the top of a kettle grill resting in a fire pit.

He said, "We might as well cook it while it's fresh."

I went to the plastics pile and got a JumButter tub and helped him dip from the cistern. The coals were still smoldering. Remmer went to his stack of books and threw some labeled "encyclopedia" on the ashes.

The fire leapt as Remmer poked an old paper journal—*Reader's Consumption*—into the flames. He ran the burning paper across the turkey, charring off the pinfeathers. He leaned over and plopped the turkey into the water.

"Now all we do is wait."

He went into the cabin and returned hoisting the rug woven from plastic bags.

"Are Eve and Layal still going at it?" I asked.

"They're happy. We might as well rest a while. This won't be done 'til morning."

He set the rug next to the fire.

I said, "Not so close. Those things are flammable. Plastic is made from oil, you know."

"It is?"

"Yes, we import those bags. Cochtonville doesn't have a reliable source of plastic despite our love for it."

Remmer moved the rug away from the fire. Some errant form of motherly love rose within me. This guy was going to need a few more pounds and a little more scientific knowledge to make it through the winter.

"Better sit on it with me before it blows away," he said. "Thanks for the help. I don't know what they would have done to me. Your device was effective. Of course, we will have to live with the hunters in as much harmony as possible as time moves forward, especially in the winter when there is nothing to gather but acorns."

I'd probably disrupted their relationship. I changed the subject. "How's your scratch?"

"Healing. A little dirt is nothing compared to manure runoff."

"Maybe a wing in the eye *would* be worse."

"Yes, but I won't tell them. How's your bruise?"

I lifted my t-shirt and inspected my side. I couldn't see much in the darkness but my skin had a blush of purple. Remmer put out his hand and brushed his fingers across my tingling body.

"Does it hurt?"

"Not really. A raw turkey isn't a match for me." I unclipped my gadget belt and put it on the ground behind me.

"You've got a vicious weapon if it could stop NezLeigh."

"It's not a weapon. It's for testing. M-my feelings for you made me do what I did. We have those people back home, too. They coerce my mom into doing illegal things."

"Thank you for your help. Cali, will you be staying here for a while? To quote Francis Bacon, 'without friends, the world is but a wilderness.'" He put his arm around me in a simple but inspiring gesture.

A light breeze came up and tickled my skin. Crickets chirped. He smelled like smoke and thus like my dad. This gave me pause. Well, he might be a little like my dad if my dad stopped drinking. I hated myself for my weird feelings of compassion, curiosity, and wanting to be with him. *How often am I going to get the chance to study a young man?* Oh, I hated deviating. *This is my only opportunity.* No. Yes. Where will I find a spare young male? *I will probably be assigned to bear a son. I should know more about males for his sake. I should learn all I can.* If I was going to cast my lot here, it wasn't going to be halfway; I was risking too much by taking time off from my project for halfway.

"Remmer." I put my hand on his thigh, just below the green plastic Cochtonville Market bag he'd made his pants from.

"Yes, Cali."

"Remmer, if I stay, I'm not going to be just a friend."

CHAPTER EIGHT

His amber eyes went blank.

"What do you mean?"

"Put your arms, both arms, around me and we'll bask together. You know, let our feelings wash over us." For me to say something like this about feelings was out of character, but this man had me dizzy and dare I say it, hopeful. "It's easy. I've seen Eve and Layal do it when they're happy. We're happy since we met, aren't we?"

"I'm happy with you. You're not a rival. We're mates. We're meant to share. What if we could be a family like the one I lost?"

And the one I never had where both work together.

"I'd like to be your mate."

He gave me a tentative hug. "It's so soft."

"Give it time."

He kneaded my arms with his strong hands. "I'm not accustomed to this reality."

Delight and curiosity ran though me. I wasn't used to someone touching me, especially someone so firm and muscular and wearing only plastic bag clothing that crinkled provocatively. No one in Cochtonville was particularly experienced with any sort of touching, particularly not with someone you might care about, someone who lit you on fire. I knew one thing, he was not soft, no, not soft in any place at all. He was coursing with hot blood, and so was I.

"I-I don't think it's soft."

He gazed into my eyes. "It's you. Your skin is soft; it yields, as if you've had regular meals. Everything here is harsh and lean. Words are rough and meat is tough. Take me with you when you return to your place. We can eat together."

I gazed back. "You wouldn't like it there. Everyone is perfectly normal and dull or depressed or mean. Isn't your job *here*?" It was freeing to have this guy holding me. Owning so few possessions beyond my gadget buoyed me. I didn't want to think of Cochtonville and all its troubles. If I had known last week that tonight I'd be sitting with—lusting for—a young man wearing plastic bags I would have thought myself ridiculous. Yet here I was, reveling in each perfect second.

"Remmer, the stars are so bright out here."

He took my chin in his hand. Being near him had me drunkenly unstable. He said, "Do they have birthday cake?"

"What? Cake? In Cochtonville? Yes, they do. Corn flour with corn syrup frosting."

"I had one once. It had candles. Each one burned a different color. Orange for sodium, purple for potassium. My dad told me."

"Your dad was a chemist?"

"I'm not sure. I had parents. We were happy. They called me... I can't remember. Something other than Remmer."

"I'll give you something better than birthday cake." I leaned into his face. I had instincts. He had to have them too, didn't he? He was made to be erotic. Why wasn't he interested? Was it me?

He gathered me in his arms and put his chin on my shoulder. He pulled me to the crinkling rug, burying his face in my hair. His breath was hot on my tingling scalp. His lips brushed across my ear. I wanted to pop from the delight of it all. I was afraid and fascinated, like crossing a rickety bridge. I was swaying and looking over the edge—an explorer. His body pushed against mine. A thin layer of my corn fiber and his plastic separated us. We moved together in a new oscillation, a pattern to break all loneliness.

"Cali," he whispered. "Cali. I can't believe you found me. I'm so happy. I could hold you like this forever."

"Rem."

"I hope I am not imposing my will on you, for it would be wrong."

"Rem, we're in this together. It's how it must be. We're equals. We share, as if covalently bonded. If we were elements, we'd be the same, or at the very least, have nearly identical electronegativities."

His breathing slowed.

"Rem?"

"It's been a long, splendid day." He rolled onto his back and quickly fell asleep, softly snoring in my ear.

I got up and went into the shadows to go to the bathroom. I was goose bumpy and distressed with my own impatience. An impatient chemist was a dead chemist, dare I say a damned chemist. I'd take it slow, as he wanted. Even out here, p-cresol hung in the air in dilute concentration with its foul sweetness. The chemical p-cresol, or para-cresol as it was sometimes called, was in pig manure. I'd done a gas chromatography lab with the stuff. It attracted mosquitos, too.

Cochtonville blinked in the distance like an irritated eye and the well-lit drones rotated above it. Despite my parents' mild griping, I'd always seen the city of Cochtonville as a safe place, an island of stability in the chaos of the surrounding United States where people were thugs and crazy, or so we were told. Being out here was distorting my perception. I could almost see Cochtonville's radon glowing, the arsenic creeping into the wells, and the sewage lagoons overflowing.

I returned to the mat and snuggled into Remmer as the fire's light danced on my face. He drew me in with his smoky arms.

"Stay close," he whispered.

"Give me a reason," I whispered. This was going to take longer than I'd planned.

After the sun rose and Eve and Layal came out from the cabin, we sat by the fire and gorged ourselves on the turkey, eating the warm meat with our hands, the grease running down our faces. When we could eat no more, Eve, cool and perky in her HotNot, declared we should dry the meat by the fire and make jerky. I suggested we let it sit in the ashes for the salt.

"We need something flatter than this grill lid to put the meat on," she said, confirming we'd do it her way. She held out her fingers and Layal licked them clean.

"Let me go find something for you," he said. "Remmer, we can scrounge today, don't you think?"

"Well, sure. I'd hate for this to go to waste. Cali fought off the hunters for it."

"I've got bruises to show it," I said, lifting my shirt to show the purplish area where I'd been slapped with the turkey. "And she bit me." My arm had an elliptical mark from NezLeigh's mouth.

"Ouch," said Eve. "And you've got blood on your shirt as well. Rinse it in cold water before it sets."

"The cistern is getting low," said Layal. "There's only water left for drinking until it rains again."

"I'll wash in the river," I replied. The blood looked gruesome and this was my only shirt.

"I'll go with you," Remmer said.

"No, man," said Layal. "You're coming with me. I might need help with the carry. She won't get washed away before, you know, you, ah. You're taking it slow, aren't you?"

"Cali, be careful where you go. It's shallow where we crossed," said Remmer, ignoring his friend. "Stick to our side of the creek and you won't run into NezLeigh."

"Who's NezLeigh?" asked Eve.

"A mean little Pesto," I replied. "A little jerk."

"Out here?"

"On the other side of the river," said Layal. "Mouthy Pestos live in the trees. They're an annoying fact of life. There's no need to fear.

Remmer is babyish about them, but they are harmless. Go to the creek. Get some water. Remmer and I will hike to the WasteBin and return with a flat pan for drying the meat and a tarp to hang in the loft between our beds for privacy. Truth, you accompany your friend and return with her safely. I'll be half alive until we're together again." He grabbed her and tickled her side until she screamed and the grease from his hands left finger smears on her shirt.

As soon as the men were out of sight, we made a beeline to the river, following the worn path, leaving the turkey simmering on the dying coals. I wore my gadget belt in case we ran into NezLeigh. And honestly, I didn't care to be without it. All it would take was the right crop of rocks and I'd be in the money with the resource. I beamed a rubble pile. Limestone again. There was a mile of limestone between the cabin and the tree line, and who needs limestone when you have plastic?

As we neared the trees, the hard dirt sprouted a blush of green. My heart skipped a beat. Was it a hint of copper? I beamed the patch with my UTI. Damn. Chlorophyll. I bent down to study the tiny clusters of three bright leaves. Poison ivy? No. I smelled jasmine. I poured through the molecular profile on the UTI. Yes, jasmine. These were baby graveyard plants. Had I introduced an invasive species out here? I tried to discreetly squash a few of the new sprouts with my foot.

"What are you finding?" Eve asked.

"Not much," I replied, embarrassed. I pointed straight ahead. "In here."

We ducked into the humid shade of the tree canopy.

"It's so dark!" Eve exclaimed. She put her hands to her head, holding her HotNot as if the trees would snatch it from her.

"You'll get used to it," I said, glad to be the one in the know.

We stopped in front of the bushes covered with bulging raspberries.

"Try one," I said. "Remmer and I picked them and traded them for the turkey. Those little jerks are afraid of the thorns. All you need to do is use your fingers carefully to pull them off the stem. Like this." I plucked one and handed it to her.

She took a hearty bite. "Mmm. I've had more delights these past two days than I'd get in a year in Cochtonville. What am I eating?"

"It's called raspberry. My Lady is some sort of scientist. She made these."

"Mmm, so juicy I can eat and drink at the same time. Ack. I got juice on my shirt. Let's move on to the water. We've got more spots than a Guernsey."

We reached the creek. I wasn't sure if I should take the bank or venture onto the flat stones carefully placed between the shallow banks. In the center, they were barely above the water racing between them. They had to have been placed because of a murky bottom or snapping turtles. I removed my shoes and inched onto one. I pulled out my shirt with one hand, leaned over, and scooped the water with my other hand to soak the corner. I was sure the UTI had to be waterproof, but Nell hadn't mentioned such, which left me cautious about getting it wet. I squeezed the shirt and examined the dissolving stain.

"They wash out." I moved a few stones down, leaving room for Eve to join me. She did so and pulled off her shirt, dunked it in the water and rubbed it together. The sun beamed between the trees and their leaves tossed in the breeze.

"It's so liberating to not have to worry about society's restrictions," she said. "It's as if I am finding my own voice, not the one my parents expect. Free speech!"

"My forehead is freer already," I said, happy to not be constantly pressing it when the flag went by. I remembered who I was talking to—the daughter of the commissioner—and I hastily added, "With all of this sunshine on it."

"Sunshine on your forehead? That's random. You look like such a doof with your belt full of gear." She laughed. "Do I sound like you? It's Calispeak."

"I've never used the word 'doof.' Don't blame me for your free speech."

"Ha. You know what would make a good resource—the raspberries. You don't even need a UTI. So there. Haha." Her laugh was as cute as she was, a little feminine trill. It, and the notion that the UTI was useless, got the best of me. I splashed her. She jumped away and fell on her rump in the water. It was only a couple of feet deep. She grabbed for her shirt as it half sunk in front of her. As she did so, her HotNot fell off.

"My beret!"

We both reached for it at the same time and clunked heads.

"Sorry, so sorry," I said.

She screamed, "It's getting away! We'll swelter out here without it."

She struggled to her feet, pulling her t-shirt on over her head and hurrying toward the beret at the same time. The white cap was carried along on the current, not fast enough to signal it was gone and not slow enough to let us catch it easily. The water remained shallow, and we followed it as I apologized constantly. She was right; with no air conditioning and summer fast approaching, we needed that material. The creek bent and we went around the bend, and then another, as if the water was showing off and becoming more an elegant S than a little river. We vowed to stop if we didn't catch the beret in the next minute. Eve didn't seem mad, more determined, but the water made each step a slog even as it pushed us along.

It widened to about thirty feet—not enough to be frightening; the rocks were slippery as if the water had gotten fatty, though not enough to be dangerous. I took the UTI from its holster and beamed the water. "Animal fat, protein and blood," I said. Eve took one last lunge at the HotNot before her feet went out from under her and she fell face first into the water. The beret floated out of sight. She sat on her butt in the water and slapped the creek. "Rocks are slippery. Who knew? This place is the heart of darkness. My dad is going to be so mad at me."

A splash answered. A deer drinking near the bank jerked its head from the water. The bottom half of its face was a yellow mass. At first, I thought it was a gaudy tumor, but no. The animal had gotten its head stuck in a plastic ear of corn-shaped bucket used to hold popcorn on Cochtonville Days. The strap was behind its ears and the colorful yellow cob with a smile and green leaves was lodged across its snout. The animal stood in the water, its head bowed.

"I'm not sure if I'm fascinated or horrified," Eve said.

"It can't eat. Poor deer must be starving."

"Can we catch it and kill it? Then we'd have our own meat," Eve replied.

Shame flushed through me at the thought of killing this frightened thing instead of helping it. The truth remained. We'd be more self-sufficient if we killed it.

"I don't want to go splashing about with my gadget," I said, making an excuse not to tangle with the deer.

"Don't worry, I've got it. We'll strangle it. *I'll* strangle it. It's already weak," she said.

The deer shook its head and mounted the bank toward an oak tree surrounded by mounds of sticks and leaves as water dripped from the bucket and dirt streamed beneath its hooves. A mosquito bit my neck and I slapped it. We both moved toward the animal. The stones beneath our feet were slick, covered with rotting leaves. The deer slid down the bank and tumbled into the water. It fell onto its side. It was drowning again and struggled to its feet. This deer was going to die anyway. We might as well make some use of it.

"I can't get solid footing," Eve said. She put her hand on my shoulder and we both lost our balance and took a dip. I kept my head out of the muck and struggled to my feet as I eyed the banks, deciding which one was closer. We had to get out of this water. We were shivering and my gadget had taken a dunking.

This place was eerie. Except for the water, it was drenched in shadow. Nothing was static. The leaves bobbed; a bird flitted from one leafy tree to another. An eagle swooped onto a white-barked tree hanging over the water. The tree squeaked like a hinge on the gate to hell. A half dozen triangular mounds of sticks and leaves protruded from the farther shore. My first thought was they were burial sites, pyramids, a mass grave. Something slunk between them, crouching down like a bobcat. We were told the cats were out here and it was a reason to never visit the countryside.

Back on her feet, Eve crept toward the deer as it sat stunned in the water. The crouching form on the bank slinked toward Eve. I froze and whispered, "Stop. Animal." Eve paused. The animal rushed forward, barking hoarsely. It was the dumb dog of that little jerk Kola. Amidst high-pitched shouts, plastic bag-clad girls poured out of the stick and leaf mound lean-tos.

CHAPTER NINE

"It's mine."

"I got it."

"Right on!"

There were a half dozen tiny-eyed girls, shouting, bones and clubs swirling above their heads like ceiling fans. They slithered down the bank and swarmed the drowning deer. That pug-nosed bitch NezLeigh and dimwit Kola led the charge with younger girls sliding behind them. One of them was the orphan I'd seen the night Dad got hauled away—the same child Remmer and Layal had pulled out of a garbage bag. She was tear-free now as she brandished a big femur and yelled fiercely. NezLeigh pummeled the deer's head with a bone. The plastic broke off and spun into the river.

Eve slogged to my side. "Are those the mean girls?"

"Yes. Shhh. They can't see us out here in the light." The deer still had fight in it. It bucked and kicked at the children.

"Maybe they can help us."

"Help drown us is what they'll do. They're nasty."

"Nonsense. They will know about the resources of this area. You need them."

"No. They're crazier than hoot owls. We're getting the hell out of here. Come on."

I knew we had to get away. Home was upstream. My legs were as heavy as if I was walking on Saturn. My feet went out from under me and I fell with a splash. Filthy brown water—the kind of stuff that harbored fecal coliform—flew up my nose. Even worse, my equipment went under once more. Eve grabbed my arm and helped me to my feet. "Can you swim?"

"Of course not." Only rich people had pools in Cochtonville. "But I can learn."

"Now is not the time." She fell with a little yelp, poorly timed between dog barks; her cry startled the girls. They halted. The deer yanked away and swam downstream.

"Hell's bells. Who are you?" NezLeigh yelled. "We off intruders."

This was more bravado than any adult would attempt, considering they couldn't see us and en masse weighed maybe three hundred pounds. The Pestos were known for being more go than show. Their men crop dusted in wind storms. The women killed themselves when threatened. They followed through in dangerous ways. This reputation wasn't lost on Eve.

"They've such a savage nature. I can't understand half of what they say. We can't pass up this opportunity to study youthful tribalism in such a raw form." Eve wrapped her arms across her chest. "And I'm getting bit to pieces by all the bugs out here."

As a chemist in charge of a large lab, as surely I would be if I ever got out of here and finished our presentation and was awarded InVitro status, I'd make quick decisions. I'd be flexible and work with what I had. What did I have at this moment? I pointed downstream.

"We've got to get to the opposite shore."

We'd have to slip past these girls *with* the current—we'd been good at slipping, at least—and get where there was a sandbar.

We moved through the water like light through darkness. The rocks grew slimier. The bottom was covered with rotting acorns with sharp caps. We both fell.

"Damn. Intruders." NezLeigh put her hand over her eyes and stared in our direction. A cloud rolled over the sun, casting us in shade.

"It's bitches! Dungo! Dungo!" Kola screamed as the dog bounced to the edge of the bank and barked at us as we struggled to our feet.

"Hello, friends. Do you speak Cochtonian?" Eve called. "We need assistance."

"No, we don't bow to the culture of our oppressors. Ya hip? Looks like your asses are in a sling," NezLeigh yelled.

Eve hollered, unaware of her naivety. "If you help us, we'll be in your debt."

"Debt like a payday loan." NezLeigh pushed Kola.

"Dungo. Fetch. Fetch," said Kola.

The dog waddled, then paddled toward us with his wet mouth open. I was thankful for that time back home when a bat had fallen on me from the ceiling and I'd needed a series of rabies vaccines. They'd set my parents back most of their savings, but now, as the dog's slobbery mouth clamped down on the rear of my pants, I didn't have to worry about a virus as he shook his head, and pulled me toward the shore. This was no rescue, more like an interception. I fell several times but kept my neck and my gadget out of the water as I was inched toward the bank. The dog growled and wagged his thick tail as if this was a game. NezLeigh waded out and grabbed me by the arm.

"That's a trick for the little ones, getting stuck in the slimy spot." She was a kid, not even five feet tall. Despite her stature, she had me rattled. My blood whooshed through my chest as if I'd downed ten cups of Sleep No More fortified corn beverage. The little orphan rushed forward and embraced me.

"She's a friend!" I was wearing the same clothes as on the fateful night of our meeting, and yet I was still surprised she recognized me. Her advocacy calmed me down a little. I gave her a hug.

"You know this humping bitch, Purceel?" NezLeigh said.

The little one scratched her butt. "She fed me candy when Mama became a martyr." I guessed her name came from the detergent bottle found the day she'd landed in the WasteBin.

I took a slow breath. "Good to see you again, NezLeigh." I tried to keep my tone casual.

"*See?* Is that a joke? It's a miracle you didn't put my eye out with that light you attacked me with." She fingered my UTI in its damp holster. "Does it still work? No tricks or I'll slit your throat."

I made up my mind to be honest with her and cooperate. I didn't understand her enough to lie to her. "I don't know. I've dunked it twice, three times, maybe."

"Turn it on."

I drew my UTI from its holster.

"Stand back, cutie," I said to Purceel. I held my gadget at arm's length and dialed it through the wavelengths from 400 to 700 nanometers. The bands of sequential colors bounced across the lingering twilight, flashing the color-changing beam on the water where the dog was tugging Eve by the waistband.

"It works," I said, flush with happiness as I returned the UTI to the holster.

"Damn fine. Mark me down as an admirer. Your weapon isn't useful with those pansy gatherers and I betcha they don't appreciate it or you. You're with us, ya dig? We're using your bitchin' contraption to our advantage. You heard what your friend said, you're in our debt."

Kola waded into the water and grabbed Eve's arm. "This way, my miss, this way, my miss. Good Dungo, good boy, good boy, Dungo."

"Your dog slobbered on me," Eve complained as she climbed up the bank with Kola.

"Crybaby and his pretty boy friend live upstream. Tell it like it is. Are you sent as spies? Are you spies?" Kola asked, shoving her face into mine so close I could see her crooked bottom teeth.

I wrung out the hems of my shorts. "Why would we spy? He claims you're friends."

"Everyone knows a woman never leaves her home unless driven out by an old man," NezLeigh said.

"You're right." Dripping, Eve wiped away a tear. "We were sent to this place, not by our Crispers—by our evil...our evil overload, Sir Bux. He's a wicked man who wears a uniform and has..." she flicked her hand under her chin, "a little goatee and a potbelly. He eats well and banished us here to starve." She gripped her stomach.

This was a genius story, and NezLeigh and her army leaned forward, listening sympathetically. The Pestos would be sensitive to banishment and repelled by a uniform. Even better, it was true enough that I could go along with it.

"We had no warning," I added. "One day home, the next exiled."

Eve shook out her hair. "He lied to us. He said nothing was here and no one. Yet we found you brave huntresses."

"We're clandestine," NezLeigh said. "We know men lie. You should stay with us."

Kola said, "Those men you suck face with are douchebag losers. Losers. We keep them alive."

"We're grateful to you," said Eve. "But as grateful and indebted as we are for our rescue, we must return to them, for unlike you, our hearts are foolish."

NezLeigh said, "You cost us dinner and a month's supply of poop-berry barter. You owe us a favor."

"Of course," Eve said, "we're at your service. What can we do to make this right?"

"Ever killed a pig?"

"No," we said together.

NezLeigh grabbed me by the arm. "That thing of yours is going to help us."

I pulled back. "It's not a weapon. It's a measuring device. You shine light through something and see how much the beam is weakened. The degree of weakening is proportional to the amount of substance in it. It's called Beer's Law."

"Spare the details. We're too young to drink. Listen up and

listen good. The wild pigs eat at night. Light attracts them. Can you make it set on green?"

"Yes, the entire ultraviolet-visible spectrum."

"You'll help us then."

"Do we get to go home after?"

"Home? Dig that. She calls it home. You *are* sleeping with Crybaby."

"I'm trying to, but you little jerks are interfering," I said in frustration.

"Bummer. We've got the fix if you do what we want," NezLeigh said.

Eve said, "We'll get you some extra berries. Help us get out of here."

"Sure we will, but your knees are knocking together. Take off those clothes and wrap up in plastic bags."

We stripped as she suggested, goosebumps popping, our nipples as hard as field corn, the Little Jerks eyeing our bodies. NezLeigh handed us a couple of plastic bags.

"Whez-damn," she said as she looked at my bruise, already turning blue. "That'll teach you to tangle with me."

With help from the girls, I made a vest from bags and a skirt from bags tied to a plastic bag waistband. Eve ended up in a similar miniskirt, the length of a single-use grocery bag, and a crop top.

"How exciting to be dressed as a native," Eve said. "I can't wait to show Layal. How do we get back? You mentioned a pig and a light. Let's get the details."

"First, we need breakfast," NezLeigh replied.

The middle two Little Jerks, Wama and Starb, roasted small bits of dead animal over a fire. We each got a skewer with meat burned on the outside and raw in the middle. We passed around two chipped cups of acorn tea. I was chilled and thirsty and tried not to think of cross contamination. The ground was cold on my bare bottom. My garb was both smothering and chilly. I couldn't see dressing like this through the winter. Fortunately, I wouldn't be here in the winter.

NezLeigh sat leaning against a tree, the littlest Little Jerks crowding around. Eve and I sat beside her, listening to the plan.

"We'll bring you to the rock where we meet the men and you can get back to your humping when this task is through. First, we need your help to catch the wild pig that roams through the corn and down to the river for a drink. It's fast and slippery. We need you to beam your light in its eyes. We need green light. Pigs sense traps. They won't fall for bait. They'll follow a green light though."

"How do you know all this?" I asked.

"Our people farmed. They raised pigs 'til our land was tooken," Kola added. "Tooken against our will."

"Here's how it works. We dug a pit." She motioned to a hole a couple feet deep and about five feet in diameter. "You take the pig to the edge. Show it your light. We drop the pig and kill it as it's trapped. We'll hoist it out on a rope, gut it, let the blood drip out, drop it in again. Cover it with sticks. Light them. Cook it up. Gotta cook them to kill their worms and such. Let me warn you about this pig. It's modified to be lean and stupider than most pigs from what I can tell, but it's wild and skittish and hungry as a stoner. A gnarly blue flamer, too."

"Blue flamer?"

"It lets off gas strong enough to kill an army. This is a discontinued pig. Some sort of escapee. We get a lot of them out here but most won't come near. This one raided our camp."

"If we help, you'll give us a portion of the meat?" Eve asked.

NezLeigh said, "You misunderstand hunting. Of course we share. It's a community event. We'll all eat."

I added, "And when this little shindig is over, you for sure get us back to our men. Ya dig?"

"This one speaks our language," NezLeigh said to Eve as she put an arm around me. "I'm changing my mind about you. Of course we'll get you and plenty of pig to the men. But tell me, what's he like?" I found her dirt smeared pug-nosed face full of fury compelling. What sort of Midwesterners acted with such emotion? "Tell me all about him and you. What's your heart burning with when you're near him?"

"You don't have to answer to her," Eve said.

"It's burning with curiosity and confusion and...and hope," I said.

"You got emotion."

"I try not to."

"He brings it out of ya. What do you bring out of him?"

"I-I don't know."

"You'll find out, hehe."

"If you get us back."

"Give it time. We need you tonight and tomorrow night, and after, you go with everything you can carry, ya dig? Those men of yours need pork, dontchathink? Imagine the feasting. The celebration. The love making. Give the men a nice dinner—slam!"

NezLeigh and I rubbed ourselves over with tree bark to hide our scent. We wrapped our feet in plastic bags to protect them from pebbles and acorn caps. I hugged Purceel goodbye, and NezLeigh and I ducked into the cool tree cover, its shadow falling over us. She walked on the balls of her feet, her strong calves bulging, the bags swishing with each careful step. Following behind, I tried to copy her. Oh, I was already shaking.

She viewed our time alone as an opportunity for a combined information and interrogation session. "This is a dumb pig, which is why we're on it, but it can smell us and see us. We go at dusk. I got my heart set on this pig like you're set on Crybaby. You help me, I'll help you. I know more about Crybaby than you. He's not Pretty Boy. Even I can see his nose is big. What do you like about him?"

I talked to the back of her swishing skirt. "He's thoughtful and...a man."

"Nah. You like Crybaby because you are incomplete. You don't cry. Not even before your period. You might get mad, not sad, not emotional. He cries. He emotes. Men don't have a period to cry before. He cries anyway. He has his angst as his period. It's erratic, but it's there."

"Bullshit." I was grateful my dad had taught me to swear. She was right about my lack of sadness—if I had any humanity I would have sobbed at the thought of Dad being hauled away. "Having emotions is shitty. You get let down. They mislead you. I once thought my dad was a businessman, but he was a drunk, ya dig?"

She stopped and turned. "I like your language. Maybe we should hook up. You and me. Touch each other, talk filthy. 'Cause even worse than no man, you've got no people, no society, no customs. You're alone, and baby, let me tell you, people aren't meant to be alone."

I tried to read the emotion on her scrunched-up face. I wasn't sure if all of them talked dirty or if it was a symptom of adolescence. "You're too young for such savage thoughts."

She turned her back on me and kept walking. "You're too old to be so naive. Hasn't anyone told you about men? They don't stick by you. They move around from one leaf hut to another."

"What are you talking about? I'm not living in a leaf hut."

"A freaking figure of speech. I'm telling it like it is. A man won't keep by a woman. They forage for more than roots and berries. If they get stuck with you like in Cochtonville, they beat you or abandon you emotionally. A man isn't enough for any woman. You need other women. Let's be friends. Here's the deal: I like Crybaby too. You can have him now, and I'll take him later."

A chill went through me. Not that I saw her as competition for limited resources. Who was I kidding? Of course I did. "You're wrong. He's loyal. May the best woman win. And since you're a *girl*, that would be me."

"I won't be a girl forever. I'm older than I look. In fact, I think I feel a cramp coming on." She grabbed her belly.

"If you keep flapping it you'll get a cramp in your jaw. And I've got a pill for it." In truth, my mom had the pill, but NezLeigh didn't need to know any more about my family life.

"I'm the leader of my people. You are a follower. You put your dirty hands down his tiny pants because you are searching for what you don't have, something is missing but you don't know what it is. I know what I'm missing."

"Well, aren't you a know-it-all?" I said. I added, "A fucking know-it-all," to give it some clout.

We walked. Sweat drained down NezLeigh's neck and dripped across her muscled calves.

"Okay. What is it? You said you knew what you were missing. What are you missing?" I asked.

"My damn land. That's what I'm missing. Are you hip?"

"You must not have had the deed to that land."

"It was in the county court house as required by law. We followed the law."

"And?"

"The courthouse was burned to the ground. There was no record."

"No back up?"

"Seems like there wasn't. The Cochtons sent their land managers from farm to farm. They said the land was theirs, purchased from the county. My grandparents got a knock on the door. They knew it was coming. Neighbors had warned them. They could work for Cochton Enterprises or vacate our property. My granddad called them assholes and dung-crawling losers. They left and he went to the barn, so pissed off, he didn't want the family to see him that way, he said as he left. Granny found him next to the combine with three bullets in his back. My dad signed up to be a Duster as they demanded and the Cochtons took the farm. What do you care? They gave *you* a cushy job, so screw it. Why would you care? I'll clue you in. Crybaby was told the same thing happened to his family except nobody was killed. They went peacefully, the dweebs. Sold it. Got something for it. Guess that's privilege."

"I'm sorry. Life is shit. I'm not some princess. My dad sold his farm, too. For a song apparently because we live next to a graveyard and our house has rotten stairs and I got bit by a bat."

"I get it. You're common. I'm not sure about that friend of yours. I'd watch myself around her. I'll stop ragging on *you* on account of you understanding why we need our land back. I've got goals. I'm gonna stick it to the Cochtons, those cocky savages, sit on my land, and drink a toast to myself with their blood."

"The Cochtons have too much security."

"All you need is smallness."

We came to a split in the path. NezLeigh chose the narrower split.

"The pig turns here. I've watched her. You know what my granddad did before he died?"

"Wrote his killers' names in blood on the barn floor?"

"No. He kicked a switch to let the pigs out so the Cochtons couldn't seize them. He was the last man alive who did anything to stand up to them. He died free."

We walked farther.

"We had two dogs, but the pig ate one and the pups within. Poor Gunga. It's why we must kill the pig. For revenge as well as eats."

The path became haphazard and crooked. The ferns along the side were dug up and the moist dirt and broken roots gave up humidity and terpenoids, smelly as hoppy beer.

"It's here. The plants are busted up, aren't they? I can smell them bleeding. Shh. Look." NezLeigh stooped down and put her hand on the ground. I bent over to examine thick split hoof prints in the dirt. "It's tracks," she said.

I ran my fingers over the indentations. "Tracks alright."

"These are like tears. The earth is crying cuz of this pig. Shh, it's close."

The scent of p-cresol—an irritant and bad for the pancreas— made my eyes water.

"Stinks like the devil's pits," said NezLeigh, rubbing hers.

"It's p-cre—"

"No, it's shit. Damn, you folks raised in the city know nothing at all."

The whole thought of manure tossed me into a waking dream of Remmer. How had their time at the WasteBin gone? Was he missing me and wondering where we were?

"When do we get this over with?" I asked.

"Stay cool. Not all life has a time clock. They're not nocturnal by nature, but they don't sweat so they come out at night in the summer when it's cooler. Tonight is reconnaissance. If we see it and it sees us you can test your light. Shine it ahead of it and see if it follows. Don't mess with its damn eyes. Give it a lead with the light. Watch your step." She put her arm across me to keep me from going farther.

"That's its scent and caterpillar-fat turd alright."

"I can't see a thing. Can you?" I fumbled for my gadget, drew it from my belt, and flipped on a spotlight.

"Turn that off. It's dark enough I can finally see," she said, taking her club and breaking apart the stinking dung. "I'm looking for any trace of Gunga. A fragment of bone. Her black hair." She pulverized the turd. "Oh man. What a drag. I'm too late. I've nothing left of my dog. When I go to the ashes, I'll go with her, for she alone was in my camp. The finger of fate has been cruel. This world is nothing but weeping." It was too dark for me to tell if she was seriously sobbing for her life or faking it. "I cry and you stand there unmoved. Is this how you people survive?"

A cracking ahead of us sent shivers down my spine. I stopped and reached for the UTI with a trembling hand that had turned to an amorphous blob. A dog-eating pig could become a people-eating pig.

"We're coming up on it. See? It's one of the purple ones Cochton E made years ago—the Purple Eater, a descendent from my grandfather's, perhaps."

"A-a p-purple people eater?"

"Shhhh."

Through the dappled fading light, the buxom lavender rump of the pig swayed and glimmered like violet hams, swarmed with mosquitos beneath the corkscrew tail. It was, in fact, not a pig at all but a hog, huge and full-grown. The pig in all its glory walked the path, veering off the trail to rub on trees. It snorted like my dad burping—if he'd weighed a couple hundred pounds more—and it snuffled. Distracted by the mosquitos, it grunted.

"Don't move." NezLeigh put her hand out to stop me although I was already stopped, a fountain of fear, weak in the knees, ducking as if it could swoop at me. The swine turned and faced us.

NezLeigh squeaked. "It's gonna charge. Flash your light. Green. Green light."

I turned the UTI over. My fingers were dubnium—an element heavy and useless. I'd drawn a blank. The wavelength for green was what?

NezLeigh inched away. "The light. The light. Get off your flabby ass and shine the light." She dropped her club and scrambled up a river birch.

This UTI was never meant to be a weapon. It was designed to put radiation through materials to measure how much of certain chemicals were in them. The stress was making me stupid. Green was mid spectrum, wasn't it? Between 400 and 700 nanometers. A halfway color but a little more blue than red. I quickly poked in 532 nanometers as the pig stared at me in confusion. Or was I projecting my own confusion? The animal softly snorted. Its lavender ears were erect. Its snout wiggled. The two of us were locked together, neither wanting to break the stare. The pig flicked its tail. Instinctively, I flashed the beam in its eyes. It was green, gloriously green. The eyes didn't reflect. The pig shook its fat head. I backed up, feeling for the tree with my entire body. The gadget worked at short distances. The beam fell away from its eyes.

Without the light, the pig advanced cautiously. Curiously. How stupid could it be if it was curious? To be curious was to have a sense of wonder and intelligence and an innate boldness.

Hypothesis confirmed. The pig *would* react to the light. I aimed the beam at its face, which halted the progression of the pig.

"You lit it up," said NezLeigh from her perch. "Way to go!"

"Yeah, it works," I said. I switched off the beam. "And my ass isn't flabby."

"Now beam on the ground like I told you, before it gets mad."

The pig snorted, put down its head, and charged at me. Flooded with panic, I rushed behind the birch tree as NezLeigh yelled. Flicking its tail, the pig trotted around the tree. Again, it regarded me with reflectionless eyes. I met its gaze. It opened its vulva-pink mouth. I screamed, pushed the switch, and beamed the light on its face. Once again it stopped when the green hit its eyes. I couldn't do this all night. My battery wasn't up to it.

I shone the beam on the tree beside me. *Follow it, oh please follow the light.* Wagging its lavender tale, the pig went for it. As soon as I saw the buggy rear and before the pig could turn around I took off running up the path with my light off so as not to attract the pig. I couldn't see a thing. I fell and lay surprised with a skinned knee in the dirt. Which way had I come from? Where was I going? Nothing out here was long-term planning. It was react, react, react. Patience was a sin.

I scrambled up and ran forward. Who knew what was out there? Sticks cracked beneath me. My feet slipped on moss. I was out of breath, tumbling over a log, down again with hands and cheek on soggy ground. I rolled onto my back. The only sound was frogs croaking to each other. The pig was gone and I was near water!

I tucked the gadget into its holster and struggled to a stand. I'd get to the water and then, I didn't know. A crack of twilight peeked through the draggle-droop branched trees ahead. I stepped toward the light, toward the frogs. The ground bobbled beneath me. It was rotting vegetation. I sunk quickly above my knees as adrenaline sent my heart racing again. My first thought was my UTI, precariously close to submerging. My second thought was: I was stuck. And I wasn't sure this pit had a bottom.

CHAPTER TEN

I kicked my bagged feet in a bid to get to the surface of the gunk. Instead, I sank farther into it. My femoral arteries were covered and their cold immersion gave me a shiver. I tried to calm myself. *You're mostly water. You should float. Except you have this gadget belt pulling you down faster than mercury in dry ice.* I had to ditch the gadget, my beloved gadget, along with my hopes and dreams.

"Oh bummer. You like our boggy fen? Like no other. Special area all our own. Keeps the pig from rooting around here. A couple other hogs went down. Good thing you don't weigh 300 pounds or you'd have sunk deeper. Your crotch is about ready to go under." NezLeigh was a foot or so from me. Her labored breath whistled through her tooth gap. She could almost touch me.

"Yeah. I could've sunk farther. I can't feel the bottom. How deep is this thing?" I was slowly sinking. I could tell; the bog was creeping over the bottom of the UTI as it hung like a Washer pistol in the belt. around my waist.

"Who the hell knows? Can you feel any pig carcasses?"

"I can't even feel my legs. Can you find a stick for me to grab? I keep sinking."

She bent over and stretched out her hand. "I'm surprised someone smart enough to have a gadget needs me to break the news: you're too heavy. Hand me your weapon and take off that belt." It struck me she would probably steal the UTI and leave me here. It was all I had for collateral. I couldn't keep it and I couldn't give it to her. I took it from the holster and put it under my arm as I fumbled to unclip the belt. My idea was to get rid of the belt first and see where that left me. Maybe I could force her to rescue me to get the gadget if I waited her out. My armpit was slick from the plastic. The UTI slid. I reached a hand across my chest and grabbed it.

"You're leaving this to the finger of fate, I see." NezLeigh got on her hands and knees and held out an arm. "Come on now. Stop playing chicken. I won't five-finger it. You're sinking fast. Any last words?"

"Nothing I wish to share."

She was being dramatic. I was stuck, sure, but plenty of me wasn't even submerged. I reached for the edge. My hand touched the surface in front of me. It sprang like a sponge.

NezLeigh hovered over the ring of flowers at the bog's edge. "Freaking weird, isn't it? Would you call it solid or liquid?"

"A non-Newtonian fluid would be my guess. It changes viscosity under stress."

"Stress, huh? Here's something for your brain to consider. If you go down too far, pulling you out can yank you in half. Happened to a pig. Of course, we ate the half we pulled out."

My legs were simultaneously itchy and dead.

NezLeigh continued. "Gets cool this time of night but we still got ticks, ya dig?"

My back tickled at this mention. It was surely my imagination, although I shuddered and this sunk me a quarter inch.

"You're not too tall. Not a lot of time left. You got any regrets you wanna talk about before your head sinks under?"

It would be hours before my head sunk under...if I could keep myself from moving. There was, however, not much hope of a rescue without her assistance. "If I talk about them, will you help get me out?"

"Maybe."

I searched my mind for a regret. Having no regrets was a part of life in Cochtonville.

"What about your work?" she asked. "Anything you're proud of you want to talk about?"

"I figured out our fast-growing corn isn't lacking vital nutrients."

She whistled through her teeth. "I'm sure that's going to help a lot of people."

"Otherwise, I haven't done anything great. Not like I take risks or anything."

"Sounds like a regret."

"I suppose. Now, how about helping me out?"

"First, the weapon."

My skin burned. My throat seared. I'd either swallowed some sand or was dehydrated. Yes, the latter—I was weak. I had no choice. I had to get back to Remmer. I'd give anything to see those eyes again, to listen to his banter about caves and birthday cake. My hand shook as I handed the klepto my UTI. It was better to lighten my load and sit here and starve or even let the pig eat me than to smother in the filthy fen as it sucked me in. NezLeigh jerked the UTI from my grasp, nearly dropping it. I didn't want to give it up even as my life hung in the balance.

"You did the right thing. This sucker's heavy." She rose, smiling. "Easy peasy." She turned her back to me, her bag skirt bouncing as she stepped, quickly and gleefully. I unbuckled the belt and let it drop. My descent into the bog stopped. I floated like a cork in wine. NezLeigh put the UTI on the ground, came back, and again got on her hands and knees.

"How about the belt?"

"I dropped it." I swished my numb feet, trying to feel it, to kick it, but touched only emptiness below me. On the plus side, I stayed in place.

"Bummer. I do like you, although you are dumb for an adult."

An owl hooted. "Love that sound. I don't imagine you like the dark as I do."

"Can't say I do like the dark or anything about this situation."

"We're not made for each other then."

"We could be. If I could fix your eyes, would you get me out of here?"

"What do you mean by 'fix'?"

"Help them not hurt when you are in the light."

"Make me a day tripper like you?"

"It would give you that choice. It's drops; a drink of water for your eyes."

"What's the catch? You people always have a catch."

"I'd have to go to Cochtonville to get the fix. I guess that's the catch. You could come or wait here."

She whistled through her teeth again. "You know what will happen? I'll be stuck working day and night. You sound like a person desperate to get out of a predicament, offering a bogus fix."

"I am...desperate." And yet, I wanted to cure her, although I wasn't sure why.

"I don't want to be fixed. I'd see how ugly I was in your eyes. Keep your cure. Any other last words?"

"I don't feel like a success right now."

"Let's have a pity party for your ego. You're nothing but a charity case. Sure as shit I'm benevolent. Would you like some canned goods?"

"I'd like to get out of here."

"It's not hard to spring yourself. Flatten and inch over." She kept her arm outstretched as I wiggled toward her, my mind envisioning a helium balloon, a black bug skating on the surface of a dirty creek, a bubble moving through paint. One summer when we tried to paint the house, Mom had explained to me that bubbles in paint move to be together. It was unnatural to be alone. I needed NezLeigh, damn it, I did. Our hands met. Her tiny fingers dug into mine.

"Easy now or I'll rip you in two."

NezLeigh crawled back as she slowly tugged me from the swamp. She was right. It hurt like a wing in the eye as the boggy fen held me back and her tiny fury pulled me forward. My skirt stripped from my waist. I lay on the damp spongy ground with my bare butt in the moonlight.

"I gotta rest," said NezLeigh. "My hand is killing me. Float there on top bare ass naked for a sec. You're almost out." Reluctantly, I unleashed her. As she promised, I hung on the spongy surface, sprawled, with my legs still trapped, considering how I'd never done anything great, while she shook her hand. From this angle the outline of the boggy fen was as clear as if there had been a warning sign. White flowers and swaying reeds marked the perimeter, delineating it from the firm dirt of the forest. This was how NezLeigh knew where the edge was. At last, she held out her hand again. "One more thing," she said before grabbing me. "Why are you here? The man exiled you. For what?"

I decided to be honest. "To see if we can find a use for the WasteBin."

"It's already being used. You plan to bring people here?" She took my hand flaccidly. "I don't want regrets for saving your butt."

"Not here. To the manure lagoon. Maybe. We don't have a plan."

"Keep it that way." She groaned with one last effort to free me. My legs popped out with a sucking sound. I was naked from the waist down and covered in goo, splayed out on the ground, humiliated.

"Success! It's not 'cause I like you. I can't read the buttons on your thingy. I still need you. And your ass is cute." She gave me the UTI. Without the belt, it threatened to pull my weak arm out of the socket as we walked together, coyotes howling, me slopping and itching and shifting the gadget from one hand to the other as I burned with thirst and cursed Sir Bux for sending us on an impossible mission filled with fens and wild kids and a man so tempting I might give up everything for him.

"It works!" NezLeigh announced to the rest when we finally

made it back. They sat by the fire, Eve holding the little ones in her lap while the other two sharpened sticks. I walked straight past them to the creek and sat where the deer had almost died, the mud billowing off my body and rushing downstream as the last of the bog clung to my calves. Eve rushed to me, bobbing at the edge with her plastic bag skirt flowing.

"You look like hell. Your ass is showing. What happened?"

"Ever hear of a boggy fen? I fell in one. Would you bring me some bags?" Once again, I took the hand of another as she helped me up. This was getting to be a bad habit, all this hand holding, me needing others. I stood by the fire to dry myself, still warning the others not to get close and light their plastic. Starb handed me a chipped mug of hot water with acorns floating in it. Wama rubbed my rashy legs with turkey fat. Purceel quickly assembled a skirt for me. I blew on the water. My throat was as scratchy as if Mom had taken Ruff Dog Heel Exfoliator to it. At last I drank and sat by the fire as Kola doled out bits of greasy opossum. I'm not sure if it tasted like pork or if I had the pig on my mind. A peace fell over me as NezLeigh went over the plan.

"Kola, you and Dungo will come with me to drive the stinking pig in the direction of the pit. Nookie Number One will stay behind and roost in that tree, and from there she'll lure it in with her light, drawing a green line across the dirt and into the hole. The pig will fall. Wama and Starb, you'll stab it. Blood and squeals will fill the air. We'll feast after."

"How deep is this hole that it will keep a pig in?" Eve asked.

"Deep enough," Kola said. "We dug it until Purceel couldn't climb out. We'll cover it with branches to hide it. She don't have to stay in long. Deep enough. It's deep."

"Show it to me," Eve said.

As I listened, I hung up my plastic bag skirt and wet top and dressed in my dried clothes. Never had a t-shirt and khaki shorts felt so luxurious, nor a plan sound so childish.

"It *isn't* deep enough," Eve insisted as she viewed the hole. "It's more like a dip than a pit. It needs to be big enough to trap the pig but not so deep we can't get the meat out easily. This deep," she put her hand to just below her breasts, "and twice this wide." She held out her arms and her bag skirt jiggled. "And long enough for any of us to lie down in it." She took her hands and dug, tossing dirt to the side of the pit. The Little Jerks crawled in and helped her. As she dug, I crept into a leaf hut, enjoying the coolness, the earthy smell, and the soft moss bed. I lay down, folded my arms over the UTI and used it for a pillow. Oh, I loved this gadget, I needed this gadget, even though it had discovered nothing but trouble.

CHAPTER ELEVEN

The late-day light dappled us through the trees. It had been an off-kilter golden afternoon. The Little Jerks woke at dusk. Eve and I had been up at dawn and were sleep-deprived, our biological clocks confused by reversing days and nights. She and I sat waiting for the pig to be herded our way by NezLeigh, Kola, and Dungo. After my fall in the bog, I certainly wasn't going to go back out there.

Wama and Starb sharpened sticks with rocks from the creek. Purceel braided my hair while Tyde snuggled into Eve's lap and sang to her. In Cochtonville we only sang "Bombs and Tassels." The songs of the littlest Little Jerks were vaguely longing. "Here is where I have my home. No longer will I seek and roam," with *here* being almost anywhere, and then, "So many mouths to feed. Who is there to meet my need? Where do my people lie? Why do my people cry?"

"That's very sad," Eve remarked.

"*You* sing us a song," tiny Tyde begged.

Eve sang in a clear voice. "Bombs and tassels, tassels and bombs, come father, come brothers, hear the sound. As bombs and corn tassels burst around."

"Not that one. It stinks," I said as Purceel pulled my hair tight.

"LouOtta is my supervisor now. She's vain, but you can't argue with prizewinning lyrics," Eve said.

"And undeserved."

"Kept her from being Sir Bux's wife."

"No! Ew. I can't blame her, but the song is dumb. We have few fathers, fewer brothers, and no bombs. And burning tassels sounds like a disaster."

"What's a bomb?" Tyde asked.

"A thing that blows up," said Eve. "A weapon."

"It's based on an exothermic reaction," I said. "It releases heat and creates entropy—you know, disorder. It starts in a concentrated spot and radiates fire outward."

"Our anthem writer was jealous of another country that had bombs in their anthem," Eve added.

"Fire intimidates enemies," Starb said, sharpening her stick again.

The night was warm and we'd kicked off our bag shoes. Eve continued to wear her plastic clothes, having given Kola hers. She insisted she felt closer to nature and to Layal dressed as a native. Frogs chirped. The river rushed beside us. The hot little breaths had me nearly asleep. It was peaceful here without the sirens, the Vice Patrol, and announcements of danger. Of course, there *was* danger and warning. The distinct smell of a p-cresol-laden flamer drifted to our campsite.

I sat up, charged. "Smell that?"

"Yeah."

"Time to get in position," said Starb, brandishing her stick.

Wama addressed the two little ones. "You girls get into the huts, ya hear? This pig is dangerous and you're small."

"You're not the boss of me," Tyde objected. "I want to see the pig."

Purceel grabbed her hand. "Is it coming?" She was as white as a Yorkshire sow.

"Yes, can you smell it?" I said.

Tyde hesitated. "I like bad smells and so does Purceel, the baby butt scratcher."

"Go or I'll smack your bottom," Wama threated. It did the trick. The girls scurried into the leaf huts. Eve and Wama boosted me into a white-barked tree close to the pit. I wrapped my legs around a low branch as Starb handed me the UTI. Testing it, I shone green light across the lid of loose boughs and branches covering the hole. My breath labored through my nervousness. This was not the largest or deepest hole but still, it brought back sensations of the boggy fen. I was already sorry for the pig and at the same time, worried it would climb right out and eat Purceel.

"Looks good. The beam's right on target," Eve said. "You gonna be okay up there?"

"If it doesn't take too long." I wasn't a tree climber, Cochtonville having very few because people didn't like to rake leaves. My legs were still rubbery from my dunk in the boggy fen, and I feared falling. "This is a dumb idea."

"Except I'm starving. If we're going to live out here, we need to learn the ways of the wild. And can you imagine how happy we're going to make the men? It might start something for you."

"Let me worry about my own love life." As much as I wanted to know Remmer better, the idea of living to make a man happy loomed before me like a pit. Wifehood was not for me and neither was sitting in trees or wearing plastic bags for the rest of my life. This wasn't my idea of success. I had to get back to Cochtonville and prove myself.

The ground shook. Eve scrunched behind the tree as Wama and Starb crouched behind the leaf huts.

"Hey pig, move your ass."

"Sooie, ya bitch, sooie, pig, pig, pig."

NezLeigh and Kola waved sticks and drove the hog toward the hole. Dungo nipped and growled at its heels. The pig grunted in alarm, running toward the green light from the UTI as random sticks along the path cracked beneath its quick hooves. It dashed toward the green light as if it was rushing to safety. My stomach dropped. I was going to help kill something, and yet I salivated. I beamed the light in front of the pig, onto the boughs. It cut through the mist from the river like a sword. Green as a clover, a mantis, a leaf, a sprout. The lavender pig followed it as if pulled by a string.

"Come on, baby, come on," I said to myself, holding focus although my hand shook with the weight of the UTI and my legs shivered as they clung to the tree. The pig came on. The joy of being part of a team flushed through me. No wonder NezLeigh was the destined leader of her people. She was a brilliant strategist. The pig did her bidding and so did I. A few steps more and it would be done. Without warning, the UTI grew warm, the green light sputtered. The pig stumbled. The light flickered; the pig stopped at the lip of the pit. Frantically I pushed the button, but the light went out. The pig snorted and swung around to challenge her pursuers.

"Squeee, wee, weee," she squealed, stepping toward the drop-jawed girls. They didn't move. Even the frogs were silent. The pig put her head down and rumbled like a rusty, ethanol-powered lawn mower. NezLeigh raised her club slowly. Frantically I pushed the button again and again. Click, click, click, like rain dripping from a gutter.

The tan dog stretched his neck and howled. With a snarl, he crouched, his eyes glued to the pig.

"Oh shit." Kola lifted her stick.

The pig didn't want a fight. It looked both directions, at the leaf huts as the older girls came forward with sharpened sticks, at the creek with the steep bank, at the branch-covered pit. Frantically I shook the UTI. I sobbed as I pushed the buttons and saw the message: "Lamp overheated." I shook the gadget. "Excess dark current" it read. Damn. Damn thing. It slipped from my tired hand and crashed onto the bough-covered pit. The pig grunted, let out a cloud of blue flamer, and darted left, toward the leaf houses where the girls peeked out, watching it all unfold.

My terror erupted with billowing spontaneity. We all screamed.

The pig charged on. Starb rushed forward with her stick. Dungo intercepted. He snapped the pig's face, right between the eyes. Starb paused, unable to tell pig from dog in the blur. The pig screamed, thrashed, and backed up as the dog relentlessly bit it and herded it to the pit. With a lunge the dog clamped between the pig's eyes, and the dog and the pig fell in the pit, crashing through the cracking branches.

I couldn't stand to hear the cries of the hurt animals. It was as if I too were screaming in pain and fear for my life, a life that until now I hadn't appreciated, maybe even complained about. The sulfur from blue flamer burned my eyes and nose. My legs slipped from the tree. I held onto the branch as Dungo yelped three times, then howled while the pig squealed continuously. Their pain jumped out of my guts and into my mouth and seared across my arms as I dangled over them.

"Dunny!" Kola cried at the edge of the pit. "The pig is pinning him. And it's shitting."

Eve rushed to help me. I dropped from the tree as gracefully and deliberately as I could into her strong arms. I gasped for breath amidst a cacophony of yips, squeals, and shouts. As Starb and Wama stood with sticks poised, unable to act with the confusion of the dog in the pit with the thrashing pig.

Eve leapt into the pit. The pig struggled on its side, smashing Dungo's back leg against the wall of dirt. Eve heaved the grunting pig off the dog and snatched him in her arms, holding the pig with her back to the wall. She handed Dunny to Kola as if she'd bought a new purse, not moved a 300-pound pig. The dog relaxed in his master's arms and the two locked gazes as Eve hoisted herself from the pit. Starb and Wama moved in for the kill.

"Hold your fire. That's not shit," said NezLeigh, standing beside the pit. "It's a baby." Her eyebrows shot up and her shoulders relaxed. "It's so cute." She was correct. A squirmy lavender piglet, shiny and slick with a delicate pink cord hanging from its belly crawled to the pig's engorged teats. The trouble was, the UTI was in its way.

"It might need a little help." NezLeigh slid into the pit, grabbed the UTI and heaved it out with a thud. I grabbed it from the edge of the hole.

"Get the nuts out. She's gonna bite you any second," Kola said. "Unless she's almost dead. Kind of not moving. Not moving." The pig lay there but she *was* moving. Her tail was twirling, her eyes wildly white. The pig gave a grunt and another piglet slid out. This one was white and still.

NezLeigh put the first piglet on the teat and picked up the next one. The lavender sow made no move to bite as the tiny piglet snuggled in to nurse.

NezLeigh held the white piglet by the back leg. "Good. It's dead. We may be able to eat it." She tossed it out of the pit. The sow twirled her tail as another piglet slid out. This one was alive, as red-purple as a little beet. My stomach growled as NezLeigh placed it on a teat. It grunted and sucked vigorously next to its littermate.

"They sure pop out quick," Tyde said.

"They do. This pig is like no other," NezLeigh said. She ventured a brave hand toward the pig and stroked her side. "We're keeping her. We'll start our own farm. At last a place to hang our hats."

"We're not eating her?" Eve asked.

"No," NezLeigh said. "No, we're not eating them. From now on, this'll be our home, our farm. We'll have this pig. These little babies."

"We can keep her and eat some of the babies when they get bigger. They'll have better flavor," said Kola. "Better flavor."

The pig grunted. Tyde and Purceel squealed as a blue piglet popped out. At the same time, the pig grunted out a red blob, like liver.

"The placenta, I'll be damned. She's gone for quality, not quantity," NezLeigh said, giving the organ to the pig, who slurped it down. Kola was correct about the pig. This suddenly tame version had me uneasy. Yes, she'd been chased and given birth, but pigs, I was told, want to kill you, especially the mamas. Was she injured?

NezLeigh held the lavender piglet to her cheek and the words of the old woman at the market came back to me. We need something more. We need something to love. Something to touch. Something that stops crying when we are near. The isolation of Cochtonville washed over me—always working, always striving, no time to even touch anything or connect. Of course, it was driven by valid insecurity. What good was love or friendship when you lived in poverty?

"Nookie Two, hand me some water." NezLeigh said urgently.

Obediently, humbled by the failure of the UTI, I fetched water and gave NezLeigh a cup. She poured the drink into the pig's pursed mouth. It drank with surprisingly dainty slurps.

NezLeigh handed me the empty cup. "I've pushed my luck enough," she said, climbing from the pit. "Damn, she's either tamer than I thought or hurt."

"You're full of crap," Kola said. The dog yelped as he lay in her arms. "Ah Dunny, I'm not trying to hurt you. Look at your leg, it's broke by the fierce pig. How will you walk and hunt? I won't abandon you no matter. I'll die with ya, for life has sparse pleasure without ya. Oh my Dunny. I'd do anything for ya. Anything."

"I can help. I've set an arm before," I said.

"You? It's your fault. You shut off your light. The light shut off."

"No, I didn't. The lamp overheated."

Kola buried her face in the dog's neck. "Get out of my sight. I'll bloody your nose like you bloodied my dog."

"Put him down and let her look at his leg, you dork, unless you can do better," NezLeigh said.

We all settled on the ground, a safe ways from the pig as she and the piglets grunted softly. Dungo whimpered.

Kola cried. "You gonna help my dog like you said or are you going to make a mess of things? A broken mess and broken light."

"I'm going to set the leg. I helped set my dad's arm. I can

stabilize the leg and it will heal naturally. I need some bags and a couple sticks the length of the leg."

The little ones ran about the camp snatching sticks from below the trees and bags from the brush. With my supplies in hand, I had a renewed sense of competence. Mom had talked me through the process. I could redeem myself after the horrible failure of the UTI.

"Eve, help me with the dog. Kola, hold him tight. Eve, hold the leg." I ran my hands across the leg. Dungo yelped when I touch his tibia. I felt the clean break under the skin.

"It's a lucky break," I said. "Not too messy." I did as I'd done with my dad, gently pulled the leg in place, as Kola held him in a headlock. I wrapped it with the plastic, setting a stick next to it with a splint, and wrapped it again. "I can't do much for the pain."

Kola stroked the dog. NezLeigh came and crouched beside them. "Lie still, Dunny. I got something for you." She got the dead piglet and held it to the dog's mouth. Dungo snapped the white mushy body while everyone agreed he deserved it, having saved the little ones. The day was just beginning for the Little Jerks, but I was weary and defeated yet hopeful.

"He can eat. That's a good sign."

"He's gonna rip it right off," Kola said.

"My clothes?" I put my hands to my chest. I'd been daydreaming about Remmer.

"No. The bag." She was right. The dog of course would chew the plastic if the leg irritated him. I wasn't sure how long the cast would last.

"We could make plaster by heating limestone. We have to cross the creek, but there's plenty on the other side."

"Have you made plaster before?" Eve asked.

"No."

"It sounds like a long process."

The little ones fell beside the dog and smothered him with kisses. Although he was eating, he didn't growl. This was a good dog, and I had to do all I could to fix him. I itched my leg and thought about it. My rashes from the boggy fen were still irritatingly with me. The goop! I could dip some strips of cloth in the goop and wrap them on the outside of the plastic. My shirt would provide some fabric and Kola's the rest.

"I know what we need for the dog. I have to go back to the boggy fen, get some of its slime, and coat the cast with the goop. It dries hard. It's irritating, so he won't nibble it off. Come on, NezLeigh. Let's go."

"You're shittin' me. You want to go back?"

My heart tripped like I had A-fib. I didn't want to go back. I *had* to. I had to help the dog. I worked to keep myself in control. "We need some fen slime. I can't do it alone."

"Okay. I'm with you. It's a beautiful dark night. Kola, you good here with the pig?"

"Hell no. I hate the pig."

"I'll watch the pig," Eve said.

NezLeigh and I grabbed a few cracked cups and ducked onto the trail as coyotes yipped and owls hooted. Only NezLeigh knew the way. I put a hand on her shoulder, unable to figure out where I was going. I had no shoes and neither did she. The leaves shuffled beneath our feet. We were fixated on this goal, forgetful of protections, driven to help the dog.

Alone again with NezLeigh, it was the perfect time to learn more about her. "How did you get here? It's not like you were born here."

"I ran away. We did. Kola and I are sisters. We left home and family."

"How long ago?"

"Just last year. Our mother, she died and we had nobody at all. Just our dad, who didn't want the burden. Grandmothers had already been done away with as fat to be trimmed."

"Grandmothers?"

"Yes, you know, our parents' moms. Do you have one?"

"No. They went to the US and never came back."

"So you were told. Dig this, they were exiled, not sent. No room for the old here."

"My Lady at the Welcome Mart proves you wrong."

"An exile. As for me, I had no mother. No grandmothers. I was going to be sent to school. I didn't want to go. Dad got me and Kola dressed up in our best skirts. We stood outside in the wind, waiting for the school bus to come up the gravel road. We saw it headed our way through the dust.

"'They're coming to get you, NezLeigh,' Kola teased me. But they were! We grabbed hands and ran for the dumpster by the barn."

"What type of school was this? We don't have public schools."

"We weren't going to school. We were going to freaking prison. It wasn't a school bus coming for us. It was a Washer van. It sure as hell was. We didn't dare leave the dumpster. We huddled in there for so long, not knowing if it was day or night, if the Washers were waiting or not. The WasteBin truck rumbled up the drive. The fucking truck came and emptied us. It was painful falling into the hopper. We almost suffocated with rotten meat and discarded corn fiber clothing. Next stop, a dead sow was dumped in with us and a shit ton of cracked eggs dripped all over.

"The truck took off down gravel, twisting and turning. We were scared out of our minds. Where does waste get taken? We ended up by the WasteBin, almost tossed in to drown in the filth where the dead sow went. For better or worse, Crybaby and Pretty Boy pulled us out of the garbage. They named us after other things they found in the trash. After a while, I forgot my real name. Who cares, right? We got along for a while, but the food they collected just sucked. Nuts and berries. Even worse, they read all the time and talk on and on. It's unnatural. Still worse, they get visits from the Blood Bankers, and we'd have to hide. They're no better than Vice Patrol. We'd be captured. We'd never get our land back, ya dig?"

"Blood Bankers?"

"Yeah. They come in a fricking helicopter."

"The Cochtons?"

"No. Two guys wearing white, packs on their backs filled with needles and tubes and flexible PVC bags about 0.25 mm thick. Got some plasticizer in it. Good stuff, ya dig? They come and bleed Pretty Boy once a month. The blood flows into the bags and they take it to the men. He's got the same blood type as the Cochtons. He keeps them young with the transfusion, or so they say, ya dig?"

"People bleeding him? How disgusting."

"He'd freak out and tell us to hide since we weren't supposed to be there. They came with no warning, so you might even be taking a crap one minute and running like hell the next. It got old. Some things shouldn't be interrupted."

After we'd walked a ways, I smelled the ferns and their terpenoids. My stomach twisted. I stopped to urinate. NezLeigh made fun of me for having the piss scared out of me. Shortly after, the ground wobbled beneath our feet. The wet sponginess made me gasp. My blood ran cold. We were back.

"Whoops, back up," NezLeigh said, putting her arm across my back. "I'll get the goop. You tell me when I've got enough. She took a cup and crawled forward. The boggy fen made a sucking sound as she dipped the Hot Dog Haven cup into its surface. The frogs chirped in the trees.

"Careful," I called. "Careful."

She brought the cup to me. I stuck my fingers into it and was instantly sorry. Now they itched. I measured the cup by its weight instead.

"We need double this amount."

The second cup in hand, she crawled on hands and knees to the boggy fen as I wiped my fingers on my pants and pictured once again the size of the dog's leg wrapped in plastic and splints. She brought the catch back for my assessment.

"This is enough," I said. We headed back to camp with our thick heavy cups of goo. I kept one hand on NezLeigh's shoulder as she skillfully traversed the shadows. I should never have offered to "fix" her eyes. They were more useful than mine tonight.

Back at camp, I tore the hem off my t-shirt. The dog was munching on the pig, but the tranquility wouldn't last once the last bit of tail was swallowed. I dipped the shirt in the goop, using a plastic bag to protect each hand. I wrapped the fabric over the plastic on the dog's lower leg while Kola held it in place.

"I need part of your shirt," I said to Kola.

NezLeigh took the sharpened popsicle stick from her hair and slashed the bottom of the shirt. Eve tore a long shred of hem and handed it to me. I smoothed it around the leg, holding the fracture in place.

"Everybody keep calm while it sets," I commanded. Kola held the leg while the little ones constructed a mound of moss and leaves. Once the goop had hardened, Kola rested the leg gently on the mound. All was well.

The night couldn't have been more beautiful. With Eve joining them, the hunters had killed a squirrel apiece for each of us. We ate our fill and had enough leftovers for the dog and the pig. We let our food digest and drank acorn tea by the fire, our backs to it, of course, to protect sensitive eyes. Motherhood or perhaps hand-feeding had settled the pig and her adorable piglets. Calm was upon us.

"The leg will swell and then shrink. You might have to make a new cast. I'm sure you can, or I can come back and visit." Not only was I feeling guilty, the wild was growing on me.

"I might like that," NezLeigh said.

I went to the creek to wash the cups. Purceel followed me.

"Can I help?"

I didn't need help but gave her a cup to rinse. She swooshed it under the water and inspected it until she was satisfied it was clean, then she gave it to me proudly. We went back to the fire and she cuddled in my lap.

"I don't have a mommy," she said. "Do you?"

"Yes, but she's far away."

"Is she all alone?"

"Yes, she is." I stroked her matted hair. She needed some of

Mom's conditioner and body wash.

"How'd you get these little ones?" I asked NezLeigh.

"Some people throw away kids. No shit! The men pulled them out of bags and delivered them to us at the trading rock," NezLeigh said as she braided plastic bags into rope.

"This one is new," I said, giving Purceel a kiss on her dirty cheek.

"Purceel? Yeah, just got her."

"Her mom killed herself. I was there."

"A martyr. It happens."

"I saw Purceel shoved in a rendering truck. I didn't know what to do. Other Pestos came for her mom's body, but nobody wanted her."

"Pestos? What's this Pesto you are talking about?" Kola said angrily.

"People who work with pesticides and live out of the city," I said.

"We call ourselves Agros," she replied. "Pestos is your evil word for it. We're Agros."

"In any case, you owe them. You all owe Remmer and Layal your lives," Eve said.

"We do," said NezLeigh. "Kola, you got to admit it. This life out here is better than any we could have imagined. If the men like the bitches' company, and the women can put up with them, we'll sure as hell reunite them."

"Pestos sounds like an infestation," Kola said. "Infestation."

"Stop ruminating. You're not a cow. Tomorrow at sunrise we'll trade them for food," NezLeigh said. "Then we'll come back and nab some freaking needed sleep."

"Trade us for food?" I said.

"That'll be the ruse. We'll refuse the trade. We're gonna let them rescue you. Let's be clear about Crybaby. He's the classic case of a hero in need of a rescue. You'll be in peril. I'll be a powerful villain. He'll feel like such a man and deserving. It's going to happen." She held up her middle finger.

"What's that mean?"

"It's what goes down before you have a baby."

I covered Purceel's ears while a vision of naked Remmer danced in my head. "Why are you so obsessed with my sex life?"

"It's my dad. I got daddy issues."

"Doesn't everybody?"

"He said no man would have me, not even as a hooker, 'cause of these damn eyes. All the hopes, the dreams, the curiosity—I'm living it through you. You got nearly all I ever wanted. You got two good eyes. And you got Crybaby, too."

I didn't remind her I'd offered to fix those eyes. Fixing the eyes wasn't going to do it. No matter what you have or don't have, Cochtonville teaches you that since you aren't one of the Cochtons, you aren't good enough.

"You get the men, we get the shit. The shit," Kola said. "I sure as shit wish you'd never come."

"I sure the hell am glad they're here. We wouldn't have the pig," NezLeigh said, as the pig and her babies grunted contentedly in the pit.

"She's gonna bust out and eat us all. We got more to feed, more trouble."

"Why don't you build a fence around the pit if you're so worried?"

Kola snatched the UTI from the ground beside me. "This thing. This thing is to blame."

"Put it down. Please put it down. It's a delicate instrument," I said, panicking.

"Quit your bitching, Kola," NezLeigh said. "I wish to enjoy these last few hours with these cherry popping chicks. Stop obsessing over the pig. It's like your mind is constipated."

"All's well that ends well," said Eve, petting drowsy Dungo. Casting his leg had gone perfectly and the boggy fen gunk hardened to a paste that resisted chewing. "Your dog is content. Come sit, put the gadget thing down, and say goodbye."

Kola shoved the UTI in NezLeigh's face. I made a swipe for it as Kola spat on the UTI. The spit spattered as if Kola had bit into a juicy cob of corn and accidently splashed NezLeigh in the face.

NezLeigh blinked and held out her hand for the UTI. "Damn. Keep your slobber to yourself. It smells like you've been eating snails again. I told you those things were bad for you. Come on, give it here."

Kola hunched her shoulders subserviently and shoved the UTI at NezLeigh again. I relaxed as NezLeigh grabbed for the gadget. Before NezLeigh had it, Kola pulled the UTI away, twisted, and heaved it into the fire.

"What the—?" I cried. NezLeigh leapt at Kola and pinned her to the ground. "Kola, you twat. You shot me up a wall. How are we going to control the freaking pigs?"

Dungo tried to rise and fell with a yelp. Eve held him down with one hand, stroking him to keep him calm. Kola fought back by grabbing NezLeigh's hair. I groped for sticks and used them to fish the UTI from the flames. It looked as if nothing had happened to it. I moved to grab it as the heat poured off and the two girls—showing their age—rolled and scratched each other while Purceel and the others piled on. I fanned the UTI with my hands as Kola bit NezLeigh's arm. NezLeigh crunched Kola's finger and she yowled in pain.

"They are not mature enough to be left here alone," Eve said as the girls wrestled each other. "We need to contact someone about them."

I aimed the UTI at a tree and pushed a button. Nothing.

"Or have them live with us," she added.

"No. They're too destructive. It's messed up." I tossed the UTI aside and put my hands over my face. Without my gadget I was utterly helpless and alone. I had nothing. No data beyond the preliminary tests at the WasteBin. Our mission was jeopardized. We were nearly to the point where there was no sense in going back. I missed Remmer so much, I wasn't sure I cared about winning the competition at all.

CHAPTER TWELVE

In the coolest part of the night, NezLeigh tied our hands behind our backs with rope woven from plastic bags. Kola rang the farm bell and it pealed its deep, somber call.

"Let's go," NezLeigh said. "This is gonna be good."

It was the four of us—me, Eve, Kola, and NezLeigh. We walked parallel to the river, up closer to the cabin, the WasteBin, and the Crispers. Provoking a rescue was the dumbest of ideas, made dumber by the hands behind the back. Without my hands for balance, dips in the path jolted my spine and nearly tripped me when I stepped into them.

The rustle of leaves was broken by the first morning birdsong. It was dark in the trees but at the edge, day broke. I'd be in Remmer's arms soon.

The men sat on the rock. Layal carried a bag of dried leaves and a bag of berries. When they saw us, Remmer burst into tears. "You had them!"

"How grateful we are." Layal oozed sincerity. "We found the shoes they'd left by the river. We feared they were lost or had fled."

"Hey, it's Pretty Boy," NezLeigh said to Layal.

"Pretty stupid," Kola added.

"And Crybaby."

"Give us the goods or you'll cry more, ya dig? We like your trade or else we keep the chicks. We keep the chicks," said Kola.

Remmer wiped his eyes on the back of his hand. "Hey, NezLeigh, we've got some things for you, all good stuff, so let's not dilly dally. Cut those ropes, release our friends, and we'll get on our way."

NezLeigh shook her bag dress playfully. "What you got, Crybaby? It might not be good enough. I might keep her for myself and show her lovin' like she's never known."

Remmer leapt forward and grabbed NezLeigh by her plastic shirt. "Stop playing around. What have you been doing to them? We thought they'd drowned." NezLeigh's mouth fell open and her eyes were as wide as Lavender's rear.

I wiggled my hands against my bonds. "It's okay, Rem. She saved us from a wild deer and we helped her catch a pig. Take us home." He released NezLeigh. She fell to the ground. He bent down, put his arms around me, and tossed me over his shoulder. I hadn't been swooped up to a shoulder since I was a child. I didn't need this rescue, which made it utterly thrilling. I squealed like a kid.

"Let's go, Layal." I'd never seen Remmer so decisive, and never had he spoken to Layal like this.

"Yes, Layal, come get me," Eve added as Kola held her wrists loosely. Layal looked from Eve to Kola, wearing Eve's clothes, as if he was confused.

"You're getting scooped by Crybaby," Kola said to me. "Scooped."

"Aren't we going to have a moment of bartering?" Layal asked.

"Give me the damn bags and take this bitch. They been trouble. Trouble," Kola said, untwisting Eve's wrist bags. "And toss in a kiss while you're at it. For *me*. A kiss."

"At your service." Layal dropped the bags at Kola's feet, bowed, and gave her a smooch on the hand before kissing her cheek. "It's a pleasure."

"First to be kissed," she said proudly, shoving Eve into Layal's arms. "Me before NezLeigh."

"Damn," NezLeigh said, blinking. "The sun is stabbing me. I didn't see a thing." Impatient, Remmer took off running. NezLeigh flashed me a V made with her fingers.

Remmer carried me across the worn path through the trees. My arms were goosebumpy as I twisted my hands from the loose wrist wrap and let myself be carried by his rhythm.

"Have you been injured?" he asked as we bumped along.

"No. I lost my UTI, my gadget, though."

He let out a rush of breath. "We'll barter for it next time."

"No need. It's broken. Thanks for negotiating our release." I rubbed my hands across his crinkling plastic back. "You were brave."

His voice cracked. "I thought you were dead."

Breathlessly, I told him what had transpired as we rushed past the raspberry bushes without stopping. We broke out onto the dirt, causing a pair of crows to caw in alarm. Two stars hung in the pink-blue sky; the ground was splotchy with green and smelled like jasmine as Remmer tromped over it. We got to the cabin and Remmer stopped at the cistern. I slid down, lingering across his chest, marveling at his stamina, as my feet touched the ground. He dipped out a cup of water and gave it to me.

"We didn't find a tarp," he said, breathing deeply and fixing his eyes on me.

"Tarp?" I tried not to be jolted from my dreamy state. A tarp was the last thing on my mind.

"To separate the loft into two private bedrooms if you and I want some privacy, now or in the future."

"I'll take privacy now, with or without a tarp," I said. His run had left him glistening and me breathless. I handed him a cup of water and watched his throat bobble as he drank it, struggling to keep my eyes from his plastic pants. The oblong shape of the drinking cup put butterflies in my stomach. I hated and loved these hormones but drank them in.

I stretched. "I might need to go to bed. We slept in leaf huts and NezLeigh kept us awake all night."

"Like you, I'm tired," he replied.

"I need to get out of these dirty clothes."

The logs of the cabin were strong and smooth. Each wooden shingle hung down firmly. The long-handled knob had me tingling as I opened the door. Each step on the boards, the climb to the loft with *him* behind me, the sequence and light touch of his breath, had me pounding all over. As I sat on his bedroll, bursting with emerging feelings, he stacked books around the bed, a makeshift wall.

"They won't be here soon," he said. "I ran the whole way."

"Layal is probably still there talking," I said.

He put his last paper book on the stack and sat beside me. He was bred to be a treasure with his even features and bright eyes, gold with sincerity. I couldn't keep my hands off him as I fell into his orbit. I fluffed his hair, smooth and soft as corn silk, with my fingers and drew it across his forehead, beading with sweat.

"Perfect," I said. "Ah, perfect."

He opened his mouth to speak, but attraction overwhelmed us. Our first kiss was shy, a lick of raspberry ice cream. I shivered with delight. We paused to share a look of surprise and giggled with relief. We leaned together. The taste of each other drew us in deeper, to where time and space merged, and ache and balm became one. I was ravenously curious as desire rose with each touch of his mouth. He lay on top of me, pressing himself on me, and where our bodies met, a primitive force emerged.

"I need you," he said. His yearning filled me with power. Being with him at this moment was the pinnacle of my life, the most important, most necessary, most achingly honest moment I'd ever had.

He drew back. His pupils were dark.

"Don't stop. The others will be coming." I did my best not to sound desperate.

"Cali," he said, my name resonating in his throat. "Cali, I've been thinking about what you told me; how we should be more than friends. You make something grow within me. I want to be irrational when you're near. I want to be achingly in love. Truth isn't beauty. It's love."

Now that he was coming on to me I had to reason it through. Did I want to hook up because I was curious? Because I wanted to make sure NezLeigh didn't get with him? Was it his physical perfection or the ridiculous rescue? If it was those things, it wouldn't be fair to continue. There had to be something between us. He was that kind of a guy.

"Truth is love or beauty is love?" I put him off to give myself time to think.

"Love is truth. Let us be equals."

"Love among equals. I'm with you."

"How will we know if we are equals?"

I pulled him nearer. "We already are. We are." There was a wonderful moment when our faces were close. Again, we quivered with anticipation.

"I remember something about my mom."

"What is it?"

"She said people who love each other work together. They make life easier because they are one. Cali, we need to help each other. It has to be about more than...more than emptying the hopper."

"Emptying the hopper?"

"That's what I was bred to do, to make you tingle with the force of my auger, to open my valves. Yes, but I want to be more than a machine for you. I want to love you. You're what I want." He took me in his arms as I had him in mine. "It's more than action or duty. I think of you constantly. Every movement reminds me of you, turns my thoughts to what we might do together. I can't stop thinking about you. Being apart from you was like death. I must never let you go again. I want to get close, to lay together. No longer will my fears hold me back."

"I-I've been thinking of you too. I can't get you out of my mind. It's like being tipsy," I said.

"I don't know what that is." He moved in and kissed me again. It was the most wonderful feeling; we were melting together, our lips, our tongues, his forceful hands tucking themselves beneath my t-shirt. He kneaded my breasts. We throbbed together like two lobes of a heart. It was so beautiful it hurt. I was open to the world. I could do anything now. I would walk the land with the strength of a human bond. This is what Cochtonville was taking away from its citizens with their InVitro and forced marriage—the ability to love a peer of your choosing.

"I will part you with my fingers and with my tongue. There are all sorts of ways to proceed from there—ways of connecting. Positions they are called."

"You are so technique oriented. You'd make a great scientist!" The way he spoke of it so technically had me flooded with excitement.

"We can start off with the most pedestrian and move from there. It won't hurt. It will help us sleep better, stay younger, and boost our immune systems."

He spoke my language with his mention of physiological benefits. Never would I find another man like this one!

"The only pain is going to be not doing something." I was tingling and pounding as if something stung me. Remmer was the only way to cure this delicious itch.

"How many thrusts do you want? Or would you prefer minutes? What size is best for you? I'm adjustable."

"Are you sure you aren't some sort of robot?"

"If I was a robot, I would not have mentioned it to you, for love has no room for lies. I'm human but I'm trained."

"Trained?" I shouldn't have continued the conversation. I was going to pop with desire.

"I trained with female robots, more accurately animatronic dolls; robots do work and these dolls simply made measurements."

"Measurements?"

"They evaluated me. My performance was measured by the dolls and appraised by a team of scientists, older men who claimed experience in lovemaking. I would have passed inspection except I'm erratic. I underperform at times such as when shown photographs of real women."

"Performance-based review? No."

"Layal and I should have told you earlier. We were *trained* as erotic repeats as young men. This was why we were made."

"You mentioned it, but I didn't want to ask then. What is an erotic repeat?"

"There are wealthy women who buy such erotic services. We were failures. Layal talks too much and I-I can't overcome my shyness. I'm not the performer I was bred to be."

"You were to be a performer?"

"In a way. I wasn't comfortable with it." Remmer shifted and touched his tattoo. "Read it."

"Clustered regularly interspaced short palindromic erratic repeats. *Erratic?* A spelling error?"

"No. *I* received the stamp of disapproval. We were sent here as failures. Some mysterious benefactor purchased us, but not for sex. The condition was we would never interact with this person and would take on tasks for the good of Cochtonia. This spared our lives. The isolation I'd thought of as bad, now seems good with you here."

His tale touched my heart. I could help him gain his confidence.

"What kind of women did you practice with?" I said gently.

"None. I'd have to be approved for such."

"There's the problem. Those dolls couldn't see you or touch you or talk to you or-or kiss you or run their hands across your chest. They didn't know you. May I take off this plastic bag, by the way? I want to touch your beautiful skin." I ran my hands across his body. I was exothermic, giving off heat, with high entropy, exploding with compassion and lust for him.

"At your service." He stood up. With a hiss of plastic, he slowly ripped off his bags and tossed them to the floorboards. Standing over me, he flexed his pectoral muscles and rocked his hips while holding his hands behind his head. His regular pulsing movements, his symmetrical, hard body, his eyes fixed on mine—he had me charmed. He bent over me. I'd been starving and I hadn't even realized it. I thought I might faint.

I grabbed his face and pulled him close. Our lips met and I knew joy and yearning as I hadn't before. I held out my arms and he fell upon me, kissing me, touching me, undressing me. We became lovers. It was as if a bomb went off. In our hearts burned the hope that we'd sealed our friendship and it would last forever.

As the days passed between us, his confidence grew and I learned a love deeper than my own dreams of success.

CHAPTER THIRTEEN

"We need soap," Eve said as we stood around the cistern rinsing our bowls after a meal of mouse stew. "And we need to store food for the winter. How do we get started?"

We'd been here a month. Yes, I was happy. I knew love and I knew friendship. Without agriculture, I'd lost weight and was leaner and harder than a Purple Eater pig and far more heat tolerant. We'd adjusted to the temperature. Life was simple. We were always out gathering food or in making love or reading paper books—dark but soothing in their pages—and talking about the meaning of life, about which we had no conclusions.

There had been less trading with NezLeigh and her band than I'd envisioned. Yes, we'd gotten two rabbits, which NezLeigh skinned herself, digging her nails into the back of each animal and ripping off the skin. Kola delivered a bag of mice, skinny and furry. She complained that the pig was eating anything extra.

"And we need our own meat," Eve added.

"Truth, darling Truth, worry is living in the future. Don't go there," Layal said, handing her his bowl. "We'll have enough. We always do. If I grow weak, we can get some provisions delivered."

"What's that supposed to mean?"

I was totally shocked by Eve's reaction and I knew Remmer

was too, for we had grown a cosmic connection, feeling each other's thoughts and sensations. Yes, I was as sure of that as I was taken aback by Eve, although I agreed with her. Either we made plans to stay or we went back. This uncertainty was gnawing at me even as I was happy.

"You're beautiful when you're mad, my Truth."

"Either you commit to our future here or you don't, in which case I call for a ride home." She handed him his dirty bowl. This mood was worse than a maize borer in a field of Big Yields corn.

"I can make soap," I said, putting my bowl on the branch we used for a drying rack.

"In a few months we can collect walnuts," Remmer added. "And we have the new greens."

The graveyard plant had grown abundantly, nearly to the edge of the cabin. We pulled them up and used the leaves as a seasoning. It added floral notes to salads.

"Don't worry your pretty little head. We can make this place as you wish, keeping in mind that material goods are a burden." Layal took the plastic cup from the cistern and rinsed his bowl onto the dirt.

Eve persisted. "This place needs to be safe and comfortable. Make yourselves useful. Aren't there some nuts you could gather?"

"Mushrooms, maybe. It's too early for nuts," Layal said.

"Mulberries," Remmer added.

"Did I see some grapes? Is that what you call them?" I asked.

"Men, go get as much as you can. Cali will stay here with me and make soap."

Although the education system in Cochtonville was spotty, my dad had discussed how we might make soap if we had to survive government oppression or shortages. Mom had explained the chemistry, which wasn't tough—take fat and add some alkali to turn part of the fat into a water-soluble head with a fat-soluble tail dangling behind. Since like dissolves like, soap can remove about anything. The grill lid still contained congealed turkey fat—we occasionally used it as a lotion. Using a single use plastic spoon and makeshift plastic bag gloves, I mixed ashes with water in a can and let it sit to create alkali. Eve crouched beside me, her arms on her knees.

"Careful," I said, "it's going to be caustic."

"I needed to talk to you. Alone."

It had been a while since we'd talked alone. I'd hooked up with Remmer; he was all I thought about and the only person I confided in. Eve had kept busy making new plastic outfits and had woven a privacy tarp. When we'd gone gathering, it was Eve and Layal in one direction and Rem and I in the other. I missed her.

She moved away from the alkali on my instruction. There was something off about her. Her hair was shaggy, but so was mine. She was missing something. Her No Regrets 2.0, the device meant to keep us from getting our periods, was gone. I was surprised I hadn't noticed sooner. I'd been so love-blind, I hadn't seen anything but Remmer.

"You lost your bracelet?" I said, hoping I didn't sound upset about it.

"Yes, during the rescue. It's what I want to talk about. I'm not bringing a baby into this dump. And besides, I'm not attracted to Layal anymore."

"Not attracted to him? He's the handsomest man in all of Cochtonia. What don't you like? Is it his personality?"

"He's so overbearing since the rescue. My mom says hormones make the worst men look good sometimes. Was it the bracelet giving me attraction or do I really care about him? I'm beginning to wonder. He's getting ideas. He wants me to call him MegaStud and Johnny Jackalot. Where does he get these fantasies living out here all alone working as a garbage tosser?"

"The men were bred but also trained to be erotic escorts, but they were trained by old men with no idea what women want. No doubt one of the dudes told him those pet names are what women want. Tell him what you *do* want."

"Cali, there's more to it. Since I lost the bracelet, I've been having second thoughts more and more frequently about staying.

I'm modified, but it's not like you think. I had extra chromosomes. I had material removed as well as traits inserted. Without this genetic intervention, I wouldn't be myself. I'd have cognitive and facial deformities. I might not even be alive. The treatment left me strong, but it wasn't done to give me strength. What I'm saying is, I'm not sure if I should reproduce and certainly not here. It *must* be InVitro if I want motherhood. I should go back."

"We can," I said slowly. "At least for a while. If something happens and you get pregnant here, my mom can help."

"She's a midwife?"

"No. She has this device."

"Good to know."

I, too, was having second thoughts, but in the other direction. I wanted to stay here with Remmer and away from Cochtonville.

"We'll have to share the bracelet," I said to Eve. "You'll be happy again when you don't have to worry. One week on, one week off. It will mess us both up enough to work like it should, I hope." Hope was exactly what I held in my heart—hope, innocent hope, naive hope, artless hope the world would make sense and I'd be happier than my mother had been. And oh, I wanted *him* and if the desire in his eyes never quenched, I would be in eternal ecstasy. I might never leave this place.

"Share a bracelet? Are you serious? You've got the dopiest look on your face. Don't tell me you're falling for Remmer."

"I am. I want to see if I am without the bracelet. Nothing bad will happen. This is where we're meant to be."

I poured the liquid from the ashes into turkey fat in cans that, according to the labels, once contained pork and beans. It made me hungry just thinking of food with sugar in it, except now each can contained caustic potash. I wasn't sure of the correct ratio of base to fat. I made three trials with each can. I filled one can a third of the way with the fat, one half way, and one with mostly fat. I stirred each can with the spoon, averting my eyes in the process. Each can was as hot as the pits of Vulcan. The one that was mostly lard took a soapy firmness; the tallow was saponifying. It was tan and runny and smelled like poultry—unless I was imagining it. The other cans were alkaline messes. Of course, those weren't going to work. You couldn't have extra caustic in the mix. Theory worked so much better than trial and error. I added more fat to them.

This was all Eve and I had to do today—make soap, and let it sit for a few weeks as it hardened. Life was easy with so much time left for sex. How did people have real jobs?

We set about bringing a home to our cabin. I wanted my future to be here. The fight between Layal and Eve had passed, and I saw her in a new light, a vulnerable light. Equally important, my feeling for Remmer never wavered when I gave Eve the bracelet. Our love was real.

The four of us were in the cabin, each couple cuddling in bed, skin on skin, cheek on cheek. Morning light and the sounds of energetic crows had been trying to wake us, but the loft was still cozy and dark. On the other side of the plastic curtain, Eve talked lazily about what tasks we might do. She mentioned catching frogs for meat. The crows' caws were cut by the whir of blades. This was a normal sound in Cochtonville, but not here.

Eve screamed, "It's my dad. Get dressed. Pretend we're here doing research."

We scrambled for our clothes. Quite a lot of dealing with the Washers was having a plausible story and cooperating. My mind sifted through several stories—we were examining the water, we were studying the foliage—none explained why we were here without our packs. Eve hurried down the stairs.

"The helicopter has a red drop on the tail," she called up.

"It's the Blood Bank. Don't let them see you. The Bleeders are thugs." Layal pulled on his plastic pants. "Remmer, climb in bed and pretend to be sick. Truth, Cali, climb out of the window. Don't come back until twilight. They won't stay past dark." He rushed down to Eve, kissed her, and slipped out the front door.

"I thought you could have visitors," I said, my voice rising in fear as Remmer folded himself into our bed and closed his eyes as he pretended to be sick.

"Layal is overly frightened of these guys, but do as he says."

Someone outside yelled what sounded like, "Hey, Men at Arms. Time to come to the service of your country."

I was weak from fear. I wanted to say more to Remmer but I dared not. "Go," he said. "Layal will need something to eat after this. It's hard on him. It would be cool if you gathered."

My heart gushed with fear. I rushed down the stairs to the back window and ran my hand across the sill as I listened to the male voices.

Layal spoke loudly as he attempted to both warn us and hold the Blood Bankers off.

"Why are you here so soon?"

"Last bag of blood was thin. We need more."

"Not today. No blood today. I'm under the weather. If you'd allow me any sort of communication device, you wouldn't have wasted your time coming here."

"We got plenty of time. Things are slow in Cochtonville today. Besides, we have a report to share with you."

Following Layal's command, we opened the window. We didn't dare speak. There wasn't time to make plans or work things through. Eve bent over and formed a step with her intertwined hands. I put one foot in and she hoisted me to the windowsill. Carefully, I hung one leg over the sash. I straddled, a leg over the edge, one inside. How far was it? A breeze blew my hair across my face. Eve put her hands on my waist to steady me. I gripped the frame and hauled my second leg over the sash. It was about four feet down. Eve placed her palm on my back. I scooted forward and dropped to the ground, my knees buckling beneath me. I fell but picked myself up, then held out a hand to help Eve, already perched on the ledge. She jumped and landed gracefully. We walked as softly as we could. Layal cried out. We stopped. So did the cries.

We raced for the trees, stumbling across the dirt in panic. It was too far—we were obvious out there in the open and had nearly a mile with no cover. My lungs and legs already burned. My nose dripped. Salty sweat stung my eyes. I gasped for air, pushing harder until we finally broke the canopy of trees around the river and collapsed into the dry leaf litter that crinkled beneath my chest, my heart aching like it had been stomped on by a wild pig.

The dirt was musky, a smell as wild as sex, as if an animal had urinated here. Not wanting to be intimate with the earth, I pushed myself up on my elbows. Beside me, Eve was on her knees and heaving. As if I'd been stung by bees, my skin prickled. We'd been doing the things Report 'Em Raw reported. Instead of being contestants, we'd be convicts. My mouth was dry and it was a half-mile to the dirty creek. At least we were in the shade.

Eve sobbed. "Who are they? I know all about the law and I've never heard of Blood Bankers. Are they hurting him? Why did we run? I don't understand any of this." She put her hands on her stomach. My stress manifested as an eye twitch. I took a breath. We mustn't panic. We had permission to be here.

"They get these visits at times. They mentioned them and so did NezLeigh." I didn't want to bring up the reason for the unfriendly call—to take blood from Layal because the older Cochtons thought it kept them young. "Let's hustle to the creek, take a bath, catch something, and go back tonight. I smell like bad cheese."

"Umm. I could go for any type of cheese," Eve said, relaxing slightly. "Not that I don't stink, too. If my parents knew how gamey I'd gotten they'd disown me. Of course, if they knew what we were doing..."

We headed to the creek.

Eve brought up the unsavory topic. "It only takes a few minutes for a person to bleed to death. My dad told me."

"They aren't killing him. He's being drained slowly."

"You're making me nervous. I don't understand why *he* must give blood."

"He could be the universal donor."

"He is very giving," she said, eyelashes batting.

We arrived at the creek. Frogs leapt from the bank and

surfaced farther down, eyeing us from a safe distance. We took off our clothes and plunged into the water, rinsing and combing out our shaggy wet hair with our fingers.

"Think we could catch a frog?" I said, approaching one slowly, my hand stretched. It sat until I bent to grab it. With a croak, it dodged away.

"They're tricky suckers," Eve said, darting toward one as it ducked under a rock. "This one got itself into a corner." She pulled it out, holding it over the water by its fat middle. "I don't think we should eat this." It had a white tumor on the left side of its face and eyes the size of peas, not the bulbous visionary lenses of an average frog. She dropped it and it scooted beneath the water. "This day gets creepier by the minute." The acrid scent of pesticides drifted in the breeze.

"Smells like Dusters," I said. "Why would they be here?"

"Why didn't we hear the plane? I'm dying to check on Layal. I thought I heard the copter leaving."

"He'll need food."

We dressed quickly. Still damp, we followed the trail through the trees and picked a bag of raspberries before heading back. We raced toward the cabin. All was not well. The soap was spilled. The dirt around the cabin was kicked about. The cluster of vines was wilted, the big leaves collapsed, the tendrils shrunken—killed by herbicide. In the middle of it all was the white helicopter of the Vice Patrol. Eve's dad and Washer Ursula stood on the porch along with the chubby Washer I'd seen before and a young Washer, female, with large glasses. White hats, white coats, white leggings, white boots, white belts with white guns and communication devices. Remmer and Layal weren't in sight.

"Where are the men?" I said, panicked. "Why is your dad here?"

"I don't know," she said. "But Daddy is always on my side. He'll help us. Don't say much."

Eve threw herself at her father. Her words tumbled out, almost like sobs. "Thank the Cochtons! Dad, I'm so glad you're here.

Have you met the residents? They've been utter gentlemen. Have you heard of the Blood Bankers? They're creeps."

"I've been hearing all about it," he said.

"Where are they? Did you see them?"

"You're going home. A Blood Banker was strangled with a plant."

"One of the vines out here? They're innocent. We've been picking them."

The commissioner said, "The plant was firmly around the agent's neck. Nobody could get it off. Those so-called gentlemen gave it a go, but like everything they were sent here to do, they failed. We got an emergency call from the surviving agent. Eve, I thought something had happened to you. It's a relief to know you're safe."

A killer plant? The story was unbelievable. As if she read my mind, Ursula put her hand on my shoulder. "We had to spray this whole place down to get rid of the murderous vegetable. Fortunately, the other Banker was able to deliver the transfusion to Mr. Cochton."

Eve embraced her father. "What about the residents? Are they safe? Where are they?"

"The Banker took them back to Cochtonville. We handcuffed them at first, of course."

Eve wept—beautifully, of course. "Don't hurt them. I entreat you. They didn't do anything. They gave us water."

Ursula said, "They had a job to do and they didn't do it. They'll be kept close and put to use in Cochtonville."

The commissioner said, "Why are you all the way over here? This isn't the WasteBin. What have you been up to? I've seen hookers dressed better. Where's your gear?"

"At the shack on the hill."

"Ursula, go fetch it."

Eve's voice had water in it, as if she was drowning. "We are working on our presentation, Dad. We are toying with the idea of a survivalist camp. We lived on our own to see if it could be done.

We ventured here to get away from the flies near the WasteBin. It's impossible to concentrate with them buzzing."

"Where's your HotNot?"

"I lost it, Dad, and I still survived. I survived. Aren't you proud of me?"

"Your boss has been frantic. The competition is three days away."

"We had a tough assignment. We took our time and did it right, like you always say."

"This project was suggested by Bert Cochton himself. He's keenly interested in it. It's a wasted resource begging to be exploited. Eve, you'd better come up with a smashing presentation. Van Winkle, you are going to keep out of contact with my daughter until the presentation. She will come up with an idea with my supervision. You will support her and go along with everything she says. You got that?"

The crows were cawing. I was going to have to ride in that helicopter. Remmer was somewhere in Cochtonville, and Eve and I would be separated. I understood the horribleness of it all.

"I dig," I said.

"What did you say? Where did you hear that phrase?"

I hated the emotions washing over me—sorrow, fear, hatred. I wasn't going to get anywhere with them. I wouldn't find out what happened to Remmer in this state of mind. I'd never get him back. I swallowed my emotions. My throat was dry, but I managed to say, "Sir, I'll comply."

Ursula escorted me into the Cochton Enterprises building, past the guards and up the elevator.

"No hard feelings, right?" she said as we rode to my floor, my eyes nearly burning from the brightness of her HotNot uniform. "Like you, I do my job. I don't care for some of it, but we're all in this together."

I was too wrung out to argue with her. I didn't know why she was chatting with me.

"You'll make it," she said, her face as fierce with determination and short teeth as NezLeigh's. "You and I will make it here. I got instructions to take you to your lab. Where is it?"

Hoping we wouldn't run into anyone and I'd have to explain, I led her down the accusing halls—*the ladder of success is built on you.*

Keep it Simple, Stupid.

The first step is hard work. And the second.

The only I in Cochton Enterprises is near the end.

The Cochtons loved slogans and they screamed in green from the bright yellow walls. Each one hit me like a turkey carcass; they wouldn't hurt me but each one left a mark. When we reached my lab, my name was on the door. Ursula didn't have to doubt my sincerity. She held out her hand and I shook it, my mind a crumpled mess.

"Thank you for your hostility," I said. She furrowed her forehead at my mistake. Hurriedly I corrected myself. "I mean, hospitality."

She squeezed my hand harshly before releasing it. I'd botched our moment of friendship.

"You look immature with your dopey pig backpack," she said. "Everybody knows pigs are mean suckers." I watched her walk away, her broad shoulders hunched as she traversed the lonely hall with its demanding advice.

Although I was as hollow as a rotten log, my lab held out its arms and drew me into its bosom. Here were the tall windows with light streaming through, the labeled chemicals in rows on the shelves, flasks and beakers ready to be used, brown and clear bottles of liquids. Here was where things worked out, where reactions were predictable, where science yielded to persistence. I slumped down into my ergonomic desk chair. I'd missed this lab and the measuring instrumentation that sprung alive at my touch.

My computer was on my desk, exactly as I'd left it. I turned it on, located the file marked UTI data, and tried to open it. It was empty. After a moment of panic, I remembered the backup drive. I took it from my dopey pack. All it had was the first two days' worth of data on it, but that was enough. I downloaded the manure pit data, searching for some component of the rocks or feces that was a unique resource. Yes, I'd find a resource and Remmer, too. This lab reminded me I could do it. I could find logic in this messed up land.

My fatigued eyes jerked over the data. Besides the expected nutrients, the manure was high in calcium and iron. It would be easy to recover these, especially the iron, using electrolysis. I took a pad of paper from the drawer and sketched out a diagram of a giant battery docked at the edge of the manure lagoon. Of course, I needed more. We had to go overboard to win.

I studied the fat layer, then ran the information through a database—swine fat. Dead pigs had been tossed into the site. I'd seen it. The fat could be made into candles and, of course, soap. I ran my fingers through my hair. It needed a wash. Manure pit shampoo. I couldn't see it being a best seller.

I was drumming my fingers on the lab bench when Nell, the microbiologist who had been our driver to the WasteBin, came in carrying a plastic tray filled with microbe-colony culture tubes capped in plastic, labeled "biohazard."

"I heard you were back. I met the officer in the elevator," she said. I didn't want to explain how the Vice Patrol brought me back because of an alleged strangling plant, a Blood Banker hauled away the love of my life, and on top of it all I'd lost the UTI. I had to tell her though, at least about the testing device.

"Yes, here I am alone, so very alone. The UTI got...it got stolen. It wasn't working properly so it shouldn't be a security risk or anything. I'm sorry."

"How could it get stolen out there?"

"There are a few critters living hand to mouth in the wild."

"Did you get enough information before it was lost? You're going to win this thing, right?"

I pretended to be positive. "Of course. I spent plenty of time studying. The WasteBin is dank."

"The potential?"

"If you only knew."

Her big, blue eyes dug into my brain. "What's your proposal?"

I was relieved she let the theft of the UTI pass so quickly even though she was acting way too much like my boss and not my co-worker. I floated an idea past her. "What do you think about making iron from manure?"

She put the plastic tray on my desk. "Good idea. There's an iron deposit a hundred miles from here but in an area highly populated by Pestos. Cochtonia doesn't like to set up operations there. How much iron can you get from the manure?"

"A gram per liter. I'd only need a million liters to get a ton and it's continuously replenished. Of course, we'd need to get a high voltage source out there or transport the sewage. And Cochtonia doesn't use much iron. Everything here is plastic. Aurgh. I wish I had more brains and more time."

"No worries. I brought you something from the outside. Read it as you get time. But hurry." She lifted the culture tubes with one hand and fished a thin paper book from beneath the towel they rested on.

"Paper?" I said.

"It's a magazine. Look at the headline. *Money from manure.*" She handed it to me.

I reached for it. I wasn't afraid of paper, it reminded me of Remmer, and yet, what good would I do Remmer from a prison cell or rehabilitation center? "Where did you get this?"

"It's from the American Chemical Society."

This was going too far. I withdrew my hand. "I don't do American. It's subversive."

"You will if you want something creative. It's got my fingerprints. Blame me. Say I left it here."

I pulled a pair of High Density Polyethylene disposable gloves from a box on my desk and slipped them on before tenuously taking the magazine.

"That's the spirit. You need to take a risk to win it all." She pressed her finger to her forehead, crossed her eyes, stuck out her tongue, and left me holding the magazine as it flopped between my hands. I was guilty for looking, mad at myself for being loyal to such a 404 place as Cochtonville. I used my thumb and forefinger to turn the pages as they tried to slip from my grip. I flipped to the lead article and read about the chemical potential of manure. *Nobody else will have this.* Paper was such an intimate means of communication. It was personal, not readily shared, easy on the eyes, and could be burned, which was what I'd do with this once I'd absorbed its information. The buzz of an incoming phone message made me jump out of my skin. I put the magazine in my backpack and read.

"Cali, dear Cali. How worried I was. Did something go wrong? I asked the Patrol to find you. The presentation—it's soon. Didn't you get my messages?" I pulled off my disposable gloves and tossed them in the trash can. The lab door opened and in he came, Sir Bux in his ridiculous garb and sash, putting his phone in the baggy pocket of his uniform pants. I hadn't noticed before how his pants were so high and ballooning on his waist and so tight at the ankles. It gave him the shape of a ham. I salivated.

He stopped at the door and opened his mouth and closed it like a carp longing to be caught and eaten. "You shortened your shirt. It shows so much midriff. Oh, why are you dressed in that shocking manner?"

"I could say the same for you." Clearly the time in the wild hadn't helped my office manners.

"Did you find something?"

"More than you can imagine."

"You must pull yourself together. Get yourself cleaned up. Take the rest of the time until the presentation to recuperate. The judges will expect you to look enticing. It shouldn't be difficult. Even in that get up, you've got me hard."

"What did you say?"

"You've got me hard pressed to find fault with you. You made excellent use of the UTI at first. It stopped transmitting data though, and I got so anxious."

"Transmitting data. Did you confiscate my data? The file on my computer was tampered with."

"We couldn't leave things to chance. Cali, forgive me for leaving you vulnerable out there and exposed and dressed in almost nothing. The horrid place is nothing but limestone and pig waste. The transmissions stopped after a few days. Did you quit because you became frightfully discouraged?"

"No. The gadget broke and was burned. I lost it."

With medals clanking, he fell to his knees and embraced me. "I beg your forgiveness. Even I didn't know the full extent of the assignment. I was acting on orders. Yes, I was promised great rewards beyond my wildest hopes, but I didn't know where the instructions came from except from above." He put his face in my pubic area. "I want you to know how proud I am of your sacrifices for Cochtonia and for me."

I wasn't sure how to react to his sincere yet vulgar display. Looking down on his head, I could see the neon tinge of Mom's product—Hair Raiser. If only it was Remmer with his face in my crotch and not an authority figure subjugating himself before me. I cried at the pure unfairness and sorrow I had for both of us.

"Cali, your heart is tender. I put my life in your hands at this moment."

"My hands need to get to work," I said, pulling myself away. "I must contemplate how to make the presentation a success."

"Cali, I want you."

"Sir?"

"I want you to be a success."

CHAPTER FOURTEEN

I went home, my mind as tattered as a plastic bag on a barbed wire fence, and fell into bed. I slept for a day, sweating under my comforter with my head on my firm, slick corn fiber pillow. Twice I walked to the bathroom, startled by the mirror, the person in the mirror with such dark eye circles, and astonished by the thundering toilet flush.

I roused at light through my bedroom blinds and the sound of the wrens dulled through the window glass, only to have exhaustion pull its covers over me for the remainder of the day. I felt Remmer's hand on my back and together we chased a plastic bag across the hard, packed soil. I snagged the bag, a spotlight hit me, and sirens sounded. My eyes popped open. It was Mom, light through the blinds, and a siren in the distance.

"Do you have a project to work on?" Mom said gently.

I stretched. "Yes, the mission. I've got this idea...I'm not ready to share it. It needs time to gel. It's going to be a winner."

"I'm glad you're on top of things. I was worried without a word from you. What were you doing out there for two months?"

"Living as hunter-gatherers, mostly on the gatherer side. It was so freeing. It left me wondering about what success is. Mom, I even had a mate."

"As in someone on a boat?"

"Kind of."

"What's happened to the person?"

"He's here in Cochtonville too. I don't know where. We were extradited at the same time. I need to find him more than anything."

"The best thing to do is make yourself valuable to Cochtonia and hope he does the same."

"He's a Crisper, Mom. He was exiled for being erratic, but I rehabilitated him."

"A Crisper? I've heard the term."

"Yes. A man designed to please women. He's more to me. He's a friend and a human being."

She gently took my hand. "I know the place to start looking. The Union Station bar! They advertised a Crisper display last month and InVitros say they rent them out. It's a recent perk because having a baby isn't fulfilling enough. Surely, he'll pass through. For now, let's get working on your project. You need to look smashing. It's going to make all the difference."

I tossed on my robe, soft and warm against my dirty skin. I stood in the shower rubbing my skin with body wash until the hot water ran out. It was hell/heaven to be back. Instead of scurrying about for a morning meal, I plopped myself in a chair at the kitchen table with the blue tablecloth. The old analog clock swept away the seconds with a faint grind of gears as Mom made coffee. I drank a cup black. It was bitter and brought the new, clear day and its chores thundering upon me. I drank another with cream. Then I drank a cup brimming with nothing but cream. Agriculture had its tasty advantages. My stomach churned. A rabbit hopped by the window. I tensed until I remembered I didn't have to kill it for food.

Mom cracked open eggs and fried them in corn oil. She topped them with cheese and gave them to me on a plate. I took a bite using my fingers. Oh, they were good. Mom handed me a fork. I was satiated and awake—such a weird feeling—and ready for a day filled with tasks. There wasn't one task like what we had in the wild, such as picking berries or sorting through trash. There was the presentation, dressing for success, having aspirations.

Mom said, "I've expanded the shop. I've hired a stylist. Come with me today and

we'll get you ready to meet your dreams and make this place a little easier to live in."

"Yes. Dream on!"

I was broken by the loss of Remmer and being back in Cochtonville against my wishes. Despite this, a fire burned in my belly. My idea for the resource was going to be the pinnacle of my life as a scientist. I had to admit to myself that a career in science had been a matter of practicality. I didn't love it. Except now maybe I did love it, or loved my idea and the usefulness of it. It was enough to bestow me with an enthusiasm for the ritual sacrifices I'd have to make to boost my appearance enough to be taken seriously at the presentation. The idea—and the chance to see Remmer again—gave me everything to work for.

Jane, the stylist, wore her blonde hair piled on her head and a gold hooded sweatshirt with matching pants along with her white sneakers. She reminded me of the Cochton's gold-plated limo. She bustled me to a cushy seat in the new aesthetics area, opposite Mom's medical area. My hair was standing up in several places.

"You've got some cowlicks to work around," Jane said, brandishing a comb.

"I appreciate all you can do for me. I must put the best head of hair forward."

"True. The Cochton brothers will be watching."

She combed through my hair. Deep tangles remained from my time in the wild. After a bout of tugging out the snarls, she snipped it precisely; the tiny bits of hair fell around my face like dust.

"You're going all out for InVitro."

"It's my goal and has been for a long time."

"You have to take what they give you. There's a dark side, these days more than ever from what I hear. How about a deep conditioning?"

"Yes. Whatever it takes."

"Most young women aspire to InVitro. I'll make your hair look fabulous for the big, life-changing contest. Never underestimate the power of great hair. This InVitro thing used to be experimental, you know. People were guinea pigs. It wasn't the glamorous award it is now."

"Yes. I-I've heard. From a reliable source." My heart dropped for a moment, thinking of Remmer.

Jane washed me, conditioned me, and sprayed my head with aerosol carrying a whiff of almonds. She gave me a curly updo, traditional, as would please the Cochton brothers.

Mom came in from a walk around the block. "You should go next door and check things out," she said urgently. "It's a Crisper show. You'll need cash. I've got some bills for you."

My heart skipped a couple of beats.

"A Crisper show?"

"New men. Tonight only, the sign says."

My head spun. I had to go. I had to see if Remmer and Layal were there. But tonight? The night before my presentation? I didn't know what Eve had in store. I didn't want to be tired and out of it tomorrow. My idea deserved full throttle. Except for loving Remmer, it was the highlight of my life.

Jane said, "Honey, you should go. Take your hair over there and make sure it doesn't fall. This will be your trial run. I have to warn you from experience, when it comes to Crispers, don't get your hopes up. I've been there before and never saw what I was looking for."

I did, however, get my hopes up. The men had to be somewhere. Remmer had display-based moves. He could have been sent back and put to work in a cheap local bar. Coincidences happened.

"Yes, for sure I want to go," I said.

I hurried to the bar. A sign on the heavy wooden door read "Crisper Show. New Models! Tonight only!" Two Agro kids with stringy hair and swinging long skirts hung by the entrance.

"Here comes another nympho," one said as I reached for the door. She was about a year older than NezLeigh, with round eyes, nearly normal sized, the same pug nose, and skin as blanched as WasteBin limestone.

The other, nearly identical, held up a plastic bag. "Can I bum a light, skank?"

"Nah, she won't have one. She's a flake, look at her."

A woman in a Union Station t-shirt and a miniskirt came out and tossed them each a pork stick. "Now skedaddle. Stop harassing the customers."

"What? No beer?" said the kids as they snatched the meat and stuffed it in their mouths. I'd been there myself with a gnawing ache tossing away the ornaments of civilization.

"This is all I got. Get your asses out of here," the door keeper said. "This show is for successful grownups. You're bothering people."

"It's okay," I said. I reached into my pocket, drew out a couple of bills and handed them to the girls. "You're too young to be out alone, dontchathink? Get off the streets, ya dig?"

"Screw this life of charity," one said, taking the money.

"It's not charity. I'm paying you to get your carcasses off this block."

"Hot damn, solid. Happy hunking."

The bouncer gave me a warm smile as the girls scampered away.

"First time?" she asked.

"No, I'm used to kids."

"I mean at our Crisper show."

"Yes! I'm looking for someone. Are these all the latest men?"

"They are the latest and greatest."

"Do you get new ones all the time?"

She cocked her head as she thought about it. "It's hard to say. We just started this business."

"Do any of them seem wild?" A couple women stood behind me, waiting to get in.

"They're all wild," one of them said.

"As in captured?" I asked.

"Honey, you're holding things up. Go in. Love your hair by the way."

The place glistened from Tiffany lamps above the serving area. A huge portrait of an ancient general, his nameplate reading "U.S. Grant," hung behind the bar. U.S. Grant had brooding eyes and a trimmed beard. Damn if I didn't find him attractive. It had been two days since I'd had sex. I was already a basket case. Crispers meant Remmer. I was close, yes, close. I had to be. If he wasn't here, perhaps I'd find someone who had seen him or talked to him and knew where he was.

Women milled about. I sat at a crowded table with two women in sexy street clothes—tight pants and low-cut tops, earrings, glittery hair bands. By contrast, I was in drab work attire—a polo and khaki pants. Except for my fabulous hair, I looked nothing like a woman who had a Crisper lover. This made me smug. What if Rem walked out and we locked eyes and immediately fell into each other's arms? These women would freak and I'd run away with him. Yes, I'd do it, because who needs status when you have love?

A woman with red hair draped across one eye—the bartender who had sold Purceel's mom the vodka she'd used to ignite herself —came to the table.

"Want a drink, ladies?"

The other women ordered a beer and a glass of wine. I was afraid of drinking before my presentation tomorrow. My idea was going to wow them. I couldn't wait to tell Remmer.

"Nothing for me."

"Just here to look?" she said, not recognizing me. "Be sure to get out your tips. It keeps 'em frisky."

A woman who appeared old enough to be in prison, the other bartender, climbed onto the wooden bar. She had slim, athletic legs, which she showed off with a mini-skirt.

"Women of Cochtonville, your pleasure is my pleasure. What type of pleasure is your favorite—slow burning pleasure, detonating pleasure, hasty pleasure, idle pleasure? Let your mind imagine your deepest pleasure. Nothing gives me greater pleasure than giving you pleasure. Well, almost nothing. How about some rough riding to start things off? Atta, the cowboy, will hog-tie you."

A Crisper, tall and rugged with an aquiline nose, sauntered from behind the bar. He wore a black bandana, boots, a big belt buckle, and black cotton underwear and carried a rope. He flexed his biceps and the crowd cheered. He moved through the ladies and they ran their hands across his smooth chest. He put his hands behind his head and undulated as Remmer had done for me. Finally, he roped a woman and pulled her to him, close enough to almost let her touch him. He fixed his eyes on her, mouthed some words, tipped his hat, and left her standing breathless.

"Timber! You'll fall for our next stud," the woman on the bar announced.

Treert, the lumberjack, a blond in jeans, boots, a checkered shirt, and a knit cap popped from behind the bar. His walk was hulking, as if his leg muscles were trees. He tugged the front of his pants and they broke away to show boxers emblazoned with a hefty axe. He rubbed his neck like it was sore, then turned his back to the crowd and shook his butt. A woman jumped from her seat and grabbed it. He swung on his heel, axe in hand, and she stuffed a bill into his thong.

Sas, the sexy-ass Scotsman, gave me a twinge of hope, but he was taller with hairier legs and a smaller nose than Remmer. He did a handstand and his kilt fell around his waist, showing his tight, tiny plaid undies. Hunnuh, the Hun, rambled through the crowd, hoisted women onto his loin cloth made from animal fur, and tossed women two at a time over his shoulder.

Women cheered while I studied each man. These guys were taller, bulkier, and more confident than Remmer and lacked Layal's protruding forehead. Why were they here? What purpose was this display serving? I was bubbling over with anxiety and self-hatred for desiring these men and for losing the one I had.

"Good stuff, huh?" the woman beside me said.

"You know what's sexy? Getting to know someone." I tried to cover up the attraction I felt and my disappointment—none of these were Remmer.

Her friend leaned toward me. "Know them? No chance, sweets."

The woman on the bar said, "My friends, it's been a delight. We're at the climax of our performance. The next performer has me shaking in my boots. You might want to grab your identifications and clear the room because here he comes, our mystery man, Ohho."

The women gasped as Ohho walked from behind the bar, his face covered with a hard white mask and a white Stetson over his forehead. He wore white boots and a white coat, much like the Vice Patrol. Certainly, this was a violation of decency, a mockery of our law enforcement, which we all knew deserved mockery although we were too afraid to mock. The swing of his arms, the thrust of his chest convinced me this was Layal. Layal was brash. He'd do this.

He slipped off his coat and dropped it in front of him. He was wearing a white thong and nothing else. Was this the chest I'd seen so often? The tattoo was there. He stepped on his coat, and the women fell silent—enticed and afraid. Ohho fell onto the coat and writhed over it, violating it and the law it represented. Most women had their hands over their mouths, eyes bugging in shock. I was transfixed. Would we be allowed to talk to the performers afterward? I had to ask the owners.

I lurched from my chair and inched through the stunned

crowd. Ohho, or was it Layal, grabbed my ankle as I walked past and pulled me to the ground with him. He mounted me and feigned humping, never really touching me. The man had control. The crowd screamed in delight at this.

"Layal," I said. "Where are they keeping you? Where's Remmer?"

"I'm Ohho," he grunted, his voice muffled by the mask. "Enjoy this."

The crowd yelled and expected more. Obviously, he wasn't going to reveal who he was in front of everyone. I smiled and wiggled beneath his undulations as I studied his face. It was a blank slate of plastic with pinpricks for the eyes.

"Who has you? Do you know me? Where are you held?" I asked.

"You wish to be held?" he replied in a deep voice. "I'm here to serve. If you like what you see, my rental is available for the right woman, gorgeous." He stood and swooped me into his arms, then quickly inverted me. My head was in his crotch. You'd think all those weeks looking at the plastic shorts would help me make positive identification of Layal from this angle, but I couldn't.

The crowd cheered. A lock of hair popped from my up-do and dangled toward the floor. I fixated on the tattoo. Yes, it read "erotic", as Layal's had. They were all erotic. All except Remmer. Ohho spun me, inches from his groin, until I was dizzy. He righted me and set me on my feet. I wobbled into his arms and played along by running my hand across his chest. The room was hot and the elevated carbon dioxide and the spinning had me dizzy and needing to pee.

"You like it?" he asked.

"I must find a Crisper known as Remmer," I answered. "Can you help me?"

"Renner?"

"Remmer. Remember without the b and the second e." Layal was not this dense. My heart tripped and fell. No, it wasn't Layal.

Too dumb. I was going to wet my pants before I learned anything of value from Ohho. Still, I had to try.

"Do you know any stripping philosophers?" I asked. "Have you met a red-haired guy with a roundish nose who's new in town?"

"Philosophers?"

"Someone who wonders about what if we lived in a cave? That kind of thing."

"A caveman. Good idea. We'll add one. You get a free pass to the next show."

"Thank you. I'm sure I'll be back. I gotta go."

"Not so soon, my beauty."

I had to give it one last try. "Is Truth beauty?"

"There is no truth," he replied.

"The truth is, I'm going to pee my pants."

He grabbed my arm. "Put money in my thong." I fished a three Cochton note from my pocket and stuffed it in before running to the bathroom. When I came out, the men were mingling and collecting tips. I decided to make nice with the owners and get more information.

"Is this legal?" I asked the announcer in the miniskirt.

"Sure is. These guys need training and exposure to women in the flesh. They used to make the trainees go at it with testing devices. They couldn't get into it. It freaked out the early models." Remmer's story about practicing with dolls was holding up. I could only imagine how he'd hate this raucous crowd.

"Where do you get them?"

"Rented from the State Crisper Facility."

"I want to visit. Where is it?"

"The location isn't known. You need a display permit to have a show, but women with the right status can access the View Book and rent a Crisper. Do you have status? I think Ohho has a thing for you. You could rent him indefinitely."

"Status? Not yet. Soon if I'm lucky. I'm competing for InVitro tomorrow."

"Come back and see me when you get your InVitro permit.

We'll go through the View Book." She handed me her card. *Wilma's Wild Ways. Crisper Parties and Rental.* "You'd better make it an early night. I'd love to see you back here."

I swayed back to Mom's, clutching the card.

"How'd it go?" she asked.

"Need a tiny bit more hairspray."

CHAPTER FIFTEEN

Mom gave me a melatonin pill and I slept deeply, waking up feeling as if I'd had my face in the pillow all night. I was groggy as we waited for Jane in the shop, and surprised by the first customer of the morning, Lady LouOtta Maliegene, the InVitro who wrote our national anthem. She had her nanny in tow, pushing a baby in a fancy stroller.

"I have a line," she said to Mom, pointing to a faint crease peeking from the bridge of her nose to her eyebrow. "I need to get rid of it now. I am on stage tonight." The bubbly voice she used in public was replaced with harshly barked orders. She bent forward and stretched out her long, smooth neck so Mom could examine her.

"You have got to do something," she said, pointing to a worry line near her brow.

"Come sit behind the screen, Lady Maligene," Mom said. "We'll have it smoothed in no time. I have an e-mag skin plumping device that will give you little to no downtime and banish your line by tonight."

LouOtta went to the place where the Agro woman had her procedure long ago. The round-faced nanny in a dumpy jumper frowned at me.

"I need a new toothbrush."

We had a basket of giveaway items on the counter. Some of Mom's customers were wealthy like Lady LouOtta but others struggled, and this poorer group included nannies, who were underpaid servants, even lower than married working women like Mom, not even allowed to leave the house alone. Basically, all this girl got was room and board in exchange for her services, and once the kid was sent off to school, she'd be out of a home. Mom was quick to provide the basics for her customers for no charge. It was part of the reason our house was falling apart. Clearly I wasn't an employee, but I thought I'd be nice, so I tipped the basket toward the nanny. "These are complimentary."

She rummaged through the toothbrushes, tampons, and small samples of lotion while the baby fussed.

"There aren't any pink ones," she said grumpily. I thought I might tell her to eff off. I didn't care about her toothbrush. Instead, since I wasn't NezLeigh, I went to the Smile Aisle and got a pink toothbrush and gave it to her. She quickly slipped it in her jumper pocket as LouOtta stumbled from the screened off area holding her brow.

"It will fade within an hour," Mom assured her.

"I certainly hope so. I can't be mutilated tonight." She touched the area where the wrinkle had been. A smooth red line remained.

"On the house, " Mom said. "No charge since you are not satisfied, Lady Maliegene."

"I sure as hell hope so."

A siren went off, making me jump and sending my heart to my throat. This was followed by a broadcast—a woman's voice warped by speakers. "Alert. A security violation has been reported. Citizens, remain inside."

People ran past shouting, holding hands over their noses. Voices tumbled over each other like a pack of Little Jerks after a possum. A dozen Vice Patrol, the Washers, ran past in the opposite direction, their white coats flapping. The baby cried.

"It's those dirty Pestos," the nanny said, picking up the baby and bouncing it. "What do they want, anyway? Do they want our jobs?"

"Causing trouble for everyone. Now I'll be late," LouOtta said.

"You should wait here for fifteen minutes anyway. I'll get you some orange juice."

"No. Too much fructose," LouOtta said, eyeing the expensive Mercury purse in the case. Not only was it the color of a sunny sky, it had been designed by Mrs. Bert Cochton—our patriarch's third and youngest wife. It was part of her Impression collection and to own it was a sign of utmost taste and national loyalty.

Jane, dressed in gold, blonde hair piled high on her head, stumbled into the shop, a wave of manure odor following her.

"Oh Lordy," Jane said. "That's a whole lot of crazy."

"Jane! Are you alright?" Mom said in alarm.

"What's happening out there?" LouOtta demanded.

"A stink bomb. Mercy. I haven't smelled such a thing since the days when I used to neck in the country near the confinement operations."

"Shame on you for even mentioning it and shame on those who perpetrated this atrocity. They should be shot immediately," LouOtta said coldly.

"Looked like some kids," Jane said.

"A prank? Not at all funny. Can you imagine stinking up peaceful citizens? Where are their nannies?"

Mom flipped on the audio alert system and we all listened.

"Citizens. We are under attack. Roaming bands of Pesto youth have disrupted our city just before the opening ceremony of the Corn Days Festival. We must allow our Vice Patrol to take back control. Remain inside until the all-clear is sounded."

"Why would they do such a thing?" LouOtta said. "They should put effort into finding jobs and acceptable attire."

"The Cochtons took their farms and they want to make trouble until they get them, or a place of their own, back," I said.

LouOtta gave me a stare that made NezLeigh look tame by comparison. "Sacrilege. The Cochtons provide. Those savages shouldn't bite the hand that feeds them. You sound like a traitor."

"My daughter has risked her life for this country," Mom said, "by putting herself in a dangerous place to find new resources."

"This situation is unacceptable," LouOtta said. "I'm featured in the awards ceremony tonight. I need to get this baby back home, not sit here in this stinking shop."

"Oh, it won't take long at all to scoot those kids off the streets, Lady LouOtta," Jane replied. "Sit in my chair and I'll pluck that hair on your chin. It's gray."

LouOtta grabbed her chin. "No." She flopped into the chair.

"Yes," said Jane, pinching some tweezers LouOtta's way.

As Jane predicted, the all clear blasted after five minutes and LouOtta and her entourage rushed away.

Jane watched the door close behind them. "Do I have class envy or is she the worst?"

"I can't say she's the worst. She's a steady customer," Mom replied.

"Steadily cheap. She got a free line removal and a free plucking," Jane said.

"And her nanny got a free toothbrush from the Smile Aisle," I added.

"Nannies struggle," Mom said. "I'm sure hers struggles doubly. But forget them. We've got to get Cali ready."

"I hope you're next, the very next to walk up the ladder of success, and I will help take you there. Come to my chair," Jane said. "Wait one second." She sprayed it with disinfectant and wiped it down. "Now I'm ready."

———

By afternoon, my hair was thicker than it had ever been with nary a split end and swept up on one side as was the style—Jane had suggested going for a slight modification of last night's 'do. My lashes were full and fat, my lips cherry red. My dress was form fitting. I had never looked like this before and hoped I never would again. It'd taken the entire day to achieve.

"You look so professional, prepared, and under control. Take the purse," Mom said.

"The Mercury? No. I can't afford it."

"Yes, Cali, you can. I'm giving it to you. You've got to appear as if you're already there. Someday you might end up caring for me, and if the purse helps get you financial security, it's worth it. Besides, you can return it and we'll put it on sale. She unlocked the display case, took out the robin's egg-blue handbag, and handed it to me. The processed pigskin was candle smooth and soft as Purceel's little cheek. I tucked it under my arm. "I'm ready."

"I'll drive you. I don't want your hair to fall."

The ride turned out to be a good idea. Burning plastic bags littered the sidewalks. The Fire Patrol extinguished them—one on every corner—as the black smoke lingered.

"It'll be safe once you get there. The pavilion security will be a priority," Mom assured me.

She stopped in front of the Pavilion of Agriculture's auditorium. The pavilion was a squarish building decorated with kernels of corn, giving it a golden hue. The double front plexiglass doors were flanked on each side by bundles of corn stalks. *Corn*, I thought nervously, *would burn well and release plenty of smoke.*

I stepped out onto the green carpet. For the first time ever, I was relieved to see the Vice Patrol lining the sidewalk as cars pulled up and people in evening attire exited. I would do this— wow Cochtonia with science, find Remmer, and get dignity for Mom. Everything depended on this night. I knew I could do my part, but Eve, she was fickle. The black hole once again pulsed in my stomach. The jitters.

Ursula stepped from the squad to escort me. I did everything I could to make up for my slip of the tongue.

"I'm so glad to see you here," I said enthusiastically. "I'm in the best of hands."

"Don't mess things up for the comish's kid," she said. "I'll find a reason to arrest you otherwise."

We walked through the halls, past the refreshment booth serving popcorn and pure corn whiskey. My stomach churned at the thought of eating or drinking anything.

Ursula showed me a spot to the left of the stage in the two-thousand-seat auditorium. Eve was already there waiting in a strapless white dress with a short fluffy skirt, much like the plastic bag skirts we'd worn. Her dad and another Washer sat behind her. Ursula took a spot behind me.

"Cali! You look great," Eve said, almost in surprise.

"You, too. Are you channeling your inner Little Jerk?"

"Sure am. Nothing's going to stand in my way. I've got some big ideas. You might not like them but it's for the best for all."

"What do you mean?"

"Can't divulge with everyone listening. It's surprising. Play along as I click through the slides. Do you have a resource?"

She had me scared. "A resource. I do. Yeah."

Her dad muttered in my ear. "One more word and I arrest you."

The program began with the image of the flag projected on a screen filling the back of the stage. I pressed my finger into my forehead extra hard and put on my most serious expression, even though I was so nervous I wanted to bust out laughing. The Keep It Tidy Icon in front of me had tears of emotion pouring and stabbed her forehead so hard she scratched herself and drew blood. Next, we sang "Bombs and Tassels." Everyone was off key, but that didn't stop the shower of golden glitter dropped on the stage from the rafters during the crescendo.

Lady LouOtta got an award for her service to the nation—it was a year of escort services. Tears running down her cheeks, she thanked Cochtonville for this surprise.

I whispered to Eve, "Note, tears are mandatory."

"I'm on it," she said. Her dad leaned forward and squeezed my shoulder.

It was time for the competition. We sat uncomfortably listening to the presentations of the other teams. The first team dressed in identical white dresses with black stripes, carrying magnifying glasses. The Icon was the Private Eye—the media personality who warned people the Vice Patrol was always looking, always ready to stop criminal behavior. They discussed how an abandoned library, a place once used to house those clandestine tomes known as paper books, now infested with bats, could be made into a prison. The resource was guano, a fertilizer with 8% nitrogen, 2% phosphorus, and 0.6% potassium.

I rubbed the soft leather of the purse to calm myself. Cochtonia didn't need more fertilizer. It needed less shit.

The next group wore matching chicken feather hats. Had Eve and I missed the memo to dress identically? The Icon was the Report 'Em Raw girl. She warned the citizens of Cochtonia how unapproved sex would not be tolerated. Sexual union needed to be approved by the State and strictly man-woman. This group, the scientist being an employee of the chemical stockroom at Cochton Enterprises, discussed how a chicken farm with chicken skeletons hanging in every cage following a sweeping plague would be made into a prison. A video of chickens transforming into deviants accompanied the presentation. The resource was chicken manure. It could be made into biogas, fertilizer, and calcium supplements.

I clasped my hands together nervously. These two were creative in their wide use of the resource. The presentation ended with a zoom in to an egg, alluding to the prospect of 100% Cochtonia approved InVitro. My soul sank to the floor and was stomped on. Hadn't we also talked about a prison? *Everyone* was using feces as the resource. Cochtonville loved private prisons, but it wouldn't be cost effective for us to propose another prison-for-profit in the WasteBin compared to a nearby abandoned farm. The costs of transportation, building, and guards would be prohibitive. Plus, Cochtonville liked visible reminders of where you went if you didn't toe the line.

I had my plan about the resource, a unique one, but no idea

what Eve had come up with. Why had her dad forbidden contact? We were two individuals and not a team. I wished for something we had worn in common—shit emoji hats or something. No time to fret now. The usher stood beside us. It was our turn. The walk down the green carpeted aisle and up on stage was more frightening than facing the boggy fen. My legs were rubbery. I thought I heard screaming, but it was only the blood whooshing through my head.

CHAPTER SIXTEEN

We stepped in front of the audience, positioning ourselves beside the podium. I looked upon the "better half" of Cochtonia—the employees at Cochton Enterprises—and my mom far in the back of the balcony. In their own elevated box, behind a plate of everything-proof glass, sat the Cochton family, not that you could see them clearly, but certainly the two patriarchs, Bert and Clarence, were there, the sister being dead from overwork.

The stage lights blinded me. I was caught in a current and not sure what to expect. Eve had a clicker and enough composure for both of us. The lights dimmed as she showed the first video clip— a shocking cut of the immolated woman with Purceel crying beside her in her two-tone dress and matted hair. This had to be a photo from Eve's father. Yes, she had an in, but where was she going with it?

She began. "Everyone has seen the fate of the Pesto children. They are kept from a successful future by the actions of their parents. As of late, they run wild, playing with fire on the streets. Is it because they are bad? No. They have nowhere to go with their energy and nothing to do with their active hands. We have found a place for them—the WasteBin. This barren, rocky area of nothingness with its magnificent manure pit offers a unique resource, a bleak landscape suitable for training. With nothing of beauty, the only sounds being the death cries of birds, the wasteland has nothing to offer, and there lies its strength."

The grizzly death scene blended into a view of the manure pit.

"It is well known that landscape imparts a sense of identity. These children have been raised on the streets. They are tough. With the proper training in the sparse wilds, they can be economically efficient. We will train them to survive on nearly nothing. To do as they are told. To look to us for guidance and as role models. We propose to offer camps with crafts and activities to boost their cooperative skill building. We'll recruit the children, rehabilitate them, teach them to work, to assist us in the struggle for growth. They can be pre-identified as maids, servants, night custodial. This will work because everyone needs to find their path to fitting in with society. The tiny eyes, with their ability to see in the dark, will be useful for overnight work. Parents will no longer see their births as tragic."

I was blindsided by Eve's plan. Yes, it would be a good thing to help the discarded Agro children but to train them to be servants? It was a betrayal of their deep wish for freedom.

A spotlight shone on Eve's legs in her revealing skirt as she continued. "How can we recruit them? We entice them with a parade. And vitamin supplements supplying steady nutrition," Eve said. "Everyone has a place."

She moved to a slide of a camp overlaid onto the observation area. There were small cabins with cheery names on each door—Lapping Waves, Whispering Winds, Bursting Berries. The WasteBin pit loomed darkly behind.

"We can reward them with ice cream, praise them at every turn. They are different, but in diversity lies strength," Eve added. Our competitions' faces were painfully twisted as their chance to win slipped away. Sir Bux leaned forward, his eyes glistening.

"But that's not all. We have abundant and unexploited resources on site waiting for the hand of Cochtonia to manipulate them."

I was stunned by her presentation. I had to believe her father had forced her to come up with a way to get rid of the "Pesto" problem. I wasn't on board with this. Yes, on the surface this dealt with the immediate concern of abandoned children, but it did nothing to address the hopelessness that had led the Agros to this point. It was a solution that only someone who did not fathom its intricacies would propose. Eve knew better than this. If I subtly revealed my lack of support a pop-up law would land me in one of the proposed prisons—something like "lack of enthusiasm for Cochtonia's mission." With Ursula's gaze on me, I had no choice but to enthusiastically follow.

"Abundant resources," she repeated. "We have the scientific member of our team, chemist Cali Van Winkle, here to tell us about them." She showed the clip of me using the UTI for the first time. The video ended in a shot of the WasteBin in all of its sludgy glory.

I gripped my purse and the notes within. I didn't need the notes. All I'd discovered was burned into my mind. I knew what could be done with the WasteBin, and despite my misgivings about Camp Cochton, my enthusiasm for the scientific end of the project and the chance to clean up and use the waste creatively, swept me in.

I said, "Feast your eyes on the massive pool of sewage. This waste is all we need to produce miraculous products, al-along with the help of our hearty campers. We will of course need to contain the smell for the sake of the trainers, er, camp counselors. I have the thing—ConTain. If the manure pit contains one point three million gallons of sewage and one drop of ConTain will neutralize a gallon of waste odor, all it will take is fourteen and a half gallons of ConTain." I was at last being useful to the presentation. Encouraged, I jumped into it, nearly rambling with fervor— everything based on an article Nell had slipped to me.

"Imagine, not a pit of malodourous manure, but a rich source of bacteria-produced PHAs—polyhydroxyalkanoates—natural polyester. Polyester—it's plastic, folks. Yes, polyester can be made from natural sources including tree resin, but who wants to make it from messy trees, laborious to harvest, and taking up space that could be used for corn or soybeans, when we have manure in plentiful supply, a brown lagoon waiting to be harvested? Imagine if you will a world made from our polyester resin—boats, planes, automobiles, building materials replacing that cement in the photo, shower stalls and hairspray, yes, the ticket, all beginning from our own Cochtonia manure.

"My device, the Universal Testing Instrument, detected the building blocks of PHAs at a concentration of 750 parts per million in the WasteBin sewage lagoon. The fatty acid rich sludge will be seeded with *Cupriavidus necator*, a harmless Level 1 Gram negative bacterial organism, to produce the biodegradable plastics at an acceptable rate, especially above eighty-one degrees Fahrenheit. The lifeless soil is perfect for maintaining this temperature, and the copper wastes left in the mine stimulate the process." Yes, I had learned much from the UTI, may it RIP.

The crowd murmured in approval and clapped as Eve clicked through her presentation and came to a clip of a plastic bag blowing beside the pit. My mind scrambled for a way to pull the threads of our presentation together. How did this fit with a camp?

"One word: plastics," I said. "Not from oil. From a never-ending supply of our own sewage. We will establish a plastics plant and have our own well-trained P-Pesto workers collect the resin in the form of malleable micro-pellets. Plastic snow, ready to be used for camp crafts, our own raw material production, or sold to other countries at abundant profit."

"Total transformation," Eve added. "WasteBin to Money Bin." Large denomination bills arose from the image of the WasteBin as the plastic bag image transformed into a purse. This presentation looked like we had collaborated extensively.

Eve and I basked in applause. Perhaps as an Icon she was used to it, but I had rarely been so well received for an idea I was proud of. I wasn't a fan of Camp Cochton, but my plan to use a manure pit to produce biodegradable plastics was genius. To top it off, Eve stood gazing at the Cochton family booth with tears, real tears, streaming. We had it all: emotion, science, greed, and citizen approval.

Eve's father stood up. This brought the entire audience to its feet in a standing ovation. He, however, wasn't clapping and neither was Ursula. They marched to the stage, each step clicking starkly over the warm swell of clapping, as if we'd committed a crime. It had to be performance, but still, I trembled. As the applause swelled, Commissioner Whitehead held up his hand to call for silence as Ursula beamed an image of the flag onto the curtain on the back of the stage, blotting out the final image of money rising from the WasteBin.

"It's much to my sorrow that I find I must arrest these women," he said into the podium microphone. My legs got wobbly. I grabbed the side of the podium as the pavilion swirled around me. I could see the people in the audience put their hands up to their foreheads, stifling any protest.

"The charge is Word Crime." My mind spun. What kind of hokey crime was this? The night in front of the bar came back to me. *Word criminals. The dreck of society. The poison of ideas. A canon dangerous.*

"The use of the forbidden word 'natural,'" he said.

The crowd muttered at this flagrant pop-up law. It made sense such a word would be banned here in Cochtonville, where science made all things better or at least more convenient, but until this moment, it hadn't been outlawed. Ursula pinned my bare arms behind my back so harshly, a strand of hair fell from its perch.

"And also 'diversity.'" This too made sense. Cochtonville wanted to be one homogeneous material. I could only speculate Eve had tossed that word in to explain our lack of matching costume. Her father yanked her arms behind her back, nearly causing a wardrobe malfunction. A flash of gold came from the Cochton box. A man stood up and put both palms on the glass. The flag clicked off. Surprisingly, the audience clapped. Of course. They had no notion of Eve's relationship to the commissioner. This was one more

Beautiful and Damned episode to them, live, on stage. He put his hand to his ear, receiving a wired message with some stock nodding. He released Eve and addressed the crowd.

"The Cochtons have requested a reprieve."

"Long live the Cochtons," a woman called out, and the crowd exploded in cheers and applause.

The officers marched us back to our seats.

We sat nervously through a presentation led by the Keep It Tidy girl that was all about picking up loose garbage. She and her partner proposed making bombs from the urine in the porta potties and the Styrofoam cups left over from the Harvest Festival. The presenters ended by singing "Bombs and Tassels" and the crowd joined in. Listening to the citizens sing those hated lyrics gave me a sinking feeling. Why did Cochtonville need urine bombs? Not to mention it was clearly derivative of the stink bombs of the Agros. Not making sense was a way of life for the Cochtonville citizens. This presentation had a nonsense advantage.

The whole time, Eve's dad lurked behind us. I wasn't sure if his attempted arrest was genuine or performance. I took a tissue from my purse and dabbed my forehead. Lady LouOtta announced an intermission. I raced for the bathroom along with everyone else. After waiting far too long, finally it was my turn for a stall. As I attempted to lock the door, Eve burst in and shut the door behind us.

"I think we've got a shot," she said breathlessly as I urinated.

"After the stunt your dad pulled? Was he serious? And are you serious? Making the kids into maids?" I whispered forcefully.

"It's better than being dead. Even more importantly, what do you think will happen to us if we don't get this status? You told me it was important to you and it sure is to me."

I stood up and flushed. "It is. I'm pretty sure the men are here, being rented out to rich women. We *must* be rich, it's true. If we get this, we can visit a rental center and lease them, maybe even free them. We must win."

"Leased to rich women? That explains it." She kept her voice low as she sat holding her poufy skirt carefully.

"Explains what?"

"I caught a glimpse of Layal in the Cochton box." She ripped off a strip of toilet paper and dabbed her eyes.

"Impossible."

"I know what I saw. In any case, we must free them. I don't understand why you're mad about the presentation. What's your problem?"

"Did you have to bring the Agros into it? They aren't cut out to be servants. Who ever heard of someone serving you a meal or vacuuming a rug and cursing you out at the same time?"

"They have no mothers. They are going to kill each other out there."

"Open up." It was Ursula pounding on the stall door. The door clicked open and there she stood, holding her breaking-and-entering device, her arms crossed in a scolding manner. Why was I always in trouble with the law? I didn't aspire to be a criminal; I was just tasting success.

Eve stood up and fluffed her skirt. "Ursula. So good to see you. Your turn." She pushed past the officer as I followed her. She failed to stop at the mirrors. She was running on confidence and I was in her wake. Once back in the auditorium, I peeked in the nosebleed section for a comforting glimpse of Mom, but the people were tiny blurs. We took our seats as the lights dimmed and Ursula squeezed in behind us.

LouOtta came from backstage and towered above the podium. "This has been an exhilarating example of capitalism and womanhood at its finest. When given the sourest of assignments, these brave girls were able to make lemonade, which we all know is constructed from two corn-based products—corn syrup and citric acid. Each team deserves a round of mild applause along with a gift basket containing eight ounces of citric acid, four-hundred and seventy-five milliliters of corn syrup, a dinner for two at Hot Dog Haven, all in an adorable corn husk gift basket from Stalkers, the boutique for all your gifting needs. And don't forget to follow your favorite Icons on Statebook.

"The Cochtons have handed down their judgment with which there will be no disagreement. First runner up will receive a two-year supply of CochaCola CornSoda." I thought how I would hate to win a feed truck worth of the corn syrup and phosphate laden bone cracking drink. It would be better to win nothing at all. I would content myself with not being imprisoned rather than get this horrible burden of a prize. Lady LouOtta put her hand to the receiving device in her ear, receiving instructions.

"First runner up is, hold on, I'm getting the final decision... Alright, our runner up, in recognition of fighting fire with fire, is..." *Please not us. We'll have to appear on some talk show drinking that stuff and carrying on about the fun of poisoning ourselves with it.*

"For teaching us how to fight fire with fire, the first runner up, winners of our national beverage, is the Keep It Tidy Team. Here's to plenty of urine bombs in our future."

I slumped with relief. It would be all or nothing. If we didn't win, I'd set out to find Remmer on my own. Nearly every woman in town came through Mom's shop at some point. I could ask customers subtly and have my mom keep her ear to the ground for any mention of an erratic Crisper. Eve poked me and I clapped for the runner up team as they accepted the award with tears.

"And now, our winner..." Again, Lady LouOtta put her hand to her ear. I was filled with dread. I wanted to move forward with my project, but what were the implications? What would happen to the woman at the Welcome Mart? Would it disrupt the life of the Little Jerks? How were they surviving without the gatherers? And the Camp Cochton idea—was it feasible, let alone moral? Maybe these presentations meant nothing. No one would act on them. Or maybe they meant everything. In the past, I hadn't been privileged enough to know. Regardless, we'd gone forward and completed our absurd assignment without asking why. Damn if we hadn't done a fine job with it.

Lady LouOtta smiled stiffly as she listened to her instructions.

"Our victors were highly creative and wore the shortest skirts." Eve grasped my hand. "They narrowly escaped arrest but the strength of their contributions to our society show justice is not blind and winners take all. Please come forward and say a few words, Team Beautiful and Damned."

The ushers escorted us onto the stage to the drumbeat of applause. I was frightened and excited, scared and hopeful. Whatever came, I'd accept it. I'd relish it. Our mothers came from the wings to congratulate us. Eve's mother was tall and shapely. Mine was small and huggable. Each wore a green t-shirt proclaiming "Cochtonville's Best Grandma." Mom embraced me and said, "It was all worth it."

"Love you, Mom, and thanks for everything."

Once again, we stood for a rendition of "Bombs and Tassels". Sir Bux was brought up to join us for photos, jittery with excitement like a pest that had been dusted. Lady LouOtta presented him with a silver corn pin—the Order of the Stalk. Eve waved to the audience and I followed her lead, not sure if I should keep my fingers together or leave some space between them.

"Alright everyone. Hold tight," Lady LouOtta said into the microphone. "We have an announcement on the big board."

Once again, the screen sprang to light and to everyone's surprise, Bert Cochton appeared, small featured with a stretched face, live from the box.

"We congratulate the winners and commend the care and thoughtfulness they've shown in addressing multiple problems seen in Cochtonia today, those being what to do with our untapped resource of lagoon waste, how to increase our export capability, how to incorporate the WasteBin into our landscape, and how to integrate and absorb the Pestos into our glorious society. Additionally, the short skirts brought extreme joy to old men, and that can never be discounted.

"I am so inspired that I will immediately release funds to cover all expenses of this project. Construction of Camp Cochton and the plastics plant will, with input from our winners, begin at once. Lady LouOtta will now present you with your InVitro microchips."

A stage hand came forward with a microchip gun on a green pillow decorated with golden pigs and tassels hanging from each corner. A microchip? No one had mentioned it. Of course. I should have expected as much. I had one thought: if anyone stuck that chip into me, I'd be bound to the conditions of it. To refuse would tempt arrest for me and for Mom. I had to do it.

Lady LouOtta cradled the device in her hands. *At least she's picky. She'll be precise in her placement. Unless she recognizes us and remembers the line on her forehead and my comment about the Agros. The line's gone, thank goodness.*

Lady LouOtta snapped a tip onto the device and went for Eve first. "Show me the right side of your neck." Eve tilted her head to the left, exposing her smooth, splendid muscle. *How clever to put a chip in the neck where it can't be removed by an amateur.* LouOtta placed the gun on the side of Eve's neck and pulled the trigger. Eve didn't flinch. Her mom gracefully hugged her as the audience applauded.

"As for you." She changed tips, and in the stage lights, this second tip looked wider. She put the gun on my neck. I titled my head to help her find the spot as Eve had done, and as I moved, she injected me. It burned like a cut. She put the device back on the pillow. My neck became cool and I touched the spot. It was wet with blood. As subtly as I could, I opened the Mercury, retrieved a tissue, and dabbed the spot as Mom watched. To my horror, I'd smeared blood on the purse.

Bert Cochton clapped from his box and once again talked to us via the screen. "You have all privileges of InVitro status. However, we must hold off on the fertilization process until Camp Cochton and the plastics plant are in full operation. We can't risk the loss of your expert advice, and I for one would like a few more months to enjoy those youthful figures of yours."

Mom grabbed my hand. This would make her a tidy profit from her patented ConTain. I was happy for all of us. I was as happy as a woman alone could be.

CHAPTER SEVENTEEN

It was after midnight when Mom and I got home. We changed into our most comfortable sweats and sat on the back deck. The woodpile possum was out, her dark eyes glittering as she bustled in the grass, looking for slugs.

"What an ordeal you went through," Mom said, handing me gift basket lemonade. "Your presentation was so creative. The near arrest had me on the edge of my seat! And your manure to plastics plan! I need to get started on formulating the ConTain. I imagine you'll be going back to help civilize the place."

"I'll be going back to make plastic from manure. Mom, the place is already civilized. I met people I can't forget. Girls live there in the wild. It's a refuge for abandoned kids. The Crispers there saved them. The child from the night Dad got hauled away is one of them."

"I'm glad she's safe. Poor things. No wonder you want to have a camp for them."

"They don't need a camp to train them to be servants."

"If only kind people would hire them..." Mom stared at her lemonade, knowing how hollow she sounded. I let it drop.

"Sorry about the purse. I'll buy it from you," I said. "I'll be able to afford it."

"Don't worry about it. I'll have my own money now. LouOtta drew blood on purpose, I'm sure." She put her hand to my neck and examined it in the porchlight. "Your injection is bleeding again. I'm going to give it a dash of antiseptic and a butterfly bandage. I've got some inside." She put her lemonade on the deck and went into the house, leaving me alone with the owls. I wouldn't be alone for long. I'd fetch Remmer from the State Crisper Facility. As sad as I was for the Agros, things would be better.

A car came down the dead end, the lights casting harsh shadows. My heart picked up a beat. Nobody came out here. It had to be Dad. Or Remmer magically finding me. Yes, he could. He was smart. He knew my full name. Or the Vice Patrol, warning me to stay away from Eve. I sat listening. A door closed. It was Mom, returning with her first aid kit.

"Let's see your neck."

I tilted my head. "Someone's coming. Did you see the car lights?"

"No. Car lights? Out here? How about we go inside to do this?"

Mom was nervous, which made me concerned. We slipped into the house and I locked the back slider. Trying to keep cool, Mom sprayed antiseptic on my neck as we stood in the kitchen. I could practically hear both of our hearts beating. Her hands shook as she placed the bandage and closed my wound.

"It's probably some autograph seeker," she said. "I suppose we'll be needing more security."

"I don't think coming up with a plastic factory qualifies me for cult status."

"They would've turned off the lights if they were trying to sneak up."

"It could be Dad."

"Of course, he's returned at a happy time to get in on a celebration he did nothing to earn." She studied my neck. "I noticed that Washer hovering near you. Did anything illegal happen out there in the wild?"

"A state agent was killed. The theory is one of those graveyard plants wrapped around his neck."

"How horrible. They have graveyard plants out there?"

"They do now. I planted them accidentally. It's beside the point. The Washer simply doesn't like me."

The doorbell's harsh ring startled us out of our skins.

"I'll answer it. Don't say much," Mom said. "Keep out of sight."

I hurried up the stairs, my mouth dry, heart ripping through my chest, and peeked out the window. In our drive, with its cracked cement and encroaching graveyard plants, was a tan sedan. Only Cochtonville Hire a Lift used those. Someone was here, traveling incognito. I rushed to the top of the stairs as Mom, holding up the spray can of antiseptic as if it could be a weapon, opened the door. A woman spoke.

"Sorry to bother you. Is Cali here? It's urgent." It was Eve in a pulled-up black hoodie and jeans.

"At this hour? What's happened?"

I rushed down the stairs. "Mom, it's Eve. Eve, what's up?"

"Cali, I'm so glad you're here. You said you lived near a graveyard. Not many houses fit that description. We've got to look for the Crispers. Immediately. My parents are asleep. The lift is waiting for us. It's my only chance to do this incognito."

I'd never been downtown at such a late hour, not even the night my dad was hauled away. Cochtonville was generally regarded as safe for law-abiding citizens. This was why people were willing to put up with the pain of the finger press. Vice Patrol walked the streets to keep it so. At our age, it wasn't a crime to disobey our parents, and we were certainly old enough to be out at this time of night. However, Eve's dad had warned us to stay away from Layal and Remmer. Instead, we were searching for them, entering the mouth of the volcano—the Crisper rental service run by Madame Wilma out of the Union Station bar. We watched a Washer van turn the corner past the laundromat and out of sight before leaping from the lift and slinking through the heavy door of the old bar.

The place was packed with women playing pool, laughing over drinks, and teasingly touching a Crisper cowboy, lumberjack, and Viking as they mingled with the crowd. The bartender, a compact man with dark curly hair, was carefully drying a beer glass while the red-haired owner pushed frothy pints across the bar to a group of patrons dressed in their sexiest short dresses.

"Wow," Eve mouthed as I walked to the bar. "These guys are Crispers?"

"Yes, and strippers."

"They make them big these days."

"We're here to rent," I told the sexy bartender.

"Let's see your necks, sweethearts," said the red-haired woman, the one who'd mentioned Word Crime the night of the immolation. We tilted our heads, Eve revealing a red pinprick and me the butterfly dressing.

"Do I need to take off the bandage?" I asked.

"Oww, brutal, huh? Na. I recognize you from the files that came through tonight. Have you checked your instructions? You ain't dressed as you should be. InVitros dress up."

"I like women who aren't afraid to dress down," said the bartender. "It shows confidence. Congratulations on your achievement, and thank you for your service to Cochtonia. You must be magnificently clever."

"It was nothing, really. A little brainpower and lots of stamina." Eve smiled at the bartender.

"Stamina, huh?" He put his hands on the bar and flexed his muscles.

"I like what I'm seeing," Eve said. "Are you a Crisper for rent?"

Did he blush or was it the light through the Tiffany fixtures? "I'm at Wilma's command. And I'm not even a Crisper. I'm here on a work permit."

"A foreigner? Here?"

"You don't have enough men in Cochtonia. It's a problem. You can't have women getting unmotivated. Sex has always been a motivator," he said.

"I'd say," Eve replied, putting her hand on her hip and batting her eyelashes. "This place is hopping."

"It's getting late. We're anxious to talk to Wilma," I said. Eve had a thing for dark curly hair but this was not the time.

"I like women who aren't afraid to go after what they want." He pushed a button beneath the bar. "Walk this way." We watched as he walked, in his tiny shorts, to the door to the left of the bar and opened it to a set of stairs. "Watch your step."

Wilma, in red satin pajamas, her hair in a long white braid, appeared at the top.

"Thank you, Gus, darling. Ladies, you're eager beavers. Come on up and let's see what I can do to help."

Her office was in the front of her apartment. Life-sized holographs of some of the performers lined the wood paneled walls. Eve gasped at the sight of Ohho's image. "No. Oh no. I'm going to have to leave," she said.

"Does he look like Layal to you?" I asked.

"No. I'm sure this is illegal. It's mocking the Vice Patrol."

Wilma got a tube of lipstick from her pocket. "The customer is always right." She waved it in front of the hologram and Ohho became Atta, the cowboy.

"Being at ease is an important part of claiming your female sexuality. You've made a wise choice to speak up at the slightest discomfort," she said, motioning for us to sit in plush armchairs. "How can I assist you in keeping every part of yourself in top shape?"

The door to the adjacent bedroom was conspicuously open. A glittering chandelier illuminated a bed with rumpled shimmery-white sheets and a pink wand on the pillow in an obvious display of consumption. I wanted to run over there and grab the wand, it reminded me so much of Remmer. Losing him hurt so bad. This love stuff was worse than a wing in the eye.

Eve's head bobbed like she was on a bumpy road as she took in the apartment.

"This place is lush," she said, reviewing the sex-themed tapestries on the walls with the cavorting naked people and various positions, some I'd never tried.

"We're looking for Crispers," I said pointedly. "Not just any Crispers. We have two in mind."

"Before we go any further, I need you to sign my agreement. No physical or emotional violence is permitted with my rentals."

"Of course," I said. Eve and I eagerly signed the electronic form.

"Thank you, ladies. Do you have photos of the men you desire? I can facial match any real or virtual image to assure complete satisfaction."

"We do." Eve pulled up the shots she had on her phone. Wilma scanned them with her lipstick tube and the image popped up on the wall in front of it. There were the men, a little blurry but standing in their plastic with no shirts.

"Nice. What was their jam? Hauling your trash?"

"Something like that," I said.

"Plastic fantastic." She tapped her lip with her finger. "Look like early models. I never work with these."

"They are. They're flawed but we love them," I said.

"They'll be on discount. Let's look at some full-body photos of Crispers for rent and see if we can pull up a match." She pushed the end of the lipstick tube. A screen snaked down from behind a tapestry that featured a nude woman reclining on an enormous seashell.

"Show me the matches," she said.

A photo of Remmer in a skimpy fireman costume popped onto the screen. It was certainly him and all his shyness. He looked down, ready to cry as he hoisted a hose over his shoulder.

"It's him! How much to rent? I'll pay anything."

"You won't have to. He's a second, one of the earlier Crispers. Are you sure you don't want Ohho?"

"This one is all I want with all my heart."

"Show location and availability," she said.

An image of a hand held up to halt appeared.

"Bad news. He's got a hold. He's already being rented."

"By who? Who wants a second? I'll pay more."

"I can't say who, but someone wants to keep purse strings tight. I'll put a reserve on him for when he's returned. I can't legally rent to you until after you've had a baby."

"I have to have a baby? As in wait over nine months?"

"Being InVitro has a dark side. Renting a Crisper is a perk for successful mothers. There's a black-market for pre-moms like you, and I can get you someone, but if a man is on rent, I can't recall him or hold him for you."

My stomach tensed. "Does this mean he's here in Cochtonville?"

"Of course. I doubt he'll be out and about. But you're breathing the same air."

"He's with someone else, doing whatever she wants?"

"He won't get attached. These guys are bred to be aloof."

Not him. He's flawed.

"How about my guy?" Eve twisted the string of her sweatshirt hood.

"Could this be him?" Wilma showed a man in a business suit with shorts and an open jacket, baring his chest.

"No," said Eve. "He's better looking. His nose curves up a little." She pushed her own nose up with her finger.

"Here's the next closest suggestion." We gazed at a towel-clad man, so muscular his head looked the size of an apple.

"No, he has a big forehead. He's intelligent."

"I'm not getting a match."

"I know he's here." Eve pulled the sweatshirt strings.

"Do you have another photo?" Wilma asked.

Eve scrolled through her phone frantically. The screen snapped up behind the tapestry. Wilma put the lipstick remote in her robe pocket and stood up. "Thank you for browsing. I'm sorry I wasn't able to help. You'll be leaving now. Come back next year with the proper paperwork."

"I need answers," Eve cried.

The door flew open and Commissioner Whitehead strode in. He jabbed his index finger at Wilma. "If she comes here again, you're losing your license."

"Officer, they're legally browsing. They have chips."

"How do you think I found them? This is my daughter, not some highbrow trash, you got that?"

"Of course. I run a clean operation with no secrets."

"Eve, time to go home."

"Dad, Cali and I are celebrating our good fortune. We've made it. We're adults. Browsing adults. Aren't you proud of our success?"

"Eve, you're better than this. You're too good for this bar and these men and the company you keep. Cochtonia and I have plans for you. You're going all the way to the top."

CHAPTER EIGHTEEN

"I believe in this project," Eve told me as we sat in our private box, makeshift plywood with three sides and an uncomfortable bench, waiting for the Camp Cochton recruitment parade to process past the Cochton Enterprises buildings. Fortunately, for recruiting purposes, the sky was cloudy. Rain threatened. It was a fine afternoon for curious tiny-eyed children to be out. Now a success, I wore a tailored shirt and slacks of my choice instead of my drab work uniform of khaki pants and a green polo shirt. Once I had a kid, I'd get a gold corncob necklace from Cochton Enterprises. These were immediate perks of my success.

"We've got some girls enrolled. You'll be seeing them soon. They've all lost their mothers, so they would've been thrown away. Now they have a shot at life. I'm hiring councilors, too. Nannies are out of a job when their kids get sent off for training. I've found a place for trashed nannies. They have jobs at Camp Cochton. There's good in this project. Too bad the buildings are being tossed up like vomit. Bert Cochton's in a hurry for it to be done. And me too. I've had enough of working with him. He visits too often and pinches my butt."

"Is he so homely up close?"

Eve made a gagging motion. Our conversation was interrupted

by the flag bearer, requiring us to do the forehead finger. This was followed by a gold-plated vehicle with tinted windows, a Corn Burner, carrying the Cochtons. A few women around me fainted, and not from excitement. Whenever the Cochtons passed by, people who carried concealed weapons were detected and beamed with a brain relaxer. These gals would wake up with splitting headaches.

Next, a troupe of Washers in their white coats and Stetsons marched uniformly down the blocked off street. This was followed by a cavalcade of tractors, the drivers tossing out hard candy and vitamin packets to entice children who swarmed the streets like starving locusts. Following this came Bux on a flatbed truck, with an announcement playing on a loop. "Fit in at Camp Cochton: good times, good food, good jobs." The fitting in part would send chills down any Agro's spine and indeed, this part of the announcement wasn't for them. It was for the abiding citizens of Cochtonville.

The flatbed held a park bench, and on the bench sat three Agro girls in camp uniforms—sunglasses, green polos, tan shorts, gold socks, and sneakers. This Cochtonville garb would do nothing to appeal to Agros, and yet they crowded the truck as it stopped, for Bux, doing his part to make our project a success, was grilling pork chops over hot coals, and each little camper gnawed a pork chop on a stick and held a can of CochaCola CornSoda as she sat obediently amidst the fragrant aroma of Cochtonville's favorite meat. It was a testament to the folly of Cochtonia—the people who had a hand in growing our food were practically starving.

Groups of parents, some crying, some joyful, hoisted their daughters onto the flat bed and each tiny girl was given a stick of meat. A rehabilitated ex-nanny, dressed in a camp uniform, opened a cooler and gave each child a can of soda pop and each parent a can of Coch Lite beer. The truck blasted two quick honks, drove to the next corner and no one, not parent nor child, looked back. My throat was overcome with a sudden tickle at the thought that after all our work, this is what we'd come to—a flatbed truck, picking up kids from parents who couldn't care for them. I coughed.

Eve clapped her hands. "We have a quorum. I'll be leaving to get the camp in order. Come visit me if you can. I'll take care of them, I promise. There's more to the camp than I can reveal."

"I'd love to. I'll keep looking for the guys. I won't give up." I sniffed as, despite being covered by a roof of the plywood box, rain spattered us.

"We'll find them. We can do this," she said, but I was becoming resigned. This would be a slow process. Meanwhile, they were with other people, forgetting all about us. Like Eve, I'd thrown myself into my work, anxious to get the projects launched, after which I could go through with the InVitro process and get my name on the list for Remmer's rental. I pulled a silky tissue from my pocket and wiped my nose.

"Do you have a cold?" Eve asked. She waved to passers-by.

I sniffed again. "I'm getting one." I blew my nose. "Sometimes I hate this place."

By the time I got to work the next day, I had a sore throat. I crawled into my lab to examine the wastewater-plastic conversion system. The process required genetically modified soil bacteria that thrived on sugar and wastewater. Twenty-five one-liter bacterial growth tanks with varying sugar content, artificially constructed waste, and bacterial cultures filled my lab. I spent my days monitoring the plastic powder produced. It was a tedious process that required me to filter the gallons of water, then dry and weigh the plastic, all the while with Nell chatting away about the delights of working with Level 1 pathogens and hovering at my elbow to make sure her organisms were thriving with no contamination to me or to the tanks.

"Take the day off," Nell urged as I blew my nose one more time in front of the bubbling bacterial tanks, each stirred automatically, at a fixed pH, with a simulated atmosphere pumped through tubing. "We want gram negative bacteria growing, not rhinovirus."

"These tanks are sealed tight and you know it. And I swear I've had enough vaccines. I shouldn't be getting sick."

"You've been working too hard. Relax. I'm thinking we're ninety percent there with our formulation. The sweet spot is somewhere between mixture nineteen and formula twenty-three."

Bux came in, breathing through his mouth, his medals clanking, his nose as stuffy as mine, as if we'd been kissing instead of standing in the same rain. He cracked his knuckles and stretched his arms. He opened his mouth to speak, closed it, and opened it. A catfish.

"Cali, Lady Van Winkle, I've hired an engineer to construct the manure fermentation tanks at the WasteBin. I'm getting impatient. This project is dragging on. Have you the formula?"

A tank bubbled and Bux jumped, his goatee wagging, the smell of grilled pork drifting from his jacket.

"I'll be ready with the exact composition soon. It's only been a month. We're optimizing."

"I'm worried about your InVitro. I disagree with the decision you must hold off until all is finished, but I've been overruled."

Nell piped up. "All we need is a tweak here and there and I can prepare a colony and nutrient packet and we can start the operation. Have the engineer get me the dimensions of the tank. Cali and I will seed the wild colonies. Sir, you'll be pleased to know it's our own CocE plus modified bacteria powering this project."

"We could start as soon as the vats are constructed," I said. "If we can have at least three 50,000-gallon tanks, we can start immediately with our top trials."

"I'll request them. I can assure you, I'm a kind man." He smoothed the front of his coat. He was more trim than I remembered, as if the award had given him a new chance at life. I pulled a tissue from my pocket and blew my nose. Either I was allergic to him or I was getting worse.

Bux babbled on. "Oh, you are such sweet, young things. It won't take long, not long at all. You'll get your three tanks. I do what the company wants."

"Sir, as you know, Eve's leaving for the WasteBin to establish the camp following your strong recruiting effort. I'd like to see it, our handiwork, and assist Nell as she adds the first batches of bacteria to the plastics plant." I blew my nose.

"Even better, I'll accompany you. I want to see our success first hand and get to know you better. Lady Cali, my friends call me Bux. Please consider yourself my friend. You're sick today. You're vulnerable. Go home early and rest. Your recovery is important to me. Have a good day, both of you."

Usually after I got off of work I walked to XX Success and caught a ride home with Mom. It was too early to drop in on Mom. Yes, she would have some medicine, but I didn't want to scare the customers with my illness. I could feel the raw strips of skin beneath each nostril. I looked like a horror. I left the building and instantly felt a little better. Being outside had me breathing again. Wasn't mild exercise an immune system booster? I'd go for an urban hike and seek Remmer.

I walked the sidewalk, past the department store, past the Pavilion of Agriculture. A card swipe station imposed upon me at each stoplight and I swiped my sidewalk pass at every one. In Cochtonville, the homes in the city were inexpensive and older. The suburbs fanned out from the heart but within limits, for the deep country was an undesirable place to live, filled with hog confinements. There was an optimum distance to live in Cochtonville and at the peak of the optimum distance, on the only hill in the city proper, sat the Cochton mansion, gleaming and white with a helicopter pad on the roof. My idea was to walk toward the mansion, searching for any clue of Remmer or Layal. I'd be able to afford it.

Beyond the stoplights, I entered the medium-high income section of town, Tan Terra. Each ranch house had tan vinyl siding, some of it warping in the sun, each set on a small, weedless lawn. I stopped to cough for a minute at a corner. I was running out of dry tissues. Two cars went by and no one stopped. The concrete under my feet had a message pressed into it: brought to you by Bert and Clarence Cochton with our thanks. I hadn't passed a meter. These people walked on sidewalks for free! The only price was loyalty.

I continued my trek on through the gray section of town, Graykill. The houses were two story vinyl-clad sprawlers. I could imagine them constructed from my termite resistant plastic someday, their largeness filled with plastic furniture and appliances —whatever these people stored in such homes. Each had corn fiber curtains in the picture windows and a two-car garage. I could see the domed Cochton mansion, shining like two mounds of vanilla ice cream with corn sweetener in the distance. I walked on, even as my tissues became soggy.

The next section of town had white houses, each adorned with brass house numbers. Each had a small swimming pool. Roman-style vases sat on pillared porches. The Cochtons loved the Roman Empire where slaves, the women, and the poor knew their places, and this tier of society was closest to the Cochtons. If Cochtonville made enough InVitro children, they could raise an army and aspire to Roman glory. I put my hand on my belly. Better to stay barren than contribute? Who was I kidding. I'd just contributed a fantastic idea to this city-state. I was a full partner in this empire. This was no time for missteps. And here I was, shedding germs in front of the best part of town, Cochton Estates, set off from the rest by a series of three linked gates, flanked on each side by cement columns, each topped with a bronze statue of a Cochton—Bert on the left and Clarence on the right.

I grabbed the bars and looked into the homes, a fountain in front of each one. At the top of the hill was the Cochton mansion. I could use my new wealth, when it came, as surely it would with the success of the plastic production, to move here. I'd look for the Crispers where the people lived behind gates. I was sure Layal was stashed away, being bled on a regular basis. I hated to think what Remmer might be used for. I wouldn't rest until Remmer was *mine* again. There was no one else walking. Not a soul about. Not a dog. There were no trees with their protective canopy, no squirrels, no human voices. Nothing but isolation and white brick-and-mortar homes behind the gate, fountains in front, and swimming pools sparkling behind them.

A Washer van pulled up to the curb. I should have known this place was patrolled. Even peeking wasn't allowed. Eve's dad got out, shimmering in his whiteness—a marble monument of HotNot. Ursula, the assistant, held up her All Things Device and the image of Cochtonia's flag with its corncob and fat hog on an amber background. As required, I stood straight and pointed to my forehead to indicate I was focused on Cochtonia while my nose ran.

"You think you can walk around like this?" said Commissioner Whitehead.

"I'm not hurting anything." Pressing my forehead, I sniffed, hoping my cold would put him off. It didn't.

"It's a private sidewalk. Sensors picked you up a while back."

Ursula shut off the flag image and frisked me, her rough hands taking their time with me, picking through my pockets, confiscating my tissues, moving between my legs.

"She's clean."

"Put her in back. We'll give her a ride home." The Vice Patrol agent shoved me in the back of the white van behind a thick sheet of plastic. It wasn't so thick I couldn't hear them talking purposely loudly.

"Ursula, did you ever have a fling?"

"As in throwing something?"

"As in throwing yourself at another person."

"One time I was a body guard for the second Mrs. Cochton. I saw movement in the crowd. I threw her to the ground and laid on top of her, then whisked her to her armored car."

"I'm referring to tossing yourself at a love interest."

"Can't get paid for that."

"Exactly. You're a smart woman. I'm recommending you for

InVitro. Our suspect here is one. Not too late to turn her in and reverse it all and toss her in the gutter like her drunken father. To not do all you can for your kid, to jeopardize their future should be a crime, don't you think?"

My sinus pressure built. I sniffed back all I could. Despite this, a blob hung from my left nostril and I discreetly wiped it on my arm.

"I have a kid, the baby we confiscated. Nobody came for it," Ursula said. "My mom helps me care for her."

"I'm talking about Lady Van Winkle. Have you ever heard such a contradiction? A Van Winkle InVitro? She's living up to her Van Winkle. Walking about. Not caring for her future. Van Winkles can't handle the responsibility of success. As for you, I say go for InVitro. There's help with the kids. You don't do it all on your own."

"I don't feel the pressure to have kids."

Upon the word "pressure" my nose pressure built up unbearably. I sneezed into my hands, goop leaking out around my palms and through my fingers. The walls of the van were spattered.

We stopped in front of Mom's shop and Commissioner Whitehead marched me in, frightening two nannies who scurried out the door at the sight of us.

"I found her wandering in the high-end part of town."

"It's legal. She's been chipped and is on her way to making a tidy sum of money. Her ideas are revolutionary—I mean, innovative. Highly innovative."

"I'm worried. She's got a dangerous touch of her father."

"Nonsense. More like a dangerous touch of a head cold." She handed him a bottle of clear liquid. "Please, take this all-body sanitizer as you let yourself out."

He pinched my arm and foolishly put his face close to mine. "Save yourself trouble. I know where he is and you won't find him. Eve consorts with my permission, not with your help."

CHAPTER NINETEEN

A month later, I found myself on the rambling road, across the stretched flatness, the machined conformity of rural Cochtonia. I would have been galvanized about meeting up with Eve if it hadn't been for Bux sitting in the back seat while Nell and I hugged together like two rabbits hiding in a hole up front. We'd had three days of steady rain, but at last the sun had broken through. It wasn't the only cheery thing. Bux prattled on like a hyper kid. "There's still time, time for the Crisper son of my dreams." I could see he'd been passed over for much of his life. His eyes sagged at the wrinkly corners. I was ready to be sorry for him, but he crept out a hand and put it on my neck. My skin crawled front ways and back. I'd done this to Remmer when I was attracted to him. Oh, I was grateful Remmer had been gentle about it and not slapped the intrusive hand as I now wished to do.

"Is there something you need to tell me?" I asked. Yes, he was my boss, but I was more at ease questioning his actions now that I was Lady Van Winkle. There was nothing official about our change in relationship. My success had made me bolder.

He withdrew his hand to his lap. "I thought you were falling asleep."

Of course, that was nonsensical. We'd just been talking.

"You wanted to wake me up?"

"Yes, so you could enjoy the drive with me."

As if to spite him, the road swerved and so did our autonomous car, dust flying and wheels skidding. The car straightened itself and moved on. A wild turkey ran across our path. The car jerked to a halt, or tried to. It spun in a circle before stopping. Nell took the wheel and hit the accelerator. We crossed the bridge with a rattle of boards. On the other side, gravel hit the car.

Beyond the pass station was a new road sign: "Camp Cochton 5 miles." The excitement of returning, even though I knew Remmer wouldn't be there, lit a hope within me. *If I go back, I'll recapture the time I've lost.* It was indulgent to even imagine going back in time. So much had happened.

The Welcome Mart was repainted white with colorful splotches of paint and so was the old bus. A new sign read: Camp Cochton Canteen and Trading Post. Campers in their uniforms and sunglasses sat at round tables on the new deck, licking ice cream cones. They had to be Agro but already they were plump with wide faces and chubby arms.

"Hello!" they called out in a friendly fashion, so cheerfully it made me nervous.

"Let's go in and tell My Lady we're here," said Nell, taking an insulated bag of bacterial colonies and a sack of concentrated glucosides from the back of the car.

My Lady was perky in her own uniform with a Camp Cochton t-shirt and hiking shorts showing boney knees.

"Hey!" said Nell, giving her a hug and a fist bump.

"Oh, Nell! Great to see you."

"This headquarters looks superb. All paid for by Bert, I hear."

"Yes, I can't thank him enough." She and Nell exchanged a sinister laugh, or was I imagining it?

I shook her hand. "I trust you remember me, Cali Van Winkle." Before, I could barely eke out my last name, but I was a success now and not afraid to use it.

"How can I forget? Thanks for all you've done to make things right here."

"And this is my boss, Sir Richard Bux."

The woman put her hand to her heart and gasped for air. "Who?"

Her reaction surprised me. Bux did look imposingly formal standing there stiffly in his uniform, his eyes sagging, but not so much he'd strike fear into a heart. If anything, the wild ride had terrorized him. He lifted a shaky hand to his mouth as the woman said, "Bux! It's you? Do you know who I am?" This was a dangerous question to ask at any age and Bux looked as blank as a dead deer.

"My Lady?" Clearly he wasn't making a connection.

The woman pulled up her t-shirt and tugged down the waistband of her pants to reveal a tattoo of two blue birds swooping around a heart, which read **Ways of the Wild**.

Bux was stricken. He thumped his chest with one fist as if his heart had stopped. "Annie? Annie."

She lifted his sash, unbuttoned his pants, and tugged them until the same tattoo revealed itself on the side of his shrinking paunch.

"Ink never forgets. Bux, it's me!" She threw her arms around him.

"You didn't die at your desk?" Bux choked on his words, his feigned self-control shot to hell.

Playfully, not realizing what a creep he'd become, she massaged his uniformed chest. "Die at my desk? No. However did you get such an improbable notion? Look at your medals. I knew you were special."

He stood frozen in place. "I went to your funeral. I sat in the back of the pavilion crying inside."

"I had a funeral?"

"And a stately parade."

"What did I die of?"

"Overwork."

"A wealthy person dying of overwork? Unlikely. No one was

suspicious? All a hoax. My brothers sent me away. They cut me out. They gave me this quadrant of my own and nothing more. They even told people I'd died, apparently. No. I signed everything else to them at a vulnerable time."

"How? And why?"

"Oh Bux, you know why. Surely you haven't forgotten. Those were the happiest times of my life. You still have a firm body." She looked him up and down and peeked at him through her gray bangs. The soft folds of her cheeks pinked. She was glowing as she remembered fond times with, of all people, Bux. I saw her no longer as an old woman but as a woman only, her years falling away as she reunited with a man she'd known as no one else had. She could be me some day if fate was harsh. And it was apparent who she was: the woman of statue and photograph, Aiyn Cochton. "But a goatee? Why? You are trying too hard." She yanked it and he yelped and jumped away.

"Annie. You're petrifying me as you always have." He panted as he held his chin.

"Petrifying, yes, I recall. Are you saying you're afraid? You weren't afraid before. Not like the others. You weren't intimidated. Anytime, anyplace. We *did* have to hide it. Remember when I called you in and locked my office door? I had a lock no Vice Patrol could break. Oh, the ways we had. Only a woman has an organ made solely for pleasure. It left me foolish. I did love being reckless. My brothers said it would make me weak and vulnerable to male whims—a shame to the family name. My brothers took it away from me while designing men for female pleasure. It's pleasure without emotion. How can it be better than what we had? You have been always on my mind and in my heart since those tumultuous days."

Someone as impressive as Aiyn Cochton had once had a love affair with a man as middling as Bux? I was awash with sympathy for her, wishing he'd dive into her quirky arms. Nell leaned casually on the ice cream freezer as the former paramours reconnected. Or didn't.

A camper, her hair neatly braided, came into the canteen. "Hi, Miss Aiyn. I was good, so I have a coupon for an ice cream."

Buoyantly, Aiyn swept over to the girl. "What counts as *good* in this camp?"

"I didn't curse for two days!"

"Fuggin' A! What flavor do you want?" Aiyn opened the case and took an empty cone from the top of it.

"Blue moon," said the girl.

Aiyn scooped a generous portion into the cone. "How fitting. The perfect flavor. Keep your coupon. On the house."

"Thank you, Miss Aiyn." Licking her blue ice cream, the child skipped out to join the others.

"Anyone else want some?" Aiyn asked. "Bux, would you like a lick?" Abruptly, Aiyn slammed the lid of the ice cream cooler. "You ghosted me, Bux. I texted you and I needed help. I said I was going to lose my mind. You didn't text back."

"I received no text. I got on with my life."

"Had you come to my rescue, things would have been different for me. All these lonely years."

"Annie, it wasn't meant to be."

She marched to him and put a hand on his waist. "I want you back, Bux. I want you back. I've kept myself in shape inside. I honed my skills privately. The skills we both enjoyed."

"Annie, it's great to see you. You look wonderful. Grown up. Mature."

He pulled out his phone and texted desperately.

"I don't even have one of those out here. What are you trying to say?" She snatched the device and read it. "I owe you the truth. After all these years, I've made other plans." She tossed the device to the ground and stepped on it. Bux fell to his knees and picked up his broken phone. He lifted it, swiped the cracked screen in my direction, and returned it to his pocket.

"Annie, I've done well for Cochtonia. Show some respect."

"Change your other plans. Bux, our child has been extracted to Cochtonville by my oppressive brothers."

His face went blank. "We had a child?"

"Yes, my trouble was a boy. We did together what few could do. My brothers had him modified before birth. They sent me and him here because I wouldn't reveal your name. I protected you, Dickie. Don't leave me to grieve alone. He's been taken to Cochtonville. Help me find him."

"A boy?" Bux stayed crouching, his hand running over the shattered phone in his pocket. "What did you name him?"

"Layal."

"A terrible name. Gereg is superior. He's safe in Cochtonville you say?"

"Bux." Her tone was more demanding than apologetic and every time she said his name was like a chicken clucking. "Bux, he is strong, handsome, smart, and genetically modified, although flawed because he has independent thoughts. My brothers sent me here and he came later to manage the garbage of the WasteBin. Life here's been lonely. All I had to do is turn you in to gain my freedom. I didn't do it. I never told your name. I spared you. Bux, screw your 'other plans.' I need you at my side. I remember everything, Bux. I haven't forgotten."

He stood up slowly. "This is quite a shock for me. I'm sure you'll understand. I need time to process it all." If he'd been half a human, he would have comforted her as she stood shaking. Instead he said, "Did you meet Cali when she was here on reconnaissance? We're here to inspect the camp. Annie, you were the one who taught me a productive life is a happy life. We are making children happy. That's what we can do together now. Make the children happy. And make plastics from the wastewater. You'll have a resource at last, thanks to Cali."

I said, "Aiyn, I'll do all in my power to help you and Bux find your son. And sir, congratulations!"

Nell drummed her fingers on the ice cream cooler. She loathed Bux and her face said she was put off he'd had a relationship with Aiyn. "I have a job to do today. I must add the bacteria to the plastics producer. The bacteria are what form the plastic from the waste. I have them here in my insulated bag. I'm headed out to find the fermentation vats before they lose their viability."

"I'll come," said Aiyn. "I was a premier biologist in my day. How do you think Cochton Enterprises got so advanced? It wasn't my brothers. I worked on Big Yields corn and developed behemoth raspberries."

"Aiyn, I'd like to see Eve and the camp, too," I said.

"The camp headquarters is in the observation cabin atop the hill. Did you spend much time there?"

"Not at all. But I can find my way."

"I'll go with you. Bux, I leave you here to help the children with the ice cream. Can I trust you?"

Bux slumped.

Aiyn called out to the children on the porch. "Girls, Daddy Bux has permission to give you all the ice cream you can eat today."

The path to the cabin had new wooden steps. It was steep and had three landings with benches where a person could sit, rest, and look down at the canteen. At the first landing, Aiyn sat. "You must think me a fool. Anyone can make mistakes. The key is to not repeat them." She sighed. "How about a change of subject? Do people in Cochtonville like my raspberries?"

I had to tell her we didn't know what fruit was. Cochtonia was all about corn.

"Ah," she said. "People must be unhealthy there. And constipated, thanks to my brothers' foolish embrace of monoculture."

At the second landing Aiyn said, "We must not put much trust in my brother, Bert. His main interest is solidifying his relationship with the Vice Patrol, not the camp."

At the third landing, we sat and watched Bux run out the door with campers clinging to him. He shouted up to us but his voice was lost in the wind. "I imagine the ice cream has run out," Aiyn said. "Bux has lost his looks. Is he a good boss?"

Nell and I replied, "No," simultaneously.

She said, "Subjected to force, any man can turn bad, especially if not accustomed to it. Only deep-sea bacteria can withstand high pressure. Well, I can apply pressure, too. As much as needed."

We climbed the last set of steps and walked onto a stone patio. Footpaths made from flat limestone led to the pink, turquoise, and yellow cabins surrounding the once humble observation shed. The shed was now a white cottage with planters of pink flowers at each side of the door. Children in sunglasses and yellow uniforms—bright shirts and khakis—were bustling about completing tasks, some sweeping, some washing windows. They curtsied when they saw us and one rushed to knock on the door. "Lady Whitehead. You've got company!"

Eve, wearing a Camp Cochton uniform, opened the door. "Cali! Cali, a sight for sore eyes."

Aiyn apologized. "I'm sorry I didn't let you know they were coming. Your boss is a negligent communicator."

Eve squeezed me and held me tight. "Of course he is. What a wonderful surprise." Despite her dweeby look, she smelled hot and wildly sunbaked and windblown—a scent I could trust. I relaxed in her arms.

Her place was luxuriously furnished with multicolored rugs and overstuffed pig hide furniture. A girl came from behind a wingback chair and twirled on her toes.

"I completed dusting, Lady Whitehead. Do you have another chore for me?"

"Don't you look nice in your uniform? You'll make the perfect maid. Purceel, I'm sure you remember Lady Van Winkle."

Purceel's little face crinkled into a smile. "I do. Nookie Number One."

"Yes, dear, but remember, no lingo. Cali, can you believe it? They've got corn fiber clothes and pig skin shoes. They have three meals a day. Programmed exercise. They are learning skills. Plus, they are articulate. For the most part."

"A maid? Eve..." My elation hadn't lasted long.

"I thought Purceel would be a good match for your family someday, when she's learned all her tasks."

"She will be but...are the others here? I'd love to get NezLeigh's take on this."

"We offered to take them all but only Purceel was released," Eve whispered to me. "She had a dreadful case of pin worms we had to clear up."

A nanny came into the cabin. "Lady, another kid ran off," she said. "Took the zip line and never came back."

"Thank you for letting me know. We'll go looking," Eve said. "This happens at times."

Carrying her cooler, Nell said, "I can't help, I'm afraid. I'm off to give the bacteria their new home."

"I need to save the children from that scoundrel," Aiyn said, "and place an order for more ice cream."

"Cali and I can handle it. Purceel, will you help My Lady get home?"

We bid them goodbye, and Eve, Nell, and I walked down the hill toward a platform overlooking the WasteBin. Two cables ran across it to a second platform on the other side of the morass. On one side of the pool, the three fermentation vats sat by the edge. Each vat had a deck to it from the shore and a collection bin where the plastic would be removed.

"We'll be proud of ourselves when this is over," I said, surveying the beauty of it.

"Sure will. Refuse to refuge," Nell replied. She saluted and walked toward the tanks as Eve and I continued on to the platform.

As soon as Nell was out of earshot, Eve grabbed my arm. "Have you found them? Have you found our men?"

"No sign. I tried to get near the Cochton mansion, but your dad picked me up. He told me he'd decide who you consort with."

"That's what he's saying, but I've got Aiyn Cochton on my side."

"You know everything then? Layal is Aiyn's son and a Cochton."

"I know it. How ironic. My dad always said I'd end up a Cochton. Aiyn's playing it cool for now. She was content in her obscurity when Layal was here with her, but she's as motivated as I am. We're going to draw him out."

"And then?"

"Begin a colony here. You'll be joining us with Remmer, won't you?"

"A colony?"

"Why not? A part of Cochtonville and yet off on our own, free from their constant attention."

"As in bacterial colony. Related but apart," I said.

"Yes. What would you lose to gain your freedom?"

We reached the platform and climbed the stairs.

"Are you ready for the zip line?" she said.

"Across the lagoon?"

"It's faster. That's how the runaway got down."

"I can't swim. Remember?"

"You'll have a harness. It's safe and kid proof."

The cable and trolley ended at another platform.

"This is something fun to give the girls confidence. We don't have to do it, but we can get away alone faster in case Bux decides to eavesdrop." We laughed together over the pun. I considered if I should tell her about Bux being Layal's father. My own dad had his faults, as did hers. Would it be a big deal? I decided I'd do it later, when he wasn't lurking around. Who wants to find out you slept with your boss's son? She fastened me into the harness.

"You need a helmet," she said, taking one from a deck box and plopping it on my head. "I'll put the break on for you. I'll go first to help you land. Kick off when you're ready."

She strapped on a helmet and harness and stepped off the platform, gliding away from me.

My stomach was in knots. Wind blew through my hair. Below me lurked the dark pool of sewage with the tanks at the banks. It was beautiful, so full of rich potential. It would soon be worth something. Rapunzel couldn't have done better. I was proud and I was confident. I kicked off and skimmed through the air, wind rushing in my ears, the sewage below speeding past, and flew onto the platform, bumping into Eve like I was a raw turkey.

"Ouch. You call this Camp Cochton entertainment?"

"Of course."

"How does it fit into being a servant?"

"It doesn't. With any luck, they won't be servants."

"What do you mean?" I said with relief and confusion.

"They will be full-fledged citizens, right here."

Eve stashed the gear in another deck box and we hoofed it in the direction of the cabin.

"I know right where the girl is. She went to join NezLeigh. NezLeigh's building herself a little army there," Eve said.

"I always kind of liked her. Is she dangerous now?"

"It's always hard to say. This search is for insurance purposes by the way. We'll look for the girl and claim we can't find her. Except for Purceel, each girl is sponsored by a wealthy family. If she leaves, the family collects insurance. We'll report she's permanently missing."

"Won't the insurance company call this fraud?"

"Yes, if enough run away. For right now, it's not cost effective for them."

"How many runaways have you had?"

"Three. Four with this one. Less than ten percent. They usually spend some time at our cabin before exploring further and getting picked up by NezLeigh's gang. The dog you saved has a nose for runaways."

"Dungo's still alive?" In the distance, a discordant small ethanol-powered engine rumbled.

"Alive and some sort of retriever. He fetches the runaways and brings them to NezLeigh. Now that you and I are alone in the wild I can admit the truth—I'm not sold on this camp. I don't know if we're helping by teaching the Agros our ways. If they don't like the lessons they are learning and run away, I don't try hard to find them. I want Layal back. I want my dad off my back. Once Layal's found we can live out here together and let the Agros live in peace."

Despite their defoliation, the graveyard plants grew green and snaky. We kicked through a tangle of them to reach the cabin, as white and plain as we'd left it. Dungo sat on the porch. He barked at us and wagged his tale in confusion.

Eve grabbed my hand. "Makes you want to cry, doesn't it?"

"I've got to sit in there one more time," I said with slow, hot tears.

Dungo bounded toward me with his tongue hanging out. He stood on his hind legs, put his paws on my shoulders, and lapped my face with his meaty breath as I pushed him back down to all fours.

"Maybe I even missed *you*," I said, petting his dun-colored, overly large head. "Yes, I did miss you and everything out here." Eve opened the door to the cabin and a fair-haired child dashed out, crying like a balloon with air rushing through a pinhole. Dunny took off after her, barking at her heels as she ran toward the river.

"We should follow and make sure she doesn't drown," I said. "The creek will be swollen after the rain."

Eve stood at the door and snapped a photo of the fleeing child. "No worries. Kola's waiting for her in the trees."

I watched the girl as she ran, remembering our own harsh journey across the baked plain. When she reached the trees, safely accompanied by Dungo, I stepped inside the cabin.

"This place is just the same," I cried. With Eve behind me, I climbed the ladder and flopped onto Remmer's bed, trying to catch a whiff of him, a molecule, a trace. Yes, I could detect it. We'd been here. Here together. We'd been a thing, and I was sorrowful for the loss of it.

I snuggled my head into the crinkly mess and said, "I can't bear the thought of no more sex for the rest of my life. No more kissing. No touches. My heart's never going to beat again. You know what Cochtonia is not going to give us for our success? They aren't going to give us love. They aren't going to give us friends or a mate."

"I've thought about this, too," Eve said, sitting beside me. "That freedom I wanted...it was freedom to love. I feel real here. Natural. My wants and needs are raw."

"Look at me. I'm fake now." I sat up. "This place is real. It helps us discover what we are."

The rattle of the doorknob interrupted our discussion.

"Do people come here?" I asked in alarm.

"We get supplies delivered to the camp." Eve stood up. "To the camp. Not here."

The door creaked open. Two older men in mud spattered green jumpsuits tromped in. One had almost no chin and the other, a huge dimpled jawbone. Together, they were very average and smelled of vodka, a scent I'd learned to recognize from my days with Dad.

"Insurance adjustors," said one. "Cochton Enterprises Property Claims."

"Seeking a runaway," said the other in a voice most familiar. "Blonde. Five years of age. Tiny eyes."

I froze as Eve climbed down to confront them.

"Is it her?" Eve held up her phone and the men came forward to look. My brain was buzzing. It couldn't be, but it was, each step made me more sure. He was shaven but still the same man I'd seen hauled off several months ago.

My voice quivered. "Dad? Dad?"

"That's the kid." Dad tried to focus on the photo on the phone. "Where is she?"

I rushed down the ladder. "Dad Van Winkle?"

The chinned man looked blank, vodka flowing from his breath. "Cali. I'll be damned. You're done up."

"Nice to see you too, Dad, despite your chintzy uniform." My voice was bursting with disappointment. Shouldn't he be hugging me instead of commenting on my appearance?

"Damn, it's true. I look like a pickle and I have the blood of one, too. Since your mom booted me, I've had to take jobs as no man deserves. I'm crawling on my belly for the White Hand." He gave the hang-dog look of a person who'd gotten by on pity for far too long. It was infuriating. I was proud of Mom for having the courage to dump him and live on her own, for false love was worse than no love at all.

The chinless man spoke up. "Have you seen a kid? We need to return her to the training facility and make sure she's secured this time. We've got shackles to make certain she doesn't try these shenanigans again."

"How did you get here? Let me see your paperwork," Eve said angrily. The cabin was heating up with the windows closed.

"And who would you be?" he replied.

"Lady Eve Whitehead, director of this camp, appointed by Bert Cochton himself."

The man was nervous when faced with her title. "Lady Whitehead, we were sent by Clarence Cochton. He owns the insurance company. There are reports of missing campers."

"Are you implying the Cochtons aren't in solidarity? That's treason. I'll have you arrested."

"We're already arrested," said Dad, wiping his sleeve across his forehead. "It's why we're here."

I knew enough about drunks to know Eve was taking the wrong tactic. They'd get belligerent.

"The little bitch has run off for sure," I said. "She enjoyed our food and vitamins and with her newfound strength the ingrate skedaddled back to her farm. The question is, did she take the high road or the low road?"

The chinless man hiccupped. Dad swayed and held up both index fingers.

"Ingrates take the low road, like your mom."

"Have either of you been on the low road?" I asked.

"I've been lower than a snake." The chinless man's voice cracked.

"In that case, I suggest you go back the way you came. Do you have a vehicle?"

"Parked a ways back on the road," said Dad. He was barely able to open his eyes. "It was a hike. We're parched."

"I'll fetch you water," Eve said. "And you can rest here. We'll search the high road in case she's wily."

We went out to get the men water from the cistern. As I dipped the plastic into the cool water Eve gripped my arm. "We've got to run for it. I want to warn NezLeigh."

"We can't leave them here. This is my dad. I can't leave him here like a deadbeat." I went back to the cabin with the water. Both men were already curled up on the floor, smiling and snoring, threats only to themselves. Seeing my potbellied dad like this, so contentedly worthless, broke my heart. Thanks to him, I didn't have a stable home, didn't know where I belonged.

I put the water on the table and sat next to my dad, listening to his even breathing. He'd be okay. I cracked open a window about a quarter of an inch to let in air and then left them. Eve was already half way to the river, making a beeline for the spot where the trail went through the woods.

CHAPTER TWENTY

I finally caught up with Eve as she crossed the river in the shallow spot using the rocks, water swirling around her ankles as chaotically as the thoughts in my head. My dad out here and working as a bounty hunter for an insurance agency? He was worse after his rehabilitation than when he'd sat at home doing nothing. How was I going to tell Mom?

"They passed out. They won't be finding anything but headaches," I said, holding up my pants legs and slogging after her.

"I'm going to warn NezLeigh. The company might send someone competent next. You know, like two women."

We reached the soft bank, soggy from the rain. The hems of my slacks were filthy and my professional shoes with half-inch heels were slippery. The tree canopy was filled with spores and the smell of wet dirt, and mist, reminding me to help Mom out and clean the shower stall when I got home. Eve led me toward the camp via an unfamiliar path.

"Make noise and one of the Little Jerks will come to us," Eve said. "We won't have to walk all the way to their camp."

"I don't know how to make noise. I haven't yelled since NezLeigh whacked me with a turkey."

"How about applause? Isn't it grand? Let's pretend we're still winners." She clapped wildly. "Introducing Lady Cali Van Winkle, the scientist who saved Cochtonia from its own shit. Proud mother to—" She elbowed me hard.

"Umm, Nan."

"Mother to Nan. Owner of Remmer. A woman who has every success."

The branches reached toward me accusingly. Although I'd played along, Eve's words flushed out a nagging thought. I was a fake. I didn't deserve my success or Bux's malignant adoration. "Except..."

"Except?"

We stepped over a rotten branch on the path. "The whole thing was Nell's idea."

"The InVitro?"

"No, the manure plastic. She gave me a magazine. It had an article."

"What's the problem?"

"Shouldn't she be a lady? She had the magazine. She did most of the microbe work. It's Nell's genius, not mine."

"No. Cali Van Winkle. It's you. You gave the presentation. You went to the WasteBin. You identified the problem. You read the magazine. You made our presentation complete. Without your role in it, I would be a fraud. You are the lady." Once again, she applauded me and this time, I joined her to make noise and attract the Little Jerks, but I couldn't help but wonder why I would consider forming a colony if I was such a success at home.

We clapped as we walked and each bend held more trees. The light grew more dim. The trail faded to nearly nothing. It would be morning for the Little Jerks. Would they be curious enough to rise and find us? Had the runaway wakened them? A crow called out harshly and others joined in.

"We're being followed," Eve said as the cacophony swelled. "Stand off the path and see who goes past, but watch your step.

This route passes near a fen." The ground wobbled and my skin crawled as we ducked into a stand of birch trees. The perpetrator came closer with heavy, erratic steps and the familiar clank of medals.

"Cali! Cali! Where are you?"

It was Bux, his pant cuffs wet, his shoes muddy, his eyes on his cracked phone as he tripped over a stick and landed on the soft dirt. Shit. How had he managed to follow us when I wasn't even sure how I got here? I touched my neck. My ID. Of course! I'd never be alone again and not in a good way. Sure enough, he got up, brushed off his pants, held out his cracked phone, and walked directly to us.

"Lady Cali!"

"Hello, Bux, we're searching for a missing camper. Have you seen her?" Eve said matter-of-factly. Bux, of course, had no inkling we'd been hiding from him. With a crackle of underbrush, he threw himself at me, grasping my shoulders abruptly.

"Cali, I was so worried. Come with me. One camper isn't worth risking your neck for. Let me help you get to safety." He hadn't a clue of the irony—he'd sent me here, forced me to learn the ways of the wild, and now he didn't realize that if anyone could save anyone, it was me who would save him. If I had to. "I can't risk losing you. Every moment away from you is like hot oil dripping on my heart." Eve and I giggled. He stuck out his hand and swiped at my breast.

"These will temporarily nurture a future InVitro child of Cochtonia."

"Sir," I said, folding my hands across my chest. "Stop acting like a child."

"You plague on women!" It was Aiyn, her eyes consumed by their pupils, leaves stuck in her hair, dirt on her shoes. "It wasn't a man I protected, but a shamble of a human being stumbling around out here like a two-ton boar."

"Aiyn?" Bux said in surprise.

"In the flesh. You thought you'd slip away and find yourself alone with Cali, didn't you? How little you understand. These woods are full of the people your society rejected. Did you think you and Cochtonville could toss them—or me—away? Being rejected brings a certain cunning. I followed you easily."

Bux's goatee shook. "Aiyn. I've always respected your intelligence. Great to see you, old friend."

"Friend. That's a sanitized word for it. We were never friends."

"We'll always have our memories, and our tattoos. Remember me kindly, Annie, and calm down."

"It's time for me to throw my foolish heart in the WasteBin. Bux, all these years I pined for you, idealized you in my mind. What I was missing wasn't you; you're a creep. It was my ability to love."

A sulfurous sweet scent drifted through the rustling leaves.

"Good thinking, Aiyn. Don't let the past drag you down. You've got to get over it for the sake of the future." A green beam of light struck Bux on the forehead. He shielded his eyes.

"It was a stinking deal for me, Bux. Make it right. Turn yourself in."

Bux waved his hand over his eyes, as if swatting bright green bugs. "Aiyn, move on. You've got me so upset, I'm seeing spots."

NezLeigh, Kola, and a troop of little Agros, all dressed in Camp Cochton uniforms and holding clubs and sharpened sticks, appeared from the brush. NezLeigh waved the UTI. The others surrounded Bux, holding out their weapons.

NezLeigh said, "I'm seeing a bummer of a rotten bargain. We hate interlopers and betrayal doesn't sit well with us. My Lady, I'll revenge you."

"It's good to see you again, NezLeigh," said Aiyn.

Eve added, "You found the errant camper, I see."

Bux put his phone in his pocket. "Eye opening for everyone but me. What's going on? Who are these little savages? Why aren't they at the camp?"

Kola stepped forward. "We aren't campers. Get your stupid ass out of here now. Now." Dungo growled to back her up.

"Girl, mind your manners," Bux scolded. "Eve, control them."

He grabbed for me and I stepped away. The ground quivered. I looked down and saw the ring of white flowers marking the cursed fen. NezLeigh shone a green dot on his Order of the Pig medal. "Stand back, or you fall, ya dig?"

Bux was a prig but not stupid. "Cali," he said, "is that your Universal Testing Instrument?"

"Sure is," said NezLeigh. "I stole it. Fixed it, too."

Bux lunged at her. NezLeigh covered her eyes with one hand as the green light reflected from his medallion, but she kept the beam steady as she sidestepped him.

"Lavender," she called. "Lavender."

The underbrush splintered. Lavender busted through, snorting.

"Lavender, baby, you know what to do."

Cautiously, the pig advanced as Bux backed up. One step, two, three. The ground shifted beneath his feet.

"Watch out!" I called. No one deserved to fall in the fen, not even the odious Bux. He halted. Lavender shoved Bux with her snout. With a shout, he fell into the boggy fen and sank.

"Smooth move. You get a freaking rash from that mud," NezLeigh said. "Master Bates will be in sorry shape by tonight, as well he deserves."

Bux tossed his mucky head, getting what air he could, trying to back float. He tugged his arms from the mud and stood, sunk in to his crotch.

"Help! I'm going down."

"You won't die. You're not dense enough," I said.

"It'll keep you cozy until the law comes," Aiyn said.

"We can't leave him here," I said in a panic. "Even *he* doesn't deserve to suffer in the fen."

"Damn straight. I don't want the law here," NezLeigh said. "Leave him in until he itches. After that, we have get him off our land, ya dig?"

"Who is he?" Kola asked.

"He's Pretty Boy's father," I said. "That's his crime."

Kola burst out with a cry. "Shit, no. How can it be? How can it be?" She ripped at her shaggy hair.

"Layal's father? Bux?" Eve put her hand to her forehead and her legs wobbled as Aiyn put an arm around her to steady her.

"It's true, dear. I had a fling with him. He was a smooth talker in his youth and more handsome than you might guess. His above-status liaison with me made him a criminal but I protected his identity. With family pressures, I allowed Layal to be modified before he was born. That's why Layal looks nothing like his parents and his fatherhood couldn't be traced. The joke was on me. The only modifications being done at the time were to create a line of erotic men to satisfy high-class women who'd done well by Cochtonia. He was taken from me as a boy to be raised and trained by Cochton Enterprises. I lived alone for five years. He was rejected and returned to me with a friend to work productively for Cochtonia. I could only watch him from afar as he supervised waste disposal."

"Dumb de dumb dumb. Did you question why you had to keep away from him?" NezLeigh asked.

"I obeyed so he and Bux would be safe. I was loyal to Cochton Enterprises."

"You made a freaking flawed assumption, ya dig? Tyrants bite your ass no matter how docile you are. When they've tired of you, they betray you. Maybe your eyes are too small, you're too old, not loyal enough. Even we backward folks know as much."

"They lived," Eve said. "Bux and Layal are still with us, My Lady. You did the right thing."

"No. I was isolated and *he* was making other plans. I've been pining for him all these years. Time, however, doesn't preserve love. Far from it. I'm done protecting him. I can only hope I'll learn where our son is as part of my confession and negotiation. I'll get Layal back. Yes, I will. I'll turn Bux in. I have a plan and my confession will help hasten its reality. Deep inside me, there's a rumbling."

"It's gas," Bux said.

Aiyn's voice soared. She thrust out her chest. "It's desire. The desire to do one great and wonderful thing. I'll embrace this land for my own. We'll make it a utopia where people can be themselves and not be squeezed into uncomfortable clothes or labels. We won't be ashamed of who we love. All of us who have been outsiders will be in. No longer will this be the WasteBin or Camp Cochton. It will be a thriving city. We'll call it Camptown."

Bux groaned. "At least come up with a better name to match the rebellious spirit. And for the sake of our son, get me out of here."

Ignoring him, Aiyn grasped NezLeigh's hand. "Will you and your band join me?"

NezLeigh jumped away. "Shit no. Why would I trust any of you? Leave me and my girls in peace." She stroked the pig, who nuzzled her hand. "If you want us to join you, to scheme with your scheme, return this land to us."

"A trade agreement. I love it. I feel like a real country already. I must call the authorities to retrieve Bux immediately."

"Annie, I didn't mean to betray. Cochtonia first. We both agreed." He scratched his back.

"Shut up. Pull your legs up. Pull up. Lean back. Float," NezLeigh said.

Best I could see in the growing darkness, Bux complied.

"I don't want him or the arrest visible to the children," Eve said. "They'll be frightened."

"I'll take him to the cabin and wait for the authorities there," I said with resignation. "This is on me."

The wavelike call of the insects echoed in my head. I didn't want to help Bux, yet I had to.

"Good idea. We'll go ahead and call from camp headquarters," Aiyn said. "NezLeigh, will you be so kind as to escort us?"

"Kola, can you handle this gig?"

"Can I clean an outhouse? No."

"Cali, are you sure?" Eve asked.

"If I can get plastic from manure, I can extract Bux from the morass. I'll have him at the men's cabin."

The three schemers left for the camp. Kola and I—the sidekicks—were left with Bux. Kola brushed away the mosquitos as Lavender attracted more. "Make you feel plain, don't it, to have to deal with this mess."

"Cali is anything but plain," Bux said as he held his head above the bog.

"I believe it now. You *are* Pretty Boy's dad with your flattery. Totally believe it."

"Cali, don't get involved in this scheme. You have your whole life ahead of you. I didn't pluck you from the thorns of Cochtonville for you to rot in some colony. Let your light shine," Bux gurgled.

"You shouldn't give advice, stupid. Stupid," Kola said. She pointed at the little ones. "Fetch plenty of bags." The troupe scampered off and she and I sat petting Lavender. The wind came up as night fell and I wrapped my arms over my chest. Bux twisted and writhed as he scratched his back. With each scratch, he sunk deeper.

"Hey hound dog, stop scratching. *Slowly* creep this way, assy ass," Kola said as girls ran up with handfuls of plastic bags. Kola ripped the bags in half and tied them as Bux inched toward solid ground.

"Is everyone from Cochtonville helpless? Don't just sit there, lend a hand," she demanded, shoving the tied end at me. "Hold this. Hold." The girls did the same, some holding, some braiding as my boss inched his way toward solid ground and finally collapsed on the bank, heaving, exhausted by his escape.

Kola put her foot on his neck and tied his hands behind his back with the plastic bag rope. "I should let the pigs eat you. Now get up. Up with you. March, you hear me? Step along. Step, step. You're not too stupid to step."

We walked together to the creek's shallow spot, Kola leading Bux by a bag leash, followed by Dungo nipping at his heels and the other Little Jerks poking him with sticks. The pig, her little ones, and I followed in a ridiculous parade. Goop dripped from Bux as he loped with his head drooping and his hands tied behind his back. The green of the trees shifted to black. Finally, the light over the creek glowed ahead.

"I'll go no farther. No farther," Kola said handing me the rope. "You got to see on your own here out. May we meet again, but not him."

The Little Jerks called out goodbyes and a few jumped in the water after frogs. A quarter moon gave scant light as I held Bux by the muddy shoulders and edged him ahead of me on the rocks. Dungo splashed in the water and snapped at the rope dangling from Bux's neck, escorting me half way before running back to follow Kola. The bog residue swirled around Bux's feet and he moaned in agony. We were alone on the rocks in the dark. Much about him was unsavory and bewildering. I couldn't let myself think about that as we moved ahead. We had to pass safely together. If he fell in his condition, it would be hard to get him to his feet again.

Silently cursing my professional shoes, I said, "Keep your eyes on the stones."

At the far side, I washed my burning hands. My pants were soaked to the knees. Bux pitched himself into the shallow water, flopping onto his butt. He fell back and submerged his body. The muck washed downstream.

"Ahh," he said in relief. "Ahhhh."

When he was washed, I said, "We can't sit here all night."

He pushed himself up with his hands behind his back. He wasn't as weak as I'd imagined.

"Cali, do you really want to be a part of this lover's quarrel? I wonder if the Cochton brothers will be mad about my apprehension. I'm an innocent man. They won't take Aiyn's side.

Even before I fell victim to her seduction, there was tension between them."

"We'll let the law decide," I said. Still, he had me questioning my involvement in this mad scheme.

The half-mile walk to the cabin should have been easy, but the wind kicked up and despite the recent rain, dirt pummeled us. It wasn't cold, but it stung my face, and since Bux was wet, it stuck to his uniform and clung to the bottoms of our pants. I could manage one night with him and my dad, despite Dad's mistrust of authority.

"Behave yourself," I said. "Believe it or not, my dad is visiting." I pushed open the cabin door. The place was dark and snoreless. As my eyes adjusted to the dark it was obvious my dad and the chinless man were gone. I helped Bux sit in a dining chair. *Cali, see you at home* was written in the dust on the kitchen counter. I wiped it away with my hand.

"He's gone," Bux said. "I'm sorry. I must look a sight, not like a man to meet your father."

"Nobody looks wonderful out here."

"You are beautiful. Your eyes are kind and intelligent, your body is strong, your hair is as wild and windswept as a field of Big Yields. It doesn't have to be light for you to shine. It's day in my mind and I see you as a divinity. Is there anything about me you want me to change?"

I wasn't sure what to say in the face of this insincere flattery. All had changed since I'd gained InVitro status, as if I'd been nothing before and everything now that I would reproduce. He goaded me with his stare.

"Umm, Aiyn is right about the goatee. And I'm not a fan of uniforms."

He looked down, his chin on his chest. "Have I lost any medals?"

"How many did you have before?"

"The Order of the Stalk, the Order of the Pig, and three

copper soybeans. I should have a gold kernel, too, since I have a son."

"The medals are all there."

"I can't give up the goatee, but if you please, remove the Order of the Pig. Never again will I look upon pigs fondly."

I removed the pin and held it in my hands. It was light enameled plastic powdered with dust.

"Dispose of it. Toss it in the WasteBin."

"Sir?"

"Please call me Bux. Yes, I can't bear to have a pig in my life. Cali, could you unbutton my coat? I'd be so grateful. It is smothering me."

I'd learned from my mother not to judge people who needed medical help. My fingers fumbled with the brass buttons. Bux coughed. He closed his eyes as if he was expiring. I opened the coat as best I could.

"Do me a favor," he said weakly. "March the dreadful pin to the WasteBin."

He was either delirious or planning an escape. "I can't leave you here alone."

"You must. First, can you cut these bonds? My back is killing me."

It was an escape he was planning. Where did he think he was even going to go? "I don't have the right tool. Should I take off your boots? I don't want you to get a foot rash." I unlaced his boots and tugged them off. His toes were long and gangly.

"Cali, this place is wretched—bugs, pigs, wild children. I applaud your survival skills. Your ability to survive in this wilderness is uncanny. You've met with success and thus, I have. You'll be mine, no matter where I am." He dropped his eyes to the bulge in his crotch. I stepped back. "Don't be shocked. Even dead men get them. I have a son. I could have another."

Disgusted and worn out by his antics, I grabbed the Order of the Pig pin and tossed it out the door.

"Are you happy? Settle down or it will be a long wait."

It *was* a long wait. After a while, Bux fell asleep, his head back as he snored with a boarish ferocity. At last, I too succumbed to sleep, no longer than fifteen minutes. It was enough. When I jerked awake, a breeze on my arms, he was gone and the door hung open.

I ran outside after him, texting futilely. *He's escaped.*

The wind had died down. I ran to the WasteBin and stood at its edge, waving up frantically for help. Instead of a pit of manure, it was now a marvel of engineering and science. The plastics vats whirred as they stirred and white fluff floated on the surface of the collection pool illuminated by the scant moonlight and the glow from the light of Eve's cabin at the top of the hill. Children romped in the dark. A figure stood on the platform, her hair lifted by the wind. It was Nell, admiring her handiwork. *She* was a real scientist who did things to make the world better. I yelled for her attention.

A flash of headlights startled me. For a moment, I thought it must be the old bus in front of Aiyn's place, but the lights were too low and tore down the uneven terrain like a mouse toward a hole. I stood still, not sure what way to go to avoid the ATV as it barreled toward me, two Washers at the wheel: broad-shouldered Ursula and tall Commissioner Whitehead. In the back sat the young Washer with glasses. I held up my hands and shouted "Hey!" as they approached. Unsure of how to step out of the way, I stared down the lights as if the vehicle was an enemy. It passed to my right and skidded to a dusty stop.

"We're looking for a man to arrest," the commissioner said. "Get in and stop wandering about in the dark. You're not a Pesto."

"He's at large," I cried, climbing in and sitting between them. Immediately Ursula peppered me with questions. Why was I alone out here? Was anyone else with me who might have helped him escape? She'd been planning to make an easy and prestigious arrest. It was apparent that indeed the brothers did want him incarcerated. As we approached and the headlights hit the little cabin, Ursula slammed on the breaks and each Washer drew a weapon.

Ursula hopped from the car and approached the cabin, weapon in hand. "Does he have to be alive, boss?"

"Hold your fire. You can't fill a prison with the dead."

"He's harmless," I said, incredulous he was important enough to be wanted. The bugs shrieked like sirens in the dark. Ursula's feet crunched over a tangle of plants as she walked to the porch and threw open the door.

The commissioner held my arm. "Sit here and tell me how this all happened. The Cochtons are eager to make money from this place, but the sister says she needs her cut for turning this guy in."

"He's my boss," I said. "He came with me to the camp. The sister was here. They had an altercation."

Ursula came from the cabin. She held up the plastic bag rope. "Did you tie him with this? It looks like kids made it."

I said, "I had to use the resources available." In timely fashion, a stray bag blew past.

The commissioner said, "Stupid move. He slipped out. How long were you asleep?"

"Only a few minutes. I ran for help as soon as I woke up."

"We'll make a circle and move inward."

My stomach was in knots as Ursula slipped behind the wheel and we drove around the perimeter of the cabin, piercing headlights illuminating the rocks and gangly plants surrounding us. I'd been careless. About a quarter mile from the cabin, a pack of dogs sprinted away as we approached.

"Shit. Coyotes," Ursula said. She stopped the ATV and got out to investigate. She kneeled and reached into in an area of tangled plants. "Oh crap. It's him. You've got to see this." We got out of the ATV and walked closer.

Bux was tossed on the ground like a toy, a vine around his neck, his eyes open and blank, his tongue hanging out, a trickle of blood in the corner of his mouth, his phone in his hand. Dread coursed through me at the sight.

"What's going on?" I cried.

"Are you going to vomit? Civilians vomit at times like this," the young Washer said.

"The prisoner has passed away. He was strangled by a plant," said the commissioner. "Ursula, erect some signs from here on back. This area is officially off limits."

"Passed away? He's dead?" I couldn't believe any of this.

"That's what 'passed away' means. It's a euphemism," Ursula said bitterly. "He's dead and nobody will get what they want."

CHAPTER TWENTY-ONE

Bux was dead. Aiyn could no longer use him as leverage to get Layal back. I was farther than ever from finding Remmer. Although only Ursula directly blamed me, the others agreed he'd faked me out by pretending to saw wood. My hapless role in the death made me question my ability to solve problems. Maybe I should leave well enough alone, but I couldn't.

A person could be in a city full of people, on stage receiving applause, having a mother's admiration, and still be alone. Remmer was my firelight and my mirror. Without him, I was cold and blind. I couldn't see my way forward without him by my side. I'd spend the rest of my life eating one corn dog with pesto sauce after another and tipping the bottle more than Dad in helpless search for the comfort I'd lost. Yes, despite the hardships of the WasteBin, I'd found a comfort I'd never have in Cochtonville. A farm bell rang in my head, calling me to him. Where? Where? *Where?*

The quarantining of the cabin and everything close was good news for the Little Jerks. No one dared go near the creek. Purceel was allowed to come home with me to work for Mom and after a midnight breakfast of bacon and eggs she enthusiastically did the laundry. As we sat outside on the porch, I told Mom all about the horrible day, starting with the worst news—my boss was dead, tragically murdered by a graveyard plant. Her face froze as she stared at the plants through the sliding glass patio door. "You theorize the plant kills oppressors?"

"It seems to be the pattern."

"Was your boss an oppressor?"

"He grabbed my boob. It's all so confusing. Yes, he was. He was."

I went on to relate the story of meeting Dad, his job, and his continued drinking.

"He was drunk! I paid for nothing. What a waste! Where is he right now at this very moment?"

"I don't know, Mom. He has a job. He's halfway fixed."

"The years. The years." She stomped down the freshly repaired stairs and into the yard. The fire pit hadn't been used since Dad had been hauled away, and graveyard plants crept over it cautiously. She screamed and fell onto the grass, crawling on her hands and knees, ripping the plants as they tangled through the yard.

"You vulgar vines. I'm oppressed. Do you get it? *I'm* oppressed. And no one saves me. No one strangles my oppressor." The vines released their defense and alarm chemicals as their epidermal cells were ripped; fatty acid catabolites and L-phenylalanine derivatives volatilized into the humid air. I ran after Mom, as she tore them viciously

"Mom, calm down. You're making them mad."

"These frauds don't know what oppression is."

"You're right. We don't know what triggers them. You've got low serotonin from years of living with Dad and your adrenaline and noradrenaline are surging. You're exhaling extra carbon dioxide. Plants talk in chemical language. I don't know what you're telling them but get inside. You've got to let go of your anger." I couldn't bear to tell her what he'd written in the dust: *see you at home.*

Purceel stood in the door. "What's wrong with Dame Van Winkle?"

"She wishes the plants had killed her husband."

Purceel and I convinced Mom to go to bed. Purceel dusted and polished the stairs inside as an incentive to keep Mom in her bedroom. As fatigued as I was, it was clear what I had to do. I knew Dad well enough. He *was* coming home. I'd wait up for him. I'd make sure he didn't bother Mom. The air was as heavy as a wet sponge. I sat on the back steps listening to the crickets singing their short lives away. Wasn't every life too short? Was there ever enough time? I might not see Remmer again, or if I did, we'd be gray and forgetful with even less time left to be together. It wouldn't do. It would never do. I had to find him soon.

The moon was a bright crescent hanging next to a planet. How beautiful they were together, looking down at this dreary earth. I didn't need a free sidewalk to be happy, I didn't have to be InVitro. What I needed was love to walk beside me. It was so hard to come by here. The emptiness in my arms was unbearable. Oh, even my bones ached with loneliness. Sirens broke the night silence. Even the dead couldn't rest in peace.

Purceel came out of the house and pushed a button on the window ledge to start our robotic lawn mower buzzing across the perimeter of the yard. She sprayed the window with cleanser and wiped it down with a corn fiber cloth. She went into the house and came back with a bucket and a mop.

"I should wash the steps," she said. "You'll get dirt on your clothes."

"No need. It's late and you just got here."

"I insist. Dame will be happy when she sees it."

I stood up as the child scrubbed the bits of plants from the newly re-built stairs, water splashing.

"Did I miss something?" she said.

"No. Don't worry about a thing. Is there work for you in the house? I'd like some privacy."

"You didn't tell your mom about the yesterday incident, did you?"

"Some of it, yes."

"Did you tell her about your father?"

"My father? What's there to tell? What do you know?"

"I was warned about it from Miss Eve. He's a bounty hunter, after escapees."

"He is. Fortunately, he's incompetent," I said, carefully not admitting a thing.

"He's coming back, isn't he? He'd better not fuck with me—or her." She propped the mop on the house and walked softly into the yard toward the woodpile, her hands outstretched. The possum slipped inside the pile as she lunged.

"Didn't Mom tell you? We buy our food at the store."

"I'm trying to be helpful."

"Hey!" a voice shouted. "You're going back to training." It was Dad, green and fat as a pickle, stepping into the yard from the dark shadows of the graveyard. "This is my home, you little animal. You almost cost me my job." Treading over a tangle of vines, Dad lurched at Purceel.

Purceel jumped back. "Hands off. I belong to the mistress of this house."

"Dad, no. She lives here. She's not an escapee."

"This is my house. I'm the master." Dad was red faced, breathing heavily, as angry and aggressive as they come. If the plants were killers, why weren't the plants after *him*? Although he'd never been violent before, Dad grabbed the girl and shook her until her head jerked back.

"Dad, she's a kid." I rushed toward them, ready to rescue Purceel from his grasp.

"A kid? She's an asset. And not much more." His breath was enough to blind an owl. As I swished away his smell, it came to me. Plants excrete methanol and other light volatiles. The vines didn't strangle Dad because of the ethanol from his breath—one carbon atom and two hydrogens removed from their methanol—disguised him as a communicative plant! They did, however, sense the tension and anger in this situation. Confused, they reached for Purceel. I had to wash away her anger and aggression before they strangled her; they were already climbing up her legs. I grabbed the bucket of mop water and tossed it over Purceel and Dad as they struggled. The shock did the trick. Dad dropped Purceel and so did the plant.

"My uniform! Your mom's getting the cleaning bill," Dad yelled, wiping the water from his clothes. He'd never been like this before. Previously, he'd swallowed his anger. A vine reached out and wrapped around his knees. He gasped and fell. His extreme anger must have crossed the threshold of detection. It had cancelled out the alcohol. The plant was after him.

Purceel stood over him and clenched her fists. "You fat fucker, you're gonna pay for this in Hell." She rushed to the windowsill and poked some buttons on the lawnmower controller. The machine veered from the perimeter of the yard and headed straight for Dad.

I yelled, "You'll hurt someone. Turn it off."

The mower made a loop near Dad's head as the plant crept up his body and covered his mouth.

"Turn it off so I can save him," I cried.

"If you command it." She fiddled with the controller. "It's broken." The mower made a smaller circle, nearly brushing his foot and swooping past his hair as he struggled.

Without thinking, I snatched the robot with two hands as it passed by. I was immediately horrified at the rushing sensation of the blades millimeters from my fingers. What a stupid move! This was like holding a wildcat. I swung my body to the right and heaved the mower and its blades into the arbor vita hedge at the edge of the graveyard.

My knees were wobbly. I could have lost my fingers or my drunken father. I tossed myself next to Dad and tugged at the vine as it held him fast. It was turgid and hard, yet fluid, like a penis. I rubbed my hands across it, searching for a weak spot as the vine steadily clamped across Dad's mouth while he thrashed, making it hard for me to keep calm.

"Hands up." It was Ursula, followed by the Washer with glasses, holding the flag app high. Weakly, I pressed my finger to my forehead and Purceel, being well-trained, did the same.

Ursula said to the young Washer, "Show me your stuff."

Reluctantly, the new Washer unbuttoned her white coat with one hand.

"I don't mean flash me. I mean, what's your take on this situation? Tell me what you should do," Ursula said impatiently. "I'm asking you as part of your training. Coch forbid if all new Vice Patrol agents are like this."

She touched her glasses and lifted them slightly as she peered at Dad, writhing. "Shoot them all? You can never go wrong with that." The young Washer reached for her weapon and clumsily pointed it at Purceel. "Boss, the eyes are so creepy."

"Put that away and turn off the flag." Ursula came over to me. "Our listening devices detected noise from this area."

"Another plant, another guilty man. Take him away," I said, hoping she would return Dad to his facility before Mom knew he was here.

"According to his uniform, he works for Property Insurance. He's no deadbeat."

With a crack of branches, the mower roared through the trees. Instinctively, we scattered, except for Ursula, who aimed a device at the mower and disabled it right after it sliced through the vines and cut the toe off of Dad's left boot. Dad howled as the vine withered.

"Thanks," I said to Ursula. "You're my hero."

Wearing a pink bathrobe, her hair in a tangle, Mom came out into the yard. "What's going on with this shit show? Oh my. Not you." She crouched beside Dad, her focus on his boot with blood oozing out.

"Are you going to vomit?" the young Washer asked.

"She's a medical person, you dope. Dame Van Winkle, shall I remove him?" Ursula asked as Mom carefully slipped off Dad's boot.

"He's lost the tip of his big toe. He needs a digital block and some stitches. Release him to me. I'll take care of him."

"You deserve better," Ursula said, placing a hand on Mom's shoulder. "He's a lucky man."

"In so many ways," Mom replied grimly. "I thought *he* was the only one who held on to things for too long."

———

On the edge of town near the factory that made breakfast cereal, the Aiyn Cochton Clinic was disguised to look like a silo and blend with the rest of Cochtonville's industrial corridor. Not everyone approved of genetic modification and some were jealous of those with InVitro status, thus the clinic was unremarkable from the outside.

As I stood in front of the clinic, watching smoke puff from the adjacent boxy factory, I reminded myself this was the only way to get to Remmer and to help Mom afford a new house where she could live without Dad, who was once again lounging by the fire pit with beer, this time with a slightly shorter toe. I needed to become a full blown InVitro and have a baby as soon as possible. The time between Rem and I stretched out like a vast manure pit. If I learned anything at all from the saga of Aiyn and Bux, it was that love didn't wait like a stone. It died like a field in drought. I put my hand on my belly. Motherhood was as sticky as the boggy fen. I wouldn't be afraid. Others had done it. I could too, for love.

The industrial steel building and the thought of having a child in order to get what I wanted put me off as I shoved my reluctant self through the door. The clinic was filled with pink and blue pillows, balloons, tiny socks strung on string lights—it was unscientific and manipulative. I didn't need my heartstrings pulled any tighter; being in love with someone who'd been ripped away from me was painful enough. I took a seat in a pale pink plastic chair. I was the only person in the place. Cochtonia wasn't going to grow at this rate.

The clinic's director, scrawny as if she hadn't gathered enough food, welcomed me into the examination room. She scanned me with four different devices, running them across my head, arms, torso, and vagina before leaving me fully dressed and alone to sweat and listen to my heart beat in silence. Waiting, I took in the poster about "making a baby." A twisted helix of DNA, an enzyme cutting it like a scissors, the cell reacting in alarm, guide RNA carrying the new gene coming to the rescue by repairing the broken DNA, a happy baby showing off muscles. Except for the baby, it was standard fare. The director returned, reading my report.

"Congratulations. You passed. Welcome to the world of new motherhood. You won't have to compete for the man who provides the most care and stability. You won't have to juggle motherhood and career. We provide the childcare—for a modest cost—as well as the child. You have the luxury of the ideal lifestyle with reliable help to care for your offspring. Freedom to have a baby and freedom to get away from it." She made it sound so good. This *was* a better world.

"We have high standards. You must present a professional image. No being alone with unapproved men. We detected it from your health screening; you have experienced a man, though that's not enough to toss you out of our pool of candidates. All of us try out human nature at times." Her tone was warm yet firm, as if she was speaking to a child. Like a child, I vowed to ignore this bit of advice. Remmer meant the world to me. Cochtonville was unbearable without him.

She scanned me with her Universal Health Monitor. "Currently, you're a little high on stress hormones and their metabolites. Are you nervous?"

"A little. This is a big step."

"Relax. How about a baby shower?" An assistant brought two gifts, one wrapped in yellow mylar, the other in green.

"Go ahead," said the director. "See what's inside."

I opened the flatter package, the yellow one, and took out a one-piece fireman outfit, sized 0-3 months. I held it up as if an audience was in attendance.

"It's going to be a boy, of course. You said on your initial survey you wanted your child to be honest. Do you still?"

"Yes."

"And strong but not too tall."

"Yes, please."

"And with red hair and auburn eyes. You go for the quirky."

"It's a personal preference."

"Open the next gift if you would."

I fumbled with the slick green mylar and the taped box beneath, at last reaching in and pulling out a toy fire truck. I wasn't sure how to react to this.

The director beamed. "Based on your parameters, his perfect job match would be firefighter."

I blurted out in shock, remembering Remmer's sexy firefighter Crisper photo, "No, no. A real firefighter or a stripper firefighter?"

"A real one. You wanted honesty—he can't be a stripper or escort, considering. We need real men for dangerous tasks."

"Dangerous!" I should have known there'd be a catch—the man created wouldn't exist to be loved but to have a duty. "Aren't those jobs automated?"

She stiffened but spoke sweetly. "Not fully automated. The best of firefighters would indeed be valued and have robotic assistants. Red hair would be a cute touch. We'll feature him on our advertisements."

Unsure what to do, I put the truck on the floor and pushed it. The siren squawked.

The director relaxed. "Training begins at age five."

"To be a firefighter? I thought only...only Pestos had their children taken away."

"Theirs get taken away to work. Yours will be taken away to get training *and* education. You didn't expect a superior being would be left to your care once it becomes cognizant, did you?"

"Why would a boy destined for a dangerous job be taken away to be educated?"

"His job is dangerous, but he'll be trained for it. We need smart men in dangerous roles. We can't leave a crafted person to chance. Nature *and* nurture, you know. Your personality survey indicates your nurturing skills are low quality."

"I sacrificed a lot for this. What if he doesn't want to be a firefighter?" I couldn't believe I was arguing. I needed to do this and get Remmer, not worry about a baby I didn't have.

"He'll want it. We'll add desire. You haven't sacrificed. You've strived. Your striving isn't part of the equation. Pull yourself together and get the tractor out of the shed. We'll begin the fertilization process immediately. We have a room here where we monitor the process."

"Tractor out of the shed? I'm not a farmer." I picked up the fire truck.

"How old are you?"

"Twenty-five."

"Time to burn the ethanol. Let me show you the fertilization area."

We walked down a bubble-gum-pink hall with an array of blue doors. She opened one on the left, revealing a cramped white room with fluffy bedding and a mirror to one side. Even worse, a Roman urn with a prominent security camera sat in one corner. This wasn't going to be private. No matter, I had to get it over with. I removed my shoes.

"It won't be today," the director said. "Today is for examination only. I'm cheered to note your renewed enthusiasm."

"The sooner, the better," I said.

"I agree. To warn you, or perhaps in your case tempt you, the procedure begins with sexual encounters with a select male. Keep in mind you signed the agreement clause and the confidentiality contract."

"Sexual encounters?" This was startling. InVitro included sex? Talk about giving the wrong impression.

"Yes, you've got it. Here's the catch: we can only modify what's been created. You get a frisky stud muffin until you've been fertilized."

"With a firefighter Crisper? Of my choice?" I clapped my hands. I could request Remmer! This was all worth it.

"No. We don't use Crispers for such a thing. We use established leaders with a record of success. Here's your partner."

Although the thought was off-putting, I was willing to do about anything and anyone. She beamed a photo onto the wall next to the mirror. For the first time ever, my vomit reflex threatened to undo me. I gagged. "Sir Bux! He's alive?"

"It says here he was part of the team that got you InVitro status. This is a reward for both of you."

"A reward? Frisky? He's frisky?" My head was collapsing. What was going on? Last time I'd seen him, he had a graveyard vine around his neck.

"Studies have shown aggression aids in fertility. He'll be frisky and fierce. We shoot both of you with hormones. We started him on them when he got his promotion." She lifted the pillow to show me white handcuffs. "You might wish to be restrained."

"Aggression?" This explained Bux's weird behavior as of late. But he, himself, was late.

"We've had trouble locating him, however." She held up her hand and read from her device. "Wait a moment. There's an addendum. No. It says here your boss was strangled by a plant while escaping arrest. I'm sorry. You've lost a crucial team member."

"Now what? Can I still get my baby and my InVitro papers?"

"I don't know. I've never had this happen before. What a tragedy. This child is all planned. To never create him would be murder. Let's have you come back with your new boss."

"What if I don't get a new boss right away?"

She stared at the file. "You already have a new boss. His name is Jester Rana. And here's a plus. We've used him before."

CHAPTER TWENTY-TWO

My new boss, Jester Rana, was clearly shaken up about the situation. A pleasant gray-haired man in a drab suit with a corn kernel pinned to the lapel, fit but hardly frisky, he squirmed, clasped his hands together, and apologized as we sat in my lab among the bacterial tanks.

"I don't know how to say this. Oh geez. I'm sorry for your loss. Bux was an ambitious guy. And you're ambitious. Two peas in a pod you were. Your project is genius. The transfer of power will take some time and some ding-dong paperwork, and by golly, don't you need a vacation? All the success must be exhausting." He looked at the ceiling and its corn-fiber tiles. A dusting of dirt hung off them because Cochton Enterprises was cheap about cleaning.

"Vacation? Now?" Of all the bosses I could get stuck with on the rebound, I had to be saddled with someone who found me unattractive. I wasn't going to let him squiggle out of his responsibility. I hadn't the time. Obviously, he was the person who would need those white handcuffs. If I didn't see the corn kernel for myself, I'd swear he'd never touched a woman. I turned the conversation to our project, hoping that by using a little subtext, we could discuss this in a rational manner. "We must go at this hard. Timidity isn't the right direction. The bacterial studies are only in infancy."

"Infancy." He shifted uncomfortably and stuck with his ceiling gazing, wiping his eyes. "Yes, that's a word for it." He rubbed his eyes again.

"If you don't look up, you don't get ceiling dust in your eye," I said. "Respectfully, we must move forward on all aspects of this project, no matter how uncomfortable."

"It gives me the heebie-jeebies. The word from the bird is the WasteBin is too deadly for the long haul."

"Deadly? We've got kids there. It's a camp with ice cream and zip lines."

"The per capita murder rate is out of this world."

"No one said *you* had to go there. However, we must work together to complete what Sir Bux started." I pretended to wipe away tears. "In respect of his memory."

"You've been through heck and back with your work in the boondocks. Take the month off. By golly, how about two?"

The smell of burning plastic was strong as I walked to XX Success. The Agros were agitated, and taking some of their kids hadn't done much to soothe them. What was I even going to do with myself with no job for two months and the rejection of my boss? I was supposed to be getting my status, a success, not walking the sidewalk in the middle of the day. An Agro woman with a child left Mom's clinic as I entered, unable to hide my emotions.

"What's wrong?" Mom said. Fortunately, the place was empty and we were free to talk. "How was the fertilization?"

I smacked my fist into my palm. With each day, I fathomed NezLeigh's frustration. "I didn't get the procedure yet. It was a preliminary exam. Mom, my new boss wants nothing to do with me."

"He's in shock. Your old boss died. Give him time. Is he holding up your procedure?"

"He sure is. Mom, you know how people always say there's a dark side to InVitro? There's no in vitro about it."

"The babies aren't started in test tubes?"

"No! Our male bosses are the fathers of our babies, who get modified after conception done the old-fashioned way."

"A harem scheme? I've never heard anything more distasteful," she said, her eye on the door. "Or inefficient."

"No kidding. It's harebrained. And since when has Cochtonville done anything the natural way? As I recall, that makes it a Word Crime. If I want full status, I must go through with it. The problem is, my new boss is the opposite of a lecher. He's a prude. He's not going to get the job done."

"He needs some persuading. I'll call Jane. You can get a loose sexy style. I've got perfume with pheromones." She went to the shelves and rummaged through them.

"I'm on mandatory vacation until further notice."

"Nonsense. The spill left many men like him. All it takes is persistence. He mustn't shirk his duty."

"Mom, *I'm* uncomfortable with sexual persuasion. If he doesn't want to, he doesn't want to." This was a revelation to me as much as to Mom. I'd gone along with NezLeigh's hokey rescue plan to get Remmer to sleep with me. It'd worked, too. At least for today, I'd had enough of deceiving people. Mom chose not to hear me as she walked up and down the fragrance aisle, inspecting her collection of scents.

"Tell me more about the new boss," she said, a green bottle in hand.

"He's Dad's age. He's not bad looking for a gray-haired dude. He's humble. He's not a 'sir' or anything. He works in organic synthesis—you know, making additives and such. He avoids eye contact. He has the most unappealing name—Jester Rana."

Mom's face fell. "It can't be." She shoved the bottle back onto the shelf. "Cali, I'm so sorry."

"Why?"

"He's Jane's husband. Not only are they completely old school, all they have is each other."

My hand flew to my mouth. "He's a husband? *Jane's* husband! It's practically incest. I hope she doesn't know about it. No. I can't. Never. I wish I wasn't at such a dead end."

"We need a stand-in. Let me think about any clients who would let you borrow their boss."

"What are you saying?"

"The bottom line is, you need another approved boss."

"Mom, it won't work."

The squeak of the door stopped our illicit conversation. A tall customer in a gray, hooded jumpsuit and pointed shoes came in, a shimmering scarf over the nose, a shawl over the shoulders, weirdly dressed for what seemed like an imitation of an InVitro woman of status.

Sweat popped up on my forehead. I'd broken the law by telling Mom about the InVitro dark side and now here was someone new, a wing of the Washers no doubt.

"May I help you?" Mom asked calmly.

"Yes. I need some Bone-B-Strong and Peeptide Power," the customer said, reading off a note and mispronouncing "peptide." I clutched the counter. I would know those eyes anywhere. Yes, it was him. It was Rem. I didn't know what to do. I was humbled and yet panicked by my feelings for him and my confusion. Was this some sort of Washer trap?

"This is XX, which means women," Mom said. "You are a man, aren't you?"

"Is it so obvious?" His shoulders slumped as she stared at his list. "May I still shop here?"

"Of course. We can serve you, but I'm curious. Are you here for a customer? We have loyalty discounts."

"Yes. I'm Lady LouOtta Maliegene's pool boy and errand boy. I'm called Enane," he said.

I'd been youthfully optimistic we'd meet again, but not like this

—he as a powerful woman's pool boy. My heart leapt from my body at the sight of him, worsened by the sight of him without me.

"You are? Where is she if I might ask? She's a frequent customer," Mom asked.

Rem was flustered by her questioning. "Marble stairs. Heels. Wine. She injured her wrist and sent me in her place."

He was killing me with his failure to recognize me. "Rem," I said, his name squeezing from my throat. "Rem, it's me. Cali."

"Cali," he said blankly. "Yes, Cali!" We stood there, each afraid to make a move. "I'm not myself. I'm a manservant."

"Don't be ashamed. You're here and I'm here as you always wanted. We are together in Cochtonville."

I couldn't get my head out of Cochtonia's norms and societal expectations. I was paranoid, not free as I had been when Rem and I were together in the wild. My pride, my need to save face and most of all my fear that LouOtta or maybe the Report 'Em Raw Icon would find a way to destroy our lives had me hobbled. I was like the deer by the river with its head trapped in a Cochtonville Days bucket. He might already be in love with her. He was healthy and taken care of, fed and clothed and loved, yes. I had to admit he was no doubt loved and cherished as he deserved to be. Or was jealousy or outright phobia altering my perception of his situation? I was afraid to rush into his arms and endanger him and embarrass myself.

"You're in society, as you always wished," I said. "How do you like it?"

"It's not all I'd dreamed of. At times, I'm confused. Do you all wear painful shoes? These pinch. She says she and I can share our pain. Her wrist pains her and I must have pain."

"I'll add some medication for pain," Mom said. "I wish I had some for BS."

"We don't always wear painful shoes. They are forbidden in labs, for example," I said.

He took them off. "Do you have a trash receptacle? I'll tell her I lost them. Cali, I'm so glad I found you."

Mom took the shoes. "I've heard so much about you. Why don't you two finish your conversation in the back while I find a new home for these and get your order together? I'm expecting someone any minute. You'll be safe back there if you speak softly."

We made our way to the room where Mom stored her supplies. Among the boxes and empty jars and vials, when the door behind us clicked shut, he grabbed me and kissed me. Our first kiss was gentle as we dipped our toes back into each other. His hands moved through my hair, freeing it from its sweep. I pulled him close. Everything dead in me sprang to life. His filled-out body, his lips, his silky hair hidden by the hood took my breath away, and my fear of the Vice Patrol washed away.

"We don't have much time. This looks uncomfortable." I unbuttoned his jumpsuit. Our hands slipped across and beneath each other's corn fiber clothing. His skin was clean, shaven, and smelled mossy and wild. The excitement of him, forbidden him, had me panting. We whispered each other's names over and over. I hadn't forgotten the joy of being held, the way the world came crashing down around me, the hope, the freedom. Yes, the freedom. Where was my bracelet? Did it matter? Cochtonville wasn't known for its fertility. Falling into his soul again left me wiping away my tears. I was no longer alone.

He touched my cheek with his soft finger. "Aren't you going to leave the crying to me?"

"I've missed you." I'd never wanted anything as much as this moment.

"I've missed you, too."

He unbuttoned my high-end shirt. I stretched back, allowing his caress. "This is wrong. I'm owned by Lady LouOtta," he said, his lips on my breasts.

I could stand no more. I slipped my hands in his pants. He was wearing a thong. "She doesn't own your heart."

"I'm her servant."

"Can she own me, too? I want to be with you. I can keep house."

"It's wrong to be owned at all. We're not free to love."

Every bit of me was in dire need. Despite his reluctant words, he was ready.

"How about a thrust for freedom?"

Relaxed, sheepish, fully-dressed except for his shoes, we went into the store, our pinkies touching. Mom and Jane were there. Mom busted me right away.

"Cali found her lost love," Mom said. "They've reconnected."

"I'll be darned. A man! How did she find him? How did she lose him?"

"We met in the wild," I said. "Society parted us."

"We were parted against our will," Remmer added cautiously.

"He's Lady LouOtta's pool boy. Her Crisper," Mom said. "He's dressed as a female on an errand for her. She's under the weather and sent him here in disguise. I guess she thought we wouldn't let men in."

Jane's face fell. "Heavens, what are you saying? She's got him dressed like a wild boar. All covered up on a hot day. Has she lost her mind?"

Nonplused, Remmer held out his hand tentatively. "Pleased to meet you. I'm called Enane these days."

"I'm Jane," she said, taking his hand. "LouOtta rents you. You poor guy. Other than this getup, is she treating you well?"

"Sadly, I'm allowed an even more limited range here than back in the wild. However, I'm fed abundantly. Beef, pork chops, chicken wings. It seems like much, causing bowel complications at times. Yet I eat less than many Crispers, I am told. Lady calls me her Bargain Booty. She must be a powerful huntress as she captures the best of meats even while dressed in tight clothes and uncomfortable shoes that make her trip. I was given tight shoes as well, but after seeing Cali again, I was inspired to remove mine for safety purposes."

"I understand. My husband hates tight shoes for me or him. Aren't you a sight? Despite her ridiculous clothes, you've got 'man' written all over you. Look at those massive feet!"

His masculinity affirmed, Remmer gushed information and Jane listened. "I am reminded every day to be grateful and—and— by golly, I try. I don't dress in plastic bags anymore," he said.

"Plastic bags? Since when does a Crisper dress in trash?"

"I'm an older Crisper. I was taken from my mother years ago, trained, declared defective, and sent to the WasteBin where I met Cali. At the WasteBin, we used the resources on hand; plastic bags are abundant. Recently, I was removed from the wild and re-homed. By golly, it's been an adjustment."

Her face went slack. "An older Crisper. How much older? When's your birthday?"

"I don't remember exactly. Why do you ask?"

She dug in her purse and took out her phone. She held up her background photo—an adorable red-headed boy with a shy smile —next to his face. Rem stood wide-eyed, as if he was being scanned by the Vice Patrol. The eyes. The eyes matched! Jane and I drew in our breaths.

"I know you," Jane said slowly.

"One time, I had a birthday cake with sparkling candles with colored flames. My dad was a-a—"

"A chemist," I said, with a rush of understanding. I grabbed Mom's arm.

"Junior?" Jane said, her voice shaking.

Remmer struggled to comprehend. "Junior? The name has a familiar ring."

She pulled the hood from his head. His hair tumbled out and fell over his tawny eyes. She stood on tiptoe and brushed it to one side. "If you aren't Junior Rana I'll eat my curling iron."

"That's who I am! My name is Junior!" His eyes grew watery. "Mom?"

"Your name was Junior, my son."

He held out his arms. "Mama? Mama, hold me!"

They embraced and their sobs were so deeply intimate and primal, I put my arm around my own mother as I mopped my eyes.

Jane wiped her cheeks and his. "Junior, are you happy?"

"I want to be home with those who love me."

"I'm going to make it happen. You get that woman back here. I'll take care of everything."

The following Saturday, Lady LouOtta sat in Jane's chair as the stylist teased and subtly dripped depilatory into her hair.

"You took a nasty fall?" Mom examined LouOtta's wrist. Wearing my safety goggles and lab coat over a nondescript skirt and blouse, I looked over her shoulder. I'd changed my hairstyle to an asymmetrical shorter cut. Fortunately, she was too self-absorbed to recognize me from the contest with this slight modification.

"That's not your only problem. Your hair is coming out in clumps. Doctor, a diagnosis. Pronto." Jane held some strands of hair in LouOtta's face. They were from her stash of hair extensions but matched LouOtta's shade.

I leaned forward and examined LouOtta's scalp. "She has testosteritis," I said firmly. "The worst case I've ever seen."

LouOtta's hand flew to her head. "Tetoser—what?"

"Too much testosterone. You have a son and an errand boy. It's overwhelming your hair."

"Do something! I already look like a wreck with this swollen wrist. I can't go bald."

"We have an at home treatment. It's costly but it works slick," said Jane.

I added, "It neutralizes the testosterone and restores the scalp."

"How much?"

"Gee whiz. A bundle. Five hundred Clarences a month. Maybe more if that doesn't do it. The success rate is sixty percent."

LouOtta sat up. "Robbery."

Jane tapped her forehead with her index finger. "Using my noggin here, I'd suggest you can turn in your boy. He's the cause."

"Not a chance. I need arm candy."

"The excess testosterone in your home is making you go bald," Mom said.

"Bald? I can get a hair transplant cheaper than your product."

"You'll need more than one," Jane added.

Mom said, "I'll tell you what. Our doctor on staff will take him to the back room and give him a testosterone extraction procedure while I cast your wrist."

LouOtta grumbled. "How much is this going to be?"

"First one is free. If we see improvement, one Bert per treatment."

"It's cheap enough. Enane, give it your best shot."

I took Rem's muscly arm. "This way, sir."

We made our way to the back room. I lifted my skirt. He undid his pants. If I got pregnant from this, I would say it was his dad's and allow the state-sponsored modifications. Of course, his dad and I would need to hightail it to the clinic and go through the motions, something neither of us wanted. It was the only way to free his son. Rem and I were in a hurry. I wanted my chance to rent him—forever.

"This procedure won't hurt a bit," I said.

He wrapped me in his arms and laid me down on the cool floor. He was utterly good at his task. In less than two minutes he left me grateful, with a growing dependency on these erratic visits when LouOtta had an appointment and chose to bring him to carry her purse and fell for an excuse to let him out of her sight.

"Let him rest for the remainder of the day," I said breathlessly, as we made our trembling entrance back into the store. The quickie was as explosive as sodium azide and left me as blasted.

"It's not going to happen. He's got to clean the pool and I get to watch."

"When can I see you again? Bring yourself and your boy for

treatment. This is a serious matter. We need to monitor it," Jane said.

"I can't be pinched by this place and your phony doctor every time I drop a hair." She put her hand to her head and brushed away falling clumps.

Mom said, "Come visit our booth at Cochtonville Days and I'll give you a coupon for fifty percent off products and five free testosterone reductions for your boy."

He held out his arm to her and helped her from her chair.

"Well, leave some of it. Otherwise, what good is he?" She handed Rem her purse.

"Free facials, free tooth whitening. See you at Cochtonville Days," Jane called as they walked out the door. "Bring Enane."

Jane put her hand on her heart. "There goes my baby. I can't stand to think of him eternally in her clutches. Each day I die a little more. He hasn't even met his daddy yet."

"This situation has me exhausted," I said.

Mom said, "Don't get too complacent, Cali. I've got a delivery for you. Tomorrow you're bringing LouOtta a get-well package and delivering a message to your beau—he and LouOtta must come to Cochtonville Days."

"Tell him I'll be there waiting with his daddy," Jane said. "He's got to meet him."

"I can't get near the rich part of town," I said. "Washers will be all over me."

"She's on my subscriber list. I'll notify her about the free delivery. She'll bite. You'll have a day pass." Mom went to her shelves and pulled out a moon-shaped bottle. "I'll free your beau and get rid of your dad at the same time. Let's give both of them a little snooze and when they wake, they'll change their minds about what they want in life."

CHAPTER TWENTY-THREE

As I surveyed the white two story with a semicircular window above the door, every hair on my skin raised and every extremity rushed with blood. A security camera was tucked into a white vase decorated with dancing maidens sitting beside the front door. I didn't walk onto the porch.

Holding the basket of hair and skin products, I crept to the backyard where the glistening swimming pool sat open. My fingers dug into the vinyl siding as I peeked around the corner of the house. Remmer was there, seated on a lawn chair, kneading a plump pink pillow between his legs. The sun shone upon his lightly browned skin. He was shirtless and the muscles in his arms rippled as he mashed the pillow. The muscles on his chest tightened and the skin around his perfect belly button was flat, smooth, and tan. I was embarrassed by my hungry gaze and focus on his navel. He was more than that and I was better than this, wasn't I?

"I hope you are satisfied with the massage," he said gently to the pillow. I burned with jealousy. He was practicing giving LouOtta a backrub! The only thing that kept me from running out to confront him was the Roman urn at the edge of the patio. Certainly it contained a security camera. Remmer caressed the pillow as I scanned the area for something to toss over the prying urn. The gift basket contained a headband, but it was too rectangular and of thin material. Rem rubbed the offending pillow on his cheek.

"So soft," he said tenderly. He closed his eyes, his relaxed face sweet and innocent; I could understand why he wasn't on the stripper circuit. He hadn't an ounce of bad boy. Hastily, I unbuttoned my shirt and, creeping forward, slipped it over the urn to block the camera.

"Drop the pillow."

Remmer startled in surprise and flung the pillow to the cement.

"Cali! What brings you here? Is this a dream? I've been longing for you."

"I'm delivering this gift basket for Lady LouOtta. A token of customer appreciation."

"She's off hunting. They call it 'work,' as you probably know." He stood up and came over to me. I was still angry about the pillow.

"Yes, I do know. I'll leave the gift. I bear a message for you from your mother: come to Cochtonville Days. Your father will be there."

"My father! How wonderful. And tragic. I can't get there without my owner."

"You'll have to convince her. With a backrub or whatever you've been doing with her."

My jealousy flowed out like lava. She had him. I did not. I couldn't see anything else. I must've looked and sounded as boiling as I was inside.

"You're angry? Would *you* like a massage? She's instructed me to improve my skills."

"I'm your test dummy for her? No." I tossed down the basket. A headscarf and tubes of lotions and hair products poured out. A Squats for Locks Conditioner rolled into the pristine blue pool with a tiny splash and bobbed, cap up. Remmer stood and went to the side of the pool. He was wearing a suit tighter and smaller than his plastic bag pants. With a quick motion, he dove with barely a splash and retrieved the product. As water glistened over his body, he set it on the edge of the pool and hoisted himself out.

"You can swim? And dive?" I said as he shook drops from his hair.

"Yes. I've had lessons."

"From *her*."

"No. After I was captured and you and I were separated, I was fostered for a few days by a woman with a pool. Her Crisper taught me to swim. I could teach you. You'd have to trust me."

"Here? Now?"

"Yes. Would you like a swimming lesson? I'll bribe the nanny with something from your gift basket and Lady LouOtta won't be the wiser."

"Tell the nanny Dr. Van Winkle makes house calls. If she asks, I came to give you an extraction."

"I've been needing one," he said. "You may wish to take off more garments. For swimming."

His eyes were on me the whole time as I undressed slowly, folding my pants and undergarments and placing them on the lawn chair. Rem took my hand and we walked down the plastic pool stairs, into the bright waist-deep water. I drew in my breath at the coolness and the memory of being stuck in the middle of the creek.

"Trust me. Put your face in the water. Don't breathe it. Lady Maliegene wears some sort of cap to keep her hair dry."

Upon hearing this I thrust my head under the water, proving to myself how different I

was than my rival InVitro. I drippingly came up for air. He held out his arms and drew me close. I was naked in LouOtta's pool with her Crisper. The fear of being caught made me want Remmer even more.

He took my hands. "Hold me and kick your legs in the water. That's it. One thing I've always admired about you, besides your ability to fight for what you love and make conversation, is your strong legs. You have an office job but outdoor gams."

I kicked, strong in the rushing water.

"I'm going to let go and walk back. Move your arms and swim to me."

I thought I might explode, being so bare and so close. I pulled my arms through the water viciously, as if it was an enemy, gliding into his arms, kissing him as hard as I could. He lifted me in a fireman's carry—maybe the InVitro clinic had been right about our child—and carried me to LouOtta's house.

His bedroom—a ten by ten kid-sized space with an adjacent tiled shower—was in a corner of the house off of the pool. A large mirror to one side and a portrait of Lady Maliegene, her mouth open in song in an unflattering way, over the bed were the only furnishings other than the single bed with a white comforter. Remmer took off his suit and hung it in the shower.

"Welcome to my luxe digs. The sheets are made from corn tassels. Feel them." He pulled me down onto the small, silky bed. Our naked skin on the slippery covers and the forbiddenness of the moment filled me with runaway excitement.

"Come here," I said. "I want you more and more."

"Your wish is my command."

I put my hand on his chest to stop him. "What do *you* want? You have a right to want something."

"I only want you." He fell on me like an animal, kissing me and nibbling my neck forcefully.

"And hurry."

He loved me until tears poured forth and streamed down my cheeks.

"Shall we go for two?" he said, his body slick with sweat.

"Yes." Once again, he was mine. And again. And again.

After, we rested in lavishness. I was convinced all I needed was some time and this pleasurable intercourse would be a daily occurrence. We could be friends again and hang out, chatting about philosophy. "I'm almost a full InVitro. I'm going to rent you away from LouOtta. Then we can be together."

"I will still be a servant?"

"Only in the eyes of society. At home we'll be equals."

"I see. When will this happen?"

"I must have a child first and allow him to be modified. He is to be a fireman."

"I see."

"You will be the father of the child."

"I see."

"We don't have many choices," I added. It piqued me, the way I was with my love and satisfied, on my way to greatness, newly educated in the art of swimming, and still, Cochtonia limited our happiness.

He pulled his arm from behind my head and sat up. "Crispers are not permitted to be fathers. We are medicated accordingly. I've been on it for a month, ever since I was rented."

"Will it wear off?"

"I don't know." He wiped away a tear. "I can't rescue us. I can't. This is as good as it gets. We must appreciate the here and now."

I floundered hopelessly for a moment, my brilliant plan shot down. The futility of our existence as a couple and the thought of the rest of my life without him, and he without me, washed me with emptiness and an even deeper desperation.

"Stop sounding like Layal. I still want you. I still want to be with you. We'll find a way. Meet me at Cochtonville Days. We'll go from there."

A car pulled into the driveway. It was the end of the work day. We'd lost track of time.

"It's her," he said with a trace of panic. "Where's the gift?"

"By the pool," I said. I grabbed one of his towels, did a quick mop up, and dashed out the door. I dressed in a rush and gathered up the products. Leaving the headband and some hand lotion for the nanny, I straightened my back and marched to the front door. In truth, I'd had my back against the wall so many times as of late that it was starting to meld with the wall. I ran my fingers through my hair and rang the bell. My stomach was eating itself and acid burned in my throat. Despite this, I saw no other way out. I had to pretend I belonged here.

The nanny opened the door. The house was white with highlights of gold but sparsely furnished. LouOtta sat on a canvas couch, her cooing baby on her lap. This was so different from the bitch who came into Mom's shop. Despite her mean prejudices, even she was capable of loving—at least at times. Was Mom's plan to drug her and get her to see the world in a different light going to harm this mother-child bond? It wasn't as if her views were fully her own—our society had nurtured them because seeing the Agros as pests to poison, underpay, and strip of their land helped make money for the empire. Thinking you were better and deserved more was modeled by the Cochtons. Even I did it.

"What do you want?" said the nanny with irritation.

"Special delivery for Lady LouOtta Maliegene," I said, handing the gift basket to the nanny.

"We didn't order anything," the nanny said suspiciously.

"It's fine," said LouOtta, her focus on the baby. "I've been expecting it." She rubbed her nose on the baby's tenderly as he giggled. "How's my little man? Mommy's had a terrible day at work showing her face and repeating slogans for Cochtonia."

LouOtta's cooing put me off. I didn't want to see her care for anything but herself. I needed to hate her completely. The nanny took the basket and slipped a tube of lip balm into her jumper pocket.

"Your eight seconds on the porch are done, scram."

I bowed, turned, and walked toward XX, cursing the here and now. *She* was smooching her baby. Remmer and I had been too afraid to kiss goodbye.

CHAPTER TWENTY-FOUR

Cochtonville Days was a celebration of pride and feasting. Of all Cochtonville's holidays, it was the most bacchanalian. Local vendors sold sandwiches and corn-based items in the town square —corn bread, candy corn, deep fried corn, corn on the cob, corn pudding, corn chowder, corn fritters, and popcorn in the now horrifying plastic buckets with a smiling corn cob.

The Agros sold corn pie, corn dogs with corn pesto, and their own version of moonshine made from fermented corn. Their stands were white-washed plywood tied together with plastic ties, and they sat in front of them in lawn chairs when business was slow. Many carried a baby. Their kids ran to and fro with their corn cob buckets, the sight of which made my head nearly explode. The kicker was, the kids were out in the light, many without sunglasses. Mom had been curing them! They knew her and showered her— and us—with slices of pie, flimsy plastic plates of food, and too many drinks for Dad.

Jane and Mom set up a table and offered free tooth whitening and toothbrushes. The nannies and InVitros stopped by the free goods. Pulled along for the ride, Dad, wearing his pickle-green uniform, spent his time lounging nearby in a teetering lawn chair with a burn hole in the back from a previously popping ember.

Although Mom was slowly teaching Purceel her craft, the Agros had no interest in the shallow conformities of Cochtonian beauty; Purceel was more eager to watch the parade than she was to learn about tooth whitening. She stood at the curb waiting, eating the bounty of delights, and on occasion, raising her sunglasses. Remmer's dad and I took a post nearby, keeping an eye on her and nervously scouting for Remmer in the pressing crowd. LouOtta would certainly stop for tooth whitening, wouldn't she? Weaving through the people, Nell came by with a basket.

"Care to try the latest vaccine? It's free. I insist."

"On a sugar cube?" I asked.

"Yes. It's an attenuated version."

Nell fluttered in and out of my life at opportune times. Although I found it weird she wasn't boldly proclaiming this vaccine was a generous gift from the Cochtons, from whom all good things flowed—or maybe because of it—I took a cube. It tasted like corn sweetener. She held the basket out to Jester.

"Did I approve this?" he said, taking one. "I don't recall any paperwork on a vaccine project."

"It went through under Sir Bux," Nell said, holding out the basket to Mom and Jane.

"He's nervous," Jane explained. "We're meeting someone special. It's a big day. I'm his wife, Jane. Could I give you a tooth whitening in exchange for this vaccine?"

"I'll catch you later. I've got lots of cubes to give out."

"Did you expense this? I didn't sign a thing," Jester said.

"Last quarter. Enjoy your big day. There's sure to be plenty of excitement for all." She turned and wove through the crowd.

Sirens marked the start of the parade. People lined both sides of the street, inside the square where we were set up and across the street in front of the clothing shops, meat markets, bakeries, and department store. We watched from our table, over the heads of the citizens who'd spread their blankets out near the curb. The procession began with the tribute to Dusters, the men who applied pesticides by airplane, the Agro men, both needed and despised.

They handed out tiny plastic planes to the crowd to show how harmless their applications were, despite the birth defects their families endured. Next, the largest hogs in Cochtonville were displayed on flatbed trucks as crowds clapped and oohed and ewwed, particularly when the boar with eight-inch testicles passed by, lounging on his side, letting it all hang out. The female pigs came next, admired for their evenly spaced teats.

Following the pigs, the Washers held their weapons as they walked down Cochton Boulevard, turned on Aiyn Cochton Street, then onto Bert Cochton Road, and took another turn onto Clarence Cochton Avenue as they followed the parade route. There had to be a hundred of them. Many were mature men like Eve's dad and women like Ursula, but sprinkled among them were what looked like younger men—undoubtedly modified. Yes, of course, here's where a wave of InVitro babies was headed. They wouldn't question.

Next came floats of corn varieties, blooming out of flatbeds, each variety taller than the previous one. This was followed by tractors from every year Cochtonville had been in existence—fifty tractors, traffic-jam slow in single file. Some flew tiny flags on poles behind the driver, and at their appearance we did the forehead finger. I got a dull headache.

The parade ended with the march of men who had earned the Order of the Pig, all dressed like poor Bux. The parade was concluded by the flag bearer, requiring us to do the forehead finger yet again. I needed to cut my fingernails.

I searched for Remmer in the crowd. Had he convinced LouOtta to attend even though she wasn't part of the ceremonies? I moved to a spot where I could see the stage on the town square. It was as it had been when I'd launched my bid for InVitro status: a poured concrete slab, fifteen feet of gold-and-green curtains held up by three giant concrete hands. On one side of the stage, a gold helicopter rested. On the other, the Camp Cochton bus. The vehicles of Aiyn and her brothers hovered eerily close to each other, but what did it mean for us?

Six feet up, the mayor welcomed the citizens to the crowning ceremony. The women who vied for the crown of Miss Cochtonville came forward to be measured by the mayor and Norman Allen, city manager. The stage was crowded with dozens of females for good reason: the prize was a ride in the Cochton helicopter parked next to the stage, cash, and InVitro status. It surprised me to see Eve up there, smiling in a tight Camp Cochton t-shirt, khaki shorts, and hiking boots. Even dressed down, she outshone the others. She was taller, her hair shinier, her smile wider. She didn't need this. But she could take it. I had to admit, she was evenly spaced. This had to be part of her plan to make Camp Cochton a colony of its own. But what did it have to do with freedom?

"This is disgusting." It was Lady Maliegene, and she was correct this time. The measuring contest *was* disgusting. My heart beat so hard I could hear it, for Remmer was at her elbow, dressed in formal pants, a short-sleeved shirt, and a black tie. He looked like he should be handing out pamphlets instead of carrying her purse and a grotesque Cochtonville Days bucket, the plastic corncob smiling inanely. With his shy smile and swimmer's body wrapped in the innocent clothing, Rem was sexy enough to turn the head of Aiyn Cochton's statue.

"It's him," I told his dad as we moved closer.

"Lady LouOtta Maliegene," Jane exclaimed, rushing over to her. "You know what would help you climb on top of the world? Tooth whitening. And a toothbrush for your boy. He's one of the best looking there is. Step this way. How long do you have him?"

"You can stop poking your nose into my Crisper. This is the second time you've tried to get your hands on him. You're old enough to be his mother and I wouldn't call you a success."

"At least let me introduce him to my husband." Jane pulled Jester close. "Enane, I'd like you to meet Jester Rana."

The men shook hands, holding each other with their gaze, both blinking back tears. Washed over with stress, I knew I couldn't live like this—a father and son not even daring to hug when meeting after twenty years apart. I put my hopes in Eve and her plan, whatever it was.

"Why would you introduce them? Have you lost your mind? Enane, enough. Stop gripping his hand like you're pumping ethanol." Remmer pulled his hand free at LouOtta's insistence.

Chubby and holding a corndog dripping pesto sauce in one hand and a toy plane in another, Purceel ran up to Mom. "I saw my dad in the parade."

"Do you want to go home?" Mom asked. "I can help you find him."

"No." She threw her arms around Mom's waist, rubbing a thin green line of sauce on Mom's shirt. "I want to be a medic."

"One of the Pestos a medic? Your wishful thinking is making you a doddering fool, Dame Van Winkle."

Dad put down his cup of white lightening. "Watch what you say about my wife."

"Wife? Is this moldy creature your husband?"

I pushed LouOtta onto a folding chair next to Dad. "Do I see a coffee stain on your canine?"

"It is! Let's whiten it," Jane added, looking into LouOtta's mouth.

Dad smiled at LouOtta, his eyes squinty and half closed, his bottom lip droopy. "I don't think *she* needs to change a thing. You might have a tiny stain but you wear it well."

"I'll try the strips," LouOtta said curtly. "And hurry."

Once more, Nell came by. "Vaccine?"

Dad took a cube and put it on his tongue. "Akk, terrible. I'd rather be sick." He spit it out onto the ground. In response, Mom took a cube from Nell and gave it to Purceel. Remmer stood unmoving next to LouOtta.

"What's it for?" LouOtta asked.

"An emerging virus that jumps from hogs to people."

"How ridiculous. Hogs don't cause disease." She waved Nell away.

"At least let your boy make a choice," Jane insisted.

"Don't involve him in your conspiracy theories."

Encouraged by her mention of conspiracy, Dad leaned toward LouOtta. "You're one smart woman. I'm sure you've heard of the White Hand of oppression."

Her nose wrinkled as if she'd smelled a blue flamer. "One more word from you and I'll call the Vice Patrol."

"My, my," Jane positioned two strips across LouOtta's teeth.

Jane went over to Dad. "Open wide. You got more stains than a nursery floor."

LouOtta's head slumped and she snored.

"Sweet dreams," said Dad, nodding off.

"The whitener contained the potion. It's a mild sedative," Mom said. "We reserved treated strips for these two hooligans."

"And they're out!" Jane said triumphantly, then turned to Remmer. "He's a little fatter and grayer than you may remember, but he's got the same heart of gold. Junior, meet your father."

"Dad?" Remmer said. "Is it you?"

Jester held out his arms. "Junior!" The two men bear hugged and the tears flowed. A group of women, staggering from the corn liquor, bumped into them and fell to the ground, but the father and son kept each other in embrace.

"I'm sorry, son," Jester said, looking up at Remmer through tears. "I shouldn't have let you be taken from us."

"I almost forgot you, Dad."

"Son," said Jester. "We must plan your freedom while this owner of yours is asleep."

On the stage, the Miss Cochtonville finalists were announced.

"How long will LouOtta be asleep, Ma?"

"At least an hour. She'll wake up groggy and we can negotiate your release while her mind is vulnerable."

Remmer put an arm around me. "Mama, that's illegal. You can't drug a lady. Life could get worse."

The city manager made an announcement. "And our last finalist is iconic Lady Eve Whitehead."

"Lady Eve has something up her sleeve," I said. "Listen..."

"Eve can have some far-fetched ideas. Our safety together depends on me being complacent, Lady Van Winkle," Rem said with excess carefulness. He could have a career as a bomb defuser, if we had bombs here instead of only singing about them.

"Let's give her scheme a chance...whatever it is."

"It's making me nervous." Remmer removed his arm from my shoulder and we stood in silence, watching the show unfold. I reminded myself his caution was one quality I liked in him. He didn't shoot off his mouth or make reckless decisions.

Norman Allen spoke excitedly. "And now our finalists will vie for the crown with their talents. Give Icon Report 'Em Raw your attention. And remember, ladies, you can look at men but no touching without the proper status and paperwork or Report 'Em will write you up and out."

"Folks, sex is a perk," she said.

"We'd love to see your perky talent."

The Report 'Em Raw sang "Bombs and Tassels" enthusiastically with arm motions. The next contestant, Keep It Tidy, sang the anthem as well, but with tassels on her breasts that shook when she shimmied in an imitation of corn in the wind or possibly a urine shower. It might have been taken for sacrilege had she not kept a sincere smile on her face. The contest so far was a predictable bust. People in Cochtonville didn't have talent.

Norman Allen fumbled with his pen-sized microphone. "Good show from our important Icons. Next up is one who could be called a Mega Icon. Her camp for the Pestos is a roaring success. All we need is to round up a few more of the little buggers and get them the help they need."

A low hiss came from the multitude. The remark didn't sit well with the Agro women. The upstanding—but drunk—citizens of Cochtonville cheered to cover up the discontent of the Agros. It was a crime to hint all was not well.

Norm brushed away a fly buzzing into his microphone. "This Icon is as clever as she is talented. Please welcome Lady Beautiful and Damned."

The crowd grew silent. Eve had no reason to be here. Even drunk women knew something was going down with her. Back straight, one foot in front of the other, fresh from the wild, Eve stepped forward from the line of contestants with enough confidence to take down a bobcat. She took the microphone from Norm.

"Thank you, Norm, for your kind introduction. I'm sure we all *value* the contributions the Pestos have made to our society. In fact, I have a guest with me who has been an *invaluable* collaborator as I plan the future of Camp Cochton. I acknowledge her help in developing this out-of-the-box entertainment."

City Manager Norman Allen stuck his hands in his pants pockets and hunched defensively. Icons Report 'Em Raw and Keep It Tidy exchanged triumphant smiles. Eve would not be so popular with the regular citizens after sticking up for the worth of the Pestos. If this bothered Eve as the sun beamed onto her hair she didn't indicate it. Instead she launched into a monologue about traveling through Cochtonia and the rich heritage of hardworking people as a pug-nosed girl in sunglasses holding a purple pig on a leash came from the Camp Cochton bus. She led the hog up the stairs to Eve's side. Her hair combed to the best of its ability, NezLeigh walked stiffly, nervously in front of all these citizens of Cochtonville. People tittered at the sight.

"No, I won't be singing the anthem, but my proficient porker won't disappoint," Eve announced, her hand jingling in her Camp Cochton shorts.

"What a gas," said Jester. "A tame pig."

"What's this about?" asked Jane. "Didn't Lady Eve already win her status?"

"It's the Cochtons," Mom said. "They are responsible for any anomaly."

"Sooie! Yea pig!" someone yelled and the crowd took up the chant.

Lavender gawked at the pig-calling crowd. She released three grunts and a squeal. A few women whistled in appreciation. Not understanding, the pig looked right and left, expecting an old farmer to appear and give her supper. NezLeigh reached into her baggy pocket and pulled out my UTI. She beamed green light at Eve's feet. Lavender trotted calmly to Eve. Eve held up a finger.

"Sit," she commanded. Lavender waggled her purple rear while her tail spun like a fan blade. She wiggled her perky ears and gazed at Eve as Eve fumbled in her pocket. Eyes on Eve, the pig slowly plopped her magnificent buns onto the concrete slab stage.

"Good pig." Eve gingerly gave Lavender a golden kernel of corn. Flapping her ears in appreciation, the pig slurped the sugar and starch filled morsel, which also contained p-coumaric acid, a micronutrient.

Eve held out her hand. "Shake." The pig clumsily lifted a cloven hoof and Eve pumped it while slipping another treat into Lavender's flashy snout. The crowd clapped wildly.

"Now show your belly."

The pig sat on her haunches, displaying her milky teats.

"Look at her even spacing. Sing the anthem." Eve held the microphone near Lavender's snout. Lavender snuffled as she grunted and squealed enthusiastically while the throng added the words.

The city manager pulled his hands from his pockets to high five Eve after she fed Lavender her last treat. "We have a winner. You are clearly the audience favorite. Thank you to our other contestants. Girls, I think you have some tidying up to do. This crowd is trashed."

Eve's dad came forward with a crown and placed it on her head as the other contestants left the stage, understandably miffed.

"Miss Cochtonville, my lady, great things await you," the commissioner said affectionately.

Eve waited for the applause to die down. "Ladies, thank you for celebrating with us today. A generous donor has given me permission to share a special treat with you. The geneticists of Cochtonville have been working hard to make sure our newest entrepreneurs are well entertained. We are delighting the *entire population* with this unique event. Let's not say Cochtonville is lacking anything. We're not short on any resource. To prove it, I have for you, the Mr. Cochtonville Contest."

Murmurs of appreciation rippled through the gathering. Eve continued her banter, "We will crown Mr. Cochtonville. He could be one of the city's highly trained new professional Crispers or one of our owned Crispers. Crispers in the audience, come forth, show yourselves. We need to see the finest men our nation can make. The winner will receive five hundred Clarences, a year's supply of CochaCola CornSoda, and a private interview with Miss Cochtonville. Plus, a free gift basket for your InVitro."

Jester slapped Remmer on the back. "By golly, you got your mama's looks, son. Go on up there. Win the money, pay this woman who owns you for the remainder of your contract, and live like an honest man."

CHAPTER TWENTY-FIVE

Remmer focused on the packed-down grass beneath his restless feet. "Lady Maliegene is awfully jealous. She already won a year's supply of pop and a gift basket."

Jane gave Remmer an earnest hug. "Go on, Junior. It's money to win your freedom from that wretched woman. Collect the prize and pay her the remainder of your contract. You'll be rid of her."

"For a time. Then I'll be back for rent. Mom, Dad, she's not so bad," Remmer said.

"What are you saying?" I grabbed his arm.

He wouldn't look at me. "She's weak. I could do worse."

"She's weak so you're not going to try to buy your freedom? That's the dumbest excuse I've ever heard. *This* is the plan. Eve arranged a contest to free you and Layal."

"You won't be able to rent me for at least a year. I must stay with Lady Maliegene at this time. Forgive me."

I thought livid blood was going to squirt from my eyes. "No, I won't. Believe me I won't."

Remmer slouched, seemingly confused at my anger. "Cali, I've never been a fighter. I'm a lover. You said I had little choice about my life. It's true."

I lunged at him, tore the Cochtonville Days bucket from his

arm and tossed it to the ground. "I can't look at you and a stupid corn face at the same time. You aren't going to vie for your freedom? It's a setup. There aren't any other contestants."

He ran his hand down his tie nervously. "I can't go up there. Let's stick with the status quo."

"Bedding two women." I kicked the bucket and it spun into the crowd.

"I am not bedding two women. I have duty and I have love. I've been trained to believe duty is the highest calling. I can't shirk it. In my heart I can't give up love, and I can't let you turn your back on the well-situated life you've earned here."

I put my hand on my neck in stark realization. "I can't continue as is. I'm tracked everywhere I go. This is our one chance to be together. Buy your freedom and we can move back to the WasteBin and let society forget about us." My voice was humiliatingly desperate.

"I can't go back to the wild. We *are* together. You're a success. We're discreet. We can maintain our inconspicuous relationship. I can help with whatever life you choose here."

"You mean we're discrete—separated. Even if I do have a child to give up to Cochtonia and am able to rent you, we'll never be an equal couple. Meanwhile, I'm not going to be sloppy seconds. It's lonely. I'm going now. Goodbye." I turned my back on him.

"Wait," he called. I turned. He cried like a baby. I dragged up contempt for him to soothe myself. The way he wiped his eyes, the way he couldn't fight for what he cared about. It didn't stick. The contempt was for myself, not him. To get into bed with him, I'd pressured him, manipulated him as if he was my possession. I had to accept his decision or I'd hate myself.

"I'm sorry," I said. "We each have the right to make our own choice. I'll miss you."

"I'll miss you, too."

"Junior," said Jane. "You were bred to be used, but biology is only part of destiny. Didn't I teach you how to love?"

"I don't remember it."

His dad said, "By golly, you're not an animal to be owned."

"You don't know my life. Dad, Mom, I am."

"Are there any Crispers in the audience?" Eve pleaded into the crowd. "We need a contest. Cash prize and free beer during the competition courtesy of Union Station bar." She tipped her crown to the two bartenders, Wilma and Maven, operating a beer stand on the grass below the front of the stage. "I need a Crisper to get this and the free beer rolling."

People looked right and left for any Crisper, any man, who might be one. There were only a few Y chromosomes in the crowd besides vicious Washers, dirty Dusters, and aging Order of the Pigs. Those men were Jester, Dad, and Remmer.

A clutch of Agro women descended on Remmer like vultures on a run-over racoon, peppering him with questions.

"Who's your boss?"

He motioned to his owner as she blissfully snoozed. "Lady LouOtta Maliegene."

"That bitch. What's her problem?"

"Poor baby, you don't got her permission."

"Hey ladies, you're right," Remmer said, standing firm. "I got no rights and no permission. You've got the wrong man for the job." He looked to me as if I had a rescue for him up my sleeve.

"Eve needs someone," I said.

"Get the hell up there, ya fraking coward!" Two Agros hustled Remmer off as I watched, not rescuing him. When the opportunity came, I was going to the WasteBin and not looking back.

The women shoved Rem onto the stage and Lavender nosed him to the center.

"At last, a contestant from the audience," Eve said, gripping Remmer's arm tightly. "The free beer will begin its flow. Are there any more Crispers out there? He's awfully lonely up here."

He was more than lonely up there. He hyperventilated and flapped his arms nervously. With each rise and fall, Lavender's head bobbed in nightmarish synchronicity. In an attempt to soothe her, NezLeigh beamed the UTI across the stage. It was too hot for a non-sweating mammal to be agitated. The Purple Eater calmed and NezLeigh pushed the device into her baggy pocket.

Eve was eager. "Does he have a friend handy? How about another Crisper? Lend a hand. InVitros, are you hoarding them?"

Evidently, Crispers didn't get out much. Eve scanned the crowd from the Cochton helicopter at one side of the stage to the Camp Cochton bus on the other. The only Crisper in sight was trembling on the stage. After a long minute, Eve asked, "Ladies, do you want to see his stuff?"

The crowd yelled affirmations.

"Strip, strip," the women chanted. My stomach turned.

"Oh no," Eve said to the eager women. "You're enticed and at the edge of your seats. Hold yourselves. We're not there yet. I don't like to rush things. One man does not a contest make."

A grumble arose from the crowd. Someone tossed a half full cup of beer on the stage. Eve stepped on it, spattering her boot with beer, and kicked it back into the crowd.

"This day is too warm for anger. Not to worry. This man is an island, but we have an archipelago. Professionals, come on out." She pulled back the stage curtain and the cowboy, the lumberjack, and the sexy-ass Scotsman came forward, prancing one at a time, stepping in a circle around Remmer, patting his back in solidarity to calm him. The touch of friendly bros or the spotlight off of him did the trick. Remmer relaxed as each man took a turn at the front of the stage.

The cowboy tossed off his bandana and chaps after which he shook his ass in some plaid boxers. The lumberjack threw his shirt and jeans to the crowd, wiggling about in his checked boxers and tuque. The sexy-ass Scotsman ripped off his socks, his sporran pouch, and his kilt with glee. Disappointingly, he wore tartan boxers. As each man performed, Lavender watched him hungrily, hoping a cob of corn might appear in place of a human hand. Holding a crown, Norman Allen slumped at the side of the stage. It was rough being an average man in this brave new world.

A dozen Vice Patrol watched the crowd from various vantage points as the women of Cochtonville hooted and hollered and hugged each other. Watching the crowd, Ursula stood prominently near the front of the stage, flanked by what looked like young male Washers. As soon as the accolades reached their zenith, Eve held up her palm to settle things down. The Crispers snapped to attention in a line behind her. Remmer put his hands behind his back, then in front of his crotch, as if he wasn't sure what he should do with them as he stood at the edge of the stage.

"I don't believe I can watch my own boy as a Crisper," Jane said. "No offense, honey, but how many genes did they have to add to get him to do *this*?" Her husband put his arm around her and she buried her face in his chest.

"Gee whiz," he said. "Heavens to Betsy. I'm gonna have a cow."

"Thanks, darlings. The crowd's warmed up. Now, let's view our amateurs. We have one. Is anyone else out there? Anyone?" Eve searched the masses for Layal but no man came forward. A nanosecond of a frown flickered across her face. What had she expected? If he was held by the Cochtons he was probably chained in a dungeon somewhere and bled daily, not likely to be here celebrating. Eve turned to Remmer, acting as if she didn't know him.

"Well, sexy, it looks like it's up to you to entertain the masses as a privately held Crisper. Reveal what awaits a successful InVitro, and if you catch these rowdy hearts, the crown is yours. Can you tell us anything about yourself?"

Remmer coughed nervously and held his stomach.

"Come on, now, who has you?" Eve held her microphone to his mouth.

"I'm a privately held Crisper and one of the first created." This was followed by a squeal of feedback. Eve stepped back.

"Private, eh? How do we get you away from her and into our hearts?"

He cowered from the microphone. "In accordance with the law, I haven't the freedom to tell."

"We'll let a guy have his secrets. As a wise man once said, discretion is the better part of valor. When not entertaining your owner, what's something you do for fun?"

"I try to come up with—I aspire to have deep thoughts."

"Aww. How sweet. Can you tell me about your deep thoughts on women? You must have some."

"Err...each one is an individual."

"Aren't you darling? Deep Thoughts, let's see if you can beat any of these professional performers. Go on now." She playfully handed him the microphone and pushed his shoulder as his words crushed my soul. LouOtta was an individual. She'd obtained him legally. He hadn't asked for help. No matter how odious, she didn't deserve to be drugged against her will.

Remmer walked to the front of the stage, his strong chin brushing his collar. He was too afraid to face the audience. As I tried not to care, a lump swelled in my throat. He ran his hand up and down his tie and turned his back to the throng.

He sang in a strained voice, "Bombs and tassels, tassels and bombs."

The crowd stood at attention, not sure if this was an act gone awry or genuine patriotism. Crispers didn't sing the anthem, Icons did. No one wanted to be patriotic. They wanted to unleash lust.

Remmer continued. "Come...come."

He spun and faced the audience. Boldly, he loosened the tie with one hand and threw it to the crowd. They cheered in relief. It was all fun.

He tore off his shirt and tossed it to the boards, baring his fine Crisper chest, slightly less muscled than the others, giving him a boy next door look. He put the mic under his arm and unbuckled his belt. All the while the crowd screamed and pitched empty cups on stage to show appreciation. He stripped off his shoes. He didn't have socks. He struggled as he removed his pants. I had to give him credit for not falling on his face. He threw the pants to the hoard below him and stood at attention. He wore a new black thong with gold stars. It made me sick to think she'd probably dressed him in that thong.

He sang in a clear voice, something between masculine and youthful. "Stars and tassels, tassels and stars. Come sister, come shake those tassels tonight. As mates and friends burst around in ecstasy, enjoy our enterprise. Enjoy. Now shake, shake. Shake, shake."

He undulated to his improvisation. Once again, the crowd stood puzzled. Was this legal? Remmer did a two-step, dancing to one edge of the stage. He shimmied in front of Lavender and NezLeigh, who leapt forward and grabbed his rump. As he danced away, Lavender goosed him with her snout. The stares transformed into cheers of delight. It had to be legal—it was hilarious! Remmer danced to the other side of the stage. Eve caught him and gave him a kiss. He gyrated to center stage. He did the pony and added a hip thrust sequence.

"Boom!" He held his arms above his head in triumph, fixing his sexy gaze on a woman in the audience. The woman put her hands on her heart and swooned. Ursula rushed the platform. "Treason for desecrating our national song. You'll be singing the jailbird anthem."

CHAPTER TWENTY-SIX

Eve shielded Remmer in improvised defense. "He improved it. You can't arrest him, he's our only contestant. I'm crowning him Mr. Cochtonville. Come on, ladies, show your appreciation." The women hooted and clapped as Eve took the crown from Norm's limp grasp and placed it on Remmer's head. Norm handed him an envelope of money.

"Congratulations, Mr. Cochtonville."

"His prize is a citation and a fine. Where's his sponsor?" Ursula called to the crowd. "Whoever you are, you've got thirty seconds to take him home or you'll have to get him from the Receptacle."

Jane and Mom shook LouOtta to wake her but no go. Mom slipped on gloves and removed the tooth whitening strip. LouOtta's eyes fluttered. She relaxed into her chair, a drip of drool on the side of her mouth.

"We need to wait another half-life," Mom said. "Fifteen minutes."

"It's too long." Without other options, every cuss word of NezLeigh's sprouting in my brain, I walked across the uneven ground, past people sitting on blankets, past Washers, past women drinking beer, past kids munching popcorn from the inane buckets. I mounted the stage and addressed Ursula.

"I'm not his InVitro. I am a Stage One InVitro. I can't be responsible for what he did today, but I'll watch him until his InVitro comes around."

"You'll have to pay the fine and frankly, a guy like this isn't worth it," Ursula said.

"How much is the fine?"

"Four hundred Clarences."

I took the envelope from Remmer. The wind rose and ruffled the cash as I counted bills and handed Officer Ursula the envelope with most of the money. I gave the rest to Remmer and he tucked it in his thong. The remainder wasn't enough to buy freedom unless it was cheap.

"Despite a brush with the law, you're still our monarch of the hour, oh king, with your guardian by your side." Eve didn't have a clue Remmer and I had parted. I stood beside him, mad as hell at him for making my clean break from him as messy as the WasteBin.

"Crisper contestants, you are dismissed, as are you, officer. Free beer for your contributions to our happiness. King and loyal subject, I must ask you to stand near the precocious pig, for our next guest is larger than life. Clear the stage, the sponsor of the contest and the bestower of the prize wants to have a few words." Eve gripped a billowing curtain and pulled it aside.

Aiyn Cochton entered center stage. She was sharp in her pantsuit and wide-brimmed straw hat as she spoke into a microphone. "Residents of Cochtonville, lend me your ear. I have come with an offer. An offer of peace and mutual understanding. Two score and seven years ago, you were told I died at my desk at the age of thirty-six. The truth is, I was exiled for having an unapproved child." The crowd gasped. Aiyn paused to let it sink in. "Yes, I am Aiyn Cochton, the eldest and an heir to the fortune. I am the third hand holding Cochtonia. Yet my child and I were sent to the WasteBin for being imperfect. Our imperfection was called a blot upon our country's honor. For many of those years, I was both ashamed and waiting for a rescue that never came. My exile allowed me to think upon the state of affairs and the state of the Cochtonian nation. We need a new colony—a place where those who seek it can find new opportunities. I have negotiated for the voluntary release of a hundred people from Cochtonia to its new colony, Wowville. For those who surrendered your children with sorrow, you'll find them waiting at Wowville's Camp Cochton. My bus is ready to board. If you need to start anew, Wowville is the place for you."

On cue, the bus started its engine with a puff of corn smoke spurting from the tailpipe.

"We'll start an outpost of our own at the WasteBin—an area ripe with promise. I can't guarantee ease but I can promise flowers. They are the sex organs of angiosperms—more brightly colored and sweet smelling than a rainbow Crisper. It's home to the natural version of Let's Go called raspberries. Have you had one? They were once abundant here but were banished along with the truth. I modified them until the fleshy seed-bearing ovaries are massive enough to fill your mouth with pleasure."

Clouds piled up behind the Pavilion of Agriculture; its gleaming corn kernels lost their luster. The Agros talked among themselves and beckoned to their children. There must have been a million Cochtonville Days buckets leering at me from the grass. For a crazy moment, each became Remmer eating a raspberry, juice dribbling down his strong chin, back before he was mine. I had to get off this stage. My mind was going. I shook my head to rid it of the mocking image. The buckets resumed their brainless smirking. I was stuck here while Aiyn continued her monologue and the people of Cochtonville munched their popcorn.

"Now for the bad news," Aiyn said. "My son has been stolen by my brothers. He is here in Cochtonville. If my son is not returned to me so he can join in this endeavor, there will be no end to the stench. Brothers, you know where he is. I know you have him." Aiyn thrust her chest forward. "Release him if you value your health and comfort. The first thing one does when planning a new empire is recruit scientists to the cause, and yes, in my pathetic life of isolation I was able to do as much.

"Hogs are a rich source of viruses, many of which affect humans, and with the manure you sent my way, I had perfect soup to study. Unless I see my son, I'll release an unpleasant germ—a combination of pseudorabies and transmittable gastroenteritis causing infertility, itching, madness, vomiting, and diarrhea. It might be better to be dead, don't you think? I have a canister holding the virus strapped beneath my clothing. Would you, Vice Patrol, like to take a chance by shooting me? There's another one in my hat, so don't aim for the head. The vials are fragile and if I fall or you grab the wrong spot, they could—they *will*—burst. I, of course, have been vaccinated."

"She's serious. Give us Layal or things will get shitty," Eve said.

Aiyn said, "Give me my son, Cochton brothers. You've got five minutes to get Layal on this platform or I'll show you what it means from both ends."

Crows cawed. Thunder, no, a Washer van rumbled in the distance. I gripped Remmer's arm. Did he think I was in on this dastardly plan? His eyes were fixed on the crowd, on LouOtta as she stirred and yawned. Her mouth formed a horrified O as she focused on the stage and him in only his underwear. I crossed my arms, deliberately not touching him. A Washer came on stage and beamed the crowd with a device. Several women, those with concealed weapons, fainted. The door to the helicopter resting next to the stage flew open. Steps fell. Layal strutted out wearing a gold suit.

"Mother," Layal said, climbing onto the stage, swishing his hand in front of his nose as he passed the pig. "What's this imprudent inventiveness of yours?"

"Son, we're here to rescue you from your imprisonment."

"Imprisonment?"

"Yes, you've been kidnapped. I've come to take you home. I've improved the place and we'll be starting a new colony."

"Oh dear. There's been a fallacy of logic. I love you, Ma, but we

don't know each other. I'm not going back to the parsimonious
place. Mom, I have a job to do here. It's a secure position. I'm the
third Mrs. Bert Cochton's Crisper. Mother, he's old. She needs me
to comfort her, and I'm damn good at my job." He did a two-step
and brushed his fingernails on his suit to shine them.

"The hell she needs you," said Eve. "Your mother has put
herself at great risk to find you. I want you back."

"Eve, I won't forsake you. Bert has his eye on you for wife
number four—the mother of his Crisper son. He's allowed to have
as many wives as he wants. I'll take care of you and we'll live in
luxury. We're even permitted to be educated."

"I'm educated. I went to acting school."

"Eve, it's your chance. You can be a Cochton. I'm talking about
real education—philosophy, mathematics, Kama Sutra. No more
scrounging. We'll have more than enough. I won't go back. I'm in
the family at last." He held out his hand to Eve. "Join me. Mr.
Cochton likes your looks and we can share delights."

"No thanks," Eve said coldly.

"Come on, Eve. You're Miss Cochtonville. You won a ride in
the helicopter with me and *him*. Your carriage awaits."

The commissioner stood by the helicopter. "Eve, it's the only
way."

"Come bear the heir," Layal said, stretching out his hand. "I
insist. For both of us."

"Hell, no," Eve cried, spitting on his hand. "Hell, no."

Aiyn stepped forward. She wiped the spittle from Layal's hand
with her sleeve. "Son, stop the rapine pressure. She's with me.
Everyone who wants to leave has one chance to get on my bus and
ride to a new life. Son, I won't wait for you. I kept you safe for as
long as I was able. If you believe my brother will care for you, stay.
You'll always be in my heart. No matter where you are."

In defiance of thunderheads rising, sun beat on my face. Sweat
ran across my back and down my leg. A bead dripped off my nose
and splashed onto the cement. One of the Agros from the group of
mothers in the crowd rushed the stage and tossed a burning plastic

bag. The plastic peeled away; a bulging batch of flaming disposable diapers caught orange fire.

As the blaze burned brightly, heat and smoke billowing, sparks flying toward us on a gust, Layal hurried for the helicopter. NezLeigh jerked forward and dropped the leash. I knew what was to come. She was going to pitch onto the inferno and sacrifice herself. I wouldn't let her get away with it. As she leapt for the fire, I tackled her around the waist. NezLeigh struggled and kicked. Her resistance, her counter force, transformed what could have been a dangerous smack onto concrete into a slow burn across the rough surface. We rolled as the diapers smoked and Lavender squealed and NezLeigh and I tumbled off the platform.

CHAPTER TWENTY-SEVEN

I landed with a crunch on my back with NezLeigh on top of me, her hair dangling over my open mouth. The force flung my breath away.

"Is this how you show you like a person?" NezLeigh, a drip of pesto sauce in the corner of her mouth, put her hands on either side of me and shoved away.

I gasped and clutched my chest, struggling to pull together enough thoughts to convince myself I'd live. I rubbed the back of my head. Did I have a concussion? Did I see stars? Were my ears ringing? I drew one slow breath and struggled to sit up. It hurt to speak. Ursula was splayed on the stage with her HotNot coat, smothering the flames.

"What a stupid thing to do, you brainless dip. A Washer gets the glory instead of me." NezLeigh threw a discarded beer cup at the stage.

I drew a painful breath. "Glory? I-I'm not going to watch a-as you kill yourself. *She* has heat proof clothing. You don't."

"Kola might have gotten something out of it. Sometimes the family gets a reward." NezLeigh brushed herself off and hopped up, unfazed.

"Sometimes?" I gasped. "You'd burn yourself for *sometimes?*"

NezLeigh wiped her shirt with her hand. She adjusted her sunglasses. "I got lucky. These didn't break. Damn daytrippers. Nothing good happens in the light. Seriously, what was I thinking?"

"And there's...there's the colony."

"For you, dontchathink?"

"I can't think. I've been catching my breath."

"The wind knocked out. Lucky you didn't break your spine, ya dig? Stupid move on your part. Hot damn, the cups and diapers saved you."

I put my hand on my back. It was damp with an essence of beer mingled with ammonia. I turned. A mound of discarded cups and wadded disposable diapers was crushed into the ground. The bartenders rushed over to help me.

"Diapers? I landed on diapers?"

"And cups," said Wilma. "And you're bleeding." She poured beer on a scrape on my arm and dabbed me with a napkin. Another gust of wind whipped our hair and billowed the curtains on the stage. The commissioner marched over and stood behind NezLeigh.

"Don't turn around. Uh oh," Wilma said as he snaked out a hand and grabbed NezLeigh's shoulder.

"Get your pig before I make it bacon. It's tearing up the corn on the cob stand and agitating the boar." Several yards away, Lavender rooted in a box of uncooked corn while several Agros waved lawn chairs at her to shoo her away.

"And ladies, tear down your stand. Free beer is done."

The bartenders rushed to comply. NezLeigh pulled the UTI from her pocket. She flashed green light in my eyes before taking off with the Washer.

The helicopter wobbled from its spot near the stage as it rose slowly. The few people left nearby dispersed as the whir of air whipped our hair and clothes. The whoosh of the blades showered me with dust as I stood up, half-hypnotized by the rhythmic whir and slow ascent. The copter erratically tilted to one side, then the other, and bounced onto the edge of the platform in an aborted takeoff. I scooted away as it tumbled eerily to the ground and cracked blades as it hit. Dirt flew. It rested, lop-sided, at the side of the stage, an uninspiring, confusing crash.

I ran to the copter, beat only by Eve, who tugged open the door, lunged in, and pulled Layal from the wreckage. Blood poured from a gash on the side of his head and soaked his manly eyebrows. She held him in her arms as I examined his eyes. "Equal pupils. Good news for his brain. All we've got to do is get the bleeding stopped."

The Crispers clustered around.

"What can we do for you?"

"Let us help."

"We're at your service."

"Give me your tuque," I said to the lumberjack. He obediently took off his stocking cap. I pressed it on Layal's cut to stop the bleeding as the smells of beer and blood wafted. Didn't Mom say it took fifteen minutes of pressure to stop a wound?

"Go get my mom, over there." I gestured vaguely and the Crispers took off like show horses.

Remmer, in only his thong, trotted over. "Are you injured?" he asked me.

"I'm seeing stars."

"Did you hit your head?"

"No. I'm fine."

He knelt next to Layal. "Brother, how are you?"

Layal's eyes flickered. "I'm in Truth's arms."

"You're injured. Maybe this time *you'll* get the blood."

"Not a chance, bro. It's not how it works. I'm not an heir."

"Do you need any assistance?" he said to me. "Your arm is bleeding."

"It's a scratch. Everyone here is fine," I said, pressing Layal's forehead with the bloody stocking cap. "You don't need to hover."

"I want to. Believe me, I do. I have a duty. I can't leave Lady Maliegene in all this chaos. I must escort her home."

"Do you want to?" Sirens imposed themselves between us.

"Yes. It's my duty and my purpose."

Our past hung between us, the ripe love we'd shared when we'd had nearly nothing but. Even if I remained, Cochtonville would destroy any shred of friendship we had left and any drop of his independence. Goodbye was the only option.

"I'll be seeing you." My words broke me. I was done talking him into loving me, done convincing him to make a future with me. I'd been wrong to coerce him. My arrogance at my success had blinded me to his needs. I was sad for more than myself.

"Honestly," I said, "you deserve better than being her Crisper— or mine. You're an intelligent man. You do well with autonomy."

He blinked. "I'll find you someday. I promise."

"Do what you want and, most importantly, may you live to see the day when you pick out your own underwear."

"I'll try," he said. As he turned away I saw a black and purple bruise on his back.

Mom, Purceel at her side, hurried over with a white lunchbox.

"How bad is it?" she asked. "Is bone exposed?"

"No, but it's gushing," I said. "Might be slowing down a little with this pressure."

"He's faint," Eve added. "He's nearly out of words."

Purceel opened the lunchbox and pulled out a flexible bandage.

Mom tossed down the cap and slapped the bandage across Layal's cut.

"It'll do for now. He needs stitches. Is anyone else injured?"

"There's a pilot somewhere," Purceel said. She climbed into the cockpit like she'd been climbing into planes her whole life. She eased out a man who was holding his wrist. Once free of the plane, he hobbled away despite Mom's offers of assistance. He'd made a mistake and Cochtonville didn't go easy on mistakes.

"Here's someone else," Purceel announced. "Better catch this one."

I grabbed the slim older man around the waist and helped him to the ground. There we were, face to wormy face. This had to be one of the Cochtons. Bert. It was Bert. He'd been waiting in the helicopter for Eve. He was dressed in a loose gold robe and pants. Here was the hand I was forced to feed from, the man who had me constantly pressing my forehead and singing one song. I shook with suppressed rage. If only I could squeeze him until he popped like a maggot. I understood what went through his mind at this instant—he was evaluating *my* appearance. Was I beautiful enough to hold his attention? He closed his eyes and flopped back.

"Transfusion," he moaned. "Blood Bank."

"Layal can't give blood. He's hurt," Eve said.

"He needs a doctor," Mom added. She helped Mr. Cochton sit on the grass and examined him. "Your pupils are normal. You're not bleeding." She pressed his abdomen gently. "Are you in any pain?"

He flapped his arms and pushed her away, whapping her in the face in the process. "Blood Bank!"

"Is your neck sore? Are you having any breathing problems?" Mom asked, touching her cheek where Bert had flailed into her..

"Blood Bank! Are you having trouble hearing? I need the blood of youth!"

Two vultures circled in the gloomy sky above, searching for stray cats and possums run over by the parade. Bert's eyes rolled in his head at the sight of them. "Get me an IV, now."

"Wait for your own doctor," I said harshly. "Your stupid blood transfusions aren't keeping you young." My backtalk was chilling treason. I was to be grateful, only grateful in his presence.

"Do as he says." A fourth man put a massive hand on Mom's arm. Clearly, this was Bert's bodyguard. I hadn't seen him climb from the copter. Blood dripped from his cut eyebrow.

Vice Patrol vans pulled up next to the broken helicopter. Blood Bankers emerged and eased Mr. Cochton onto a stretcher. They pulled Layal from Eve's arms and tossed him on a second stretcher. Expertly, they strung a line from him to his uncle. Aiyn came to Layal's side. She stroked his curls as Eve hung near.

"Son, son, stay with me."

"I'm sorry, Mother. I'm running out of time. Can't join you."

"I understand. I know the enticement. I understand the processed foods melting on your tongue and the artificial scents of a house cleaned by servants. I don't cast aspersions on your aspirations, my son, and I wish the best for you. I chose to be in charge of my life."

"You're not in charge of your life if you're poor and living in exile," Bert reminded her. "Your son has more sense than either of his parents."

"Goodbye, brother," she said to Bert, tugging lightly on the IV as if she was pulling a tail. "Thank you for helping me start Wowville."

"Wowville. You're calling your colony Wowville? How childish! It's flippant. Can't you come up with a better name? Where is your family pride?"

"Having been banished from the family, I'm being fanciful and sentimental. It stands for Ways of the Wild, bro. The only ways."

"Ways of the Wild? How obscure. Wouldn't it be Wotwville?"

"Dramatic license. I learned all about it from this delightful Icon." She put her hand on Eve's arm.

"How about Shitville, sis? It's what you're getting. I've never seen a person so happy about taking a bunch of misfits to a manure lagoon." He tossed his head around dramatically. He needed makeup to draw out his tiny features.

"But it's *my* manure lagoon. Some of us see great potential in it, and so did you." He groaned as stooping, she kissed him and gave him a bear hug. Pink and energized from his transfusion, he flailed against the embrace.

"I demand the girl. Leave the girl. I must have the Icon. She's not going back to Poop Point with you. She'll stay here with the blood donor. Investments deserve their return."

"Don't speak so disparagingly about poop," Aiyn said. "You'll be far too busy recovering to care about the girl."

At this most chaotic of times, things made sense: Bert funded our project because he had his sight set on Eve. Nell was working for Aiyn during her tenure at Cochton Enterprises, designing a virus to infect the brothers in revenge.

Eve's dad came forward with a troupe of Washers, including Ursula in her sooty HotNot coat. His face was stony, and she had a melted plastic bag hanging from her chest.

"Eve, you have a choice. Go with Mr. Cochton and sit by his side while he recovers or go to jail. For the rest of you traitors, it's prison at best."

"No, these are my citizens. We agreed on it. I'm taking them with me. I give them asylum." Bits of glass sprinkled across Aiyn's feet. Her breasts were wet. The vials had broken.

"Layal, this is our last chance. Come with me." Eve let her tears flow as she bent over him.

"Eve, dear. I won't leave extravagance. I'm over the top. I wish you would indulge me."

"I can't stay now. I committed treason for you. Asylum or bust." She was a bitter mixture of blindsided anger and remorse.

"Forgive me. You're so beautiful when you're angry. You tempt me. You'll always be my queen. But no. I'd rather be a half-dead dog in paradise than a man at a WasteBin." He touched her cheek lightly with his finger in a tentative goodbye.

"Good choice," Bert said to Layal as Aiyn approached the Washers.

"Officers, would you like a hug? I'm dripping with pathogens," she said.

"We need to step away," Ursula said. "Let them go."

"Eve," the commissioner said. "You know I wanted better for you."

"Daddy, what does 'better' even mean? I love you. Tell Mom goodbye."

She turned on her heel and strode to the bus.

"I've got to go," I said to Mom. The suddenness of our necessary goodbye pressed upon the back of my eyes—a rainstorm I had to hold back.

"Yes," said Mom, shocked by the unfolding of events. Purceel bandaged my scrape while Mom rubbed her hand across the back of my neck. "How does this feel? You took a tumble. I can't send you off with a neck injury."

"I don't feel a thing."

"That's the right answer. Good falling."

We hugged, I put my head to her shoulder in an indulgent second.

"I'll be right behind you," she promised. I doubted it—she was more likely to stay behind and help others.

I ran after Eve. I put my arm around her as she choked on sobs, her crown wobbling precariously. I clung to the hope this was one more Beautiful and Damned episode and her acting was superb. It wouldn't be.

The bus loomed before us with its colorful murals and bursts. I stood by the door, memorizing the Pavilion of Agriculture, the Washer vans plugging the town square, XX Success, and the people of Cochtonville I'd leave behind.

"What about NezLeigh and the pig? We've got to wait for NezLeigh."

"She's in on all this. She's had the vaccine and the pig, too. Get in before I change my mind and become Mrs. Bert Cochton number four."

The stagnant air of the bus was like a pillow over my face. The bus driver was the bartender from Union Station. Gus's cheery smile and muscular forearms failed to lift my mood. I slid across the hot vinyl seat and sat in my resolution not to cry, not to add any more useless pain to my life. Mom and Purceel scooted into the seat behind us.

"Mom!" I said. "You came!"

I knew if I looked back, Mom's concern for my dashed hopes would push the "on" button for me bawling like the baby I wasn't going to have. Aiyn climbed into the bus, pulling herself up the stairs with the handrail. Nell, with her basket, skipped behind her.

"Welcome aboard," Aiyn said with surprising cheerfulness. "We embark on a new journey. For all who have not yet partaken, I entreat you to eat one of the vaccine-laden cubes of crystalized corn sugar developed by our Wowville microbiologist, Dr. Nell Butz. This will be our bargaining chip for any unsavory dealings with Cochtonville. As with any technological weapon, our advantage will be short lived as they develop vaccines and immunity. Quickly, we must work together and strive to make Wowville more than a colony near a sea of waste. We aspire to make it a valuable, vibrant powerhouse to be respected, not subjugated."

Her breath on my neck, Mom tapped me on the shoulder. "Microbial warfare! I can't come with you. I've had the vaccine. I must go back and help the sick."

"Me too," said Purceel.

"Mom, you can't go! Quit while you're ahead. There are too many dangers and disappointments in Cochtonville."

"I'd rather be helpful than content. People need affordable healthcare. I can't betray my clients." Mom squeezed my shoulder. I considered blubbering. *I* needed her, too. I put my arm on the back of the seat and faced her. Despite the bruise on her cheek, she was energized—eyes wide open, brows raised. Her mind was set. She was flush with purpose. I couldn't make this difficult for her. She had to stay, and I would be strong without her. It was time for me to act on my own stage.

"People need healthcare," I repeated. "There's been enough betrayal this day." Resilience flowed through me. It hardened in my belly like concrete. "I'll go on. I might even need to set a few bones. Did I tell you I mended a dog's leg? I learned from the best."

"Of course, you did! I love you, Cali. May we meet again soon." She and Purceel hurried to the front of the bus. Gus opened the accordion doors and she walked out of my life and into the chaos of the town square. I sat like a statue as the baby animal inside me whimpered. *This is what it feels like to lose your mom.* I reeked of diapers and beer. To make it worse, the rain the day had promised poured forth with a crack of thunder. The drops clattered on the bus roof and everyone closed the windows. The humidity rose as babies cried.

Nell moved through the bus meting out the vaccine doses as it lurched forward. Her composure and balance as Gus rode across the grass and onto the main street was enough to calm even the fussy babies, who each got a half cube. She'd managed to create this vaccine and the virus under Bux's nose, using the Cochton Enterprises laboratory. Remmer had been right. Eve's plan was more than a simple escape. It was an insurrection. The bus heaved, our heads jerked forward. We were leaving unimpeded.

"Hold on," Eve called. "We've got to wait for the contest's king. He's coming."

"No, he's not," I said. "He's remaining with LouOtta."

"He mustn't. She beats him. Did you see his back?"

"Yes. He stayed voluntarily. She had no control over him. She was asleep."

Eve took off her crown, pulled down the window, and tossed it out as rain spattered in. "I was part of the plan to have the contest, locate our guys, and drive off to a life together."

"We misgauged their response. Your mom was right. Love is like rabies. We were out of our minds. At least we can say we survived."

"What a sham. He expected me to be the fourth wife of some despot. I don't have time to waste with that worm. Nobody is sure of the lifespan of we modified folks."

I chilled. "What are you saying?"

"Some studies say our lives will be shorter."

"Shorter?" My voice broke. I'd never see Remmer again and he'd never know freedom. I'd have to endure a life without him or Eve. "How much shorter?"

"Mercifully, as I see it right now. Who wants an aging stud or beauty queen? When do people stop being appreciated for their looks?"

"How long have you known this?"

"Since acting school. It helps with the pathos."

"Maybe it won't happen in Wowville."

"Perhaps. I won't stop worrying about *him* though. He'll be sick and itching with that virus like he's been in a boggy fen. I should think it vengeance for rejecting me. Why am I sad?"

"Everybody left in town is going to get this virus?" The road ran with rain stampeding across the bus tires.

Eve watched the curtains of precipitation close us off from our town and those we loved.

"Those not given the vaccine," she said. "My mom, my dad, along with the Cochton brothers and their households. It shouldn't be fatal but oh, the discomfort. I'm sorry I pulled you into this. I thought it would end better. My dad was desperate for me to marry Bert Cochton. Bert's had his eye on me for a while now, but I needed to be elevated in the public eye before I was acceptable enough. I was willing but couldn't once I had a taste of the freedom I'd longed for."

"We didn't win our status on the merits of our plan."

"Not exactly. It was in the cards but would have failed if we hadn't gone through with the assignment and made an acceptable presentation. The Cochtons make no promises. I had to develop a solution for the Agro kids to make the project a winner. I learned this on our return. Your part was your own genius. It was a damn good plan."

"I was selected as your partner because it was Bux's turn for an InVitro."

"It was you or Nell. He made the wise choice. She's a double agent. She works for Aiyn, as you know, with funding from the outside. My dad never suspected."

"Everything's corrupt. Aiyn's not much different from her brothers," I said softly. "And yet we've tossed our lot in with her." The rain reminded me of applause.

"She did what was needed. You have to play tough with that crew."

A sob bubbled up in my chest, crested my throat, and burst out through my eyes.

"It's what I loved about Remmer—he didn't play tough. He was tender. He was the one sensitive thing in my life and I lost him." I was more than sad, I was desperate, smothered, my head in a plastic bucket. I'd lost an equal. I didn't even have my mom. What was I going to do in Wowville without them? Was I going to be forever gathering berries and firewood and watching plastic pellets pop from manure?

Eve took my hand. I put my head on the window and listened to the rain falling like bacon frying. The moment was punctuated by the smell of a hog confinement operation. My heart struggled on against the current.

The storm quit as the bus passed fields lush with corn rippling like green waves. We stopped for gas at a station with the fuel sign hanging lopsidedly by one magnet. As Gus went to pump gas, Aiyn addressed us.

"Women, soon we will arrive in Wowville. You'll be reunited with your children. Don't be surprised. I've fattened them. We have new bunk facilities for everyone." The women cheered and some cried with joy.

"I welcome you to Wowville where you will not be discarded. You won't be judged on your appearance or reviled as you age. We need your expertise. Martyrdom is a thing of the past. We need you. Your children won't be sent away, nor will your fertility be out of your hands. With so few men around, it will be easy to manage your fertility."

"How many men will there be?" an Agro called out.

"So far, one," Aiyn replied. "Gus here is our only male."

"Will he be prescribed? Like we rotate him through for sex?" another woman asked.

"Hey, the heart wants what it wants," Gus said, coming back into the bus. "Where's my decision?"

The women laughed as if his decision was a frivolity.

"The two kids running this place have no idea how to turn on the pumps," he told Aiyn. "We'll have to wait while they call the owner for instructions."

"Let's rest here and discuss Wowville among ourselves. What are important aspects of our society? Let's put our heads together. Come on, everyone." Aiyn's enthusiasm was over the top. I might have admired her for her optimism if she hadn't unleashed a virus in ugly revenge.

As Gus and Nell took notes, the women talked about the need for daycare for some, nightcare for others, the ability to work with their kids in tow. Fireflies came out and danced in the grass as the sun went down. At last the kids running the station came out to tell Gus the pumps were on. Eve followed him out of the bus and I followed Eve.

"Thanks for the lift," Eve sad to Gus as she and I leaned on the bus.

"My pleasure, Miss Cochtonville."

"How long will you be joining us?"

Gus took the hose from the gas pump. "I'm staying on. I was working at the bar as an undercover agent for an organization concerned about human rights in Cochtonville. I plan to help set up your society."

"You're not just stud service," Eve said.

Gus shoved the nozzle in the gas tank. "Not at all. Treatment of Crispers—the aspects where their bodies are not their own—is one of our concerns. Aiyn hired me to help write the constitution. We want to have amnesty for Crispers and equality for all."

"There's still a chance for us?"

"It will take a while. Oppression is insidious."

"Could an oppressed person see oppression as normal?" I asked, searching for closure with Remmer's rejection. I'd never stop thinking about him for even a second. At best, I'd salvage a measure of success from this failure if I understood his choice.

"Deep inside most know it's unfair, although they might accept it if they individually are treated adequately. They usually rebel in quiet ways such as feigned sickness or straying. But it's possible an oppressed person would see it as normal."

The tank filled, we got back on the bus. Aiyn's head was flopped over, her hat was in her lap, and she snored quietly.

"He's cute," said Eve, taking her seat.

I slid in beside her. "Gus? He's alright." I had my doubts about our new colony. Only one man? How were we going to sustain ourselves?

Gus started the engine and the bus pulled forward, crunching on the gravel driveway. The station lights clicked on, casting a pale glow into the growing darkness of the country. Without warning, a ghostly white pickup truck with an elevated cab on the back pulled up to block us. I thought I might go snow blind from fear. White truck—Vice Patrol coming to get us. Already.

CHAPTER TWENTY-EIGHT

"No," I said. "No. Is it Washers?"

"I've never seen them in an old pickup," Eve said. "I'll go talk to them."

"Stay here." I stood up.

"What are you doing?"

"Finding out what they want. You're an Icon. Sit tight or the whole bus is going to panic."

I inched from my seat and walked past the mothers and babies. I'd go out there. I'd let the Washers have me, and Gus could drive away.

I said quietly to Gus, "I'm checking this vehicle out. If you need to, leave without me to protect Eve and the rest. Shut the door behind me."

I stepped down, my stomach eating itself as a squeak told me Gus was following my orders. I walked to the driver's side of the truck. Doing *something* calmed me. The driver, wearing jeans, a corn seed cap, and a dirty white t-shirt, hopped out.

"Who do you want?" I said. "Let the bus pass."

The woman was broad shouldered like Ursula but shorter, with long, light hair frizzing in all directions from beneath the cap. "I'm looking for Cali Van Winkle."

"I'm her."

"Van Winkle, huh? I never would've pegged you. You don't look sleepy or drunk."

"It's my dad, Rip, who's the true Van Winkle."

"May you be better than your reputation." Muscles bulging, she opened the back of the pick-up. "Even though you left stuff behind."

NezLeigh hopped out and fell to her knees. Her hair was wet and her cotton clothes soaked through, showing her breast buds and hard nipples. Lavender leaned out of the tailgate, her ears flapping before she leapt and landed with a roll and a squeal. She stood and shook herself as the three Crispers jumped out. My heart picked up the beat. Remmer sat on the bed of the truck and slid cautiously to the ground. The driver sauntered over to him, held out her hand, and Rem pulled money from his thong and gave it to her.

"Hey!" I shouted with relief. To hell with my pride. These were my friends. I ran to them, laughing hysterically, embracing Remmer, leaping into his arms and wrapping my legs around him.

"Hope to heck you got room on the bus for a few more defectors," he said, holding me tightly. He was shivering in his nakedness. I pressed myself close, warming him.

"What are you doing here?"

"I escaped," he said, teeth chattering.

"You left on your own?"

"Lady Maliegene didn't need me. An insurance man helped her to her car. I didn't follow."

NezLeigh stood, scratched Lavender behind the ears, and ribbed Remmer. "And the man mentioned she needed to insure her Crisper or he'd give her a citation. She denied even having one."

"Hey NezLeigh, can't you make me sound more heroic?" Remmer kissed my sweaty hair.

"I don't need a hero," I said. "I need someone to love."

The truck drove off toward Cochtonville, leaving us in the

dimly lit gas station lot in the middle of nowhere. NezLeigh
pushed her sunglasses to the top of her head.

"What a lovely dark night. No moon. No stars." She gave me a
playful punch. She was wearing Eve's No Regrets 2.0. "We've been
discussing things on the ride out here. You may have noticed,
Aiyn's a little nuts. We've got to rein her in. Heed my advice. Her
colony's not going to last if it's based on anger. It has to be about
loving, ya dig?"

"Love? *You're* talking about love?"

"Gag. I said what I meant. Try not to talk about feelings or I'll
puke?"

"Got it. I'll make it about love."

She shoved Remmer. "This guy here, he's got something to tell
you. Spit it out without crying if you can, Weepy."

Remmer put me down. Blinking, he took a deep breath. "I'd
rather be Socrates in a manure lagoon than a fool in a swimming
pool in an upscale neighborhood. Cali, I can't go on without you.
May I be at your side? As lover or friend, it's up to you. I want to
be together whatever it takes."

I was going to explode with cuteness overload at his hopeful
smile and ridiculous thong. It sounds corny, but I fell into his
amber eyes and sank deep. "I don't want to go on without you
either. I mean, I could, but it would be far less pleasant."

We embraced again and cried as if we'd been apart for a near
lifetime.

"Damn right," NezLeigh said, "I give you two the green light to
be a thing, Wowville's first official thing."

"NezLeigh, speaking of green lights, how about returning my—
oh, never mind. We don't have time to worry about it."

The bus headlights snapped on and Gus opened the squeaking
door. Eve stood waiting for us. "All aboard the Freedom Express,"
she called playfully.

I took Remmer's hand, certain I could trust him, believing I
could love him for however long we had together, and knowing I
would treasure it all—the mystery, the joy, the intimacy, and even

the confusion of our new life together. He put a hand on NezLeigh's shoulder as she tugged down her glasses, pulled the UTI from her pocket, and beamed it on the steps below Eve's feet. Grunting contentedly, Lavender trotted forward.

"Let's go," I said, "to make a corner of Cochtonia more loving. And this, my wild friends, is how we'll measure success."

THE END

Thank you for reading! Did you enjoy?

Please Add Your Review! And turn the page for a sneak peek of UNREGISTERED by City Owl Author, Megan Lynch, available now.

SNEAK PEEK OF UNREGISTERED

Bristol Ray did not exist.

At least, not according to official records. The back of his left wrist, where his assigned watch would have lived if his birth had been important, was bare. There was a lump under the skin of his right hand where a tracking chip had been inserted, but he was pretty sure that was there just to scare people like him. He wasn't being tracked. His left hand was ringless, and the skin around his fourth finger was consistent in color and texture to the others. His teeth were hopelessly crooked, his brow prematurely creased, and though the lessons from his mere five years of formal school had faded, his mind was bright with life.

He stood in a shadow, clutching his homemade paper stencil to his chest, and surveyed his work on the brick wall before him. He'd painted a figure that could have been a nun. A slouching, ancient woman dressed in long robes, slicing her chipped hand open with a cross she held in the other. Getting the blood to drip from that hand hadn't been easy. For weeks he had sketched as he watched water drip from faucets to catch a glimpse of that line, that light, and once he'd seen it, his incinerator ate the drafts and roared with rejection. If his incinerator were here and had the ability to destroy whole walls, even this nun may have met her doom.

Eventually, though, the nun and her blood had to go out into the world, fully ready or not. He stepped back from it, still safely out of range of the disabled street camera. One could never be too careful.

One last glance over his shoulder was all he allowed himself. She could be there for another week, or she could be gone in a few hours when the morning sun revealed her to the commuters and schoolchildren and stunned police. He packed his stencils and paints in his backpack, kissed the air in her direction, and started home.

Bristol zigged and zagged along the dark streets in the way he always did to avoid the detection of the street cameras. He wore a glove on his left hand with an ice pack slipped inside to cool his chip, just in case. Now that it was no longer activated by his body heat, he was free from all surveillance. The only thing an unregistered person had to lose by breaking curfew was his or her life, which could happily be taken from anybody stupid enough to be caught.

A notice fluttering on a telephone pole read:

WARNING
Any persons not assigned to the artist vocation are prohibited from painting, sculpting, drawing, or working with any other mediums in the attempt to imitate Art. Violators will be prosecuted.

He hesitated a beat, snatched the notice, and added it to his bag.

His sister Denver was waiting for him at the window when he reached the house. With one of the shoddily soldered bars missing, he easily squeezed through into the bedroom they still shared. He returned her smile and handed her the notice.

"A violator you are," she said.

"And intend to stay."

"We'll have to get rid of that," she said, but he'd already taken the scissors to cut it into ribbons. She sat on her bed and yawned. "How did the blood go?"

"Not bad. It was better on the last outline, but it's done now, and I can't think about it anymore."

Denver nodded at the shreds of paper. "Better incinerate those before Mom gets up."

"She'll kill me if I don't. You're lucky."

"What, that I'm getting married?"

Bristol nodded. "And moving out."

Denver laid down and pulled the blanket to her chin. "It's not like I have a choice. And Mom's fine to live with, you know, as long as you don't have any sneaky habits."

"I promised to keep Mom out of it."

"Good. She's made a lot of sacrifices for you."

"I know." Bristol kicked softly at his backpack on the floor. He wasn't sure if Denver was trying to make him feel guilty or not, but if that was her purpose, it did the trick. "Did you get your letter today?"

"Don't change the subject."

"I really want to know."

Denver sighed and shifted. "Not yet, but that's okay. I'm sure they're going to pair me with a Four."

"A Three with a Four? You're studying to be an architect. You're saying you could end up with, what, a nurse or data-bot technician or something?"

"I'm sure Metrics will match us in other ways, personality and all that. I know they don't like to mismatch Tiers, but they'll do it in situations like mine."

"What situation?" Bristol asked, but realized the answer as the words came out. "Oh."

"Don't say oh like that."

"Sorry." He unzipped the backpack with a little more force then necessary, took out his stencil, and ripped small pieces from it. The pile containing the bits of the notice grew larger. "It's just that sometimes I forget that my life is always wrecking someone else's."

"My life is not wrecked. I can still be an architect—I'll just have to live in Four housing and stuff. My kid can still be a Three if they do well enough on their four-year-old exams."

"Yeah." Bristol mindlessly ripped away at the stencil. "It's weird your kid won't have a brother or sister."

"I know. I was thinking about that tonight." She propped herself up on her bony elbows. "Do you realize that at the end of our lives, we'll have known each other the longest out of anyone?"

Bristol sat silent for a moment. "What about Mom? You technically knew her a year before you met me."

"But Mom will die when she's seventy-five. Then I'll have spent fifty years knowing her. But then when *I* die, I'll have known you for seventy-four years! You don't know anyone that long unless it's a sibling."

"Lucky us." Bristol gathered the damning notice and piles of confetti that had been his stencils, walked out of their room, and tossed them into the incinerator. He stopped a moment to watch the flames snatch and lick their prey, reducing weeks of work to shapeless ashes that could have been anything else—a recipe card, an ad, a pamphlet on new and exciting ways to save energy. They all became the same once the fire was done with them. When he came back into the room, Denver was already dressed.

"Almost time to get up anyway," she said. "Bristol, does that scare you?"

"What?"

"Mom dying?"

"No." *Yes.* "Everybody has to do it."

"You don't have to worry. I'll take care of you."

Most people, both registered and unregistered, avoided this topic. At the same time, these kinds of thoughts were intriguing—direct thoughts about privilege shared across the divide. Even from Denver, it felt simultaneously coarse and comforting, though they'd never talked in length about their differences in Tier. He didn't like to think about it, and he certainly didn't want to talk about it. Why would she bring it up now?

She's getting married soon.

"You can live with me," she said. "I'll—"

"And what about this new husband of yours? What is he going to think of marrying someone who has a brother? I mean, what are the chances he's even *met* an unregistered? Not good. What's he going to think of you just taking care of me?" A hotness laced his mouth. "I'll tell you what will probably happen when Mom dies. You and me, we'll look at each other and remember seeing the other one in a smaller size, but we won't really know each other as we are. And you'll care more about your new family than me."

They caught each other's eyes. Denver walked over to the mirror and began brushing and pinning her hair. For several minutes, neither spoke.

Bristol rubbed his sore eyes. "It won't be your fault. It's no one's fault. That's just how the world works, Den."

The sun had begun to soak the curtains, so Bristol stood and opened them to let more of it in. With a click, he turned their blue-tinted overhead bulb off and let his eyes adjust to the color of natural light.

"Thank you," Denver said, her fingers still braiding.

"Do you think Fours have blue lightbulbs too?"

"Everyone does. These units were built right after the uprising, so they're designed to only allow the color blue for lighting."

"Why?"

"It was right after the uprising," she repeated. When Bristol made no indication of understanding, she glanced at the holowatch on her wrist. It was silent, so she stood, pushed in her desk chair, and continued quietly. "People were unhappy. Blue lights make it harder to see your veins."

Bristol nodded. Metrics underestimated how much some people needed an escape and would just invent new ways of getting drugs into their bloodstreams.

Denver sat next to him on his bed. "Listen, while we're on Metrics—"

"I know. I have to stop."

"You *have* to. You've been lucky, but it can't last forever. I don't know what Mom would do if—"

"I know, Den."

"You wouldn't have to stop drawing. I'll still bring you paper when I'm married. You can still make things here."

"You know how careful I am." He closed his eyes. For as unlikely as her offer to let him live with her had been, he could see it had been honest. *Be nicer.* "But I see your point. I'll stop someday."

Denver stood and lingered by the doorframe. "It's got to be soon. I'll see you after work."

She walked away, and an idea for a painting flashed just behind the space between Bristol's eyebrows. Though his body begged for sleep, his hands, suddenly animated by some unconscious energy, fumbled under the bed for a sketchpad and pencil. He crouched over the paper, hoarding the white space and the possibilities it offered, clutched tight the idea in his mind, and began drawing.

Don't stop now. Keep reading with your copy of UNREGISTERED by City Owl Author, Megan Lynch, available now.

Want even more sci-fi fun? Try the Children of the Uprising saga by City Owl Author, Megan Lynch, and discover more from author Catherine Haustein at www.catherinehaustein.com

---

Living the ideal life is a human right... unless you're unregistered.

Bristol lives under the watchful eye of the Metrics as an unlucky second child. The government grants its citizens the ideal life. Perfect spouse. Perfect job. Perfect home. But dare to have more than one child, and you'll become an outcast—the unregistered.

Now, he'll protest the abusive system in the only way he knows how, painting controversial murals in the hidden parts of town.

But the government doesn't condone dissent. And the frustrated unregistered citizens need to be handled. The relocation plan goes into effect and all unregistered must be sent to far-off desert states.

Will Bristol and his friends be able to escape the government's clutches, and survive long enough to discover an unknown world.

ACKNOWLEDGMENTS

Many thanks to my cohorts at the Iowa Summer Writing Festival including my teachers Amy Hassinger and Sands Hall. Most of all, thanks to Dr. Cynthia Mahmood for her books and stories on hunter gatherer cultures and for her encouragement.

High praise for my editor Christie Stratos, who pushed me in the best of ways.

ABOUT THE AUTHOR

Born under a half-illuminated quarter moon, Catherine Haustein is never sure if she favors light or shadow. Her *Unstable States* series contains ample portions of both. The author and chemist lives and teaches in a tidy town in Iowa on the shores of a lake which sometimes is cited for elevated fecal coliform levels. A graduate of the Iowa Writers' Workshop, Catherine weaves the passions and optimism of science with the absurdities of the present and dark possibilities of the future throughout her books.

www.catherinehaustein.com

 twitter.com/hausteinc1

 pinterest.com/catherinehauste

ABOUT THE PUBLISHER

City Owl Press is a cutting edge indie publishing company,
bringing the world of romance and speculative fiction to
discerning readers.

www.cityowlpress.com

Made in the USA
Monee, IL
25 February 2020

22296986R00178